Late Learner

Ciara Geraghty is a bestselling Irish novelist. She lives in Dublin and is the proud owner of one husband, two daughters, one son and a dog called Gary who still thinks he's a puppy despite being five-and-a-half. When she is not writing in her garret, Ciara loves reading, swimming in the sea and playing her violin. She also co-hosts the podcast BookBirds.

CIARA GERAGHTY

Late Learner

HarperCollins*Publishers*

HarperCollins*Publishers* Ltd
1 London Bridge Street,
London SE1 9GF
www.harpercollins.co.uk

HarperCollins*Publishers*
Macken House, 39/40 Mayor Street Upper
Dublin 1, D01 C9W8, Ireland

First published by HarperCollins*Publishers* 2025
1

A catalogue record for this book is available from the British Library

ISBN: 978-0-00-849650-0 (TPB)
ISBN: 978-0-00-849653-1 (PB b-format)

This novel is entirely a work of fiction. The names, characters and incidents portrayed in it are the work of the author's imagination. Any resemblance to actual persons, living or dead, events or localities is entirely coincidental.

Set in Sabon LT Std by HarperCollins*Publishers* India

Printed and bound in the UK using 100% Renewable
Electricity at CPI Group (UK) Ltd

MIX
Paper | Supporting
responsible forestry
FSC™ C007454

This book contains FSC™ certified paper and other controlled sources to ensure responsible forest management.

For more information visit: www.harpercollins.co.uk/green

For Frank.
For undoing knots in necklaces.
And for everything else.

CHAPTER 1

Annie McCann made a lovely corpse. The mourners didn't come right out and say it but Ronda was sure that's what they were thinking. Her mother had been a handsome woman. Tall and slim. Margo took after her. Ronda was the runt. She didn't mind. Somebody had to be.

Now, in the coffin, Annie McCann finally looked at peace. There was even a ghost of a smile across her wide face. Or was Ronda imagining that?

Ronda was glad she had insisted on the teal round-necked dress with the long sleeves. Velvet. An elegant material. Ronda straightened. She resolved not to acquiesce to her sister's inevitable demand to have the reception in the golf club afterwards. 'I'll get a discount,' Margo would say. 'Since I'm the incoming lady captain.' It was always easier to agree with Margo.

But this time, Ronda would not.

'Your mother must have been so proud of you, Ronda.' It was Mrs Murphy from next door. Joseph's mother. Relations between them had become less awkward as the years went by. It wasn't like Ronda had done anything wrong and the break-up was ancient history, but Joseph was Sharon Murphy's son, and blood was thicker than water, or so Ronda had heard.

'Staying here all these years to look after your poor mother.' Mrs Murphy gathered Ronda in an embrace so stiff and tight, Ronda's breathing became constricted. She hoped

1

Joseph hadn't come to the funeral, and if he had, that he wasn't looking in her direction.

Just like that, Mrs Murphy vanished, gone as suddenly as she had appeared. Now it was just Ronda, looking into the coffin. Even though her eyes were closed, Annie McCann seemed to stare back. Ronda hesitated before putting her hand on her mother's shoulder. The fleshy warmth of it surprised her.

'What are you mauling me for?' snapped a voice.

Ronda jumped and snatched her hand away. It was the voice of her mother. She was in her bed. In her bedroom. There was no coffin. No mourners. Annie McCann was very much alive although she did not seem especially pleased about it.

'You look like you've seen a ghost,' Annie said, struggling to a sitting position. 'Make yourself useful and plump my pillows for me, like a good girl. Did you make tea? I thought I heard the kettle on downstairs. You wouldn't pass me my iPad, would you? Oh, and did you feed Jessica Fletcher? I could hear her mewing and scratching earlier but I wasn't fit to get out of bed.'

'Was your sciatica at you?' asked Ronda, plumping each of the four goosedown pillows at her mother's back.

'Of course,' said Annie. 'And the migraine didn't help. Or the tinnitus. What are you thinking for dinner? I might be able to get something down.'

'I just got in from work,' said Ronda, reaching for the door handle. 'I'll go see what's in the fridge.'

'Something meaty,' said Annie McCann. 'I can't be doing with any of those vegetarian dishes tonight, my iron levels are low.'

'Something meaty coming right up,' said Ronda, doing a mock salute, which she thought her mother might find amusing although if she did, she didn't say.

In the kitchen, she ignored the game of chess she was losing against Berkley. She was not someone who ordinarily attached names to inanimate objects, but she'd been playing against him for so long, it was possible that she had formed something of a competitive attachment with the electronic chess set.

There was a lone pork chop on the bottom shelf of the fridge. It had been there since Saturday. Even through the plastic bag, the raw meat felt slimy and spongy beneath her fingers. Ronda opened the top of the bag, took a sniff. The smell was sharp and sour. She'd have to go to the shops. It was the least she could do. The funeral music – a beautiful rendition of Elgar's 'Nimrod' on the church organ – was still playing in the cathedral of her imagination, try as she might to lift the organist's fingers off the keys and close the lid.

She threw the pork chop into the compost bin in the side passage and put her cycling helmet, jacket and high-vis vest back on.

'Just popping to the shops, I'll be back in five minutes,' she called up the stairs. There was no answer, although she could hear the signature tune of *Murder She Wrote*, which reminded her to feed the cat. She upended a tin of cat food into Jessica Fletcher's bowl and refilled her water dish.

As she left the house, she glimpsed Mrs Murphy at the window in her front room, adjusting the net curtains.

Those net curtains were always being adjusted. She did not appear to notice Ronda.

CHAPTER 2

Ronda wheeled her bicycle through the gate of the second to last house on the terrace where she had lived for all of her forty-four years, unless you count the eighteen months she had lived with Joseph Murphy, in which case you would say her forty-two and a half years.

She put one foot on the pedal and used the other to gain a little momentum before swinging her leg up and over the saddle. She set off. It didn't take her long to reach the butcher's. Her mother preferred her meat from Hannigan's rather than the supermarket. 'He kills his own animals,' Annie said, although just what impact this had on the tenderness or otherwise of the meat, Ronda didn't know.

Even with her bicycle helmet on, people noticed Ronda McCann's face. It was no longer the colour and texture of the scar that drew their attention. Rather, it was the meandering length of it, rising on her temple and flowing down the left side of her pale face. It was also the near miss of it, skidding as it did around the delicate tissue of her eye socket before veering south to end in a thickened comma on the edge of her jawline, below her chin.

The world was divided into two kinds of people, Ronda felt. The ones who wanted to know what happened, and asked. And those who also wanted to know, but refrained from making an enquiry. The elderly woman in front of Ronda at the butcher's counter fell into the former category.

'What happened, love?' she asked, peering anxiously at the side of Ronda's face.

'I was held at knife point in a pharmacy when I was filling my mother's prescription for fibromyalgia.' Ronda's voice was a dramatic whisper.

'Go 'way,' said the woman, setting her shopping bag on the floor and leaning in.

Ronda referred to the man with the knife as 'the perpetrator'.

She told how, as the perpetrator fled out of the shop with a sack of cash, antidepressants and Solpadeine, she made a dive for his legs, brought him down like a sack of spuds.

'So brave,' the old woman marvelled.

Ronda went on to say how, in the ensuing struggle, the perpetrator had lashed out, slashing a bloody, jagged line all down the left side of Ronda's face.

'Jesus, Mary and holy St Joseph,' the old woman said, blessing herself. She jumped when the bell jangled as the door of the shop opened, dumping Ronda back into the real world where she did not regale strangers with fantastical tales. They both looked fearfully towards the door, but it was only Mr Hannigan's wife, come to count the takings.

The old woman carefully placed her parcel of meat inside her shopping trolley. When she straightened, she peered anxiously at the side of Ronda's face.

'What happened, love?'

'Sorry?' said Ronda.

'The scar?' said the old woman, nodding towards Ronda's cheek.

'Oh,' said Ronda. 'I fell off a wall.'

'Must have been a high wall,' said the woman.

'Next,' called out Mr Hannigan. 'Ah Ronda, is it yourself?' said Mr Hannigan, wiping bloodied fingers down the bib of his apron.

'It is,' said Ronda, mostly because she could never think of a better response to his habitual greeting.

'You mind yourself love,' said the old woman as she opened the door and pulled her trolley through. The bell jangled.

'And how's poor Annie today? No improvement I suppose?'

Ronda shook her head even though she couldn't possibly know which of her mother's ailments Mr Hannigan was referring to. After some further exchanges of small talk, Mr Hannigan finally gave Ronda the pork chop she requested and she paid and left.

Ronda checked her blind spot, stuck out her arm to indicate right and cycled into the centre of the road. A Tesla scorched up the road behind her and was forced to slow down behind Ronda. To make up for this inconvenience, the driver beeped the horn. Ronda had to wait for a HiAce van to pass her before she could get out of the Tesla's way. This delay further infuriated the driver, who was late for nothing and no one, but disliked cyclists and cycling as a general rule of thumb. He beeped again. The HiAce van passed and Ronda turned right, the bag containing the pork chop swinging off the handle-bar. On Sycamore Avenue, she bore down against the upward slope of the road. Her breath erupted white from her mouth, like the freezing fog that hung in patches through the bare branches of the sycamore trees lining the avenue. When the lights of a vehicle came upon her, she lit up like a high-vis Christmas tree. Garish but difficult to miss. In all her years of cycling – to work, to Margo's, to the grocery shop and the pharmacy – she'd been struck twice, once by a loud, sweary golfer in an Audi, the second time by a mortified woman in yoga pants driving a Volvo. Both were minor incidents resulting in one mild, short-lived concussion and one distal radius fracture that healed quickly, but which occasionally – in damp weather, for instance – caused her wrist to swell and throb. Ronda passed two cyclists standing on their pedals in an effort to gain the crest of the steep hill. At the top of the road, she extended her arm and turned left, onto St. Patrick's Crescent, then rounded the bend of the road onto Casino Place.

Nearly there.

She put her head down and cycled against the wind that had a habit of whistling down the narrow road. Mrs Murphy's cat – despised by Jessica Fletcher, although this was not particularly noteworthy since she found most felines beneath her contempt – was coiled like a spring beneath Mr Murphy's gleaming, nearly-new Škoda Fabia. Being black, Ronda failed to notice the cat until the animal leaped out from under the car and streaked across the road.

Up until then, Ronda had never quite known if it was considered lucky or unlucky. Having a black cat cross your path.

Now she knew.

Instinct made her jerk the handlebars to avoid the cat. Unfortunately, instinct does not have a particularly good sense of direction, because she jerked the handlebars outwards just as a car – a VW Golf – drove up behind her, and even though the driver could see, as if in slow motion, the sequence of events unfolding and turned his steering wheel accordingly, it wasn't enough to stop the back wheel of Ronda's bicycle glancing against the front offside of the car.

While it could have been a lot worse, the impact nonetheless was enough to knock Ronda off the bike and leave her winded and dazed in the gutter, the pork chop in a puddle beside her.

'Are you all right?' said the driver, pulling over and hurrying out of the car.

'I'm fine,' said Ronda, feeling her arms and legs and finding nothing broken, as far as she could tell.

'You just swerved out, right in front of me,' said the man, a peevish tone in his voice now. Ronda got to her feet. A puddle of rainwater soaked through her uniform, weighing her down. She looked at the driver. He was a burly affair with tired eyes and a smoker's puckered mouth.

'I'm sorry,' said Ronda. She pointed at Mrs Murphy's cat – Sooty – who had taken shelter under a car on the other side of the road. A Nissan Micra this time. 'The cat ran out in front of me.'

The driver hauled her bicycle – the back wheel buckled – off the road, leaned it against Mrs Murphy's front garden wall.

'Be more careful next time, yeah?' he said.

'Sorry,' said Ronda again.

'Oh,' he said then, stepping closer and peering at Ronda's forehead. 'You're bleeding.'

Ronda put a hand to her temple. It was warm and sticky. Her fingers were bloodstained when she examined them.

'You should have been wearing a helmet,' said the man.

Ronda nodded. She usually did. She must have left it at the butcher's.

CHAPTER 3

The first thing Ronda's mother did after she answered the door to the stranger carrying Ronda's bicycle with its buckled wheel in his arms was to phone for an ambulance.

Annie McCann was a fan of ambulances. Doctors and nurses too. She greeted the paramedic warmly when he arrived, wondering if he might take a look at the varicose veins that ran down the back of her left leg. 'I think one of them's bulging more than usual,' she said, turning and raising the hem of her wool skirt to demonstrate.

'I'll take a look after I check the woman who fell off her bike, okay?' said the paramedic. The kitchen door opened and Margo appeared at the top of the hall.

After she had phoned for an ambulance, Annie had phoned Margo.

'This way,' Margo said to the paramedic, beckoning him towards her with a coy smile. She tended to adopt a mildly flirtatious tone when she spoke to men. She positioned herself so that the light from the kitchen fell across her, and stood there long enough to give the paramedic sufficient time to admire her. There were few who wouldn't take the opportunity. Margo was tall and slender as a reed. Her white blond bob was knife-edge sharp and framed her angular face with its sheer cheekbones and knife edge jawline. Add the clarity of the blue eyes, the suggestive set of the wide mouth, and a high, narrow nose that might have looked a tad too high and too narrow on a different face. On Margo's, it looked magnificent.

Who wouldn't admire Margo McCann-Waters?

The paramedic did as he was bid and hurried up the hall after her.

Ronda heard all this from her position on the lid of the toilet in the bathroom, just off the kitchen. It was a small, damp room, jutting from the back of the house, like an after-thought. Ronda no longer remembered what colour the lino had once been. She noticed the bottom of the shower curtains, already streaked with mould. It didn't seem to matter how often she replaced them, the mould regrouped sooner rather than later.

She held a wad of kitchen roll against her head and plugged her nostrils with balls of tissue. Her nose had a tendency to bleed when things got a little out-of-the-ordinary. She shifted her weight. Her buttocks were numb from sitting on the cold toilet lid. Down her right side, she could feel bruises blooming.

'Don't I know you from somewhere?' Ronda looked up and the paramedic was there, standing right in front of her, smiling as if she was exactly the person he was hoping to see. He helped Ronda to her feet, then laid a soft, fluffy towel – warm from the upright chrome radiator affixed to the porcelain wall tiles – across the lid of the toilet. 'There,' he said, returning Ronda to the seat. 'That'll be more comfortable for you.'

'Actually, I'm feeling much better now,' said Ronda, flexing her right arm and leg to demonstrate.

'That's pretty impressive,' said the paramedic, 'considering the collection of bruising you've got down your right side.' Gently, he removed the wad of kitchen roll from her forehead, studying her face as he did so. 'Where do I know you from?' he asked. He was close enough for her to notice the bristles forming a dark shadow along his jaw and above his mouth. Oddly, she didn't seem to mind being this close. In fact, she was someone who was entirely comfortable with this level of proximity.

'You featured in that article in the Irish Medical Times recently,' he said then, nodding. 'You're the head nurse at Green Gables, aren't you? The photograph didn't do you justice at all. Such a remarkable career.'

Ronda shrugged. 'Just doing my job,' she said.

'There's not many like you, Ronda McCann,' said the paramedic, looking right into her eyes, right down into the very heart of her, right into the gloop of her blood, down the length of her bones.

'Sorry,' he said. 'I'm being inappropriate, amn't I?'

'Yes, you are,' said Ronda, because she was also someone who was forthright. That was another thing people liked about her.

'I can't help it,' he said. 'I'd ask you out if I thought there was any chance that a woman like you might be free? Or might be interested in someone like me?'

Even someone as assured as Ronda couldn't help feeling warmed by such ardent attention. 'Well,' she began, as a smile spread across her face, like the petals of a flower, releasing their scent at dusk.

'Don't I know you from somewhere?' said the paramedic. Ronda, startled, banged her funny bone off the edge of the wall. More bits of plaster flaked off and settled on the lino in small, sharp bits that would cut into the soles of her feet the next time she had a shower if she forgot to sweep them up. She looked around. She was on her own. Just her and the clouds of vapour that came out of her mouth every time she exhaled. Through the chink in the door, she could see Margo and the paramedic in the kitchen. The paramedic had his back to her, but she could tell from his posture that he was holding himself erect, perhaps even sneaking onto the balls of his feet.

'You're the director of the hospice in Clontarf, aren't you?' he said. 'I read that article about you in the Irish Medical Times. You brought that place back from the brink.'

Ronda walked into the kitchen and stood beside the chess set, but she mustn't have made much sound because neither of them turned around. Margo was saying something about Malcolm Junior – her eldest – and the paramedic was shaking his head and exclaiming how she couldn't possibly be the mother of an eighteen-year-old, she was much too young and vibrant. In the end, Ronda had to clear her throat to attract their attention. Twice.

Ahem.

AHEM.

It was the paramedic who turned around eventually, looking at her with confusion before registering the soggy wads of bloodied tissue hanging out of her nose. 'Oh,' he said, directing Ronda onto a kitchen chair. He lifted the sodden kitchen roll off her forehead and replaced it with a clean cloth.

'It's not as bad as it looks,' said Ronda. 'Head wounds bleed a lot.'

'You're a nurse,' he said, nodding at her scrubs.

'No,' said Ronda.

'She was nearly a nurse,' said Margo, picking up the kettle to fill it.

'I'm a care assistant,' Ronda said.

'All the stress of nursing for a fraction of the pay, ami-right?' said the paramedic.

'That's what I always say,' said Margo. 'My sister should have finished her nursing training and moved out of home years ago.'

'You two are sisters?' said the paramedic in the voice people usually used when they discovered this particular fact. When Ronda nodded, it felt like bits of her brain were banging against the inside of her head.

He took out a torch, shone its narrow beam into each of Ronda's eyes. She could feel her pupils constrict in the glare. 'I suppose you were daydreaming on that bicycle,' Margo said, crossing her arms with a deep sigh. 'She lives in a little world in her head half the time,' she told the paramedic, tucking a gleaming lock of hair behind her ear.

There was no point arguing with Margo, so Ronda didn't bother.

The paramedic reached for his medical bag. 'As you know Ronda, there's always a risk of concussion with these types of injuries, so I'd like to bring you into A&E for observation.'

Ronda shook her head. 'I'm fine,' she said. 'But thank you. And sorry for wasting your time.'

'I get paid either way,' he said, shrugging. 'I'll wash and dress that cut before I go, okay?' He steered her into the bath-room. Ronda stood by the sink as the paramedic attended to the cut on her head. She did not make eye contact. She could feel the moist heat of his breath on her face. She held her breath and concentrated on staying still, not stepping away. It seemed to take forever. Ronda went through various chess strategies in her head to distract herself. When he was finished, the paramedic handed Ronda a bottle of anti-inflammatories. 'Take two of these, twice a day,' he said. 'With food. They're hard on your stomach.'

Ronda nodded.

'It shouldn't leave a scar,' he said then. His voice was kind. Ronda was horrified to find her sight blur with tears.

'It's just the shock,' the paramedic said. 'You've had a nasty fall. Take it easy with that head wound. And if anything changes, come in to us.'

CHAPTER 4

Ronda didn't know what was worse. The bruising up and down her body and the sharpness of the pain in her head, which the paramedic had wrapped in bandages to staunch the bleeding, or the presence of her mother and her sister, sitting on either side of her on the couch in the small sitting room at the front of the house. The decor hadn't changed since Ronda was a child. Varying shades of brown, in the main. The good room, her mother still called it, even though the cabbage roses on the wallpaper had dulled to beige and the vines that held them seemed to sag with the passage of the years. It was cold too, being north-facing and never benefitting from the warmth of a fire, since carbon monoxide poisoning was one of the many perils her mother worried about. The radiator behind the rigid back of the couch had stopped working so long ago, Ronda couldn't remember the last time it had felt warm to the touch.

'I don't know why you insist on cycling that bicycle,' said her mother as Margo handed out cups of tea. 'It's a deathtrap.'

Ronda wrapped her hands around the cup and let the swirls of steam warm her face. 'I was trying not to flatten Mrs Murphy's cat,' she said.

'That cat gave this little one fleas,' said her mother, picking Jessica Fletcher up from the floor where she had been wound around Annie's feet. 'You should have flattened it.'

She made a hollow in her skirt and Jessica Fletcher

stepped into it, curled herself into a ball and fell asleep. They had been close ever since Annie had come upon her years ago, in a skip at the back of the parish hall.

'The flea incident was ten years ago,' said Ronda.

'That treatment cost me a fortune,' said Annie. 'And me on the widow's pension, trying to make ends meet.'

This was a refrain both daughters were familiar with. Margo looked at her watch.

'You were so good to come, Margo,' Annie said, petting her youngest daughter's arm in much the same way she petted Jessica Fletcher, when the cat permitted it.

'I was convinced Ronda was either dead or dying, the way you were going on.' Margo stood up and brushed the front of her silk blouse with both hands, as if there were biscuit crumbs there, which there were not because they hadn't eaten biscuits, and even if they had, Margo would not have scattered any crumbs on her clothes.

'She was gushing when I saw her,' said Annie. 'I was sure she'd bleed out. I nearly had one of my turns.' Margo bent and kissed her mother's cheek. 'I'd better get back to the hospice,' she said, 'I've still got to put the final touches on the budget for the annual fundraiser, and then I've to pick Tiernan and Sebastian up from rugby practice, collect Malcolm Junior from the library and feed the three of them when I get home. Malcolm's working late again.' She draped a long cashmere coat around her delicate shoulders, pulled on a pair of fine leather gloves and carefully arranged a beret over her hair. The coat, gloves and beret were all the same oxblood colour.

'Thanks for coming over,' said Ronda.

'You got me out of a particularly boring committee

meeting,' said Margo, striding towards the door of the good room. 'If that lot ever got their hands on the reins, nothing would happen.'

'They're very lucky to have you,' declared Annie. This was true. Margo had only agreed to organise one Christmas fundraiser, years ago, when Malcolm's mother was a patient there. Now, she was the Director of Strategy, Planning and Fundraising. She was also the chairperson of the Parents' Council at her boys' private school, the treasurer of the Residents' Association, and had a weekly slot on a radio programme about women in the workplace where she answered listener queries. 'Some people think there's no such thing as a stupid question,' Margo often said, eyerolling.

All this, and raising three children, all boys, all brilliant in one way or the other.

'Wait Margo,' said Annie, struggling out of the couch. In the end, Ronda had to put her good hand on the modest swell of her mother's buttocks and give her a gentle shove. When Annie got to her feet, she was out of breath. 'I want to say something, while I have you both here.'

'What is it?' said Margo, reaching into her Michael Kors handbag and picking out a lipstick, which she applied expertly without recourse to a mirror or even a reflective surface.

The colour of the lipstick was oxblood too. Ronda couldn't help admiring her sister's attention to detail. Annie cleared her throat. 'I'm getting my affairs in order,' she said, which caught her daughters' attention since she was not usually the sort of woman who made such pronouncements. 'I've spoken to a solicitor and he advised me to organise an enduring power of attorney. I think Margo would be best for the job.' Ronda was unsurprised to hear this. Margo was generally best for most jobs.

'It should be Ronda,' said Margo. 'She's the eldest.'

Annie shook her head. 'Ronda would hate the responsibility of it, wouldn't you Ronda?'

'Well, I . . .' began Ronda.

'Besides,' Annie went on. 'You're more familiar with this type of thing, Margo. Look how well you dealt with that court case against the hospice last year.'

Margo examined the arm of the couch, then wiped it before perching on the edge of it. 'That was a nuisance case, taken by a nut job,' she said. 'There was nothing to it.'

Annie opened the sideboard and took out a large brown envelope. 'Let's face it, girls, I'm not getting any younger, and with my extensive health problems, who knows when I'll breathe my last?' As this was also familiar terrain, her daughters no longer rushed in with contradictions, or reminded their mother that she was only 74, and so, for a moment, there was silence. Annie pressed the paperwork into Margo's hands.

'Fine,' said Margo, standing up and brushing the back of her coat with her hands. 'I'll look through this stuff tonight when I've time, okay?'

'There's something else,' said Annie.

'What is it?' said Margo with ill-concealed impatience.

Annie cleared her throat. 'I'm thinking about selling the house,' she said.

'What?' said both daughters at once.

'I've thought about it, and you're right, Margo,' Annie went on. 'A granny flat would be the best option for me. It was so kind of you to offer to refurbish the outhouse in your back garden. I know I said no, but I've had time to think. A granny flat would be easier to maintain. Safer too, all on one level. I nearly fell down the steps to the kitchen last week.'

Inside her chest, Ronda's heart was thumping. She could feel the pulse of it at the back of her throat. Margo recovered first.

'You only nearly fell,' she said, in a light, nothing-to-see-here tone. 'Which is another way of saying you didn't fall. You were fine, you love living here, all your memories of Dad are here. And us when we were babies.'

'You were the one who suggested the granny flat, remember?' said Annie. 'Last year, after I nearly came a cropper on the landing, tripping over that silly mousetrap that Ronda fashioned out of a water bottle, remember?'

'I caught four mice,' said Ronda.

'I don't know why we can't get ordinary traps,' said Annie. 'That way you know the buggers are dead. The ones you caught probably came straight back in through the back door after you let them go.'

'Let's get back to the matter in hand, shall we?' said Margo.

'As I was saying,' said Annie, 'I think you're right Margo, I'd be much better off living with you. This house needs a lot of work and I have neither the means nor the good health to see to it.'

For a brief and unusual moment, Margo seemed lost for words.

'Well?' prompted her mother, after what seemed an inordinate period of time.

'Of course,' said Margo then. 'Absolutely. That would be fine. If that's what you really want? I just . . .' Here, Margo paused. Ronda could nearly see the cogs in her brain whirring as realisation dawned. 'Is this about Dr Anderson?' Margo said, eyeballing her mother.

'What? No, of course not.' Annie spoke quickly without recourse to eye contact.

'It is, isn't it?' went on Margo. 'This is about Dr Anderson moving to a clinic in Howth, just down the road from my house.'

'It's got nothing to do with that whatsoever.' Annie rustled through her paperwork. Dr Anderson had been the family GP for years. He was – Ronda mused for a moment before she found the appropriate word – an understanding GP. Patient too, always greeting Annie warmly no matter how many times she'd been to see him that week. 'But don't get me started on that new lady doctor they've pawned me off on since Dr Anderson left. She's from, I don't know, India or somewhere,' Annie continued in a high, quavery voice that threatened tears. 'She's a quack, telling me to join the choir and take up yoga and mindfulness and all sorts. Can you imagine me doing yoga? At my age.'

Margo patted her mother's arm in the absent-minded way she had when her brain was at full tilt. 'But selling the house,' she said. 'It seems a bit . . . drastic. I could drive you to Dr Anderson's, you know.'

Annie shook her head. 'You're much too busy love, I wouldn't impose on you like that.'

Margo looked at Ronda, although Ronda wasn't sure if she was actually seeing her. Margo's mind was still wheeling, probably berating herself for ever suggesting refurbishing the outhouse in her professionally landscaped, secluded back garden. Ronda thought she might have mentioned it at

Tiernan's birthday dinner last year. Probably after the guts of a bottle of wine or two. Margo had never considered the possibility that their mother would agree to the suggestion.

Not for one minute.

'What about Ronda?' Margo said then, pointing at her sister. 'Where's she going to live?'

Ronda had the curious and familiar sensation of not being in the room. That she had no part to play in the drama that was unfolding before her. She felt like a piece of driftwood, being tossed this way and that in a current. She knew it was wrong to feel this way, and that she should say something in answer to Margo's enquiry, but for the life of her, she couldn't think of a thing.

'When I sell the house, I'll have to keep most of the proceeds in case I need to go into a home, God forbid. But I'll try and give you girls a little something too. Maybe enough for a deposit Ronda? For a house.'

Ronda nodded. She didn't mention that no bank official in their right mind would give her a mortgage, large or small. Not on her paltry wages.

'Let's think rationally about this for a minute.' Margo was pacing now, in full military mode. 'You shouldn't have to move out of the home you love just because . . .' She stopped in front of Ronda. 'How about if Ronda learns how to drive,' she declared suddenly. 'I'm sure it wouldn't take her long. While she's learning, I'll drive you to Dr Anderson's new clinic. Then, once she's passed her test, Ronda can drive you to your appointments. She works shifts, so she'll have time. And you won't have to subject yourself to the inconvenience of moving house.'

'No,' said Ronda.

'Oh,' said Annie, and Ronda wondered if she had spoken at all. Annie sat straighter on the sofa. 'That could work, Margo. I could still see Dr Anderson, and Ronda wouldn't have to cycle that deathtrap.'

'No,' said Ronda, again. Or for the first time, she couldn't be sure.

'It would be good for you,' Margo said to Ronda, on a roll now. 'Give you a new lease of life.'

'I don't need a new lease of life,' said Ronda.

'Of course you do,' said Margo, dismissively.

'I don't want to learn how to drive,' said Ronda.

'I know you're a bit of a nervous Nelly,' said Annie. 'But Margo's a great teacher.'

'What do you mean?' said Margo, confusion clouding her immaculate face.

'You have the driving instructor permit, I'd nearly forgotten,' Annie went on. 'And you've got experience. Look at how well you're doing with Sebastian. And Malcolm Junior passed his test, didn't he?'

Margo couldn't help smiling. 'He passed it first time. And Sebastian's only had three lessons, but he's already reversing around corners like a pro.'

'So it'll be no bother to you then,' said Annie, 'teaching your sister.'

Margo clamoured out of her reverie. 'My boys are an entirely different kettle of fish to Ronda here,' she said. She glanced at her sister. 'No offence, Ronda.'

'None taken,' said Ronda absently as she cast about her head for an alternative solution. 'You could get the bus to Dr Anderson's new clinic,' she said to Annie. 'I could even go with you, when I'm off duty.'

Annie shook her head, her lips pursing the way they did when Ronda put butter beans instead of beef into a stew. 'Mrs Murphy never takes the bus.'

'What does Mrs Murphy have to do with anything?' said Ronda.

'She has a husband who drives her anywhere she wants to go,' said Annie, her voice high and shaky, threatening tears.

'Let's all sleep on it, okay?' said Margo.

'No,' said Annie firmly. 'I've made up my mind. Either you teach Ronda how to drive or I'm selling up.'

Margo was momentarily silenced by Annie's authoritative tone.

'Well?' said Annie, looking at Margo for a response. 'You're always looking for new challenges.'

'This would definitely be challenging,' said Margo. 'But maybe . . .'

'No,' said Ronda.

Margo opened the door. 'I'll be late if I don't go now.'

'I'll see you out,' said Ronda, using her good arm to lift herself off the couch.

At the front door, the sisters engaged in a series of back-and-forth hissed whispers.

'I am not learning how to drive,' hissed Ronda.

'So you'd prefer to be homeless?' hissed Margo.

'I could rent,' said Ronda.

'Have you been living under a rock? There is nowhere to rent,' said Margo. 'And even if there was, you couldn't afford it on your salary.'

'I pay rent here,' said Ronda.

'You pay five hundred quid,' hissed Margo.

'Plus bills,' said Ronda.

'Even, so, that's about a quarter of what you'd pay to rent an apartment,' said Margo. 'Or even a dingy flat.'

'I have savings,' said Ronda. Over the years, she had managed to squirrel away some money into a credit union account. It amounted to ten thousand, seven hundred and eighty-eight euros.

'That's for a rainy day, not rent.' Margo spoke with such authority, it was impossible to argue with her.

Ronda changed tack. 'You said you couldn't teach me. I'm not like the boys. And you're right,' whispered Ronda. She didn't add, 'You're always right,' in a resentful tone, which is what she felt like doing.

'What I said was, we should all sleep on it,' said Margo.

'There's no way you'd have time to teach me how to drive,' Ronda went on.

'I'll make time,' said Margo grimly.

'There are rooms to rent,' said Ronda. 'I'd have enough to rent a room, I'm sure.'

'Have you absolutely no ambition?' said Margo.

There was silence for a bit after that. Ronda had always known that Margo didn't think much of her life. But there was a difference between suspecting it and knowing for sure. Margo dug her car keys out from her handbag and opened the front door. 'Bye Mam,' she called out in a bright, breezy way, as if their hissed toing and froing had never taken place. The front door slammed shut behind her and the ensuing silence felt like a drill vibrating in Ronda's aching head.

From the good room, she could hear her mother sigh, then the creak of the couch. 'I suppose I'll have to cook dinner now,' she said, shuffling into the hall. 'What did you do with the pork chop, Ronda?'

CHAPTER 5

The paramedic told Ronda not to return to work for at least four days. At six a.m. on the second day, she put on her scrubs and stole out of the house. It was so dark that, had her mother awoken and peered around the edge of her bedroom curtains, she might not have seen Ronda wheeling her bicycle down the garden path.

The bike was good as new again. While Ronda didn't have a wheel jig, she did own a spoke key, which was all she really needed. Truing a wheel took patience and time rather than skill.

It took a bit of work to get her leg – an impressive and tender carnival of bruises – over the crossbar. Her arm was also sensitive. As was the mound on her forehead, although the cut that had produced so much blood was negligible. Her fringe was due a trim and she managed to persuade a clump of it over the worst of the lump. She had stopped taking the anti-inflammatories, which, even when taken with food, had been hard on her stomach. And she took as few of the painkillers as she could get away with. She distrusted the addictive nature of codeine. Or perhaps it was her own nature she distrusted, addiction being something of a family trait.

She hadn't gone back to Mr Hannigan's shop to get her helmet. She couldn't have borne his commentary on her injuries. Instead, she clamped on her spare helmet, which wasn't as good but would do until the bruising on her face had faded sufficiently. She cycled with her usual speed and competency, although she found herself mounting the pavement whenever she heard a car approach from behind. She would have to stop that. She decided to allow herself this one journey on the path, after which normal service would resume.

It began to rain. Ronda took her waterproof trousers and her oversized rain jacket out of her pannier and struggled into both. She knew Margo would disapprove of her returning to work so soon after the accident and against medical advice, but she didn't think she could bear another day cooped up in the house.

With her mother.

When she wasn't complaining about some imagined pain or ache, she was watching re-runs of *Murder She Wrote* at eardrum-shattering volume or whispering baby talk to Jessica Fletcher. On the odd occasion when Ronda wondered – mildly – if Annie could lower the volume on her tablet, she was treated to a blow-by-blow account of Annie's tinnitus which was a curse and a scourge and necessitated the inching up of the volume steadily throughout the show so that, by the time the final credits rolled, Ronda could no longer hear the kettle when it whistled.

But even if her mother had been a different sort of person, Ronda wanted to get back to work. She knew that her colleagues' workload would not have been significantly reduced by the agency worker who had replaced her these past two days. Ronda hunched over the handlebars and went through the moves in her head for the decoy strategy she was planning to use in her current game against Berkley.

The chess set had been gifted to her by Joseph when things had been good between them. After she got the results of her first-year nursing exams. After they'd moved into Joseph's recently-deceased aunt's house up the road. After she'd bought their first piece of furniture: a small couch, just big enough for two. When she and Eileen were still friends. Before she discovered that Joseph was not the soulmate she had taken him for. A good bit before that. She had thought briefly of giving the chess set away afterwards, but she'd already started calling him Berkley by then and it seemed cruel to discard him. Apart from always reminding her of her shortcomings when it came to the game of chess, Berkley hadn't done anything wrong.

The nursing home was eight kilometres away. There was a cycle lane, but it was narrow and unreliable, given its tendency to end abruptly at sporadic intervals.

'Distract him with my queen, then advance with the bishop and weaken his defence,' Ronda said, as the rain streamed off her hood, collecting along the curve of her dark eyelashes and running down her face. 'The classic zwischenzug.'

Green Gables was neither green nor gabled, since the roof was a flat, rubber-clad affair. In the brochure, it claimed to be a 'home away from home for your loved ones', but it was a pretty generic nursing home, squat and square and beige, with long, fluorescent-lit corridors and a pervading smell of antiseptic, air freshener and shepherd's pie. Still, Ronda smiled as she cycled through the gates. It was good to be back. She undid the clasp of her second-best helmet. Her thick, dark hair was plastered to her head. Her second-best helmet was not as sweat-repellent as the one she'd left behind, probably hanging by its strap among the silent, rigid carcasses at the back of Mr Hannigan's shop.

Fatima emerged from the side door with a bulging rubbish bag. 'Ronda my darling girl, what are you doing back?' Everything about Fatima was vibrant. She was a strong, tall Nigerian woman made taller by the *gele* she wore, the brightly coloured head wrap wound tightly around her hair. She had broad shoulders, magnificent hips, and a smile that spread across her face like the sun soaring up from the horizon. Ronda, being pale, wiry and short, sometimes wondered if she was there at all, when she stood beside Fatima. 'You're not due back for another two days,' Fatima said.

'I'm fine now,' said Ronda, getting off her bike as effortlessly as she could manage, tossing her fringe about with her hands.

'You don't look fine,' said Fatima, peering into Ronda's face. 'You look pale.'

'I'm always pale,' said Ronda.

'And tired,' Fatima went on. 'You should be resting. I will make you yam soup. With peanuts, for energy.'

Fatima threw food at situations. Ronda remembered Fatima arriving for her first day at Green Gables, two years ago, like one of the three wise men, but instead of gold, frankincense or myrrh, she had come bearing a three-tier coffee and walnut cake, a lemon drizzle traybake, and a tin of chocolate chip cookies. Fergal had looked doubtful when he saw her wares and had been about to launch into some health and safety regulation rant when Fatima had said, 'Let me guess,' cutting a generous slice of the coffee cake and handing it to him, 'this is what you would have picked, isn't it?'

'It is, actually,' Fergal had said, a little suspicious.

Ronda had the unusual experience of warming to Fatima from the start. She did her best to curb her enthusiasm, but Fatima was having none of it. 'We will be friends, you and I,' she declared early on.

'What makes you say that?' asked Ronda.

'I know these things,' said Fatima, tapping her nose with her finger in such a serious way that Ronda couldn't help laughing. A laugh-out-loud laugh – there was no way she'd imagined it, she remembered people turning their heads to see what the racket was.

And that was that. They were friends. They had little in common. Ronda had never gone bowling before she met Fatima. Now, on Friday nights when their shifts allowed, she could be found at the bowling alley with Fatima and her daughter Ada. Ronda surprised herself by being above average at the game.

'Are you going to let me win?' Ada wanted to know that first night.

'No,' said Ronda. 'I'll beat you fair and square.' Ada grinned at her.

'Yam soup would be lovely,' said Ronda.

'With peanuts,' Fatima reminded her. She put her hands on Ronda's shoulders and, even though the right shoulder winced with the contact, the warm weight of her touch through Ronda's rain jacket was a comfort.

'You'll regret coming back so soon, Ronda,' she said, picking up the rubbish bag. 'Fergal's on the warpath.'

Ronda lifted the lid of the bin with her good arm. 'He's always on the warpath,' she said.

'That's true,' said Fatima, tossing the bag inside.

'What does Ada want for her birthday?' asked Ronda as they walked towards the building. 'I can't believe she's going to be thirteen.' Her right leg was not happy with the rigour of her stride, but she refused to slow down or limp. Fatima would send her packing if she did.

Fatima opened the door and ushered Ronda through. 'A room of her own, like Virginia Woolf advised,' she said, smiling. Fatima had been searching for a place for her and Ada to rent for several weeks now, with no luck. In spite of that, her resolve never faltered. 'It's just a matter of time, isn't it?' she said brightly. Ronda did not have her friend's reserves of optimism. She didn't see Fatima and Ada getting out of the direct provision centre any time soon.

Inside, rainwater dripped from Ronda onto the coarse weave of the doormat. Her hand – the one that had tried to break her fall – throbbed as she fumbled with the zip of her rain jacket.

'Let me,' said Fatima, brushing Ronda's hand away. She unzipped the jacket and tugged at the sleeves until Ronda was released. 'You should get better at asking for help,' she said, guiding Ronda into a chair and yanking the saturated waterproofs down her legs.

'Has Mrs Finnerty died yet?' asked Ronda.

'No,' said Fatima, stuffing the wet gear into a plastic bag and handing it to Ronda. 'I think she's waiting for you.'

Most of the residents waited for Ronda, when their time came. Perhaps it was her acceptance of things in general. And death in particular. She didn't seem averse to calling it by its name. She wasn't cowed by it. And so, when their time came, neither were they.

'Come in to me for soup later, okay?' said Fatima, making a beeline for the kitchen where she reigned.

Ronda made her way to her bathroom to wash her hands before starting work. She towel dried her hair and hands and face, smoothed a few wrinkles out of her scrubs. Then she straightened and glanced at herself in the mirror. She looked like a black and white photograph. With her pale grey eyes, small white face, black hair and white scrubs. She pinched her cheeks, which had no effect on their pallor.

Behind reception, Monika-from-Minsk answered the phone in her guttural, grim voice. 'Green Gables Nursing Home, Monika speaking, how may I be of assistance?' Instead of her usual curt nod, Monika waved as Ronda walked past. Ronda felt warmed by the effusive greeting.

The residents were in the dayroom sitting in a semicircle of hard-backed armchairs, singing along to a Daniel O'Donnell DVD, while Kim, the youngest of the care assistants, handed out cups of sweet, milky tea and slices of Fatima's orange and cardamom cake. 'That'll warm the cockles of your heart,' Kim told Captain Grady, handing him the tea in his Dad's Army mug. She spoke in a loud Dublin accent, which seemed at odds with her delicate frame. Ernest, the handyman from Brazil, knelt on the floor, bleeding one of the radiators. He had worked at Green Gables for two years and, oddly, Fergal liked him. Partly because Ernest was quiet and unassuming, traits that Fergal valued in his employees. But mostly because Ernest managed to complete all the tasks Fergal demanded of him, no matter how outlandish. If he didn't know how to do it, he watched a tutorial on YouTube. In this way, he had tiled one of the resident bathrooms, laid the patio in the garden, re-plumbed the staff toilet, and installed downlights in the ceiling in Fergal's office along with a dimmer switch. 'Mood lighting' Fergal called it.

Ronda knew that Ernest liked Kim. Nobody else had noticed this, least of all Kim, in spite of her never-ending and – thus far – fruitless quest for The One. Ernest, being quiet and unassuming, never voiced his feelings to Kim. Ronda smiled at him as she walked into the dayroom.

'You're not from these parts,' Captain Grady was saying, eyeing Kim with suspicion. The medals on the lapel of his uniform glinted in the harsh lighting overhead.

'You said you weren't going to be racist any more, remember?' said Ronda, adjusting his army hat that had slipped over his eyes.

'Ronda,' he said, his face dissolving into a smile as he wrapped his hands around the mug of tea.

'Room Number 23,' said Teresa, sitting in the armchair beside him. She was a tiny bird of a woman buried in layers of cardigans, cradling a doll that she called 'Baby' in the crook of her arm. 'The house was beside the bakery. We could smell the bread in the mornings.'

'Where's your other slipper, Teresa?' asked Ronda, kneeling to look under her armchair.

'I was only asking Kim a civil question,' said Captain Grady. 'Know your enemy, basic military strategy.'

'Found it, Teresa,' said Ronda, pulling a slipper in the shape of a moose from under the chair. Teresa put Baby in the crib beside her. Ernest had made it from a slab of walnut worktop he had rescued from a skip. Teresa held her foot out so Ronda could feed it into her slipper, and placed her hand on the curved wooden edge of the crib. She rocked it gently.

'I'm from Ireland,' said Kim, wiping a spool of saliva hanging from Captain Grady's mouth with a tissue. 'It's my mother who's not from these parts. She's from Vietnam.'

Captain Grady put down his cup and stood up, ramrod straight. 'The bunk house is ready to be inspected,' he barked.

'I'll do it right away,' said Ronda, putting her hand on his shoulder. 'At ease, Captain.'

'Nothing like the smell of fresh baked bread,' said Kim as she handed Teresa a cup of tea. 'Isn't that right?' Her smile widened to reveal a gap between the two front teeth.

'I thought you'd died, Ronda,' said Sheila, an enormous woman with an air of tragedy and a thatch of white hair, sitting at the end of the row. Crumbs of cake were scattered across the widow's weeds she insisted on wearing, even though her husband, Charlo, was alive and well. 'Fatima never gave me any cake.'

'I gave you the biggest slice, Sheila,' said Fatima, coming into the dayroom with a trolley to collect the cups and plates.

'She didn't,' Sheila whispered to Ronda.

'You look a little peaky, Ronda,' said Kim, 'if you don't mind my saying so.' She cut a generous wedge of cake and handed it to Ronda. 'This will perk you up. Fatima baked it this morning, it's exceptional.'

'That cake is for the residents, Kim,' boomed a voice from the doorway. 'We're trying to cut costs, not incur them.' Fergal Hutch was the general manager and son of Ronda's first boss, Senan, who now seemed like the Dalai Lama by comparison. Fergal wore one of a collection of shiny suits, with a pair of pointy-toed tan brogues. Ronda could smell his hair product from across the room, damp and dense. Despite its pungency, the gel did little to disguise the thinning barnet that he pushed over his forehead in an attempt to create the illusion of volume. Today, he was flanked by the nurse manager, Tracey Fuller, who adored her position as Fergal's 'right-hand woman', which is how he referred to her when he needed his dirty work done.

'You came back to work at last,' Tracey said to Ronda.

Fergal patted Tracey's arm. 'Poor Tracey had a nightmare getting agency staff at such short notice,' he said.

Ronda picked up the enormous slice of cake Kim had given her and held it aloft in a vaguely threatening way as she advanced on him. Fergal took a step back, alarmed.

'That's because nobody in their right mind would want to work for you on the pittance of wages you pay, you sanctimonious little twat,' said Ronda. She sank her teeth into the sticky cake. Kim was right, it was exceptional, the peppery notes of the cardamom complimenting the dense sweetness of the orange. Anybody who could stood up and cheered. The rest remained seated but cheered nonetheless.

'Ronda?' came Fergal's impatient voice.

On the television, Daniel O'Donnell was singing 'Our House is a Home' and doing his peculiar little shuffle-dance across the stage. Ronda placed the plate with the cake onto Fatima's trolley and looked at Fergal. The muscle in his cheek had a tendency to twitch when he was irritated.

'Sorry Fergal,' said Ronda. 'What did you say?'

Fergal sighed. 'I was saying what a nightmare it was, getting agency staff at such short notice.'

'Sorry about that, I . . .' Ronda began, looking around. The residents were looking at the television. Nobody was cheering. Fergal looked at his watch. 'I'm late for a meeting,' he said.

Long after he left, the smell of Brylcreem remained. Ronda could taste it in her mouth. 'I'll be in Mrs Finnerty's room if anyone's looking for me,' she said. The only person who responded was Captain Grady, who stood up and performed a stiff salute in Ronda's direction. Ronda saluted back.

On her way down the corridor, she passed Ms Gallagher's room. The door was ajar, which meant that now was a good time. If you wanted to call in. Or at least, not a terrible time. Ronda knocked gently. 'Ms Gallagher?'

'Who's there?' The Belfast accent, sharp as a blade.

'It's Ronda.'

'Well, don't just stand there.'

Ms Gallagher was one of the few residents of Green Gables still in possession of her mental faculties. Ronda wasn't always convinced that was a good thing. Ms Gallagher was a short, stocky woman, dressed in her usual uniform of runners, jeans, T-shirt and leather jacket – all black since she was in mourning for Ireland – with a black and white Palestinian keffiyeh tied loosely around her neck. The white in the scarf matched the white of her hair, which was thick and bushy and looked like it had never felt the tooth of a comb through it.

'How are you today?' asked Ronda.

'Living the dream,' Ms Gallagher said. She lay the well-thumbed book she was reading across her knees. *Imperialism, the Highest Stage of Capitalism* by V.L. Lenin. A beautiful hardback showing its age now, the velvet ribbon bookmark frayed at the ends, and deep cracks running up and down the spine.

'Where've you been?' she barked.

'I was a bit under the weather,' said Ronda. 'Nothing serious.'

Ms Gallagher shook her head and sighed. 'It's stabilisers you need, girl. Or a tricycle.'

'Who told you?' asked Ronda.

'Kim, of course,' said Ms Gallagher. 'The Oracle. If it wasn't for her, sure I'd know nothing.'

'You need anything?' asked Ronda.

'A cure for MS would be nice,' said Ms Gallagher.

'Fatima's made cake,' said Ronda.

'I suppose that'll have to do instead,' said Ms Gallagher.

'I'll bring some in to you after I've checked on Mrs Finnerty.'

'Is that woman not dead yet?' said Ms Gallagher, burrowing in her hair for her glasses and picking up the book.

Ronda's phone rang as she left the room. It was on silent as per company policy, but she felt it vibrate against her hip. She picked it out of her pocket and glanced at the screen. It was Margo. Ronda's first inclination was to reject the call, presuming that Margo was ringing to resume the argument about the driving lessons. Her finger hovered over the disconnect button on the phone, but she hesitated. Perhaps it was important? Or even an emergency, since Margo usually texted rather than phoned. Ronda answered the phone.

'Did you get that email?' said Margo.

Fergal appeared at the top of the corridor, holding the door open for a posse of men in black suits. Judging from their accents, they were American.

'Could I ring you later?' whispered Ronda into the phone, as the men made their way towards her.

'No,' said Margo. 'I'm due in a meeting in three minutes with Catherine, our outreach programme manager. I've a horrible feeling she's going to tender her resignation. At lunchtime I have to go through the annual report with the accountant at the golf club, then prep for the Parents' Council meeting. Then this evening, there's Sebastian's parent–teacher meeting and that's before I've done the grocery shop or made dinner. Oh, and I've to get to the fishmongers. Malcolm's on a new diet and needs organic seabass.'

'This way, gentlemen,' said Fergal, gesturing towards the glass door that led into his office at the end of the corridor. Ronda pressed herself against the wall as they passed in an eyewatering blast of cologne.

'The email is from Mam's solicitor,' said Margo. 'Donal something-or-other.'

'I can't believe she actually got herself a solicitor,' said Ronda. 'She won't even make her own doctors' appointments any more. I have to do it.'

'I suppose that's a jibe at me,' said Margo.

'No,' said Ronda. 'I'm just saying . . . I can't remember the last time she did anything quite so dynamic.'

'Anyway,' said Margo. Ronda could hear her fingernails tapping against a keyboard. 'He wants us to call into his office this evening.'

'Who?' said Ronda.

'Donal head-the-ball, Jesus Ronda, can't you keep up for once?'

Ronda closed her eyes and took a deep breath. Fatima was always on at her to remember to breathe when she was stressed.

'I can't afford to take any more time off work,' said Ronda.

'It's after your shift,' said Margo. 'Five thirty. Sharp.'

'Okay,' said Ronda. Her shift ended at five today. 'Where is the solicitor's office?'

'Read the email,' said Margo. 'I have to go.'

*

Mrs Finnerty's room was in darkness and it took a moment for Ronda's pupils to adjust. The outline of the hoist was the first thing she could make out. Then the rail of the bed. A dull margin of daylight skulking at the edges of the curtains. The rasp of a laboured breath. The rheumatoid arthritis – which Mrs Finnerty had suffered from since she was a teenager – had reached her lungs, inflaming and scarring the delicate tissue around them.

'Maria?' whispered Ronda. She was uncomfortable with the familiarity, but when Mrs Finnerty got her second bout of pneumonia this winter, she had insisted.

'Maria? Ronda said again, a little louder this time. She placed her fingers along Mrs Finnerty's long, narrow neck and waited. After a while, she could feel the faint flutter of a pulse through the pads of her fingers.

Mrs Finnerty opened her eyes, startling Ronda with the clarity of the blue irises.

'Ronda?' she said.

'I'm here,' whispered Ronda, picking up one of her mottled, bony hands. 'Do you need some more morphine?'

'I think I do,' she said. 'But I'm afraid that the next dose will be the one that sends me on my way.' Her words were punctuated by wheezes. 'Won't it?' She peered into Ronda's face.

'It might,' she said.

Maria Finnerty shut her eyes tightly.

'I don't want to die alone,' she said.

'You're not alone,' said Ronda, squeezing Maria's hand as gently as she could.

'Do you believe in heaven?' Maria asked.

Ronda shook her head. 'Do you?'

'I'm a Catholic,' said Maria.

'I can call a priest, if you'd like?'

The old lady grunted then, her eyes narrowing. 'They never did much good for anyone,' she said. She shut her eyes and a tear slid out of one, rolling down the side of her face, collecting in a tiny puddle at the edge of her earlobe. Ronda brushed it away with her finger.

Mrs Finnerty sighed. 'I'm tired,' she said, her eyelids coming down like shutters.

'Get some rest,' said Ronda, leaning over to tuck the blankets around the woman's sloped shoulders.

'Ronda?'

'Yes?'

'Maybe I will have that morphine.'

'I'll get the nurse.'

'Will you stay with me afterwards?'

'I will,' said Ronda. She lay her hand along Mrs Finnerty's forehead. It was clammy and warm. Her face had a pale, yellow tinge. She didn't have much longer. Ronda was glad she hadn't missed Mrs Finnerty's death. She was good at death. It was not a skill that could be easily incorporated into a CV, but it was a valuable one nonetheless.

CHAPTER 6

The solicitor's office was in a Georgian building in North Strand that had seen better days. It took Ronda longer than it normally would to cycle there with the ache down her side, exacerbated after a day's work, but she managed it with five minutes to spare. She was chaining her bicycle to a lamppost when Margo pulled up outside in her Range Rover.

'You're parked on a yellow line,' Ronda pointed out when Margo emerged, dressed in a black power suit and box-fresh Adidas trainers.

'I don't know why you bother chaining that yoke,' said Margo, looking with distaste at Ronda's bicycle. 'Who in their right mind would steal it?

'Why don't you just park down the road?' said Ronda. 'At an actual parking space?'

'We won't be long,' said Margo, throwing the keys into her handbag.

'How can you tell how long we'll be?' said Ronda.

'Will you just come on?' Margo inspected the panel of buzzers on the side of the door. She pressed the one beside a handwritten sign that read, 'Donal Clarke Solicitor'. Ronda removed the clothes pegs she used in place of bicycle clips from the ends of her scrubs and took off her helmet.

'Hello?' a loud voice boomed through the intercom.

'It's Margo McCann-Waters and Ronda McCann, we're your five thirty,' Margo said suggestively.

'Come on up, second floor.'

A buzzer sounded and Ronda pushed at the heavy door, which groaned as if in protest at the intrusion. Margo rushed inside.

The hallway smelled vaguely of damp and neglect and old age, the wallpaper peeling away from the walls at the corners. Margo clamped her hand over her mouth and nose. 'And no bloody lift,' she hissed through the gaps in her fingers. She started up the stairs, Ronda behind, doing her best to keep up.

The office was down a long, draughty corridor at the back of the building. The sign on the door read, 'Donal Clarke, Solicitor-at-Large'. Ronda was just about to knock on the door when it was thrown open and a long, hairy hand was thrust in her face.

'You must be Ronda,' said the sandy-haired man, smiling. 'Your mother described you to a tee.' He shook Ronda's hand and she did her best not to wince. He was tall and narrow and wore a pair of faded jeans that looked like they had never felt the warm plate of an iron, and a bright pink Bermuda shirt, as if he was on a package holiday in Tenerife. His eyes reminded Ronda of Jessica Fletcher. There were freckles everywhere. 'And Margo I imagine? Lovely to meet you both.' He shook Margo's hand gently, perhaps mindful of her slenderness and air of fragility, facilitated no doubt by the intermittent fasting diet she adhered to with the tenacity of a zealot.

There was nothing in the office apart from a filing cabinet – open and overflowing – a couch with stuffing erupting from it in small white clouds, a camping chair, and, on the windowsill, a house plant. Ronda thought it might have been a peace lily, once.

'Are you . . . redecorating?' Margo asked, looking around.

'No,' said Donal, ushering them towards the couch. Margo, stunned at the lack of explanation for the state of the place, forgot to inspect the couch before she sat on it. Donal rummaged in the cabinet and pulled out a slim file with the name, 'Annie McCann' handwritten in looping lettering across the top.

When he sat in the camping chair, Ronda noticed his feet, which were also long and hairy and pushed into a pair of flip-flops.

'How did my mother find you?' asked Margo. If Donal Clarke found Margo's tone disparaging, he did not appear to take offence.

'I don't do a lot of legal work any more, to be honest,' said Donal, shifting to find a more comfortable spot in the camping chair. 'Just a bit for the Citizen's Information clients. That's where Annie got my name.'

'Where did you work before?' said Margo.

There was a pause before Donal answered. 'I was a partner at Clarke, Mason and O'Brien,' he said.

'Oh.' Margo's eyes widened at the mention of the prestigious legal firm. 'Why did you leave?'

'I was in corporate law,' said Donal, smiling at Margo as if that in itself was a perfectly reasonable explanation. 'But you know yourself, people hear you were once a solicitor and ask you to give them a dig out. I just do a bit of casework here and there.'

'I cannot believe Mam forked out for a solicitor,' said Margo. Even though she shook her head with vigour, Ronda noticed how her bob remained intact and immaculate.

'I only do pro bono work,' said Donal.

'That makes more sense,' said Margo. 'But I wonder why . . .?'

Ronda looked pointedly at her watch. 'Aren't you in a hurry, Margo?' she said.

'I'm only interested,' said Margo, bristling.

'It's just, I have to pick up a prescription for Mam before the chemist closes at seven,' said Ronda.

'Let's proceed then,' said Donal. 'You're the eldest Margo, is that correct?'

'I most certainly am not,' said Margo, her nostrils flaring. 'I am younger than Ronda by six and a half years. I would have thought that was perfectly obvious.'

Donal appeared unfazed by Margo's clipped clarification. 'I assumed that you were, since Annie is bestowing the power of attorney onto you. It's usually the eldest.'

'You know what they say about assuming,' said Margo. 'It makes an ass of you and me.'

Ronda concentrated on pulling down the zip of her jacket, which was a difficult procedure with her cold fingers. Her embarrassment was familiar but no less acute for that. She was embarrassed by Margo's rudeness. And by her own lethargic role in this interaction. She had no idea what she was doing here. What was her purpose?

'You know,' said Donal, thumbing through the paperwork. 'You don't actually have to be here, Ronda,' he said, as if he had read her mind and realised that any contribution she might make would be negligible.

There was a knock on the door. 'Come in,' boomed Donal, swivelling towards the door which opened to reveal a teenage boy in a tracksuit, maybe seventeen years old, thin and grey-skinned, his eyes enormous in his bony face.

'I got the date for my hearing,' the boy said, holding up a letter.

'That's quicker than I thought,' said Donal, standing up. He took the letter and scanned it.

'Is that bad?' said the boy, chewing on his bottom lip.

'No, no, of course not,' said Donal, putting his hairy hand on the boy's shoulder. 'It's good news, Carl. Will you go and make yourself a cup of tea in the kitchen and I'll be with you in a tick, okay?'

Carl peered around Donal's shoulder and registered the presence of Ronda and Margo. 'Oh,' he said. 'Sorry to disturb.'

'Not at all,' said Margo in the high, cheery voice she used when she was ill at ease. She had seen photographs of what heroin could do to a face at one of the drugs awareness events the PTA had arranged at her boys' school. Her grip on her handbag tightened.

Carl closed the door behind him.

'Sorry about that,' said Donal, sitting back down. 'Where was I?'

'You were saying that there was no need for me to stay,' said Ronda, standing up. Margo grabbed a fistful of Ronda's scrubs. 'Don't you dare leave me here on my own,' she hissed at her. She turned and smiled at Donal. 'No offence,' she said, and he shook his head.

'You can't be too careful,' he said. 'Although my ex tells me that if I were a dog, I'd be a basset hound.'

'Even basset hounds bite, I'm sure,' said Margo. 'Now, where do I sign?'

Donal was right, it didn't take long. Despite the basic nature of the office and his informal dress and manner, the solicitor surprised Ronda by being economical with their time and efficient with the paperwork.

Afterwards, he jumped out of his camping chair and put his hand out to shake Ronda's hand again.

'Don't,' Margo told him. 'She's black and blue after a fall off her bike but she's too polite not to shake your hand.'

'Oh, so that's what happened to your forehead,' said Donal, peering at Ronda's temple. 'I'm a cyclist too, you have my sympathies.'

'She won't be a cyclist for much longer,' said Margo, grimly. 'She's finally going to learn how to drive.'

Donal rummaged in his pockets and produced a tube of cream. 'You're probably already using this,' he said, handing it to Ronda. 'But if not, arnica is a great all-rounder for cuts and bruises.'

'It looks worse than it is,' said Ronda.

'So, how long does it take for you to process the paperwork?' Margo asked.

'I'm just waiting on a statement from Dr Anderson and . . .'

'I hope Mam didn't take up half your day with her aches and pains. It's her specialist topic,' said Margo.

Donal held the door open for them. 'Old age is not for the fainthearted,' he said.

Ronda couldn't help but roundly agree.

CHAPTER 7

Outside, the day had disimproved. Dark and cold, with a light but persistent sleety drizzle.

Margo's car had been clamped.

After Margo had stopped shouting and kicking the tyre of the Range Rover, she fished her phone out of her pocket to ring the number on the clamping notice plastered across her window. She stabbed at the screen with a long, rigid finger. And stabbed at it again. And again. 'As if things aren't bad enough,' she said, flinging the phone, which had run out of battery, into her bag.

'This wouldn't happen if you were a cyclist,' said Ronda, fishing her phone out of her pocket and handing it to Margo.

'Have you thought about it at all?' Margo snapped.

'What?' said Ronda, even though she knew perfectly well what Margo was referring to. Margo glared at her. 'Learning to drive,' she said, with studied patience.

Ronda nodded. 'I've thought about it,' she said.

'And?'

'No thank you.'

'Jesus Ronda,' said Margo, pushing her hands through her hair. 'Here I am, offering to teach you out of the goodness of my heart, and . . .'

'I don't want you to teach me,' said Ronda.

'Well somebody else can teach you then,' said Margo.

'It's not that,' said Ronda. 'I don't want to learn how to drive at all.'

'You have to,' insisted Margo. Her nostrils flared when she was angry, Ronda noticed. 'You do,' Margo said, as if bending Ronda to her will was a simple matter of repetition. 'Mam will be miserable living in a shed in my back garden, you know she will.'

'She's always miserable,' said Ronda, not unreasonably.

'She'll be more miserable,' said Margo. There was a pause then, perhaps both women wondering how their mother would manage such a feat.

'This is serious, Ronda,' said Margo, gripping Ronda's arm. The good one. She didn't shake it, but Ronda could tell she wanted to a little. 'If you don't learn how to drive, Mam's going to sell the house and you won't have anywhere to live,' she said. 'Whatever about one shed, I'm certainly not building two.'

An elderly man in a Salvation Army jacket gave them a wide berth as he passed by. Margo released her grip on Ronda. 'Look,' she said, taking a deep breath. 'Driving is easy. And I'm a great teacher. Ask Sebastian. Ask Malcolm Junior. It'll be a cinch. Even easier than cycling.'

'I like cycling,' said Ronda.

'Cars are safer now,' said Margo, in a quieter voice. For a moment, there was silence between them. 'The accident was years ago,' said Margo. 'You were fifteen.'

'Fourteen,' said Ronda.

'Exactly,' said Margo. 'It's ancient history.'

The accident was mostly a blur. Ronda remembered snatches of it. The slur of her father's loud voice, singing 'Danny Boy'. The skid of the tyres, trying to gain purchase on the road as Gerry took the bend too fast. His hands skating uselessly about the wheel, trying to steer away from the bus stop. The jerk as the car mounted the pavement and the blare of the horn as Gerry's forehead smacked against it. That was the last sound Ronda remembered.

'Mam hasn't mentioned selling the house or moving to yours or the driving lessons again at all,' said Ronda. 'Maybe she's forgotten the whole thing?'

Margo took a deep breath, released it through the O she made of her mouth. 'Ronda,' she said in a pained voice. 'You need to not be you for a moment and actually face reality.'

Over Margo's shoulder, Ronda saw a taxi driving down the street. She hailed it. 'Why don't you get this,' she said to Margo, taking her phone back. 'I'll ring the Parking Services about the clamp.'

'Oh would you?' said Margo, already stepping into the street and opening the back door of the idling cab. 'I don't want to be late for the parent–teacher meeting. And I was right about Catherine. Our outreach person, remember? I've to figure out a strategy to persuade her to rescind her resignation. Oh, and I promised the boys steak and chips tonight, since they're refusing to eat seabass, organic or otherwise.'

Ronda nodded, and Margo dived into the back of the taxi. The car moved away and Ronda experienced a giddy sense of relief that the driving discussion was over. The taxi stopped abruptly and the window rolled down. Margo stuck her head out. 'Don't think for a moment that the driving discussion is over,' she shouted at Ronda. Even with the wind that had picked up and whistled up the narrow street, Ronda heard what she said and knew it to be true. She was on Margo's To Do list now. Margo wouldn't rest until she was done.

CHAPTER 8

By the time Ronda cycled home, the right side of her body ached and she was soaked through. Her mother was in the kitchen, holding a hot water bottle under the tap out of which the water alternately dribbled and spurted. 'I won't miss the plumbing in this place when I move to Margo's,' she said. Annie's use of the word, 'when' caused a peculiar sensation in Ronda's intestines. A tightening. Before Annie announced her decision to get her affairs in order, Ronda believed that the only way her mother would ever leave No. 10 would be in a wooden box. Annie turned off the tap. 'You'll never guess who I saw today,' she said. This was more familiar terrain.

'Father Matthews?' said Ronda, taking her backpack off her back and unzipping her jacket.

'No,' said Annie, handing Ronda the hot water bottle so she could tighten the lid.

'Phyllis from the Legion of Mary?'

'She died months ago, I told you.'

'Margo?'

'Sure why would that be strange? Me seeing my own daughter? She does visit her own mother you know.'

Ronda leaned against the wall. 'I can't think of anyone else,' she said.

'Joseph Murphy,' proclaimed Annie, like Jessica Fletcher uncovering the villain in a particularly nail-biting episode of *Murder She Wrote*.

Ronda's intestines were at it again, twisting and constricting. She didn't know if it was embarrassment. Or shame. Maybe both? Or perhaps it was the laceration he had scored through her heart, long scabbed over but inclined to itch every now and again.

'He pulled up next door in that fancy electric car of his,' Annie went on.

'He's just visiting his parents,' said Ronda, handing the hot water bottle – now hermetically sealed – back to Annie.

'There's more,' said Annie. She settled the bottle inside the folds of her dressing gown, hugged it to her. 'He was carrying two suitcases.' She pointed at the party wall that separated their houses. 'I'd say that foreign girl, whatsherface, has thrown him out. And good luck to him trying to charge that car. Mrs Murphy never stops giving out about the price of the electric.'

'Danielle,' said Ronda. 'She's French.'

'Who?'

'His wife.'

'How do you know?'

'Mrs Murphy told me.' No point in admitting that sometimes, in the middle of the night if she couldn't sleep, Ronda looked Joseph up online. 'Stalking,' Kim would have called it. His Instagram feed presented intimate dinner dates with his beautiful, clever, successful wife. Jumping joyfully into a pool with his adorable children, a tantalising suggestion of sandstone villa at the edge of the photograph, the tagged location exotic with its accents and double consonants. Ronda had never heard of the place. When she googled it, she was plagued with photographs of the Italian Alps, a discreet little hamlet in a lush valley that everybody would be going to next year. Closer to home, there were the stylish, well-attended parties they threw on the regular. Numerous shots of the house, taken at rakish angles in impressive lighting. Joseph had designed the house himself, since he had not only realised his dream of fortune and becoming an architect, but went on to realise his other dream, which was fame, hosting the hugely popular TV show, *Home Sweet Home*.

'How the mighty have fallen,' said Annie, filling a glass of water and popping a tablet on her tongue. 'Reflux,' she told Ronda, 'in case you're wondering.'

'He's probably just lending them the suitcases,' said Ronda. 'Maybe they're going on holidays?'

'You wouldn't lend those ones,' said Annie, darkly. 'They're much too good.' She took a deep draught of water and walked to the kitchen door, opened it. 'I managed to eat something earlier,' she told Ronda. 'So there's no need to bother with dinner for me.'

Ronda put the kettle on. She hated having nothing to do. With inertia, her mind took the opportunity to skip around the past as if it was a charming meadow in glorious sunshine fringed by magnificent horse chestnut trees with bright, burgeoning green leaves. She grabbed the sweeping brush, ignoring the groan of her body as she swept the linoleum floor. She cleared her mother's dinner dishes off the table, wiped it down and put the bottles of pills and medicine into the cupboard with all the other bottles of pills and medicine.

The kettle still hadn't boiled.

Later, as Ronda was making herself something to eat, the phone rang. It was Margo, who had obviously recharged her mobile, attended the parent–teacher meeting, persuaded Catherine to rescind her resignation, cooked steak for the boys, an organic seabass for Malcolm. Now Ronda was the next item on her agenda.

Ronda often admired Margo's dynamism. Being in the full glare of it however, was a different matter. She laid a fried egg on top of a potato waffle and did not pick up the phone.

By the time Ronda had eaten, drunk two cups of tea, washed her plate, cup and cutlery in the sink, dried them and put them away, Margo had rung a further two times. Each time the ringing stopped, the quietness in the house seemed more pronounced than before.

Margo rang again as Ronda moved her bishop to capture Berkley's knight. Even so, she did not win the game, which she put down to the tired ache in her body. Perhaps she should have heeded the paramedic's advice and not returned to work so soon.

The next call came as Ronda went outside to look for Jessica Fletcher. She wasn't coiled on her usual branch of the laburnum tree in the front garden, waiting for one of the hooded crows to lower their guard. Ronda opened the garden gate and stepped onto the footpath before she noticed Joseph Murphy's car. She was surprised he was still there. She darted back inside the house, abandoning the search. The cat was well able to fend for herself. Ronda went to check on her mother. See if she wanted a cup of the Horlicks she sometimes drank to help her sleep. She climbed the stairs, stepping over the third and sixth ones, which had a tendency to creak like old bones. On the landing, she paused. Long enough to notice how thin the carpet had become, the pattern in some spots nearly worn away with the passage of footsteps over the years. She opened the door of her mother's bedroom and stood in the patch of orange light thrown by the street lamp on the road outside. Annie was already asleep, her fingers curled loosely around the iPad, which lay on the bed. Outside the duvet and tucked into the bend of her mother's knees lay Jessica Fletcher. Even though she was an adult cat, she was small and bony and had the mew of a Dickensian stray who combed back alleys for scraps and found few. Annie loved her.

Ronda wandered into what used to be Margo's bedroom and was now a holding pen for things nobody needed or wanted. Leaning against a wall was an old mattress, with its collection of long-ago stains and sagging air of defeat. Beside it, sprouting stuffing, was the eiderdown Annie had received as a wedding present from her sister, Tess. It was the same eiderdown Ronda had used as a tidal wave to distract Margo from any shouting or shoving going on in the kitchen below, when they were children. Ronda devised a complicated game she called 'Treasure Island' to go with the eiderdown-tidal-wave, which Margo adored. Sometimes, when their father was in one of his whistling, chipper moods, he would join in, leaping onto the bed and thrashing about, pretending to be the kraken. Margo loved when he did that. Ronda, wary of how unpredictable he could be, did not.

On the table beside the fireplace, the sewing machine. Ronda thought about the shape of her mother's back, bent over the machine, her careful foot on the pedal and the speed of the needle, puncturing whatever item of clothing she had been asked to take in or let down. She had made clothes too, despite her claims of mediocrity when it came to dressmaking. Necessity had been her super power. She had made whatever the customers asked for, and in this way she had made ends meet. Ronda remembered

53

the delicate lace of wedding veils, the bolts of white satin for communion dresses, and the yards of stiff grey polyester for school tunics. It had earned its keep, the sewing machine. Which was more than could be said for Ronda's father. Annie had said it wasn't Gerry's fault. Work had been scarce in those days, even for bricklayers, and Gerry wasn't one for haring off to England like lots of the men. 'I'm not paying tax to a monarchy,' he'd declared. He hadn't paid much in the way of tax to anyone as it turned out. Certainly none after the fall on the way home from the pub that had fractured his hip and left him with a limp that got worse when it rained.

By then, Ronda was twelve. She walked four-year-old Margo around the streets of Marino in the afternoons while her mother sewed. Annie also baked. Wedding cakes and Christmas cakes, mainly. Ronda remembered the dense smell of cinnamon and brown sugar, and how the sunlight, pouring through the kitchen window in the afternoons, had made soft clouds of the flour her mother tossed through the sieve.

Margo didn't call again until Ronda was clearing out the ancient dresser in the corner of the room. She rejected the call, put the phone in her pocket.

The top drawer of the dresser was full of nothing but laminated memorial cards. Ronda shuffled through them and found her father's one. Gerald McCann. The photograph showed a dark-haired, bearded man whose face was creased in a smile. He was small and wiry, like Ronda, and had the same pale grey eyes, wide and watchful. The rest of the picture had been cut out, the original featuring Annie on one side of him and Margo on the other. Fourteen-year-old

54

Ronda had been charged with taking the photograph. She had squeezed one eye shut and peered through the view-finder. Her hands had been sweaty. The camera was heavy and the shutter was inclined to catch.

'Did you take the picture yet?' Gerry had said, his smile vanishing like a light switched off.

'Nearly,' Ronda had said.

When she looked closely at the photograph on the memorial card, she could make out Margo's skinny, white arm laced around the back of their father's neck. Closer again and she could make out the edge of Annie's gingham apron bib on Gerry's other side.

'Hurry up, will you?' Gerry had said. 'A man could die of thirst in this heat.'

Ronda pressed the shutter.

'I'll take one of you and the girls now,' Annie had said, taking the camera off Ronda and ushering her towards Gerry.

'I've to meet the lads,' Gerry had said, opening the garden gate and heading down the road. 'I won't be late,' he'd called over his shoulder.

Ronda had liked those evenings. The run of the house and her father in the pub until closing time.

At the back of the drawer, she found her mother's well-thumbed prayer book, spools of thread and packets of needles, a broken pair of reading glasses, a years old parish newsletter, and a few stray rosary beads. A small curl of hair Sellotaped to the back of a photograph of Margo, beaming towards the camera in a high chair. She'd been such a cute baby, with her white-blond hair and bright blue eyes, enormous in her little heart-shaped face. She'd been one of those babies that passers-by couldn't help smiling at and maybe even tickling under the chin when Ronda stopped the pram, perhaps at the side of the road waiting for the green man.

As a baby, Ronda's hair had been mousy, the colour of stagnant ditch water, fine in texture. Even so, she couldn't help reaching further into the drawer to see if there was any little keepsake her mother might have squirrelled away.

Which is how she ended up with a paper cut from the sharp edge of a rectangular piece of card skulking at the back of the drawer. She pulled the card out and examined it as she sucked on the thin line of the cut at the top of her finger. The invitation was stiff, yellow with the passing of the twenty-two years since it had been printed. And now there was a bloody fingerprint on the top right-hand corner.

Ronda still cringed when she thought about her mother, ringing the guests, telling them the wedding was cancelled.

'Cancelled or postponed?' one of her mother's cousins had wanted to know.

'Cancelled,' her mother said grimly.

Aunt Tess was the only one who hadn't wanted to hear all the gory details. She had been the one who insisted on Ronda keeping the wedding china she had gifted her.

'She might go again,' Tess had said.

'She most certainly will not,' said Annie, with uncharacteristic authority. As if she had resigned herself to this calamity long before it had taken place.

The humiliation Ronda had experienced in the days, weeks and months afterwards was acute, like a toxic appendix, exploding and spewing bile along every nerve in her body. Even now, thinking about it, she became convinced that she could feel it again. The maddening itch between her legs. The one that had taken her to the doctor's office three weeks before the wedding, believing she had a severe case of thrush. Or a urinary tract infection perhaps.

It was severe all right. But it wasn't thrush. Or a UTI. It was syphilis, gifted to her by her betrothed, Joseph Murphy, who got it from her friend, Eileen, who got it from a one-night-stand on a weekend to visit her sister on the Isle of Wight.

'I only slept with her once, I swear,' Joseph said, when it became obvious he wasn't going to weasel his way out of this one.

But whether that was true or not didn't matter.

Once was enough, as it happened.

Ronda tore the invitation into tiny, indecipherable pieces. The phone rang again and this time Ronda turned it off. Margo's persistence was exhausting. Ronda could not think of one single time when she had won out against her sister. She wondered how long her mother had been thinking about selling the house? Dr Anderson had moved to Howth four months ago. She'd probably hatched the plan back then. Ronda tried to imagine herself renting a room in a stranger's house with other tenants. Sharing a bathroom. Other people's hair in the drain. The sound of meat, spitting on a pan. The smell of feet. Coming up from the carpet, wafting off damp shoes left under a table in the hallway.

Ronda wished it was the day before the pork chop day. Wednesday. It had been such an ordinary day. Mr Lacey had had a peaceful death, Mrs Finnerty's grandniece had visited. Fergal had been at meetings all day, so hadn't had time to annoy any of the staff or residents. Sheila had been in great form, with the arrival of a pair of finches on the window-sill outside her bedroom where she scattered nuts and seeds when she remembered. Ada, on a half-day from school, had stopped by to show Fatima and Ronda the one hundred per cent she had scored on her history test, then entertained the residents with her dance to Taylor Swift's 'We Are Never Ever Getting Back Together'. Even Tracey clapped along. Fatima had brought in a cake she'd baked for Baby's Christening. Every so often, Teresa worried about the stain of original sin on Baby's soul, so they'd 'christen' her in the prayer room. They used tap water, poured it into the mortar Fatima used to use for crushing spices. Ronda had cycled home, eaten dinner with her mother. Cheese omelettes with a side salad and a slice of bread and butter to plump it up. Their usual exchange. An enquiry from Ronda as to how her mother's day had been. Then Annie would be off, usually starting with a list of symptoms. Maybe an account of a visit from Father Matthews or one of his disciples. A hope that Margo might bring the boys to visit on Sunday. Then questions.

Did you feed Jessica Fletcher?

Yes.

Will you cut my toenails?

Yes.

Did you hear Stella Grogan died?

No.

Did you hear Mary Turner died?

No.

Did you hear Paeder Smith died?

No.

Nothing untoward. What else? A game of chess. Berkley won, but it was close enough for Ronda not to feel unduly bad about it. She'd put away the board and ate a Weetabix for supper. Then she'd brushed her teeth and gone to bed.

Just an ordinary day. She should have paid it closer attention. Appreciated it more.

Ronda was sitting on the floor, reading her old copy of *Anne of Green Gables* she'd found behind the dresser when the phone rang again. She mustn't have turned it off properly. She glanced at the screen. It was Margo. Of course it was. She would have to answer it. What was the alternative? Ignore her for ever? Margo would not permit it.

'Hello?'

'Finally!' yelled Margo. Ronda held the phone away from her ear. 'Where have you been?'

'I've been busy,' said Ronda.

'I've come up with another reason why you should learn how to drive,' said Margo, 'if being homeless isn't enough of a motivating factor.'

'Look Margo, I know that you . . .'

'So,' went on Margo as if Ronda had not spoken. 'Despite my powers of persuasion, Catherine, my outreach person, wouldn't change her mind and stay. She's gone all spiritual since she read *Eat Pray Love* and she's booked flights to India. This from the woman whose fears include snakes, tigers, crocodiles and crowds.'

'They seem like reasonable fears,' said Ronda, who was not a fan of crowds.

'Anyway, she's leaving at the end of March. And then *boom*! It dawned on me. With a little effort, you could easily have your licence by then.'

'What are you talking about?'

'You'd be perfect,' said Margo. 'The outreach person drives to people's houses. People who want to die in their own homes.'

59

'I don't have any qualifications,' said Ronda.

'You have years of experience,' said Margo. 'That qualifies you. Plus you're my sister, and I'm the boss.'

'That's nepotism,' said Ronda.

'It's only nepotism if you're terrible in the role,' said Margo. 'Which you wouldn't be.'

'I like my job,' said Ronda.

'You get paid minimum wage,' said Margo.

'It's enough for what I need.'

'It won't be if Mam sells the house.'

Ronda couldn't think of a response to that, so she said nothing.

'Will you at least think about it?' said Margo. Ronda could hear the snap of Tupperware lids as Margo packed up school lunches for the next day.

'I actually think you might make a good driver,' Margo said then.

'That's probably the least true thing you've ever said.'

'I'm trying to be positive,' said Margo. 'Meet me halfway at least.'

'I'm sorry,' said Ronda. 'I appreciate what you're trying to do, but I just, I can't learn how to drive.'

'Is that your final answer?' said Margo.

'Yes,' said Ronda, trying to inject as much authority into the word as she could.

Margo hung up.

CHAPTER 9

Joseph's car was still there when Ronda stepped outside the next morning at six. She closed the front door softly behind her and unlocked her bicycle, cycling away with more haste than was habitual, her hood pulled tightly over her head. She kept up her furious pace until she reached the Malahide Road, then slowed a little to rest her leg which was much improved but remained tender to the touch.

It was the last Tuesday of the month, which meant management meetings at Green Gables, which meant that Fergal and Tracey weren't around in the morning.

The staff loved the last Tuesday of the month.

It also meant the attendance of Graham Cleary, a chiropodist, to clip the toenails and pare the corns of the residents of Green Gables. Ms Gallagher, who had ticklish toes, refused to let him at hers, insisting that Ronda do the job instead. She found that Ronda's method of silently gripping the foot with one hand and clipping quickly and rhythmically with the other while not indulging in small talk was preferable. Today however, Ronda's mind was not as focused on the task as it usually was.

'Take it easy, will you?' complained Ms Gallagher.

'Sorry,' said Ronda, arranging her charge's left foot on the footrest of her wheelchair and picking up the right one, rubbing the hard skin on Ms Gallagher's big toe with a piece of pumice.

'You're gripping that stone like it's done you a disservice,' said Ms Gallagher. 'What's going on with you these days?'

Ronda set the stone down and picked up the clippers again. 'Mam's threatening to sell her house if I don't learn how to drive,' she blurted.

'Ah, the weaponising of the estate,' said Ms Gallagher. 'A classic move. The quest for control and purpose. I hope you don't expect tea and sympathy from me? Us auld ones have to employ whatever methods that remain at our disposal, which are few.'

'I don't expect anything,' said Ronda, dipping a tissue in a glass of water and using it to pick up the shards of Ms Gallagher's toenails that had fallen to the floor.

'So that's why you've been distracted,' said Ms Gallagher, whacking Ronda's shoulder. She was a strong woman with wide hands that could still pack a punch.

'Sorry, that's your sore side, isn't it?' said Ms Gallagher, looking momentarily abashed. 'I don't know my own strength sometimes.'

'I wish I had that problem,' said Ronda, rubbing peppermint cream into Ms Gallagher's heels.

'Are you close?' asked Ms Gallagher, peering intently at Ronda. 'You and your mother?'

Ronda thought about it. 'I'd say she . . . appreciates me, since I'm a carer and she is often unwell.'

'So, no then?' said Ms Gallagher, summing up the situation in her usual brusque manner.

'We're not particularly demonstrative, I suppose,' said Ronda. 'She's closer to Margo. She's the youngest. And also, you know, a pretty impressive person.'

'Was she close to your father?' asked Ms Gallagher.

'You're full of questions today,' said Ronda, gathering the scissors and nail file and peppermint cream into a bag.

Ms Gallagher sighed. 'I'm wile bored, so I am,' she said.

'I think she loved him,' said Ronda. 'Especially after he died.'

'How does that work?' asked Ms Gallagher.

Ronda shrugged. 'I suppose she recreated him a bit,' she said.

'She wouldn't be the first woman to do that,' said Ms Gallagher. 'Nobody wants to admit they married a dose.'

'That's true,' said Ronda, smiling.

'You know, I've been thinking about my own affairs recently,' said Ms Gallagher. 'Let's face it, I'm not a young woman.'

Ronda did not contradict her. Ms Gallagher was likely to wallop her again if she did. Although it was true that she exuded a certain youthfulness. Perhaps it was her bearing, the way she sat ramrod straight in the wheelchair, despite the MS, eating away at the myelin around her nerves like a plague of locusts through a field of ripened wheat. Or the belligerent intelligence of the woman that gave such expression to the features of her face, sharpening the dark blue of her eyes and the rigid line of her jawbone.

'Do you know a solicitor I could contact?' she asked.

'I do, as it happens,' said Ronda. 'Well, I don't know him, exactly. I only met him once, recently.'

'They're all charlatans, of course,' said Ms Gallagher, shaking her head. 'But needs must.'

'He seems . . . okay, I suppose,' said Ronda.

'You don't sound very sure,' said Ms Gallagher.

'He's a little unorthodox.'

'Oh, that's a good trait,' said Ms Gallagher.

'In a solicitor?' asked Ronda.

'In anyone,' said Ms Gallagher. 'Are you finished with my feet? I want to ring this unorthodox solicitor of yours.'

'I am,' said Ronda, reaching for the tricolour socks she had hung on the radiator to keep warm. 'Unless you'd like me to paint your toenails?'

'Do I look like the sort of woman who paints her toenails?' asked Ms Gallagher.

'I'm not sure,' said Ronda.

'I am a Latin scholar, I'll have you know.'

'I'm sure some Latin scholars might appreciate a coat of Bird of Paradise,' said Ronda, picking up a bottle of orange nail polish.

'Well, I'm not one of them,' said Ms Gallagher.

In the kitchen, Fatima had taken the trays out of the ovens and was scrubbing them with a ferocity that was both effective and alarming.

'You'll snap that brush in two,' said Ronda when she went in to make a coffee, mid-afternoon. 'What's up?'

Fatima put the scrubbing brush on the counter, the bristles flattened by her industry.

'I got excited about a room for rent in Swords,' she said. 'I happened to see it, only one minute after it went up on the site. But when I rang, the landlord said it was already gone.' Fatima's face looked empty without her usual bright smile.

Ronda tore open a packet of Jammie Dodgers. 'Here,' she said, handing one to Fatima, who ate it absently.

'We have to move out of the centre,' she said. 'Ada will soon be a teenager. There is no privacy for her there.'

In the absence of any solutions she could provide, Ronda handed Fatima another Jammie Dodger. Ronda had only been to the direct provision centre once. She knew Fatima and Ada shared a room with another family; a mother and her fourteen-year-old twins. Fatima was always at pains to say how lucky they were, to have a roof over their heads and a dry, safe place to sleep. Still, she did not like inviting Ronda to the centre, preferring to meet somewhere else. Anywhere else. 'When Ada and I have our own place, I will invite you to dinner,' Fatima liked to tell Ronda. 'I will make you jollof rice and coconut sorbet and you will think you have died and gone to heaven, I promise you.'

Fatima looked at Ronda, worry darkening her face. 'Did I tell you there're new people coming from southern Nigeria next week?'

'No,' said Ronda.

'They might know Noah,' she said. 'They might give us away.'

Ronda didn't bother with reassurances she couldn't guarantee. Fatima wasn't prone to exaggeration. Her husband had his fingers in a lot of lucrative pies and was well known in business and political circles in Nigeria. Ronda didn't know the full story. She didn't like to pry. Their's had been a brief courtship, during which Noah was charismatic and attentive. After the wedding, Noah moved Fatima into the secure compound where he lived with the rest of his family and his security staff. It became clear very quickly that Noah was in charge of everything. He was the one who gave Fatima permission to go out to shop or to see family or friends. He was the one who gave Ada permission to attend school, play with her friends, go to her dance classes. Increasingly this permission became less and less forthcoming as Noah's moods became more and more volatile. When Fatima summoned up the courage to leave, she hadn't asked for permission. They'd slipped away in the night, her and Ada. That was two years ago. Noah had been looking for them ever since.

Ronda took out her phone. 'What's the landlord's number?' she asked.

'The room is gone,' said Fatima.

'Maybe the landlord might know of other rooms for rent in the area?' Ronda said vaguely.

'Of course,' said Fatima, grabbing her phone out of her pocket. 'Why didn't I think of that?'

She called out the mobile number and Ronda dialled it. A man answered on the third ring. 'Hello,' said Ronda. 'I'm ringing about the room for rent in Swords Valley? Yes, that's the one, number 112. I was just wondering if . . . Oh . . . Really? When? Right, well, yes, that would be fine, thank you, goodbye.' She hung up and could not look directly at Fatima. 'He said it's available to view tomorrow night at seven,' she said. Fatima put her coffee cup down and pulled Ronda out of her chair, danced her across the kitchen floor, then hugged her.

'My wonderful friend,' she said.

'He's a racist,' said Ronda.

'A racist with a room to rent,' said Fatima. Her capacity for hope was considerable. Ronda felt the expanse of it fill the room. 'I could come with you,' she said. 'If you fancy a bit of company, I mean?'

'Would you?' Fatima's smile widened. Ronda nodded, diverting her eyes. She was no better than those saviour types, appearing on the horizon on a white steed with her white skin and white accent that could open doors. Like the door to the room for rent in Swords.

Tracey barged into the kitchen. 'The minute I'm not here to supervise, it's bedlam out there,' she said. She pointed at Ronda. 'Sheila's after wetting herself, will you sort her out?' She turned to Fatima. 'Fergal and I have visitors in the boardroom, can you bring in a tray of sandwiches? I think one of them's a vegan. Or a coeliac. Bring a selection, okay?'

'Of course, Tracey,' said Fatima, jumping up. 'Right away.'

Tracey followed Ronda into the dayroom. 'There's going to be a staff meeting on Friday,' she told her. 'Four p.m. sharp. Can you let everyone know?'

'Sure,' said Ronda, stopping at Sheila's chair. The smell of ammonia hung in the air like smoke. The front of Sheila's pale grey trousers were dark with it. 'Let's go make you comfortable,' she said, helping Sheila out of her chair.

'My husband died,' Sheila said, tugging at Tracey's sleeve. 'My lovely Noel. His eyes were sea green.'

'Your husband's name is Charlo,' Tracey told her, pulling her sleeve out of Sheila's grip.

'No,' said Sheila, shaking her head as colour rushed into her face. Ronda linked Sheila's arm. 'Will we see if Fatima's cinnamon buns are out of the oven yet?' Sheila's rigid shoulders softened. She nodded.

'I'll send an email about the meeting of course,' Tracey went on, 'but you know what this lot are like, they probably won't bother checking in time.'

'Noel Gregory,' said Sheila, reaching for Tracey's sleeve again. Tracey stepped out of her range. 'You got all that, Ronda?' she said.

Ronda nodded. 'What's the meeting about?'

'I'm not at liberty to say,' Tracey answered.

Ronda did not pursue the matter.

A staff meeting was never good news.

CHAPTER 10

It was good to have something to do after work the next day, other than go home. After her shift, Ronda cycled to Swords to view the room for rent. Fatima got the bus straight from Green Gables, having arranged for Ada to have dinner at a schoolfriend's house. With the heavy traffic, they arrived outside the house at the same time. The evening was dank and dark with a chill to the wind that cut through Ronda's layers, leaving her cold to the bone.

'This is exciting,' said Fatima, who never seemed to feel the cold.

Ronda felt she should do something to curb Fatima's enthusiasm, but could think of nothing practical. She examined the facade of the house. A two-storey semi-D that looked like it hadn't seen the benefit of a fresh coat of paint since the estate was built. Late nineties, Ronda guessed. There was a touch of Celtic tiger carelessness about the place. Sodden weeds drooped from the moss-stained guttering, and the net curtains pulled across the windows were yellow with age and torn in places. The square of concrete at the front of the house was crammed with two rusting bicycles, four tyres – all flat – a dolls' house with the roof caved in, and a row of overflowing wheelie bins.

'The location is perfect,' said Fatima. 'The bus stop is just at the end of the road.'

Ronda rang the doorbell. A man opened the door after the third ring.

'Are you early?' he said, introducing himself as Paul, the landlord. He was one of those men whose age is impossible to guess at. Maybe 40s? Maybe 50s? Possibly 60s? He was mostly bald with a large, circular face, his features clustered in the centre as if they had been intended for a much smaller visage. He was dressed entirely in beige. A slacks and V-neck jumper combo with a polo shirt underneath.

Ronda examined her watch. 'You said seven, didn't you?' she said.

'This is Ireland,' he said, grinning. 'I wasn't expecting you 'til at least ten past.' Ronda didn't mention the housing crisis, the shortage of rentals. As a landlord, she assumed he must be aware of it.

'You gave me a fright there,' he said, when Fatima stepped into the light of the bare bulb hanging from the rafter of a small, wooden canopy over the front door.

Fatima smiled and held out her hand. 'Hello Paul,' she said. 'Thank you so much for allowing us to view your beautiful home.'

There was a moment's hesitation before he extended his hand, which Fatima pumped with enthusiasm. 'Which one of you is after the room?' Paul asked, pulling his hand free and burying it in a tight arm fold.

'It's Fatima here,' said Ronda, who thought it best not to mention Ada at this delicate stage of the proceedings. 'May we see it?'

Paul waved them inside and climbed the stairs, the tread of his shoes loud against the bare boards. Ronda held her breath. The smell was a solid thing, filled with old shoes and the ghosts of a hundred different TV dinners.

'Make sure that door is securely closed behind you,' Paul said. 'It's not the safest neighbourhood I'm afraid.' He stopped at the top of the stairs to regain his breath. 'A lot of . . .' he looked at Fatima, 'ne'er-do-wells around the place these days, looking for trouble. I blame the welfare system of course, they make it too easy, giving money away to every Mohammad and Abdul that washes up on the tide, amiright?'

'Is that the room?' asked Ronda, pointing at the only door on the landing that was ajar. From behind the neighbouring door, she heard the clipped, assured tones of a newscaster on a radio or TV. Behind another, music, percussive but not loud.

Paul rapped his knuckles against the door. 'I told you to keep it down in there, Deirdre,' he barked. The music stopped abruptly. Paul held the door to the room open. 'After you,' he said, smiling at Ronda, reaching for the light switch. Ronda blinked in the sudden glare, releasing the breath she had been holding. It collected in the frigid air, too cold to dissipate. A double bed took up most of the floor space. At the end of the bed was a rail to hang clothes. There were no curtains at the window, and the wallpaper – beige with beige swirls – was pulpy with damp.

'The ad mentioned an en suite?' said Ronda.

Paul pointed to a chipped, stained hand basin attached to the wall near the door. 'And there's a big bathroom down the hall,' he said.

'It's great,' said Fatima. In the harsh light thrown by the naked bulb, her smile did not seem as vibrant as usual.

'Rent is five hundred euro a month,' Paul went on. 'I'm

keeping it low because, you know, trying to do my bit and all that. Payable in cash, obviously.'

Fatima and Ronda followed Paul down the corridor. The bathroom bore the hot, sulphuric stink of a recently excavated bowel. Fatima and Ronda observed it from the doorway. The shower cubicle was surrounded by the type of nylon curtain that, once wet, would be difficult to peel off whatever bit of your body unfortunate enough to glance against it.

'There's someone in the kitchen, cooking,' Paul told them as they walked back down the stairs. 'So I won't bring you in. But suffice to say it's got all the mod cons, fridge, toaster, sandwich maker.'

'Does it have an oven?' asked Ronda.

'Just so I'm clear,' said Paul. 'The prospective tenant is this lady here, right?' He gestured towards Fatima, who nodded. 'There's a microwave,' said Paul, at pains to look only at Fatima as if Ronda did not exist.

'Just so I'm clear,' said Ronda, stepping in between Paul and Fatima so the hideous man had no choice but to acknowledge her presence. 'Are you telling me that you believe this kip to be suitable for human habitation?'

'Of course it is,' spluttered Paul, taking a step back. Now his back was up against a – paint-peeling – wall.

'Do you live here?' asked Ronda.

'Well, no. No I don't.'

'Of course you don't,' spat Ronda. 'Because it's a squalid, comfortless hovel.'

'How dare you,' shouted Paul, his face flooding with heat.

'I will be reporting you to the RTB as well as to revenue,' Ronda told him. 'I'm sure they'll be interested in your cash-only rental transactions.'

'Go ahead, I've nothing to hide,' said Paul, but there was a touch of panic in his voice.

Bingo! Ronda thought. Another tax-dodging slum landlord taken care of.

'Just so you're clear . . . about what?' Paul prompted her. His voice sounded distant. Ronda stared at him, struggling to collect herself.

Fatima surged forward. 'Ronda was just wondering when the room is available,' said Fatima. 'The sooner, the better, as far as I'm concerned.'

'Do you not have to give your current landlord notice?' he asked. Ronda shot Fatima a warning look. Fatima was inclined to tell the truth and struggled to know why this was sometimes not a good idea. However, this time, she got Ronda's message loud and clear and did not mention that she was an asylum seeker waiting to be called for her Personal Interview at the International Protection Office.

'I'm staying with Ronda,' she said, linking Ronda's arm with her own. 'While I'm looking for my own accommodation.'

Paul pushed his hands into his pockets. 'Well,' he said. 'Technically, it's available now. But I've a few people viewing it tomorrow, so don't go counting your chickens, chicken.' He grinned at his wordplay as he opened the front door. 'Now if you don't mind,' he said, gesturing them out. 'My wife is expecting me home, it's date night.'

'You don't have to wait with me,' said Fatima when they reached the bus stop.

'The bus is coming in five minutes,' said Ronda, reading the digital display.

'I know you don't like the room,' said Fatima.

'It's Paul I have concerns about,' said Ronda.

'I have to get Ada out of that place,' said Fatima.

'I know you're worried about Noah finding you, but it's been two years, and . . .'

Fatima shook her head. 'It's not just Noah. It's the people with their placards. They're outside the hostel every night now. I pull the blinds down and close the window, but Ada knows that they're shouting at us, no matter what I tell her.'

The bus appeared at the top of the road. 'Maybe there are other rooms we could look at?' Ronda said.

'This is the first room I've managed to view,' said Fatima, shaking her head. 'It's affordable, and if Paul says I can have it, I'll take it.' She put her hand out to flag the bus. Then she turned to Ronda, took her face between her hands and kissed her cheek. It was a delicate kiss, her lips warm against the frozen skin of Ronda's face. 'Don't worry,' she said. 'All will be well.'

She waved as she boarded the bus. Ronda waved back, doing her best to smile as if Fatima was right. All would be well.

CHAPTER 11

Joseph's car was gone when Ronda got home. She hadn't realised she'd been anxious about it until then. She got off her bicycle and wheeled it through the garden gate of No. 10 Casino Place. Relief freed up some space in her head and she realised she was hungry. She had the pasta bake in the oven and was crushing garlic for the bread when she realised something else. Margo had discontinued her barrage of phone calls. She checked her phone to make sure she hadn't missed any calls. She hadn't. And there were no texts or WhatsApps either.

'Something smells nice,' said Annie McCann, appearing in the kitchen with Jessica Fletcher draped over one of her shoulders, like a baby.

'It'll be ready in ten minutes,' said Ronda, shoving her phone back into her pocket.

'Please tell me you didn't use aubergine,' said Annie, leaning down to peer through the oven window. 'It sets off my reflux something terrible.'

'I didn't,' said Ronda, opening the fridge and taking out ingredients for a salad. 'Did Margo phone today?'

'Sure, didn't she have that board meeting this morning?' said Annie. 'Then she had to bring Malcolm Junior to the open day in Trinity and organise the panel for the school's technology night. Where on earth would she find the time to ring me?'

Since this was a rhetorical question, Ronda did not respond. Instead she set the table for two. Her mother sat in her usual spot beside the radiator and Ronda sat where she always sat, on the chair closest to the oven.

'What kept you tonight?' asked Annie, as Ronda dished up.

'Had to work late,' said Ronda. Sometimes, the truth didn't set you free. In this instance, it could re-ignite the argument they'd had, months before, when Ronda had talked about the possibility of Fatima and Ada moving into Margo's old room. 'Temporarily,' she'd assured her mother.

'This is no halfway house for unvetted refugees, Ronda,' Annie had said. 'We know nothing about those people. Nothing about their families. Their values.'

'Fatima is my friend,' Ronda had said.

'Well, Mrs Murphy is my friend,' Annie had said. 'You don't see her begging to move in, do you?' Ronda hadn't pointed out that Mrs Murphy already had somewhere to live. Or that she and her mother were not friends. Merely neighbours who had engaged in a persistent and monotonous game of one-upmanship for historical reasons that may or may not have its roots in the brief, turbulent engagement of their offspring.

Before she switched Berkley on, Ronda checked her phone. Still no call from Margo. She must have given up. Which would be the first time she'd ever done that.

Ronda texted Fatima. **Any word from paul?** It gave her some small degree of satisfaction, giving him a lower case *p*, although she conceded that it achieved nothing, in terms of the balance of power.

Fatima texted back immediately.

She didn't get the room.

When Annie went to bed, Ronda googled rooms for rent in Swords for €500 and found one. It was the room she and Fatima had seen earlier. It hadn't been taken off the site yet. The only reason Ronda recognised it was the address. The accompanying photographs bore no resemblance to the room they had seen.

Knowing about the housing crisis in a vague, theoretical way and being shoved up against the coal face of it like this were two very different sensations. Margo was right. Even with her white skin and traditional Dublin accent, the chances of Ronda affording a decent place to live, if her mother sold the house, were minimal.

At best.

Ronda would have to learn how to drive.

The alternative was not an option.

CHAPTER 12

Now it was Ronda phoning Margo and getting her sister's voicemail. The text she sent went unanswered. So did the one after that. She followed these with a WhatsApp, which allowed Ronda to notice that the message had been read a minute after it had been sent.

No reply was forthcoming.

Ronda phoned Margo's landline, but nobody answered. She phoned the hospice and left a message. She even tried the golf club and was told that she had just missed her. In desperation, she phoned Malcolm, but could only get through to his personal assistant who said that he was unavailable and responded that she was not at liberty to say, when Ronda asked where he was.

While she knew that this behaviour was vintage Margo when she didn't get what she wanted, Ronda couldn't help worrying. It was not impossible that Margo had already solicited tenders from local builders, compared costs, timelines and quality of materials and given the green light to one of them who was, right at this very moment, demolishing the outhouse and laying the foundations for their mother's granny flat. Except that it wouldn't be called a granny flat. It would be a hub or a pod or a den. Something like that.

This went on for two days, during which time Ronda worked two twelve-hour shifts, Fatima got excited about a lead she had received from a friend about a possible room for rent that turned out to be a mattress on the floor of a utility room in Hartstown, a two-bus journey from Green Gables, Kim went on a dinner date where the guy she met on Tinder scarpered before the bill for their three courses and a bottle of wine arrived, Teresa lost Baby, which rendered her almost catatonic with grief and necessitated the turning upside down and inside out of her bedroom, the dayroom and the dining hall, and, when Fergal wasn't holed up in his office with the door shut, or attending more meetings with the powerfully scented Americans, he walked the corridors of Green Gables, whistling and looking very pleased with himself. Which was never a good sign. Something was afoot at Green Gables and Ronda presumed whatever it was would be revealed at the staff meeting at four p.m. that afternoon.

'Mrs Finnerty is asking for you,' Tracey told Ronda after breakfast. Her look was pointed. Mrs Finnerty did not have long left. It felt like the universe was reminding Ronda that nothing stayed the same, everything changed, whether you wanted it to or not.

She stayed with Mrs Finnerty for most of the day, sitting in an armchair beside the bed. Her breathing became sporadic towards the end, the sound wet and strained when she exhaled.

'Does it hurt her? The death rattle?' her grandniece, Sharon, whispered across the bed to Ronda.

Ronda disliked such terms. 'She's very comfortable,' Ronda said. 'It won't be long now.'

Sharon began to cry. 'I need some air,' she said.

As soon as she left, Ronda noticed something. Some small change in the atmosphere in the room. A dimming. She picked up Mrs Finnerty's hand. 'It's okay, Maria,' she whispered. 'You can go now, if you are ready.' Ronda couldn't be certain, but thought she felt a faint tightening of Mrs Finnerty's fingers around her hand. The room grew quieter and the breaths further apart, as Ronda sat there in the dense stillness.

And then she was gone.

Ronda didn't need to check with a stethoscope. She never did. She always knew. The pallor that stole over the skin. The absence about the body. The vacant face. Something was no longer there. People had different words for it. Spirit. Essence. Soul.

Ronda held the old woman's hand and waited for Sharon to return. She couldn't say that she felt sad, exactly. It was Mrs Finnerty's time and she had had a long life and a peaceful death, the best kind. In those moments afterwards, with death lingering around the edges of the room, Ronda often felt like her best self. All her senses heightened, as if she was plugged into the mains of the universe. She felt alive. The feeling was fleeting, no matter how hard she tried to hold onto it. But, for a little while, the sensation seemed to earth her in some tangible way.

The staff meeting was already underway in Fergal's large corner office. Fergal broke off in the middle of one of his long, meandering monologues, subject to various clauses, sub-clauses and dramatic pauses, coupled with the construction of a pyramid with his fingers, to wither Ronda with a glare as she entered the room. Tardiness was one of his pet hates. 'As I was saying,' he said pointedly, gesturing towards the projector at the top of the room where a PowerPoint presentation was in full swing.

With her blood pushing at her pulse points and her hand still warm from holding Mrs Finnerty's, Fergal's words glanced against her like drizzle, only a few of them soaking in. Still, Ronda managed to get the gist. It turned out that the Americans, whose teeth were as white as the shirts beneath their pinstriped suits, were brokers for a hedge fund. They had washed up on the shores of Green Gables with dollars spilling out of their pockets, which they were anxious to throw in the direction of one Fergal Hutch, if he was open to the idea.

Fergal Hutch, a big fan of dollars and many other currencies, was most certainly open to the idea. Sitting behind his enormous solid walnut desk, with the mission statement his father had commissioned embroidered on a long stretch of linen hanging on the wall behind him ('Let Our Family Look After Yours'), Fergal told his staff that Green Gables had been sold to an American investment fund. The deal had been formalised earlier with the signing of contracts. He assured them that nothing would change, that he would still be in charge of the smooth running of Green Gables, and that their jobs were safe. He said all these things with the casual tone of a man who had been given everything he ever owned and presumed it was because he had earned it.

CHAPTER 13

On Saturday morning, it took Ronda fifty-five minutes to cycle to Margo and Malcolm's house in Howth. It would have taken less time if it hadn't been for the wind – a gusting north-easterly – blowing straight into her face. Ronda secured the bike to the garden fence with the heavy-duty chain she carried in the basket, and took off her helmet. In spite of the cold, sweat had pasted her fringe flat against her forehead. She wiped her face with the sleeve of her anorak, then walked down the path towards the house. It was a spacious, white-brick, two-storey affair, the last house on the cul-de-sac, by far the most modern with the refurbishments it was subjected to regularly. She rang the doorbell. It played a tinny version of Ireland's call, the rugby anthem. There was no answer, but both Malcolm's and Margo's cars were in the driveway, along with a sailing boat, the hull of which was being painted by a handyman called Jack about whom Margo spoke often and with great affection.

'Give it another ring,' said Jack, nodding towards the bell. 'Margo's in there all right.'

Ronda rang again. And again. Eventually, Margo reefed open the door and glared at Ronda.

'Jack said you were home,' said Ronda.

'Oh,' said Margo, glancing at her handyman. 'Hi Jack, I didn't realise you were working today,' she called, arranging her face into a broad smile and lifting her arm to wave at him. 'Do you want a Nespresso?'

Jack gave her a thumbs-up before turning his attention back to the boat. Margo looked at Ronda again, the smile sliding off her face. 'What do you want?' she said. She was dressed up as usual, as if she was going out to dinner in one of those Michelin-starred restaurants she and Malcolm liked to frequent. A chocolate brown velvet dress with sequins around the neckline and wide, statement sleeves out of which her long, toned arms poked. Red high heels with an impossibly pointy toe. Her hair in its usual immaculate bob, and the careful application of what she called her daytime make-up. 'More discreet,' she'd said, when Ronda asked about the difference.

'You haven't answered my calls and texts,' said Ronda.

'Well, you didn't answer mine,' said Margo.

'I did,' said Ronda.

'You took your time,' said Margo.

'Sorry,' said Ronda.

Margo shrugged. 'I didn't see the point in continuing the conversation, Ronda,' she said. 'When you had already made your decision.'

'Any chance of one of your macaroons to go with the coffee?' Jack's hopeful voice penetrated the air around the sisters.

'Sure Jack, no problem,' said Margo, beaming in his direction. She stepped back, holding the door open. 'You better come inside. God knows what Jack thinks of us.'

Ronda followed Margo into the bright, spacious hall, doing her best to walk on the heels of her boots so as not to besmirch the white tiles underfoot.

'I'll put your jacket in the cloakroom,' said Margo, her hand already out, waiting. Ronda pulled her anorak off.

'Thanks,' she said.

Margo held the garment at arms' length as she walked away with it. Ronda supposed it was a little grubby, but that's what winter cycling did to clothes.

Through the glass door into the open plan kitchen that spanned the width of the house, Ronda smiled when she saw her nephews, sprawled along the length of an L-shaped couch, eating mountains of cereal from deep ceramic bowls. Sebastian and Malcolm Junior were concentrating on a chessboard, but twelve-year-old Tiernan spotted her and ran into the hall, smiling wide so she could see the glints of diamanté along the brace clamped against his teeth.

'I'm playing the winner,' he told her.

'Which means he's playing me, obviously,' called out Malcolm Junior, the heir to the throne, as Malcolm Senior called him. Ronda ruffled Tiernan's mop of black curls, which he hated, then got him in a tight-fitting head lock and swung him around, which he loved.

'What's the most important thing to understand about chess?' she asked as he struggled to free himself.

'Control the centre,' yelped Tiernan.

'No.' She reached into his armpits, tickling him.

'Castle early,' he shrieked.

'Nope.'

'Protect your king,' he roared.

'Can you keep the noise down please?' Malcolm called from upstairs. Probably from his office. A lot of his clients were overseas and did not appear to observe the traditional Monday-to-Friday work system. Ronda released Tiernan and followed him into the kitchen, perching on the arm of the couch.

'I can't hug you yet, Ronda,' said Sebastian, frowning at the board. Ronda could see that Malcolm Junior had the upper hand, but only by a fraction. She had taught them well.

'So?' said Tiernan. 'What is the most important thing about chess then?'

'Your opponent,' said Ronda.

'Lucky I'm only playing with this clown then,' said Malcolm Junior, grinning.

'You haven't won yet,' said Ronda.

'Yeah, loser,' said Sebastian, sliding his rook up as far as it would go. He glanced at Ronda, who discreetly nodded her approval.

Malcolm Junior leaned towards Ronda and issued a lengthy and detailed whisper in her ear.

'An ambitious strategy,' she said, 'but it's doable.'

'Is that dirt on your boots?' said Margo, walking into the room and pointing at Ronda's feet.

'I don't think so,' said Ronda, examining the soles.

'It is,' said Margo. 'You're worse than the boys.'

Ronda picked a tissue out of the pocket of her jeans and swiped at the soles of her shoes. One smudge of dirt came away. 'I don't know how you managed to see that,' said Ronda.

'She's omnipotent,' said Tiernan.

'Impressive word,' said Ronda.

'It was our word of the day in English yesterday,' he said.

'I'd prefer if you took them off,' said Margo, pointing at the shoe rack inside the hall door.

'Auntie Ronda, will you play the winner of the game between me and Tiernan?' said Malcolm Junior.

'You heard Ronda,' said Sebastian. 'You haven't won yet.'

'I'll play whoever wins,' said Ronda, taking off her Docs.

'There's a hole in your sock,' said Margo.

'Good ventilation,' said Ronda. Tiernan laughed. Margo did not.

'Darling, is the front door open? It's blowing a gale up here?' There was an edge of strained patience in Malcolm's voice.

Margo ran into the hall and shut the front door. 'Ronda must have forgotten to close it, darling,' she called up the stairs.

'Sorry,' said Ronda, remembering she was trying to get Margo on side.

'I'm going to make Jack a coffee, I suppose you want one too?' Margo said, returning to the kitchen.

'I made chocolate chip cookies at school, Ronda,' said Tiernan. 'Would you like one? You don't have to say yes because you love me.'

'I would love one,' said Ronda, who wasn't all that partial to chocolate chip cookies. She walked into the hall and arranged her boots on the rack.

'The cookies come with a side order of food poisoning,' Sebastian shouted after her, and now Ronda could hear the friendly fire of brothers, thumping each other with cushions.

'Don't spill milk on the new couch,' Margo shouted at them, 'or I'll flick your bare legs with a tea towel the way my mother used to.' Then the whistle of a towel through the air and the smack of the fabric against the couch and the laughing of the boys as they ducked for cover. Ronda sat on the burgundy leather wingback chair in the hall. She did not put her feet up on the matching ottoman. She felt that Margo might not approve, given the hole in her sock.

Margo swept back into the hall in a fug of Jo Malone carrying a tray with coffees and a plate of colourful macaroons and one lone, misshapen chocolate chip cookie. 'Strong, black, no sugar,' she said, handing Ronda one of the cups.

'Thank you.' Ronda took the coffee as well as Tiernan's cookie. Margo set the tray on the hall table and carried a coffee upstairs to Malcolm. Then she went outside with Jack's. With the oversized sleeves and the clatter of her high heels on the porcelain floor tiles, she looked like a kid playing dress-up in her mother's clothes. Which she used to do, notwithstanding the dearth of stylish clothes in Annie McCann's wardrobe. 'I'm going to be a famous fashion designer,' ten-year-old Margo had told her sister, parading around in one of their mother's housecoats and a pair of long, satin gloves Aunt Tess had worn to a dress dance in the seventies. Ronda never told her sister that the realisation of her ambition to be a famous fashion designer was highly unlikely, given her humble circumstances. Back then, Ronda felt that her own ambition was more achievable. There was a nurse who lived at the top of the road who used to let Ronda put her stethoscope around her neck sometimes.

'Ah Ronda, you're looking well.' It was Malcolm, coming down the stairs in wide cargo pants and a pair of deck shoes that looked like they'd never seen the outside world. The outline of his ferociously muscled torso strained against the thin fabric of his tight T-shirt. He admired his reflection in the glass on the side of the front door as he descended the stairs, pushing his hands through the luxurious ripples of his blond hair. She supposed he was handsome, if you were into that manically-groomed, perma-tanned kind of thing.

'I hear Margo wasn't able to persuade you to take driving lessons?' He winked at her in what he probably felt was a charming and boyish way.

'Actually, that's why I . . .' began Ronda.

'Don't let her pressure you,' said Malcolm, putting his hand on Ronda's shoulder and petting her as if she was Bubbles, their miniature Chihuahua. 'You know what she's like. She gets one of her little ideas, and *boom*, she's off, amiright?'

Ronda used her – strong, cyclist – legs to push the chair back, leaving a deep and unapologetic scratch in the ceramic tiles that had come all the way from Milan.

'Unhand me, you bloated bucket of steroids,' she said, flinging his hand off her shoulder. 'And stop patronising your wife,' she went on. 'Her ideas are not little. They are often big and brilliant. How you persuaded her to marry you is something I will never understand.'

'How dare you,' said Malcolm. 'Insulting me in my own home.'

'I can insult you outside, if you'd prefer?' said Ronda. She couldn't help admiring her quick retort. The hint of humour about it. She loved how she was never lost for words. It was a gift that she would never take for granted.

'She gets one of her little ideas, and *boom*, she's off, amiright?'

Ronda, trapped in the chair, could still feel the clammy weight of Malcolm's hand on her shoulder. Short of shrugging it off, there was nothing she could do about it, being as far back in the chair as it was possible to get. She thought about pushing the chair backwards, but worried that it would mark the floor.

'You're right to stick to your guns,' Malcolm said, finally lifting his hand from her shoulder and straightening. 'Margo always gets her own way. And I don't mind your mother moving in so long as the Kube is far enough away from the house and sound-proofed, amiright?'

Malcolm laughed.

His phone rang and he fished it out of his pocket. Margo had bought the phone for his birthday. She said it was the same cornflower blue as his eyes. Malcolm flipped it open with his thumb. One slick flick. 'Sorry Ronda, I have to take this,' he said, backing off. 'It's the east coast.' He turned and took the stairs two at a time.

Margo returned from the garden, rubbing her hands up and down her arms to warm them. 'Well?' she said. 'To what do I owe the pleasure of your visit?'

'I'll do it,' said Ronda. 'I'll learn how to drive. I'll try to, at any rate.'

'Why have you changed your mind?' asked Margo, studying Ronda's face with suspicion. Ronda drained her coffee and stood up. 'I just have,' she said.

'You never just do anything,' said Margo.

'I don't want to move out of No. 10,' said Ronda. There was an edge of panic in her voice.

Margo nodded. 'Okay,' she said in a quieter voice. She got her phone and opened her calendar, swiping through the days. 'The hospice AGM is at the end of next week, so I won't be able to give you your first lesson 'til after that.'

'No problem,' said Ronda, trying not to sound thrilled with this unexpected stay of execution.

CHAPTER 14

Ronda had presumed that things would change once the private equity firm took over, but she had also presumed that these changes would be gradual. Which turned out not to be the case. Things like the toilet paper in the staff toilets, which had been replaced with a thin, fragile affair that you had to prise out of a tiny hole at the bottom of the new dispensers. The paper tore as soon as you pulled at it. The toilets for the guests retained the original holders and aloe vera scented soft paper, so the staff, naturally, began using those facilities, albeit surreptitiously.

Then there were the windows, which were usually cleaned every Friday morning by a local man – a retired shopkeeper – called Stanley, who wore paint-spattered overalls and a peaked wool hat. But the following Friday, Stanley didn't show up, and when Ronda enquired after him, Tracey shrugged and said she couldn't be expected to know about every tiny thing that went on at Green Gables. Except she usually did know. She made it her business to know. The following Friday at four o'clock in the afternoon as the meagre February light leaked out of the day, a contract cleaning van pulled up outside and two men jumped out with brushes and buckets and ladders. They had the job done in half the time it took Stanley. By the time Ms Gallagher complained about streaks on the window in her bedroom – which Stanley would never have permitted – they were already gone. Ronda assured her she would speak to the cleaners when they returned next week. But Monika said they weren't due back for a fortnight.

The next casualties of the takeover were the three cleaners – sisters from Donaghmede. They weren't let go as such. But they were no longer directly employed by Green Gables. Instead, they were offered zero-hours contracts with Sanitation Services Ltd, and instructed to carry out the same work in less time and for less pay.

Centralisation. That's what Fergal called it. 'So much more efficient,' he said.

Then there was the gardener, a keen horticulturist fresh out of college who had started her own business the previous year. She tended the grounds around Green Gables, mowing the lawn, pruning the blackthorn bushes, weeding the flower beds and feeding the roses that climbed across the trellises she had fashioned out of pallets she got from her dad, who worked in a warehouse.

No announcement was made in this regard. Alice simply didn't turn up on Thursday afternoon to feed and prune the great monstera plants dotted at intervals along the humid corridors. She had grown them from seed in the polytunnel she managed in her community garden. Now, as well as taking over the cleaning, Sanitation Services Ltd were also responsible for the watering of Alice's monstera plants, one of which died the very first week, as if it had seen the writing on the wall and thought it best to leave on its own terms.

Why Alice was let go soon became clear when diggers and cement trucks drove into Green Gables, put up hoarding around half of the grounds at the back of the nursing home, and proceeded to dig foundations for a prefabricated extension that would accommodate another twenty units, which is what the investors called the residents.

Ronda dealt with things in the usual way, pushing it deep down inside her, and trying not to think about them. In this way, she got through the days. It was not that she forgot about the takeover exactly. Or the driving lesson she was yet to have. These things were like gallstones. Before they lodge in a duct and cause a blockage.

In spite of the changes, Ronda found that work always helped, even though she felt that nothing she did at Green Gables ever really made a difference. The residents who suffered from dementia were still demented at the end of her shift. Ms Gallagher remained in her wheelchair. Visitors had come and gone and would come again, to hear the stories they'd heard a hundred times before. Fatima's tea brack had been baked and served and eaten and would be baked again tomorrow. Or the day after. Nathan Carter would instruct his mama to rock him like a wagon wheel on a loop, and most of Ronda's charges would never tire of hearing him sing it.

This was not the case on Thursday. When Ronda arrived at work, Monika gave her a warning sign with a widening of her eyes and an upward inflection of her eyebrows. As an alarm it was effective, given the depth, length and volume of Monika's vigorously manicured brows. Using a clipboard as a shield, she jabbed furtively towards the waiting area, where Charlo, Sheila's husband, was reclined in an armchair, manspreading a good half metre, knee to knee, pulling a sheaf of papers out of a large brown envelope. He was a fleshy fellow in a black wool suit that looked like it had shrunk in the wash. Even the toupee he wore across his freckled pate did not quite manage to cover all of his scalp, patches of pale pink seeping from the perimeters.

Charlo was a self-declared 'people person', but the declaration did not seem to include people with dementia. He visited Sheila sporadically, briefly, and almost always outside official visiting hours. 'Sheila is having her breakfast at the moment,' Ronda said, unzipping her anorak as she walked over to him.

'Good morning gorgeous,' said Charlo, winking his customary wink at her. 'Breakfast sounds good, I didn't manage to get any grub myself this morning. Sheila'll love that, it'll be like old times. Could I get a cappuccino too?' He shuffled the paperwork on his lap. Something official at the top. Ireland State Savings. Alarm bells rang in Ronda's head. This wasn't the first time Charlo had arrived with documents.

'I'll let Sheila know you're here, okay?' said Ronda, buying some time.

'No rush, love,' said Charlo, reclining on the armchair.

In the dining room, Ronda spotted Sheila, who was having breakfast with Teresa and Captain Grady, whose son, Sean sat on a chair near their table, scrolling on his phone. Sean was a once-a-week, taciturn visitor, who kept looking at his watch and left exactly thirty minutes after he'd arrived.

Teresa was crying. 'I've lost Baby,' she said when Ronda squatted beside her and wiped her face with a tissue. The scrambled eggs on her plate were untouched.

'I'll find Baby,' said Ronda, 'if you promise to eat some eggs.'

'They took her,' said Teresa, shaking her head.

'Don't worry,' said Captain Grady, struggling into a standing position. 'I'm on duty here.' Sean sighed, expelling air through a rigid circle he made with his mouth. 'You've become very helpful, haven't you?' he said.

Captain Grady did not register his son's sarcasm. Instead, he clicked the heels of his shoes together. They made a smart smack. 'Always happy to assist,' Captain Grady said, smiling at Sean, who did not smile back. The resemblance between them was undeniable. Both short, solid men with steel grey hair, Captain Grady's cut tight to his scalp, while Sean's could have done with a trim. Captain Grady's uniform suggested a rigid posture and keen sense of purpose, while Sean, in loose grey track pants, a black T-shirt that had been through too many wash cycles, and a grey hoodie, seemed worn out and apathetic.

'At ease, soldier,' said Ronda, smiling at Captain Grady, who sat back down.

Sheila did not look up from her plate, steadily making her way through one of Fatima's most popular dishes, the full Irish. 'These potato cakes are delicious,' she said.

'Don't speak with your mouth full,' said Captain Grady.

'Don't speak at all,' said Sheila, pointing her fork at him.

'I can't find Baby,' said Teresa, tugging at Ronda's uniform.

Ronda pulled out the sofas, looked under the cushions of the armchairs, and eventually located Baby behind the television. 'Now will you eat some eggs?' she asked Teresa, handing her the doll. Teresa tucked Baby into the bend of her elbow and picked up her fork.

'My husband died thirty-five years ago, you know,' said Sheila, pulling a piece of rasher rind through her front teeth.

'I'm sorry to hear that,' said Ronda. She couldn't remember what she had told Sheila the last time Charlo had visited. 'Your . . . partner is here to see you, Sheila,' she settled on.

Sheila studied her with suspicion. 'I don't have a partner,' she said.

'Charlo, I mean,' said Ronda.

Sheila shook her head. 'What kind of a name is Charlo?' she said. She whipped a piece of toast off Teresa's plate, although the theft went unnoticed as Teresa was winding Baby, who had reflux.

'Short for Charles,' went on Ronda. 'Charles Grattan.'

Sheila carried on crunching her way through Teresa's toast.

'Your husband, dear,' said Tracey Fuller in the voice she used for people with dementia as well as people who were hard of hearing and people who spoke perfectly good English but with an accent that was not the full Irish. 'He's going to join you for breakfast, isn't that lovely?'

'What?' Sheila looked fearfully at Tracey.

Ronda shot Tracey a warning glance, but the nurse was focused on Sheila. 'Your husband, dear,' Tracey shouted.

'My husband is dead,' said Sheila. 'He died years ago.' She clambered out of her chair, banging her elbow against her teacup, which went flying off the edge of the table and smashed onto the floor. 'Look what you made me do,' shouted Sheila.

'You'd better sort this out, Ronda,' said Tracey. 'You can't lie to the clients. Or leave their visitors in reception. It's not on.'

'For starters, Tracey, they're not clients, they are residents, this is their home,' said Ronda, noticing how measured and assertive her voice was. 'Secondly, this particular visitor is unwanted by Sheila. She should not have to receive any visitors she does not want to see.' Ronda was infused with triumph. It fizzed, as if a bottle of champagne had been shaken, then opened inside her body.

'And have this mess cleaned up before I bring Charlo down,' added Tracey, pointing at the spill of tea on the floor. 'Someone's going to slip and fall on that, and then we'll have an insurance claim on our hands, on top of everything else.' She turned and swept out of the room.

Kim mopped at the spill with a cloth. 'Someone should tell that one that they're residents, not clients,' she said rubbing angrily at the puddle of tea on the floor.

In the kitchen, Fatima was stacking the dishwasher. 'You don't drink cappuccinos,' said Fatima, looking up as Ronda prepared Charlo's coffee.

'It's for Charlo,' said Ronda.

Fatima snorted. 'I keep the arsenic in the back of the cupboard if you're looking for it,' she said. She looked tired. It was in the way she leaned against the counter, like she was glad it was there to hold her up.

'You all right?' asked Ronda, getting a tray out of the cupboard.

'Fergal was in the kitchen for ages this morning, asking questions,' said Fatima.

'What sort of questions?'

Fatima sighed. 'How long does this task take, who is in charge of that task, how many of us are involved with the cooking, the cleaning, endless questions.'

'He should know all that already,' said Ronda.

'He had a clipboard,' Fatima went on. 'He kept writing things down.'

'You know Fergal,' said Ronda. 'He's probably just bored, he'll have forgotten all about it by the end of the day.' Fatima did not look convinced. Neither was Ronda. Fergal avoided the 'floor' as he called it – anywhere residents might be – with dogged deliberation.

Ronda put Charlo's cappuccino on the tray, buttered a slice of Fatima's freshly baked soda bread and slathered it with cherry jam. 'Charlo's brought some application form with him. From the Post Office I think.'

'Sheila does not have the capacity to sign forms,' said Fatima, her hands full of knives for the cutlery drawer.

'I know,' said Ronda. 'But I don't see how we can stop him. He is her husband.' She picked up the tray and headed towards the kitchen door. Down the corridor, a door slammed shut in a draught and Fatima spun towards the sound, startled.

'You okay?' said Ronda, putting down the tray and removing the knives from Fatima's hands. She settled them into the drawer and pulled out a chair.

Fatima sat on it. 'I'm pretty sure one of the men who moved into the centre last week is on to me. I told him my husband was dead, but he won't stop asking questions.'

'Just try to keep out of his way,' said Ronda.

'That is easier said than done when we live in such close quarters,' said Fatima. She rubbed her eyes.

'You need to rest,' said Ronda. 'You've been working too many night shifts.'

Fatima nodded. 'I like to be at the centre when Ada gets home from school. I don't want that man talking to her. He could worm the truth out of her, she's only a child.'

'How about we take her bowling?' said Ronda. 'A bit of distraction might be good. For the two of you.'

Fatima shook her head. 'I have a meeting with my case worker.'

'Next week then?' said Ronda.

Fatima produced a watery smile. 'You are good, Ronda McCann,' she said.

'I'm not,' said Ronda. 'You're in crisis and all I can come up with is bowling.'

'I'd better get going,' said Fatima. 'I'm supposed to be timing my tea round.'

'What on earth for?' asked Ronda.

But Fatima was already pushing the tea trolley out of the room.

From the dayroom came Charlo's booming voice. 'There she is, my beautiful wife, looking radiant as always, the jewel in my crown.'

'I'm Noel's wife,' Ronda heard Sheila say. She picked up the tray and hurried out of the kitchen. Charlo had already set up shop in a chair beside Sheila, who was staring at the telly where Red Hurley was singing, 'Broken Promises'.

'Noel was your first husband, remember?' said Charlo, blotting his thumb with his tongue and riffling through the sheaf of papers he had set on his knees.

'He had sea green eyes,' said Sheila, looking at Charlo for the first time.

'Whatever you say, dear,' said Charlo. He took a pen out of his breast pocket.

'Charlo,' Ronda said, rushing towards him. 'I brought you some breakfast.' She held the tray towards him and he lifted the paperwork off his lap and put it on a footstool then took the tray from her and laid it across his knees.

'All my favourite things,' he said, his eyes sweeping across Ronda's body.

'Yes,' she said. 'Soda bread, still warm from the oven. And a cappuccino with extra froth and two sugars, just the way you like it.'

Charlo beamed. 'I can't understand why you're still on the shelf, Ronda,' he said, taking an enormous bite of the bread.

Ronda glanced at the page Charlo had shuffled to the top. There was Sheila's name in bold font, today's date and a space where her signature would go.

Charlo nodded at Ronda's left hand. 'A man notices these things,' he said, tapping a wide gold band that occupied most of the space along his short, chunky ring finger. A paste of masticated soda bread lined his gums.

'What does the engraving say?' Ronda asked, sitting in the chair beside Charlo. 'On your wedding ring?' She didn't think stalling him would help, but she couldn't think of anything else she could do.

Charlo thrust the ring towards Ronda's face. 'It says "*Sheila, mon amour, toujours*".' Sheila didn't stir at the mention of her name. Her eyes remained glued to the screen, as if Red Hurley might vanish if she looked away.

'That's French for all my love, by the way,' Charlo went on. 'And that's the date we were married, nearly thirty years ago now.' Ronda didn't correct his French or even ask him why the engraving was in French, since neither he nor Sheila were from France or any other French-speaking part of the world. Charlo took another enormous bite of soda bread and washed it down with the rest of the coffee. 'Sheila's one says the same,' he said. 'Doesn't it pet?' He picked up Sheila's hand and she resisted, but Charlo held on, pulling at the ring, trying to remove it. It wouldn't come over the swollen knuckle of her finger. Charlo dropped Sheila's hand. 'Except her one has my name on it, obviously,' said Charlo, using his finger to collect the remaining froth in his cup.

'Noel and me were married on the first of June in 1975,' said Sheila.

Charlo rolled his eyes. 'And you and me were married on the fifteenth of November in 1996,' he said. 'Noel died? Remember?'

Sheila looked at Charlo as if he were a suspect in a line-up. Ronda took her hand, lowered it. She couldn't help noticing the band of white, pulpy skin at the base of Sheila's finger, where her engagement ring used to be. The ring had been Sheila's mother's and was noticeable in its absence, with its three generous diamonds, clustered on a gold band. Each diamond was topped with a tiny emerald, which had been Sheila's mother's birth stone.

'I'm having the engagement ring re-sized,' said Charlo, following Ronda's gaze. 'The band was digging into her skin, wasn't it love?'

'Sssshhh,' Sheila hissed, dragging her chair closer to the TV.

Charlo looked her over. 'I think you lot are feeding her too many cakes,' he said. 'She's getting as big as a house.'

Captain Grady marched into the room, stopping in front of Ronda to click his heels and salute. 'Is Private Sean Grady reporting for duty tonight?' he asked. Ronda looked around. Sean must have left already.

'He reported for duty earlier,' she said. 'He'll be back next week.'

Captain Grady took off his peaked cap, picked at the edges of it. 'I think there's something I need to brief him on, but it keeps slipping my mind,' he said. He closed his eyes as tears ran down his face. This was not an unusual occurrence, even though Ronda was certain that the previous version of him wouldn't have stood for such an open display of emotion.

Kim slipped her hand around Captain Grady's arm. 'How about a game of cards?' she asked him. He examined her face with suspicion, but allowed himself to be led to the games room.

'I don't know how you cope with all the madsers in here, Ronda,' said Charlo, shaking his head. Behind him, Ronda could see Fatima approach, carrying a large jug of water and wearing what Ronda called her resolute face, her mouth held in a tight line and eyes narrowed and focused. They were focused on the bank forms Charlo had brought, in a bundle on the footstool. Ronda tried to catch her eye, shake her head, but Fatima's gaze never faltered. She walked around them and tipped some water into a potted palm near the television, then turned and headed their way. Afterwards, nobody could really say what had caused Fatima to trip. Perhaps Baby's soother had fallen out of her mouth and landed, unseen, on the floor. Or maybe it was a slip. On a spillage that had gone unnoticed, perhaps. As Fatima approached the footstool, the water in the jug cascaded out, formed a brief but beautiful arc that caught the fluorescent lighting and softened it, before pouring down, all over Charlo's paperwork.

'Jesus, no,' shouted Charlo, jumping up and reefing the sodden pages off the footstool. He rubbed at the top page with the sleeve of his jacket. Ronda tried to make out the title at the top of the page. Something about a deposit account. Name to be added. The words ran into each other, like a panicked crowd. The cuff of Charlo's sleeve was wet where the ink had soaked in. 'Bloody hell,' he said, doing his best to wring the inky water out of the material. 'These are important documents pertaining to Sheila's care,' he said, not quite shouting, but not far off. Kim patted him down with kitchen paper and Fatima apologised over and over so Charlo couldn't get a word in edgewise.

Sheila never looked away from the television.

CHAPTER 15

The hospice AGM took place on a Friday and Margo rang Ronda on Saturday morning to arrange her first driving lesson. It was scheduled for Monday evening at seven o'clock. Margo reckoned seven would be a good time, since rush hour would have abated. She didn't say anything about the fact that it would be dark by seven. Or that Ronda would be tired after finishing a twelve-hour shift.

'Don't worry, I've insured you on the car,' Margo had told her on the phone. 'It cost nine hundred and sixty-five euros: you can Revolut me. Plus whatever petrol we use, obvs.'

Ronda logged onto her current account. Even though she had just been paid, the balance was skimpy. She would have to dip into her savings account. There was €10,788. Soon to be €9,823. Probably less again, if Margo charged her for the lessons, which was not out of the question.

At seven o'clock on the dot, Margo pulled up outside No. 10 Casino Place. She blew the horn. Three short blasts. She waited for thirty seconds, and when Ronda did not appear, she turned off the engine and jumped out of the car. She rang the doorbell – two short blasts, followed by a long, impatient one, then rapped forcefully on the hard wood of the front door. 'Ronda?' she shouted through the narrow mouth of the letter box. 'You better not be backing out. I drove through thick traffic to get here.'

Ronda was in the kitchen with her hand on the door handle. She knew she'd have to open it, sooner or later. Margo would not take kindly to second thoughts. It occurred to Ronda, standing in the kitchen with her hand on the door handle, that she hadn't instigated much in her life. Most things just seemed to happen to her. Like her scar. Like her broken relationship. She'd been a bystander. Passive. Accepting. Compliant.

And now, here she was again, being corralled into places she didn't want to go. Like Margo's car.

Her sister's insistent voice thundered through the letter box. Ronda wondered what it would be like, to be that certain of yourself.

'Ronda! Open this door! I'm freezing to actual death out here!' shouted Margo.

Ronda's hand tightened around the doorknob.

The cat flap rattled and she looked at it, but it was just the wind, lifting it. Even Jessica Fletcher was out in the world somewhere, doing her own thing.

It was her mother who came down the stairs from her bedroom and opened the door in the end. Ronda could hear the pair of them speaking in hushed voices in the hall. They were probably talking about her. Or maybe not talking about her. She wondered which one was worse. She was procrastinating. She was well aware of it. What if she walked outside and there was Joseph? His car was still there, she'd checked after dinner. She could walk outside just as he was feeding his charger through the window of what was called the lounge in their house. Not the good room.

'RONDA!' shouted Margo down the hall.

Ronda opened the kitchen door and walked up the hallway towards them. Annie shook her head. 'If anything happens to you . . .' she said. 'I'll never forgive myself.'

Ronda could feel her stomach muscles constrict and, with them, the grilled cheese sandwich she'd eaten earlier. Anything could happen. Still, she couldn't help feeling warmed by her mother's concern.

'You with those three wonderful boys to look after, they'd be lost without you.'

'Don't worry, Mam,' said Margo, stepping into the circle of Annie's arms. 'I'll be careful.'

All the way down the garden path, Ronda made a conscious effort not to look in the direction of the Murphys' house. She focused on the gate in front of her and ignored her peripheral field of vision.

'So now you're in a hurry,' said Margo, struggling to keep up with her. 'What took you so long? I had to hear all about Mam's bowel movements. Did you know she went twice today?'

'Yes,' said Ronda, on the path now. The Murphys' house was mercifully in darkness. 'Once at eleven and then again at four when she was just settling down to watch *The Chase*. She missed the first ten minutes of it.'

The light from the street lamp across the road formed a sort of halo around Margo's blond bob, lending her an ecclesiastical hue. She was tightly belted into a pale grey cashmere coat that stopped halfway down her shins. Her feet were encased in a pair of high-heeled ankle boots, white with a furry trim.

'You won't be able to drive in those,' said Ronda, nodding at the boots.

'Just as well I'm not driving then,' said Margo.

'Well, I can't drive,' said Ronda. 'Not on the first lesson, surely?'

'Let's start as we mean to go on,' said Margo. 'Come along.' She stopped at the door of a small black Opel Corsa.

'Where's your car?' Ronda asked, looking around.

'You think I'm going to trust you behind the wheel of my Range Rover?' said Margo, her sculpted eyebrows arching into peaks. 'Do you have any idea how much they cost?'

'Fifty grand?' Ronda guessed.

'Maybe in 1989 they did,' said Margo. 'This is a little runabout for the boys. It's got manual gears. Better to learn in a stick shift.' She opened the door and sat in the passenger seat. 'Get in,' she said. 'I haven't got all day.'

The last time Ronda had been inside a car was the day Ms Gallagher had had a seizure. When she'd come round, she had been a subdued version of herself. Also, politer. 'Please come to the hospital with me,' she'd asked, slipping her shaking hand into Ronda's. 'I don't want to die in an ambulance all by myself.' Ronda had concentrated on the blare of the siren and the flash of the lights and the grip of Ms Gallagher's hand in hers. From time to time, she'd said, 'Nearly there,' and those two words, softly spoken, seemed to provide some comfort to both of them.

That had been two years ago.

The interior of Margo's car was clinically clean, the pinstriped upholstery like a power suit fresh out of the dry-cleaners. There was a complicated panel of buttons and levers and switches and dials and already some of them were blinking and flashing and Ronda hadn't even turned the key in the ignition.

'This seems . . . very complicated,' said Ronda, her throat suddenly dry.

'It's not, it's easy,' said Margo dismissively.

'Easy for you maybe,' said Ronda.

'Can we keep the pessimism to a minimum please?' said Margo. 'It's playing havoc with my chakras.'

'Sorry,' said Ronda. 'I just wish I didn't have to do this.'

'How do you think I feel?' said Margo. 'I could be home right now, on my second glass of Chardonnay and spending quality time with my boys, and yet, here I am, stuck with you in a car on a freezing winter's night. But by all means, don't bother feigning a bit of gratitude or enthusiasm on my behalf. I wouldn't want you to go to any trouble.'

'Sorry,' said Ronda again. 'I'm . . . a bit nervous.'

At the admission, Margo seemed to deflate somewhat. When she spoke again, her voice was not as shrill.

'We'll take it slowly, okay?' she said, handing Ronda a key. 'You need to turn the key and press down on the clutch at the same time,' said Margo. 'You know which one is the clutch?' Ronda nodded. She had memorised the PowerPoint presentation Margo had emailed to her.

'Anytime today,' said Margo, drumming her fingers on her black leather clutch bag.

'Shouldn't I check my rear-view mirror first?' said Ronda.

Margo sighed. 'Knock yourself out,' she said.

Joseph Murphy's face was in the rear-view mirror. The same impossibly handsome face she remembered from her adolescence, with the lantern jaw and wide blue eyes. The blond hair was grey now, which in no way compromised the quality of his luscious locks, the ends of which grazed the collar of his blindingly white shirt. He was on the phone, sitting on the pillar outside the Murphys' house, kicking his long denim-clad legs against the brick. Ronda couldn't hear what he was saying, but knew by the deliberate gesticulation of his hands that he was irked. Now that she had seen him, she couldn't seem to un-see him. Margo, twisting in her seat to see what was distracting her sister, spotted Joseph.

'That tosser's still at the Murphy's,' she said. 'Do you know how long he's staying?'

Ronda shook her head.

'Have you spoken to him yet?'

Ronda shook her head again.

'If you're not going to give him a piece of your mind, I presume you won't mind if I do?' said Margo, her face darkening.

'No, I don't . . .' began Ronda.

'He humiliated you,' said Margo, giving equal emphasis to each of the five syllables of the word.

Humiliated.

Ronda said nothing.

'Okay, let's focus here, shall we?' said Margo, glancing at her watch. 'You're going to turn the key in the ignition, yes? While pushing the clutch all the way down to the floor, okay?'

Ronda closed her fingers around the key, turned it clockwise just like Margo said, her foot hard against the clutch. What happened next was supposed to happen. In the theoretical, logical, cognisant part of her brain, Ronda knew that. When the engine started, Ronda could feel the roar of it deep inside her body, behind her eyes, vibrating down her arms, her hands, into her fingers, every one of her cells filling with sound, the fillings in her teeth vibrating with it. It was like elastic, the sound. Stretching and stretching until she felt like she would snap into pieces with the intensity of it. She yanked the key out of the ignition. For a moment, the silence was glorious, like swimming underwater, the sounds of the world muted and faraway.

'Ronda?' Margo's voice broke through the surface.

In the rear-view mirror, Joseph had jumped off the pillar and was looking up the road in their direction.

Ronda looked at her sister's face. It seemed impossible, how calm it was. 'I can't do this,' said Ronda. She sounded out of breath, as if she'd been running for a bus.

'You can,' said Margo, matter-of-fact.

'Some people just can't learn how to drive.'

'That's true,' said Margo. 'But you don't happen to be one of them.'

'How do you know?' asked Ronda.

Margo thought about this for a moment. 'You know the way Sebastian tells me he wants to do a business degree and get into finance like Malcolm?' She looked at Ronda who nodded. 'But I know that he really wants to be a librarian. He's afraid to tell us because he thinks that we'll think it's not ambitious enough.'

'I don't know what that has to do with this?' said Ronda.

'I know things,' said Margo.

'That's not the same as knowing I can learn to drive,' said Ronda, confused.

'It is,' said Margo.

'It isn't,' said Ronda.

'It is,' said Margo.

Ronda leaned against the back of the seat, rubbed her eyes. It was hard to believe the lesson hadn't started yet.

A car drove down the road. Mrs Murphy parked outside her house and greeted Joseph. They walked into the house and the front door closed behind them.

'He's gone now,' said Margo, watching through the wing mirror. 'Let's try again, shall we?'

Ronda shook her head and something about the resolute way she did it seemed to convince Margo that she meant it.

'Okay fine,' said Margo, undoing her seat belt. 'Just for today, you can sit in the passenger seat. I'll introduce you to the car, get you acquainted.'

'Really?' said Ronda, She didn't think she'd ever managed to dissuade Margo from her intended course of action.

'But the next lesson you're behind the wheel,' said Margo. 'I mean it Ronda.'

They switched places.

'I'll start by showing you how to adjust your seat and your mirrors, okay?' Ronda nodded and listened, then carefully demonstrated what she had learned.

'Bring the seat back further,' said Margo. 'Your legs are disproportionately long. And sit up straight, shoulders back, hands on the wheel at ten to two, remember?'

Margo gestured towards the panel. 'Next, I'll go through these functions and explain what they're for.'

The explanations took time. When Ronda glanced at her watch, she was relieved to see that there was only fifteen minutes of the lesson left.

'Are you paying attention?' said Margo.

Ronda pointed to the rounded aluminium head of the gear stick. 'You were explaining the gear shifts,' she said. 'It's in neutral at the moment. The R stands for reverse. To engage the gears, I push the clutch down all the way to the floor, then manoeuvre the gear stick, standard H formation.'

'Are you mocking me?' said Margo.

'I'm just repeating what you said,' said Ronda.

'Yes, but you're repeating it verbatim,' said Margo.

'What's wrong with that?' said Ronda, confused.

Margo massaged her temples with the pads of her fingers.

'Would you like some paracetamol?' asked Ronda.

'That's like throwing peanuts at an elephant,' said Margo, taking a bottle of pills out of her handbag. She shook out two of them and dry-swallowed both. She pointed at a button on the steering wheel. 'What does that do?'

'It steers the car,' said Ronda.

'No, not the wheel,' said Margo, making a stab at patience. 'That button there. On the wheel.'

'Is that a trick question?' asked Ronda.

'Why would it be a trick question?' said Margo.

'Because you haven't explained what that button does yet,' said Ronda.

'I did,' said Margo.

'You didn't,' said Ronda.

'I did,' said Margo.

'You didn't,' said Ronda.

'If you don't know, just say,' said Margo. 'I'll explain it again.'

'I never knew,' said Ronda. 'Because you never explained it.'

Margo made a whistling sound through her teeth and closed her eyes. Judging by the shapes she was now making with her mouth, Ronda reckoned she was counting to ten. She leaned towards the wheel, studied the button.

'It might change the channels on the radio,' she said. Margo opened her eyes and smoothed her bob with the palm of her hand even though not a hair was out of place.

'I think that's enough for today,' she said then. 'Don't you?'

Ronda couldn't agree more.

CHAPTER 16

Even though she hadn't driven Margo's car, there was a shake in Ronda's legs as she got out.

'Are you all right?' Margo said. 'You're white as a ghost.'

'I'm fine,' said Ronda, leaning against the garden wall. She smiled and waved, as if there was no danger of collapse. 'You go on,' she said. Joseph could be looking out of his old bedroom window at that exact moment. She didn't want to appear unhinged.

Inside the house, she closed the door and slid down the wall.

'Is that you Ronda?' her mother called from her bedroom. 'You weren't long.'

It had felt long. Ronda waited for the shaking to subside. She focused on the walls, breathed in slowly. They could do with a lick of paint. That made her think about the boiler, which needed to be replaced. The ceiling in Ronda's room leaked when there was heavy rain. The whole place needed a makeover, but Annie said, 'What's the point?' any time Ronda mentioned it. 'Sure I'll be dead soon.' Ronda felt it would be insensitive to point out that she, Ronda, would, in all likelihood, still be alive.

Ronda picked herself up from the floor and made her way into the kitchen. The chessboard was on the table. Her queen had been captured. Check. Ronda sat down and concentrated on the board. When the wind picked up, the windows rattled in their frames. 'This is the only house I know with single glazed windows,' Margo had said last week, rapping on the glass with her knuckles. 'They're vintage,' Ronda had replied. Her sister loved all things vintage. 'They're old and unfit for purpose,' Margo had said, which was probably a more accurate assessment.

Ronda persevered for another hour at the chessboard before conceding defeat. In good news, her legs had stopped shaking. She turned Berkley off and made sure the front and back doors were locked. As she was turning off the hall light, her phone rang. Ronda looked at her watch. Good news was never relayed after ten o'clock at night, and it was ten past. She picked her phone out of her back pocket and studied the screen. It was Fatima. Even if it hadn't been so late, the call would have triggered alarm bells, since Fatima always texted rather than called.

Fatima started talking as soon as Ronda picked up, struggling to keep her voice low and even. 'I just got a call from one of my friends,' she said. 'She was at the International Protection Office earlier and got talking to this man who arrived in Dublin today. According to him, Noah is coming to Ireland,' she said.

'When?' said Ronda.

'He wasn't sure. He said maybe Noah's already here.'

'Who is this man?' asked Ronda. 'Is he a friend of Noah's?'

'I don't know,' said Fatima. 'But he knows people who work for Noah.'

'It's not first-hand information,' said Ronda. 'It could be hearsay.'

'But what if it isn't?' Fatima's voice was threadbare with fear.

'What do you need me to do?' Ronda asked. Fatima was a practical woman. Ronda knew she wasn't ringing for sympathy.

'I need to leave work,' said Fatima. 'Ada is at the centre. What if Noah is on his way there?'

'I'll come in and cover for you,' said Ronda.

'But what if Fergal finds out I missed a shift?' said Fatima. 'He's been worse than usual lately. Since the takeover.'

'He won't find out,' said Ronda, with as much conviction as she could muster. Her hands tightened around the phone, thinking about Ada. She was small for her age, but she had a big personality, full of enthusiasm for a world that, on a good day, treated her with indifference. She had no idea of the danger she had been in, at the compound. Fatima had protected her from Noah for as long as she could, and then run, as soon as she realised her protection was no longer enough. Ada seemed younger than Tiernan even though they were the same age. There was an innocence about her. A happy-ever-after storybook quality that Ronda usually found so sweet. Now it just made her seem vulnerable. Easy pickings for a manipulator like Noah.

'I'm on my way,' said Ronda.

CHAPTER 17

Ronda didn't care for the night shift. Green Gables seemed to come alive at night, the residents walking the corridors like ghosts, haunting the lives they once had. The dark pressed against the windows and the artificial brightness inside the building seemed to create more confusion for the guests.

Ronda was unsurprised to find Ms Gallagher dressed and sitting ramrod straight in her bedside armchair at five o'clock in the morning when she went to check on her. Ms Gallagher was an insomniac and rarely bothered putting on her pyjamas or getting into bed any more. She now needed assistance doing both, and accepting help was not something she was good at.

What did shock Ronda was the presence of another person in Ms Gallagher's room. A man. He was on Ms Gallagher's bed, his back to Ronda. Discarded on the floor beside him was a pair of tatty runners that had been white, a long time ago. His socks were covered with smiley faces in dark glasses. A hole in the left sock accommodated the protrusion of a large, hairy toe. A legal pad was wide open on the floor, the pages full of tiny, indecipherable writing. Some of the words were heavily underlined, followed by many exclamation marks. She stretched out her arm, fumbling for the call button.

'Don't you dare push that button,' snapped Ms Gallagher.

The man, sitting cross-legged on Ms Gallagher's bed, turned his head towards Ronda.

It was Donal Clarke.

'I am having a meeting with my solicitor,' said Ms Gallagher. 'Who you yourself recommended to me, may I add.'

'The van had its annual inspection at four so I said I'd call in here afterwards,' explained Donal, a little sheepish.

'How did you get past security?' asked Ronda.

'I wrestled them to the ground,' said Donal, grinning. 'I'm stronger than I look.'

'I phoned the desk and told them to expect Mr Clarke,' said Ms Gallagher, narrowing her eyes in Ronda's direction. 'This is my home, Ronda, not a prison,' she said. 'Not that you'd know it, with you lot of sergeant majors, marching about the place.'

'I'm sorry,' said Ronda, lowering her hand from the call button. 'I just wasn't expecting to see Mr Clarke in your room.'

'Donal. Please,' said Donal, his smile widening. 'And I'm sorry too. I didn't mean to startle you.'

'You didn't startle me,' said Ronda.

'How are the driving lessons going?' he asked.

'Fine,' said Ronda briskly. 'So, you're all good here then? Do you need anything, Ms Gallagher? A cup of tea, maybe?'

'I can't believe you can't drive,' said Ms Gallagher. 'An aunt of mine taught me in Belfast city when I was a young slip of a thing, barely fourteen years old. By day three, I was zipping down Divis Street in Auntie Nell's Morris Minor with the tricolour painted on the side.'

Donal looked at his watch. 'I've to pick up my young fella at the airport at six thirty, Ms Gallagher,' he said. 'So we'd better keep at it if we're going to get your paperwork done by then.'

'In my day, we didn't ask for lifts, we stuck our thumbs out,' said Ms Gallagher.

'I offered,' said Donal. 'He's been in Scotland for a week studying rocks. Budding geologist.'

'Fine then,' said Ms Gallagher, picking up her iPad and swiping her fingers across the screen.

'Your forehead's healing nicely,' said Donal as Ronda moved towards the door.

'I thought you said you were in a hurry?' said Ms Gallagher, peering at Donal over the top of the tablet.

'I'll leave you to it,' said Ronda, ducking out of the room.

At the top of the corridor was Tracey, striding towards her. Ronda turned and hurried the other way, but Tracey had clocked her. 'What are you doing here Ronda? I didn't think you were rostered for the night shift?'

'I asked Fergal if I could switch with Fatima,' said Ronda.

'It's me you should have asked,' said Tracey. 'You know that.'

'You were in a meeting,' said Ronda. This was a gamble, but since the management spent more than half their time at meetings, there was a chance it was true.

'The innovation meeting?' asked Tracey.

'Eh, yes,' said Ronda.

'Well, make sure you ask me in future,' she said. 'I don't want Fergal dealing with trivial matters, he has a lot on his plate at the moment.' She glanced up and down the corridor, then stepped closer to Ronda. 'Between you and me,' she began in a lowered voice, 'there's going to be changes around here, if you know what I mean.' She eyed Ronda, who nodded as if she knew exactly what Tracey meant.

She didn't.

But she could hazard a guess.

CHAPTER 18

Because Ronda had been busy worrying about her second driving lesson, scheduled for Tuesday, she had neglected to worry about Joseph Murphy, whose car continued to sit outside his parents' house. Given this oversight, Ronda felt she had only herself to blame when her first interaction with him since their break-up and Ronda's subsequent return home to her mother – who had failed to register much surprise at her daughter's misadventures in matters of the heart – took place that Tuesday evening, a mere hour before the driving lesson. It was dark and cold. The street lamp outside the McCann's house guttered through the bare branches of the laburnum tree, the light it cast no match for the viscous darkness of the night. Ronda dismounted and wheeled her bike through the gate, parked it, and then struggled to get the shackle of the bicycle lock into the double deadbolt. Her fingers were rigid with cold. She cupped her hands around her mouth and blew in an effort to encourage some heat into them. Then, she hunkered down to get a better purchase on the lock.

'Hello Ronda.' Joseph had one of those chameleon voices that adapted to whatever environment he found himself in. Tonight he was using his old voice. The boy-next-door voice. The most noticeable accent had been his English one, very pronounced after spending six years there, after he had left school. 'How do you do, Ronda?' was how he'd greeted her that July, when he had returned. There'd been some misunderstanding at his uncle's architect's firm where he'd worked. He hadn't been fired, he'd been quick to assure her. He'd chosen to leave. Ronda heard he'd had a girlfriend. Bianca. But when he'd arrived back home, there had been no sign of her. He had been on his own.

He'd seemed quieter. Or at least no longer the centre of the universe amongst his peers, as he had been at school. Lots of his friends had moved away. Or moved on, made other friends. Joseph Murphy was at a loose end. Ronda, who had been working in the local supermarket since she left school, understood how that felt.

They'd got into the habit of chatting over the garden fence. Joseph had done most of the talking, complaining about living with his parents again and having no money and nothing to do. Ronda had been a sympathetic ear. Once, after a particularly lengthy and vitriolic rant about a job interview that hadn't gone his way, he'd looked at Ronda, as if he'd just noticed her. 'You've grown up very nicely, if I may say so,' he'd said.

Ronda – who had mooned after the impossibly handsome Joseph Murphy all through her adolescence, had been surprised and gratified by his attention. He started calling into Ronda's house after interviews. She made him tea and fed him custard creams, which were his favourites. Listened to his woes. About the job market in Dublin being too small for someone with his zeal and ambition. 'You could go back to London?' Ronda had said, straining to sound offhand. He didn't go back to London.

Joseph had rarely mentioned Bianca. He'd described the break up as 'mutual', his tone performatively casual. It had happened after the misunderstanding at work. Ronda hadn't asked for details.

It was Joseph who had wondered why Ronda didn't use her savings to put herself through nursing school. Ronda had wanted to be a nurse since Elaine, the nurse at St James Hospital, had removed the stitches in her face. Elaine had been dexterous, meticulous and – best of all – hadn't made any glib comments about the scar not being all that noticeable.

'You have to take what you want in this life, Ronda,' Joseph had said. 'Nobody is going to give it to you on a plate.' He couldn't believe it when she went ahead and registered for the course, started it that September. He took a job as a clerk at an architect's office in Donnybrook, even though he considered himself vastly overqualified for the position. Then his great aunt had died, and Joseph had moved into her now empty house, a mile away.

Ronda presumed she wouldn't see much of him after that.

But he continued calling in. He complained about his boss, who was a clueless hick. And about his colleagues, none of whom had a creative bone in their bodies. One Wednesday evening, Joseph couldn't believe it when Annie opened the door instead of Ronda.

'Where were you?' he'd asked, a little peevish, the next time he called.

Ronda had joined the chess society in college. The club met every Wednesday.

'I missed our chats,' he'd said, sounding surprised by the admission. So was Ronda. And by his subsequent enquiry. Would she like to see the new James Bond movie with him that Friday night? Ronda wasn't a fan of James Bond, and the film did nothing to alter her opinion. She'd bought pop-corn for them, but couldn't eat hers, her mouth being too dry with nerves. Joseph polished it off. When he'd taken her hand in his, she'd worried about the clamminess of her fingers. The boniness. His hand was smooth and soft and appeared hairless, but only because he was so fair, this blond, blue-eyed boy. The boy next door. He had never so much as glanced in her direction growing up, and now here he was, in the dark, eating her popcorn and holding her clammy hand.

Joseph had found it difficult paying the bills on the pit-tance he earned. Ronda was paying rent at No. 10 Casino Place. Why didn't she move in and pay rent at his place instead? Joseph had suggested.

So she did.

'I knew this day would come,' Annie had said, pulling her shawl tighter around her shoulders as Ronda dragged her suitcase down the hall. 'You and Margo, gone.'

'I'm only down the road,' Ronda said. 'I'll call in every day.'

For a while things were good. By day, Ronda was top of her class. She did four shifts a week at the supermarket, mostly at weekends. At night, she was the shoulder Joseph leaned on as he struggled to gain a foothold on the career ladder.

Joseph proposed to her the day of his first promotion.

'Why?' Ronda asked, shocked by the proposal.

'The traditional answer is yes,' Joseph said, amused.

Was that why he'd asked her? Tradition? Or elation, get-ting a decent job, finally free of the stain London had left on his CV? Perhaps he liked how she catered to his needs without ever really expecting much in return. All she knew for sure was that, from the moment he proposed, things had changed. Joseph had changed. Or maybe he had just reverted to the person he'd always been. Confident, ambitious, surrounded by successful people, attracted by his success.

He stopped using her as a sounding board for his work-related angst.

He was at home less and less, citing work commitments.

And when he was home, Ronda had the distinct impression that he was somewhere else, in his head. Or that he wanted to be.

And then, he gave her syphilis.

'I knew it was too good to be true,' Annie had said when Ronda returned, her savings depleted as well as her already paltry store of confidence and self-esteem. Instead of registering for the second year of her nursing degree, she'd dropped out, having neither the funds nor the self-belief. She'd quit her job at the supermarket, completed a six-week carers' course and started work at a nursing home the following Monday morning.

'Hello Ronda,' came the voice. The old voice. The boy-next-door voice. She looked up and there he was, on the other side of the garden fence, looking down at her. With his hands in the pockets of his jeans and the way he kicked at the pillar with the toe of his trainer, he looked less assured than usual. 'I wouldn't blame you for ignoring me,' he said.

Ronda realised that she was no longer cold, despite the frigid chill of the night. In fact, a tide of warmth flooded through her. Her body tingled with the sensation, even her fingers, which now moved with great fluidity when she flexed them. The shackle slid into the lock with ease. When Ronda stood up, she noticed a couple of things. For starters, she was taller. Now, it was she, looking down at him. Also, her hair was different. Still dark, but long now, in a sophisticated up-do. Some loose silky strands framed her face which was perfectly made up so that her grey eyes, in the light from the glowing street lamp outside the Murphys' house, were an expanse of seawater, deep and unfathomable. Joseph blinked several times, as if his eyes were having trouble adjusting to her.

'You're even more beautiful than I remembered,' he said in a breathy voice.

Ronda picked her helmet off the handlebars. 'I'm afraid I don't have time for small talk,' she said. Her voice was low and steady. Assured.

'You'll be delighted to hear that Danielle kicked me out,' he said.

Ronda shook her head. 'I bear no ill-will toward you, Joseph,' she said with great dignity, pulling a sheet of tarpaulin over her bicycle to protect it from the elements.

'She wants full custody of the kids,' Joseph said then. 'And the house. And a pound of my flesh, while she's at it, why not?' He shook his head. 'Sorry,' he said. 'I have no right to complain to you of all people,' he said.

'No,' said Ronda. 'You do not.'

She walked away with the kind of grace people covet. Understated. Effortless. She reached the front door, the key already in her hand. The door opened easily. Inside, the house was warm and bright with the smell of roasting vegetables – courgettes, peppers and butternut squash, if she wasn't very much mistaken – wafting from the kitchen, which had benefitted from a fresh coat of paint – duck egg blue – and some new press doors in a delicate shade of pearl. The ones that closed with a whisper no matter how hard Annie shut them. And there was Annie, in a jersey dress the same shade of blue as her eyes, setting the table for two. 'There you are,' she said, beaming as Ronda opened the door and walked into the room. 'Your timing is perfect.'

'Hello Ronda,' came a voice. The boy-next-door voice. Ronda dropped the lock and it landed on her foot. She yelped.

'Sorry, I didn't mean to startle you.'

Ronda looked up.

'Hello Joseph.'

'You haven't changed a bit,' he said. Ronda was aware of her hair, plastered against her head after the confines of the helmet. She resisted the urge to peel her fringe off her forehead.

'It's nice to see you,' he said. Ronda nodded. 'I suppose you've heard,' he went on. 'The whole neighbourhood's talking about it, no doubt.'

Ronda said nothing.

'Danielle kicked me out,' Joseph went on. 'She wants full custody of the kids. And the house. And a pound of my flesh, while she's at it, why not?'

'I'm sorry to hear that,' said Ronda, dragging a sheet of tarpaulin over her bicycle to protect it from the worst of the wet and cold. She fumbled in her pockets for the front door key. Joseph's phone rang.

'I'd better take this,' he said, glancing at the screen. 'Maybe I'll see you around.'

Before Ronda could formulate a response, Joseph was

gone. Ronda was anxious to be gone too, but had to put her shoulder to the front door and heave before it gave way.

Inside, the house was cold and dark. Annie had left a note on the kitchen table.

Gone to bed. Swollen glands.

Ronda sat down, still in her coat. While her hands and face were cold to the touch, she burned with a humiliation that did not seem to have abated over the years. And of all the speeches she'd made to him in her head over those years, never once did the word 'sorry' get a look in.

Except that's exactly what she'd ended up saying.

CHAPTER 19

The second driving lesson, which began forty minutes later, was much worse than the first. Margo picked Ronda up and drove them to a shabby little industrial estate with 'For Lease' signs outside more than half the units. She drove down one of the side roads and pulled in at the kerb. Two trucks roared by, despite the 30 kph speed limit and the frequency and depth of the potholes.

This time, Margo insisted that Ronda sit in the driver's seat. 'I'm not ready,' Ronda told Margo.

'I'll be the judge of that,' said Margo.

'I learn best by observing,' said Ronda. 'So if you could just . . .'

'This isn't going to work unless you do exactly what I tell you,' said Margo.

'Sorry,' said Ronda. 'I'm just . . .' But what word could she use that would make her fear acceptable to her fearless sister?

'You're wasting time,' said Margo, glancing at the clock on the dashboard. 'I told the outgoing golf club captain I'd drop in on my way home for what he's calling a "walk-through". Which is when he tells me everything I already know and takes his sweet time about it.' Margo's perfume was dense and the vapour rushed up Ronda's nose, making her sneeze three times in succession. Margo handed her a tissue. 'I hope you're not coming down with something contagious,' she said, opening the window and beating at the air with her hands.

'I could be,' said Ronda. 'Maybe we should . . .'

'Are you doing a Mam on it now?' said Margo. 'Pretending to be sick?'

Margo's phone rang and she reached into her bag and grabbed it, glared at the screen. 'I told Malcolm I was giving you a lesson. He never listens to me.' She stabbed at the disconnect button, then opened WhatsApp and typed furiously with her thumbs.

Ronda did her best to collect herself. She knew that a cursory glance would find her composed, but a closer inspection – under the bonnet, so to speak – would reveal several cracks in her chassis. She asked herself what was the worst that could happen.

The engine could catch fire, causing the car to go up in flames and they could both die of smoke inhalation and first degree burns.

Then there was the more likely car crash. Even though she'd been in a car crash before, Ronda's recollection of events was hazy.

She tried to think of something positive. Nothing occurred.

'Now,' said Margo, tossing her phone back into her handbag. 'Where were we?'

'We had established that I am raring to go,' said Ronda. When Margo smiled it was sudden and unexpected and very, very bright, given the regularity with which she got her teeth whitened. Such was the sudden, unexpected brightness of it, Ronda couldn't help smiling back.

'Do you remember everything I taught you last time?' asked Margo.

'I do,' said Ronda.

'Okay, turn over the engine,' said Margo, snapping her smile off and belting herself in.

'Shouldn't I do all the mirror adjusting stuff first?' asked Ronda.

'You've already done that,' said Margo. 'Can you please stop stalling?'

Ronda turned the key and pushed her foot against the clutch, as Margo had shown. The engine roared into life and Ronda felt the power of it through the steering wheel around which her fingers were gripped, her knuckles terror-white.

'What next?' said Ronda. Her voice sounded breathless, like a femme fatale in a black and white film.

'Indicate,' said Margo.

'Left or right?' said Ronda.

'And you were the clever one, according to Mam,' said Margo, shaking her head.

'She never said that,' said Ronda, prising her hand off the wheel and pulling at a lever. The windscreen wipers came on.

'She told me you got enough points to do medicine,' said Margo. 'That's pretty much all the points anyone can get.'

'I can't remember where the indicator is,' said Ronda.

'It's on the other side,' said Margo, trying – not very hard, Ronda felt – to sound patient.

After a while, Ronda managed to turn on the left indicator, check her mirrors and put the car in first gear.

'There're no cars coming,' said Margo, twisting her neck

this way and that so that her hair swished around her face, as bouncy as a shampoo ad.

'There's a van,' said Ronda, peering in the rear-view mirror.

'It's about a million miles away,' said Margo.

'Maybe I should wait and . . .'

'Pull out,' barked Margo. 'I'm ageing here.'

Ronda waited for the van to pass. Margo said nothing, but her silence was loud and clear. Ronda turned the wheel. She leaned her foot ever so slightly against the accelerator pedal.

Nothing happened.

'You have to press harder,' said Margo.

'I am pressing harder,' said Ronda, who knew she was not pressing any harder than before but seemed powerless to proceed. She was hot with frustration. She was not a cowardly person. She had done hard things. When Captain Grady got into one of his moods and became aggressive, it was Ronda they sent in. She wasn't afraid of the way he curled his hands into fists and swung for her. Or lifted one of his booted feet to kick her shins. She wasn't afraid because there was no malice in his actions. Only confusion. Once he had grabbed her hair. She'd hurt her neck that time. Had to have physio. Tracey Fuller said she'd have to report it to Sean, put him on notice that if he did it again, they would be within their rights to have his father removed from the facility. Ronda had begged her not to. 'He didn't mean it,' she'd said. Besides, where else would Captain Grady go? Green Gables, for all its shortcomings, was his home. Who would have him? Apart from Sean, nobody visited.

'He's always been a bully,' Sean had said when Tracey went ahead and told him. 'The only reason my mother didn't leave him was because she had nowhere else to go, God rest her.'

Tracey had offered to transfer Ronda to a different unit at Green Gables. So she wouldn't have to interact with Captain Grady. Ronda said no. Fatima told her she was brave. Ronda hadn't felt brave because she hadn't felt afraid.

But here, in Margo's car, her fear was a physical thing, hammering a hole through the wall of her chest, squeezing the breath out of her lungs, making a beeline for her sweat glands.

'Ronda?'

'Sorry, yes, I know,' said Ronda. 'I was just . . .'

She pressed harder and the car jerked forward. Ronda slammed both feet on the brake pedal and the car jerked to a stop, flinging both of them against their belts before catapulting them back against the seats.

Ronda screamed.

The car shuddered before it cut out.

'What the hell are you doing?' shouted Margo.

'I thought I was going too fast,' Ronda managed to say.

Margo's intake of breath made a whistling sound through her clenched teeth. 'This is going to be harder than I thought,' she said.

'How did you not know it was going to be hard?' asked Ronda, incredulous.

'I didn't say I didn't know it was going to be hard,' said Margo. 'I just said I didn't know it was going to be *this* hard.'

Ronda closed her eyes and leaned against the back of the seat.

'I'm doing this for you, you know,' said Margo, after a while. Ronda did not contradict her, mostly because there was no point, but also because she didn't trust herself to speak. If she opened her mouth, a sound might erupt from her. Something loud and incoherent and ragged with tension. Instead, she looked in the rear-view mirror, then the wing mirror, as Margo had instructed. No cars coming or going. She turned over the engine, pressed her foot against the clutch, wrestled the car into first gear. She groped with her other foot for the accelerator, and there she was, pressing it, then pressing it again, harder this time. The car moved away from the kerb and out into the road, jerky as a muscle spasm, but moving.

'Jesus fucking Christ,' yelled Margo.

'What?' shrieked Ronda.

'Nothing,' screeched Margo.

'Then why are you shouting?' roared Ronda, her grip on the steering wheel so tight, blood could no longer flow down her fingers.

'I don't know,' said Margo. 'I just . . . I wasn't expecting you to actually do it.'

Ronda kept going. After a while, Margo loosened her grip on the door handle. A little while later, she removed her hand – splayed and braced – from the dashboard and allowed herself to sit back a little, as if relaxed.

'What'll I do now?' said Ronda, approaching a stop sign.

'Stop,' said Margo.

'How?' said Ronda.

'Take your foot off the accelerator,' said Margo.

Ronda did as she was bid. The car kept going, nearly at the stop sign now.

'Now brake,' said Margo.

The car rolled towards the stop sign.

'BRAKE!!'

The car rolled past the stop sign.

'BLOODY BRAKE!!!'

This time, Ronda managed to brake, but forgot to step on the clutch.

The car cut out.

Ronda heard a roar and looked to her left. A truck was bearing down on them and the driver had his hand on the horn, which was blaring.

'Reverse,' said Margo.

'Which one is reverse?' said Ronda, who could feel sweat soaking into the cotton of her T-shirt. Sebastian had given it to her last Christmas. An in-joke he'd said. A picture of a knight with the caption, 'It's not a horse' on the front, which is what she'd told him during the first chess lesson she'd given him. Her sweat had an acrid smell, full of ammonia-drenched stress and angst.

Margo pointed at the R on the gear panel. 'R for reverse, for God's sake.'

Ronda pressed the clutch down, turned on the engine, and yanked the gear stick into reverse. As the car shuddered backwards, another truck, this one behind Margo's car, honked loudly. Ronda jammed on the brake and even remembered to pull the handbrake up before she got out of the car.

'I can't do this,' she shouted, struggling to be heard over the dual horns of the trucks.

'Get back in here immediately,' shouted Margo. Ronda closed the door. Inside the car Margo was still shouting. Ronda could see white flecks of spittle on her lips.

Ronda made her way onto the pavement. She walked up the road.

She walked all the way home.

Thirteen kilometres.

She'd never missed her bicycle more.

CHAPTER 20

Ronda did not respond to Margo's text message that she read when she finally made it home. The message contained a succinct 'WTAF' followed by several question and exclamation marks, a gritted teeth emoji, an exploded head emoji and a red-faced emoji with expletives plastered across its mouth.

Instead, she got on with things. Annie's current complaint was shingles. There were no blisters and no rash, but Father Matthews' housekeeper had it and since then, Annie was convinced she had it too, getting Ronda to scratch at the bits of herself she couldn't reach. It was a relief to get out of the house the following morning and go to work.

Fatima had spoken to her case worker who did not seem too worried about Noah and the possibility of him following Fatima and Ada to Ireland.

'She has alerted the authorities,' Fatima told Ronda. They were on either side of Sheila, helping her walk down the corridor towards the dayroom. 'I gave her a photograph of Noah and she said she'd share it with the security staff at the centre.'

'At least they're taking it seriously,' said Ronda.

In the dayroom, Teresa laid Baby in a pram and tucked a blanket under the doll's chin.

'What about the driving lesson?' asked Fatima, arranging Sheila into an armchair by the window where she could watch the birds. 'It went well, I assume?'

'I'm not well,' said Sheila. 'Today is my husband's anniversary. Noel. God rest his soul.' She blessed herself with one hand, the other laid reverently across her chest.

'I'm sorry for your loss,' said Fatima, giving Sheila a gentle hug.

'Why would you assume it went well?' Ronda asked, buttoning the cardigan of Teresa's twinset up to her chin. Teresa always looked blue with the cold, even in the tropical conditions that prevailed in the nursing home.

'Room Number 23,' said Teresa, pushing the pram to and fro as she spoke.

'Is that where you lived, Teresa?' asked Ronda.

Teresa sat down and stroked Baby's face with her hand. 'The house was beside the bakery,' she said.

There was a clatter. Captain Grady had knocked his cup with his elbow. 'I need more tea,' he declared, pointing at the puddle of tea on the floor.

'It went badly,' said Ronda, grabbing a mop from the cupboard.

'I'm sure it didn't go as badly as you think,' said Fatima, pouring tea into a fresh cup and handing it to Captain Grady.

'It couldn't have gone any worse,' said Ronda.

'Did you kill someone?' asked Fatima.

'Of course not,' said Ronda.

'Then it could have been a lot worse,' said Fatima.

'You missed a bit,' said Captain Grady. Ronda swiped again at the floor with the mop, as she told Fatima about the stop sign and the trucks and the shouting.

'Ada's dance teacher says you should get right back on a horse after you fall off,' said Fatima.

'That seems like a foolhardy thing to do,' said Ronda, reaching under Teresa's armchair for her slipper, which had fallen off her foot.

'That is not regulation uniform,' said Captain Grady, as Ronda lifted Teresa's stockinged foot and slid it into the slipper.

'When is your next lesson?' asked Fatima.

'I don't know,' said Ronda.

'We could smell the bread in the mornings,' said Teresa, pulling up the hood on the doll's pram.

'Are you hungry, Teresa?' asked Fatima.

Teresa shook her head. 'The bakery was right next door,' she said.

Fatima put her hand on Ronda's shoulder. The warmth of it seeped through her scrubs.

'The next lesson will be better,' she said.

'How do you know?' asked Ronda.

Fatima shrugged. 'That's just how it works,' she said. In her calm, measured voice, it sounded plausible.

The door to Fergal's office opened and he stepped out, wedged into one of his starch-stiff suits.

'I'd better go,' hissed Fatima, anxious not to be seen out of the kitchen without her tea trolley. Fergal had been unimpressed when she had told him she could no longer work the night shift. She was determined to keep a low profile around him. 'Text Margo,' she added.

'Ah Fatima, the very woman,' said Fergal, spotting her. 'I need a word with you.'

'Of course,' said Fatima, hurrying towards him.

138

'I don't mean now,' he said. 'I'm busy. I'll see you on Friday afternoon, after your shift.'

Ronda did not like the sound of that.

'Certainly,' said Fatima, but Fergal had already turned around, striding up the corridor. Fatima nudged Ronda with her elbow. 'Maybe he's going to offer me a promotion and a raise,' she said, grinning. Ronda tried to grin back, to show that she too was capable of rising above calamity.

On her break, Ronda pulled her phone out of her locker. She texted Margo: You still okay for a driving lesson this week?

Margo responded immediately: Is that your version of an apology?

I shouldn't have left.

You stormed off. Not even Tiernan does that and he's an actual child.

Sorry.

Margo's next message arrived promptly: Sunday. 10am sharp.

I'm working. Ronda texted.

Ronda could nearly hear Margo's tongue, clicking with impatience. Saturday then. Same time.

Working then too. Sorry, texted Ronda.

Fine then, Friday. Final offer. I'll pick you up after work.

Friday wouldn't be great. Ronda would be tired after her shift, what with the full moon due on Thursday night, which had a tendency to unsettle the residents. And Friday was hair and beauty day, which was inclined to be a bit frantic at Green Gables. Also, Kim left early on Fridays to attend her drama class. And Fatima was seeing another room for rent after her meeting with Fergal on Friday, although even she wasn't holding out much hope.

Friday good, texted Ronda.

I presume that's your version of an effusive thank you? texted Margo.

CHAPTER 21

News seemed to travel faster than the speed of light around the corridors of Green Gables. When Ronda popped into Ms Gallagher's room with a slice of Fatima's coffee and walnut cake in the afternoon, Ms Gallagher already knew about Fergal summoning Fatima to a meeting.

'I suppose Kim told you?' said Ronda.

'Who else?' said Ms Gallagher, worrying at a kernel of walnut that was trapped in a gap between two of her back teeth.

'I have a horrible feeling he's going to reduce her hours or something,' said Ronda, perching on the windowsill. 'He's been on her case a lot recently.'

'Well?' said Ms Gallagher, taking an enormous slug of tea. 'What will you do if he does, Ronda?'

'What can I do?' said Ronda.

'You can't take it lying down, that's for sure,' said Ms Gallagher. 'You've got to fight.'

'I'm not like you,' said Ronda. 'There's no way I would have taken on Ian Paisley.'

'I had no choice,' said Ms Gallagher. 'He was campaigning against legalising homosexuality, going on about saving Ulster from sodomy and the like. I had to take him down.'

'I don't know how you managed it,' said Ronda. 'He was solid as a wall and well over six feet.'

Ms Gallagher snorted. 'You don't need to be big to floor a

bigot,' she said. 'You just need a good, sturdy pair of shoes.' She pointed to Ronda's thick-soled trainers. 'Those ones would do grand,' she said. 'You give a good stamp on the foot with the heel of one of those,' she went on, warming to the topic now. 'Then, when they bend over with the pain – and they will, let me tell you – that's when you use your knee. Let's have a look at yours.' She insisted on Ronda pulling up the legs of her scrubs as far as her knees, leaning forward to inspect them.

'They're fine, bony knees,' she said, nodding. 'So, all you do, as they bend over, is pull your knee up, keep it rigid mind, up, up, up, fast as you can, until it connects with the nose. Noses break easy, you'll hear the crack. A most satisfying sound.'

Ronda winced. 'I don't think I'd be able for that,' she said.

'Everyone's able for it, if their dander is up sufficiently,' said Ms Gallagher.

Monika's disembodied voice crackled across the ancient tannoy. 'Ronda McCann to reception. Ronda to reception. Immediately.'

'Sounds urgent,' said Ms Gallagher smirking. They both knew it wasn't urgent. Monika was fond of the PA system.

At reception, Monika picked up a Post-it note on which she had written a name and number. 'This lady phoned,' she said. 'She asked about Teresa.'

'What did she ask?' asked Ronda, looking at the note. Kate Deering. A UK number.

Monika punched a button on the telephone console. 'Mr Hutch's line is still busy, do you wish to remain holding?' she said in her bored monotone. She looked at Ronda, poking the Post-it with the tip of one of her long coffin-shaped nails, painted neon pink. 'I told her we could not give out personal details about our residents,' Monika said as she pressed the hold button.

'Is that what she was after?' asked Ronda.

Monika shrugged. 'How am I supposed to know?' she said.

'Well, what did this Kate say?' asked Ronda. Monika gazed into the middle distance and closed her eyes. Ronda looked in fascination at her lashes, which made it as far as the prominent jut of her cheekbones. 'She asked if we had a Teresa Keogh living here,' Monika recited. 'I said, who are you, she said, a friend, I said, what kind of friend, she said she did not understand the question, I said I could only give information about residents to family, was she family?' Monika's eyes sprang open then and settled on Ronda.

'What did she say to that?' asked Ronda.

Monika sighed. 'She hung up.'

'Does the name Kate Deering mean anything to you?' Ronda asked when Brenda, Teresa's sister, arrived at visiting time.

She shook her head. 'No,' she said. She looked very like Teresa except she was younger with an optimistic bearing. Brenda did her best to carry on some class of conversation with her sister, but it was difficult, given Teresa's fixation on Baby and her habit of roaring out the room number she was fixated on, which meant nothing to Brenda. 'She went to London when she was sixteen,' said Brenda when Ronda asked her about it once. 'Lived there for years. But number twenty-three wasn't on any of the addresses she sent us, as far as I can remember.'

'The house was beside the bakery,' said Teresa, gripping Brenda's arm as she rose to leave. 'We could smell the bread in the mornings.'

Tracey bustled across the dayroom. 'Ronda,' she barked, holding out two pink pills in a plastic container. 'I need you to get these down madam's gullet,' she said, nodding at Sheila, who was picking at a loose thread on her skirt, studiously ignoring Tracey.

'She refuses to take them for me,' Tracey went on.

'She says they give her heartburn,' said Ronda.

'I don't care if they give her haemorrhoids,' said Tracey. 'Dr Coleman has prescribed them for her so it's my responsibility to see that she takes them.'

'I can ask Dr Coleman if there's another brand Sheila could take,' said Ronda.

'It's not your job, hobnobbing with the doctors, Ronda,' said Tracey. 'He prescribed them, she's taking them, and that's that.' Tracey shook the container with the pills in front of Ronda's face. Sheila clamped her hand over her mouth. Ronda couldn't help grinning.

'Do you find this amusing?' said Tracey.

Ronda took the tablets from Tracey and tossed them into the bin. 'I won't be forcing Sheila to take medication that she doesn't want to take,' she said. 'She is an adult and can make her own decisions.'

Tracey took a step closer to Ronda so there was no getting away from the oily stench of the tuna she had eaten for lunch. 'Sheila has Alzheimer's,' she said. 'She can't do anything on her own, in case you've forgotten.' Blood rushed up her neck and into her face.

'She doesn't have Alzheimer's,' said Ronda. 'She has Lewy Body Dementia and is sometimes able to tell us when she has heartburn,' said Ronda.

'Are you refusing to carry out your duties?' said Tracey.

144

'I'd say HIQA might be interested in a resident being force-fed medication,' said Ronda, enjoying Tracey's look of horror at the mention of the Health Information and Quality Authority.

'Do you find this amusing?' said Tracey.

'Sorry?' said Ronda.

Tracey thrust Sheila's medication into Ronda's hand.

'See that she swallows them,' she said.

'I will,' said Ronda. She presumed Tracey knew why Fergal wanted to see Fatima in his office tomorrow evening. Tracey prided herself on always having the inside track.

Sometimes, she could be persuaded to share what she knew since what was the point of having the inside track if nobody knew you had it.

But before Ronda had a chance to ask her anything, Tracey's pager beeped and she glared at it before sweeping out of the room.

CHAPTER 22

Ronda got through the rest of the week by putting her head down, attending to her tasks and trying her hardest not to think about her next driving lesson. On Friday, she went for a cycle at lunchtime to get some fresh air and clear her head. On the way back up the avenue, she heard the cough and splutter of what sounded like an old bus behind her. It was a camper van, its halcyon days far behind it. When it was level with her, the driver beeped and thrust his hand out of the window to wave.

It was a hairy hand.

Donal Clarke.

Ronda nodded in response and cycled on, but Donal stopped the van and called after her.

'Should you stop there?' Ronda asked, braking and turning around. The camper van was ungainly in size and took up most of the driveway. Donal put on the hazard lights and jumped out. He was dressed in jeans and a T-shirt, as if January was a myth he didn't happen to believe in.

'How are you?' he said.

'Fine,' said Ronda. 'What are you doing here again?'

'I have another meeting with Ms Gallagher. She's such a fascinating woman. Also, I've received the statement from Dr Anderson so I have everything I need now. One more visit to my office should do it. I emailed Margo to let her know. And to bring a witness. That'll probably be you, I'm afraid.'

'Fine,' said Ronda. 'We can do it when you get back from your holidays.'

Donal had one of those grins that his whole face took part in. 'I'm not going on holidays,' he said.

A white DPD van flew through the gates and braked abruptly behind the van. It was Sean Grady, arriving for his weekly visit. Everything about him was clenched; his jaw, his shoulders, his hands on the wheel. He looked older than the forty-five years Captain Grady claimed he was. In the passenger seat sat Sean's son, Eddie, his face in his phone. About the same age as Sebastian, Ronda reckoned. Even when Sean blew the horn, Eddie's eyes never swivelled away from the screen. Donal waved at Sean and climbed back inside the van. He leaned out the window towards Ronda. 'I live here,' he said. 'In the camper van.'

Sean beeped again, louder this time.

'I better go,' said Donal.

In the dayroom, Captain Grady stood looking out of the window at the grounds, most of which had been bulldozed in preparation for the building work due to start the following week.

'Sean and Eddie are here to see you,' Ronda told him.

Captain Grady jabbed his finger against the window. 'The perimeter has been breached,' he said, agitated. Ronda stood beside him, looked out. Since Fatima had told her about Noah, she had been extra vigilant about making sure the doors and windows were locked.

'Don't worry,' she said. 'There's nobody there.'

'I saw an intruder,' he insisted.

'How about I take a look?' said Ronda.

'You're going on patrol?' asked Captain Grady.

'Yes,' said Ronda, saluting. 'I'll patrol the perimeter, captain.' He returned her salute with an extravagant one of his own. She let herself out into the garden, pulling her arms around her to ward off the worst of the chill. The day was still, the cloud cover low. Ronda felt she could nearly touch its dull underbelly. The garden, so lush and verdant in summer, was dormant now, winter like a sheet across a corpse, covering it, tamping it down. She walked across the patio, over the lawn and along the herbaceous border, which was showing signs of neglect since Alice had been let go. So too was the herb garden Alice had planted last year in the timber raised beds that Ernest had made. The rosemary was managing all right, but the thyme, mint, parsley and sage drooped, listless.

There was nothing to see, everything was as it should be. She was making her way back to the building when a harsh sound startled her. She turned and noticed the gate at the bottom of the garden, hanging open. The latch seemed fine when she inspected it. She peered out through the gate, looked up and down the lane that ran along the back of Green Gables. There was nobody there.

'All quiet on the western front,' she told Captain Grady when she returned to the dayroom.

'What?' he said, looking confused.

The door to the dayroom opened and Sean and Eddie walked in. A smile bloomed across Captain Grady's face, as bright and fresh as Alice's wild roses.

In the corridor behind Sean and Eddie, Ronda saw Fatima, wiping her eyes as she left Fergal's office.

'Permission to be excused?' she said.

'Permission granted,' said Captain Grady. Ronda gestured Sean and Eddie into chairs on either side of Captain Grady. 'At ease soldiers,' Captain Grady said, with a smart salute.

'We can't stay long,' said Sean, checking his watch. Eddie was on his phone, his thumbs a blur across the screen.

'Fatima,' Ronda called as she hurried into the corridor. 'Wait.' But Fatima didn't wait. The starch in her scrubs made a rhythmic swish as she strode away, like the sweep of windscreen wipers in heavy rain. She reached the double doors at the end of the corridor and snatched at the lanyard hanging on a cord around her neck, pressing it against the security panel. In the time it took the automatic doors to open, Ronda had caught up to her.

'Fatima?' she said. 'Are you okay? What did Fergal say?'

Fatima did her best to smile, but it was a watered down version. 'There's good news and bad news,' she said. 'Come into the kitchen,' said Ronda, threading her arm through Fatima's. 'I'll make you a cup of tea.'

The kitchen was empty save for Ernest who was having lunch at the other end of the room with his headphones on, writing in a notebook. He looked up briefly to wave at them, then resumed his writing. When he wasn't watching How To tutorials on YouTube, he listened to podcasts about history in general and Irish history in particular.

'So?' asked Ronda, guiding Fatima into a chair and putting the kettle on. 'What did he say?'

'The good news is I'm not losing my job,' said Fatima.

'Right,' said Ronda. She supposed it was good enough, the news. 'What's the bad news?'

'They're outsourcing catering,' said Fatima. 'I asked him

what catering company would be able to make my yam fufu and okra soup. He said old people don't like spicy food.' Fatima's eyes widened. 'What's spicy about yams, I ask you?'

'So, what will you be doing then?' said Ronda, reaching for the teabags.

'I'll still work in the kitchen,' said Fatima. 'But more re-heating and cleaning up.'

'What about your hours?' asked Ronda, opening the cupboard and poking through the cups for the mug Ronda had gifted Fatima, with a photograph of Ada sitting astride a branch of the laburnum tree in full bloom last spring. Ada had been intent on 'rescuing' Jessica Fletcher. The cat had waited until Ada got close before shimmying down the tree with her usual brand of smug ease.

'They'll be reduced,' said Fatima.

'How reduced?'

'I'm not sure.'

Ronda opened the box of Fatima's camomile tea.

'I think this calls for proper Irish tea,' said Fatima, pointing at the Barry's teabags.

'And cake,' said Ronda, cutting an enormous slice of the cherry cake Fatima had baked that morning.

'That's much too big,' said Fatima. Ronda ignored her. She put the cake and tea on the table and picked up Fatima's hands, wrapped them around the mug.

'Thank you, my friend,' said Fatima, holding the mug below her chin, so the steam could warm her face.

'So when does this new regime start?' asked Ronda, sitting down beside Fatima.

'Effective immediately,' said Fatima. Ronda laughed at her pantomime take on Fergal's self-important voice. Fatima put a spoon of sugar in her mug. 'I asked Fergal if there was a chance I could be let go,' she said, stirring her tea.

'And?' Ronda held her breath.

Fatima shrugged. 'You know the way he can talk and talk and say nothing?'

Ronda nodded.

'If I lose my job, Noah will feel like he's got more of a right to drag me and Ada back to Nigeria.'

'You could look for another job,' said Ronda, trying to sound optimistic.

Fatima put down her cup. 'It took me ages to get this one.'

Tracey appeared in the doorway. 'What are you doing in here, Fatima?' she said. Fatima drained her cup and stood up.

'I had a meeting with Fergal,' she said.

Tracey consulted her watch. 'Well, there's another five minutes left on your shift,' she said. Fatima smiled at Tracey as if she had complimented her on her head wrap, which today was bright gold with purple butterflies. She stood up draping her coat over her arm. 'I will see you tomorrow,' she said to Ronda as she walked past Tracey, who stood at the door with her mouth open as if she had something to say but couldn't for the life of her remember what it was.

CHAPTER 23

Ronda's shift finished at five thirty p.m. and her driving lesson with Margo was scheduled for five thirty-five. Ronda just had time to wash her hands and pull her anorak over her scrubs before she raced out to the car park. She did not want to incur Margo's wrath by being late. Margo was fitting the lesson in between dropping Malcolm Junior to his trumpet lesson, collecting Malcolm Senior's tuxedo from the dry-cleaners, picking Sebastian up from rugby practice, overseeing the collection of raffle prizes for the hospice fundraiser and helping Tiernan with his report on seagulls. According to Margo, there were a million different varieties of the buggers, and Tiernan insisted on spelling sea with two 'e's, making it a taxing project.

Margo scorched up the avenue and into the car park at exactly five thirty-five, screeching to a halt beside Ronda. She lowered the window.

'Why do you have your bicycle with you?' she snapped.

'I just thought, maybe I could bring it along?' said Ronda.

'In case you throw another tantrum and don't fancy a thirteen-kilometre walk home?' said Margo.

'It could fit in the boot,' said Ronda.

'With those mucky wheels?' said Margo. 'No chance.'

'I've got wipes,' said Ronda, reaching into one of her panniers.

Margo did a spot of box breathing. Ronda could see her mouth the seconds as she held her breath.

'How about,' Margo began when she had finished her breathing, 'we just get through the lesson and nobody throws their toys out of the pram this time?'

'Do you promise not to get angry?' asked Ronda.

'I wasn't angry, I was terrified. I thought we were about to get crushed by a truck,' said Margo. 'Now come on if you're coming. I don't have all day.'

Margo drove with an intensity that was unsettling. Like something awful was about to happen and all anyone could do was brace themselves.

Also, she was a shouter.

'Indicate when you're turning, you moron.'

'Okay, Driving Miss Daisy, some time today would be nice.'

'The light's green you idiot. What are you, colour blind?'

The barbs were often fortified with horn blowing. She had a heavy hand with the brake and accelerator so Ronda was either being pitched forward against the seat belt or pasted against the back of the seat. Margo roared through a junction. Ronda closed her eyes as the car flew past a cyclist, perilously close. The sensation of being inside a car with her eyes closed was unpleasant. She had closed her eyes that day too. Squeezed them shut. Her father in the driver's seat, singing tunelessly. He liked to make up the words of the songs he sang.

Oh Danny boy, the pints, the pints are caw-haw-ling . . .

'Come on, little pet, up you get,' he'd said that evening after dinner. You could see the higgledy-piggledy lines of Margo's small, white teeth when she smiled. One hung on by a thread. Ronda remembered how it flapped, like a loose tile

153

on a roof. Margo tucked her hand into Gerry's and he led her down the hallway.

'Where are you going?' Ronda asked, following them out onto the street.

'Little miss nosy,' said her father, swinging Margo into the back seat of his car. He stumbled as he straightened, put his hand on the roof to steady himself. 'We're going to get some fresh air, aren't we little missy?' He leaned down to grin at Margo.

'And ice cream?' she said, always the negotiator.

Ronda knew he was going to his mother's house. His mother was more inclined to give him the few quid he wanted to 'borrow' when he brought Margo with him.

'It's nearly Margo's bedtime,' said Ronda, stepping in between her father and the driver's door. 'Isn't it, Mam?'

Annie McCann stood at the front door with her arms folded across her chest and her face pinched with the worry that had eroded her features over the years. She was colourless and stiff, like the faded tea towels that hung across the door of the oven. She wasn't even forty then.

'Mam?' Ronda put her hand on her mother's skin-and-bone arm. Her mother shrugged it off. She had long ago given up trying to persuade Gerry McCann not to do something he wanted to do.

'Cheerio,' shouted Gerry, slamming the rear door of the car. 'I won't be late.'

The keys fell out of his hand and Ronda dived for them. 'It's getting dark,' she said.

'Give them to me,' her father said, stepping towards her.

Ronda ran around to the other side of the car, opened the door and pulled Margo out.

'I want to go with Daddy,' Margo shouted.

'Let go of your sister,' roared Gerry, advancing on Ronda.

'Ronda, can't you just . . .' Annie pulled her cardigan tighter around her slight frame as she glanced up and down the street, checking for neighbours.

Ronda thrust Margo towards her mother and got into the back seat of the car.

'What the hell do you think you're doing?' shouted Gerry, breathing hard and wheezy.

'Granny said she'd give me a fiver next time I visited,' said Ronda, smiling widely to disguise the lie. Granny McCann hadn't given her anything since her confirmation, and that had been nearly three years ago.

'Really?' said Gerry, looking confused as he got behind the wheel.

The Toyota made a clanking noise whenever Gerry changed gears, and the pattern on the upholstery was bald in places. Ronda loved it when Eileen's dad gave them a lift to school. There were seat belts in Mr O'Reilly's car. Even in the back. And everyone just put them on like it was the most normal thing in the world. Nobody said they were for nervous Nellies.

'Danny Boy' was playing on the radio. Her father closed his eyes when he got to the chorus. Ronda's foot slammed on an imaginary brake any time the car approached a junction. This was how her ankle broke with such certainty, she learned years later, at nursing school.

The tension in the bone.

It started raining. Gerry turned on the indicator. 'The wipers are on the other side,' called Ronda.

'I know that,' Gerry shouted, turning to glare at her. 'You think I don't know that, Miss Know-it-all?'

'Sorry Daddy,' said Ronda, reaching for a humble tone. Her father was keen on female humility. He nodded and turned back around. He found the lever and turned on the windscreen wipers.

The rain got heavier. Ronda remembered the noise it made against the roof of the car, as loud as horses' hooves. Gerry had to shout the lyrics of the song now, to be heard over the clamour of rain.

But bring me baaaackkk, for sunshine's in the meh-he-doh . . .

After that, Ronda's recollections became hazy. She thought she remembered seeing the bench around a bend in the road. One of those comfortless, narrow ones at the bus shelter. It was empty, thankfully, lit up by the tail lights of the bus that had just pulled out into the road.

And when I come, and all the roses dy-iiii-ing . . .

Ronda remembered the way the song got caught in his throat like a fishbone. The squeal of the tyres against the wet road as Gerry realised, too late, that he had taken the bend too fast. The blare of a horn. The sickening smack of Gerry's forehead against the wheel. The shattering of the windscreen when the bonnet hit the side of the bus shelter. It was the glass, flying everywhere, that did the damage to Ronda's face. That's what the nurse said, afterwards. When she woke up in hospital with her face wrapped in bandages and her father sitting in a chair by her bed, sober.

His sobriety worried Ronda more than the bandages. She knew things must be serious.

'You're lucky,' the nurse told Ronda. 'You're a very lucky girl.'

*

156

'Why are we stopping here?' Ronda asked, as Margo parked in front of an imposing office block, all tinted glass and chrome. 'Malcolm has to work late again, so I thought I'd drop him in some dinner,' said Margo, picking up a bag with a collection of Tupperware inside. 'I don't want him ordering a takeaway with that high cholesterol of his.'

'That's nice of you,' said Ronda.

Margo bristled. 'Are you mocking me?' she said.

'No,' said Ronda. 'I mean it. It's nice. You're a . . . lovely wife. You know?'

Margo flushed a little pink. 'It's just a roasted butternut squash soup and a rice and quinoa salad with chickpeas,' she said. 'Oh, and some figs and mango for dessert.'

'Who doesn't love figs and mango for dessert?' said Ronda.

'Now you *are* mocking me,' said Margo.

'Just a tiny amount,' admitted Ronda.

'I'll be back in two minutes,' said Margo. 'Study this while I'm gone.' She handed Ronda a copy of the rules of the road. Ronda watched her go, admiring the competent way Margo walked despite the spindle-thin height of her heels. She opened the book, scanned the first page, read it aloud, then asked herself questions. She insisted on answering all the questions correctly before moving on to the next page. She was on page five when Margo returned, the bag with the Tupperware still hanging from her hand.

'Was he not there?' asked Ronda, as Margo belted herself in.

Margo shook her head and grabbed her phone out of her handbag. The call went straight to Malcolm's voicemail. She hung up without leaving a message.

'I should have phoned ahead,' she told Ronda. 'He's

probably gone to get some dinner, that diet he's on, you have to eat small portions at regular intervals.'

Margo turned on the engine and scorched away. Ronda tried to curb her nerves by reading another page of the handbook, but that made her nauseous. She looked out of the window and followed the loop of electricity wire between telegraph poles, a habit that she had developed as a child, sitting in the back seat, drowning out the sound of her father ranting about some slight, real or imagined. Or his bristling silence that seemed to Ronda back then, even louder.

'Say something,' said Margo.

Ronda looked at her. 'What do you want me to say?'

'Most people talk when they are in company,' said Margo. 'You could make some kind of effort.'

'Okay,' said Ronda, struggling to come up with something. 'How did . . . the Parents' Council meeting go the other day?'

Margo eye rolled. 'It got a bit nasty,' she said. 'There's a teacher refusing to use correct pronouns for the trans kids. Most of the parents are up in arms about it, but there's a few head shakers, muttering about wokeness and how the world has gone to hell in a handbag kind of thing.'

'You mean handcart.'

'Jesus Ronda, I'm trying to have a conversation with you.'

'Sorry,' said Ronda. 'Go on.'

'Nothing else really,' said Margo. 'Let's just say the meeting ran late and didn't end in a group hug. Some people would put years on you.'

'You could resign?' suggested Ronda. 'You've been on that council for ever.'

'People don't just give up when the going gets tough,' said Margo, pointedly.

Ronda couldn't think of an appropriate response to that. She looked out of the window again.

'Don't mind me,' said Margo, exhaling noisily. 'I'm a cranky cow, I didn't sleep well last night.'

'We don't have to do the lesson if you're not up to it,' Ronda offered.

'We're doing the lesson,' said Margo. 'But ten out of ten for persistence.'

The lesson did not go as badly as before. For starters, they did not have much time. Also, Margo seemed to realise that she had expected too much of Ronda in the second lesson.

This time, she found a large car park. It was empty apart from a couple of schoolboys in hoodies, smoking weed and swigging out of a cider bottle. 'If you leave quietly, I won't tell Mr Malone what you boys are up to,' said Margo, pulling up beside them and lowering the window.

The boys glanced at each other, then at Margo, weighing up their odds. They hoisted their schoolbags onto their backs and left.

'Do you know them?' Ronda asked.

'I recognise the uniform,' said Margo. 'The headmaster's reputation is obviously well earned.'

The car park was large enough and empty enough for Ronda to drive around without much recourse to shouting. Although that could have had more to do with Margo, who appeared distracted, than any prowess Ronda may have demonstrated behind the wheel. When Ronda graunched the gears from third to second, Margo just said, 'Go easy,' and didn't even seem to notice the brick perimeter wall Ronda was driving towards. She cut out. Again. The clutching in while braking seemed beyond her. 'I found that tricky too,' said Margo. 'You just need to practise.'

'Who taught you?' asked Ronda, stalling for time.

'Malcolm did,' said Margo. 'Believe me, you're getting away lightly.'

It was true that Malcolm was patronising. Ronda put it down to the ten year age gap. Margo was fresh out of college when she met him, Ronda having scraped together enough funds for the three-year business course in DCU. Annie had been so proud when Margo got a job in the bank. 'A permanent and pensionable position,' she'd told Mrs Murphy next door, even though the salary was barely above minimum wage and nobody had mentioned a pension. Then Margo met Malcolm. He had pursued her with the type of determination that might be admirable in an academic or professional endeavour. Malcolm was already one of the top dogs in the bank, having spent the thirteen years since he left school clawing up one greasy pole after another.

Ronda regretted that Margo didn't get an opportunity to enjoy her independence before she appeared on Malcolm's radar. He was like a collector, Ronda thought. He collected bright and beautiful things, and her little sister happened to be one of them.

Margo's phone rang. 'That'll be Malcolm,' she said, pouncing on her handbag.

But it was Tiernan, wondering if it would be okay if he put the lasagne in the oven now? 'Or I could just have a bowl of Crunchy Nut Cornflakes?' Ronda could hear him saying.

'Do you know how much sugar is in a box of those things?' said Margo. 'Who brought them into the house?'

'I think they're just Cornflakes actually,' said Tiernan, sensing danger. 'I'll see you later, Mum,' he added before hanging up hastily.

Margo rang Malcolm again, but, as before, the call went to voicemail and she hung up. 'Are you planning on making a move anytime soon?' she said, realising that the car was still stationary.

Ronda turned the key in the ignition, managed to get the car into first gear. Her neck ached from all the twisting and turning, checking for dangers through this window and that mirror and – never to be forgotten, Margo warned – her blind spot.

When Margo dropped Ronda back to Green Gables after the lesson, she rummaged in her bag and withdrew a sheaf of blueprints. 'After the disaster of the last lesson, I contacted an architect,' she said, handing the blueprints to Ronda. 'Here's what she came up with, for the Kube.'

Ronda looked at the plans.

'She's been really imaginative with the space and light, hasn't she?' said Margo.

'You sound more enthusiastic about it,' said Ronda.

Margo shrugged. 'I realise this is a long shot,' she said.

'Me learning how to drive?' said Ronda.

'Only because you're so resistant,' said Margo, taking the plans and folding them back into her bag. 'You can't blame me, having a Plan B.'

Ronda supposed that was true.

CHAPTER 24

The first board meeting since the takeover at Green Gables took place the following Monday morning at ten a.m. Ronda noticed that Fergal had treated himself to a haircut and a new suit over the weekend.

'Also a long overdue nose and ear trim,' said Kim, a stickler for detail.

Fatima, who was doing her best to curry favour with Fergal so that he wouldn't cut her hours more than he already had, made his favourite tiffin biscuits for the meeting. However, most of them had been filched by Sheila, who had snuck into the kitchen when Lawrence – the entertainer – was in the dayroom, playing his portable keyboard and belting out 'Strangers in the Night'.

Lawrence and the Machine, Kim called him. He was a big, gentle man who always wore shorts, even in winter, and white socks with thick-strapped leather sandals. His son, Peter, accompanied him to all of his gigs and was in charge of announcing the title of each song. Peter was in his early thirties Ronda guessed. He had Down's syndrome and an impressive collection of football cards.

By the time Lawrence had finished his set, the baking tray of tiffin that Fatima had placed in the pantry off the kitchen was empty. The only evidence that they had once existed were the crumbs scattered all over Sheila's widow's weeds. Nobody had been that surprised. Sheila had declared it the anniversary of her husband's death that morning, and, even though she made these declarations on a regular basis, this did not ease the pain of the loss for Sheila, who ate her feelings throughout the day.

Fergal remained unaware of the baking and subsequent theft of his favourite confectionary. He was distracted by the arrival of two Americans for the board meeting.

'Keep everything nice and calm today,' Fergal told Ronda as he checked his teeth in the glass of the grandfather clock in the hall.

'Yes,' said Ronda.

'I trust you,' he added.

Ronda took a breath. 'You know how you mentioned, a while ago, that you might consider creating a supervisor role for me?' she said. 'Well, I know that now's probably not a good time but . . .'

'You're right,' said Fergal, adjusting his tie. 'Now is definitely not a good time, let's circle back to it later. Is my tie straight?'

Teresa poked her head in between the pair of them. 'I was in room Number 23,' she said. Fergal jumped and banged his arm on the edge of the clock.

'You scared the shit out of me,' said Fergal, rubbing his elbow.

'You shouldn't say "shit",' said Teresa, pointing at Fergal.

Ronda took her hand. 'Let's see if we can find Baby, will we?' she said, leading Teresa down the corridor. They passed Ms Gallagher, who was standing at her bedroom door.

'The house was beside the bakery,' Teresa told Ms Gallagher. 'We could smell the bread in the mornings.'

'Oh do be quiet, you silly woman,' said Ms Gallagher.

'Be nice, can't you?' said Ronda, putting her arm around Teresa, who looked more confused than hurt.

'Where did nice ever get anyone?' barked Ms Gallagher.

'You know when I play chess with you and let you win?' said Ronda. 'That's where nice gets you.'

'You do not let me win,' said Ms Gallagher, incensed.

When the board meeting ended, Ronda was in Captain Grady's room, buttoning him into his military jacket. Sean appeared at the door.

'We weren't expecting you today,' said Ronda. 'Isn't this a nice surprise, Captain Grady?'

'Recreational hours are between nineteen and twenty-one hundred hours,' said Captain Grady, but with less conviction than usual and a smile on his face.

'I'm off now. I just came to get a tax form signed and stamped,' said Sean, folding a piece of paper and putting it in his back pocket.

'It's nice out now,' said Ronda. 'You two could take a stroll? At the front? The back garden is in a bit of flux with the building work, I'm afraid.' She ushered Captain Grady out into the corridor.

'I don't have much time,' said Sean, looking at his watch.

As they passed the meeting room, the door opened and a procession of men in dark suits filed out and streamed past them.

Captain Grady flinched, shook off Ronda's arm and ran back down the corridor, into his bedroom where he stood behind the door, crouched there as if he was trying to make himself smaller. Ronda could feel the shake of his body when she put her hand on his shoulder to comfort him.

'Do you think he saw me?' Captain Grady asked. There was something childlike in his voice, which held none of its usual gruff certainty.

'Who?' asked Sean, standing behind Ronda.

'The colonel said I only had myself to blame. I should mind my own business,' said Captain Grady.

'It's okay,' said Ronda, picking up his hand. 'You're safe.'

'I obeyed orders,' he said in a whisper. 'Didn't I?'

'Of course you did,' said Ronda. 'Look, they've gone.' She persuaded him out from behind the door and pointed up the corridor.

Captain Grady exhaled a long, shaky breath. 'We're behind enemy lines,' he said.

'I better go,' said Sean, eyeing his father warily.

Captain Grady straightened then, performed a smart salute and clicked the heels of his black patent leather shoes. 'You are dismissed, Private Grady,' he said.

Fatima arrived with the tea trolley and Ronda caught up with Sean in the corridor. 'I don't know what happened there,' she said. 'He was in good form earlier.'

Sean shrugged. 'He was always unpredictable,' he said.

'Was the colonel someone in the army, do you know?' Ronda asked.

'That's what he called his dad,' said Sean.

'He called his father colonel?' said Ronda.

'Yeah,' said Sean. 'He was a soldier too.' He hurried ahead, already at the top of the corridor, jabbing at the release button. When the double doors opened, Sean ducked out, past a man waiting to come in.

It was Donal. He grinned when he saw her.

'You're becoming a regular fixture around here,' said Ronda as Donal fell into step with her.

'Just putting the finishing touches on Ms Gallagher's documents,' he said.

'Can I ask you for some advice, while you're here?' said Ronda, walking towards the kitchen.

'It depends,' said Donal. 'If it's about the law or amateur DIY, then yes. Otherwise, probably best not.'

'It's about the law,' said Ronda.

Donal followed Ronda into the kitchen. 'If you make me tea, I'll see what I can do.'

Ronda told him about Charlo coming in with the documents for Sheila to sign. 'I think it was an application to have Charlo's name added to a Post Office account,' said Ronda. 'I can't be sure, Charlo just said they were important.'

'If they were that important, Sheila should have legal representation,' said Donal. 'She's not in a position to advocate for herself.'

'Maybe he has enduring power of attorney?' said Ronda, handing Donal a mug of tea.

'Then he wouldn't need Sheila to sign the documents,' said Donal. He pointed at a baking tray. 'Are they fairy buns?'

'Lemon ones,' said Ronda, giving him one. 'Fatima made them.'

'My kids loved these when they were little,' said Donal, circling his nose across the top of the bun, which was also part of Ronda's process when it came to confectionary. 'If you let me have two, you can call me whenever Charlo re-appears, and I'll come running.'

'Are you always this obliging?' Ronda asked.

'In my days as a corporate solicitor, I did some things I'm not particularly proud of,' said Donal. 'So anything I can do now is by way of some small recompense. And to make me feel better, obviously. I'm not entirely altruistic.'

'Did you do anything illegal?' Ronda asked, surprised at herself. She wasn't usually this curious.

'Not technically,' said Donal.

Ronda handed him another fairy bun, which he wrapped in a piece of kitchen roll. 'I'm going to keep this one to go with my afternoon tea,' he said. 'I need to keep my strength up, my lads are coming over to beat me at chess this evening.'

'What age are they?' asked Ronda.

'Nineteen,' said Donal. 'They're twins.'

'Are you bad at chess?' Ronda wanted to know.

Donal considered the question. 'I taught them everything I know,' he said. 'And now they know too much.'

'Can I get your number?' Ronda asked.

Donal stood up. 'Oh, sorry,' he said. 'I'm not . . . I don't . . .' Blood poured into his face as he blushed furiously. 'I don't date, I'm sworn off relationships, and also, I'm a terrible catch, I've . . .'

'No, I just meant, so I can ring you the next time Charlo arrives with his paperwork,' said Ronda, who couldn't help feeling a little amused. She'd never met a man who was a self-declared terrible catch before. She had presumed they didn't exist.

'Sorry,' said Donal, covering his burning face with his hands. 'I'm such a dope, I completely misread that. You see now? Why I'm barred from dating? I know nothing. I never did. But now at least I know that I know nothing. Which is an improvement. If you can believe that.'

'Don't feel bad,' said Ronda. 'I'm not exactly dater of the year myself.'

'Why not?' asked Donal.

Ronda shrugged. 'Loads of reasons,' she said. 'I don't think the scar helps.'

'Car accident?' Donal asked.

'Yes,' said Ronda.

'Is that why you don't drive?' asked Donal.

Ronda nodded.

'That's pretty brave,' said Donal. 'Learning now.'

'I wouldn't if I didn't have to,' said Ronda.

Donal pulled a crumpled receipt out of his pocket and scribbled his number on it. 'Here,' he said, handing her the piece of paper. 'You can phone me any time,' he went on. 'About Charlo, I mean. Obviously.' Donal clamped his mouth shut. He had a wide mouth and his lips put Ronda in mind of summer raspberries. Which was an odd thing to think about in February, she felt.

CHAPTER 25

It was difficult to get used to the kitchen without the sounds and smells of Fatima's cooking. Now, every morning, vans arrived stacked with vac-packed dinners that would be heated later and dished out. The food wasn't awful by any means. Just a bit generic and bland after the carefree pinch of this and splash of that approach that Fatima had employed.

The residents didn't have much to say about the new fare, although Ronda felt this was as a result of their varying stages and types of dementia rather than a declaration of satisfaction with the change in menu. Ms Gallagher made up for this lack of uproar by declaring the menu, 'pure slop' and threatening to go on hunger strike, although she hadn't followed through on this threat.

Yet.

Fatima and her idiosyncratic cooking style wasn't the last of the casualties of the takeover. Since the board meeting, other changes were afoot. A few days later, Ronda found Lawrence slumped on a couch in reception, his keyboard lying across his knee and his songbook on the floor, the pages pouring out of the plastic pockets. Ronda stooped and gathered up the music. She sat on the couch beside him.

'Are you okay?' she asked.

Lawrence shook his head. 'Fergal told me he was terminating my contract,' he said.

'Oh no,' said Ronda who was fond of Lawrence. Everybody was.

'And the funny thing is,' Lawrence went on, 'I don't even have a contract. He pays me out of petty cash, and some weeks he doesn't even bother, I have to chase him for it.'

'But the residents love you,' said Ronda.

Lawrence shrugged. 'Fergal says they're cutting costs. They can't afford me any more.' He laughed. 'Things must be bad when you don't have forty euros to pay for two hours of live entertainment.' He looked at Peter, sitting cross-legged on the floor, sorting through his stack of football cards. 'I don't know what I'm going to tell him,' said Lawrence. 'He thinks I'm a rock star.'

'You are a rock star, Dad,' said Peter, looking up and smiling.

Lawrence took his songbook from Ronda and tucked the keyboard under his arm. 'I'd better leave now if I'm going to make it to Twilight Years,' he said. 'Although they're closing down, I heard. Some hotel chain bought them.'

'I wish there was something I could do,' said Ronda, feeling useless.

'Maybe you could talk to him, Ronda?' said Lawrence, looking at her with a flare of hope in his tired brown eyes.

'What would I say?'

'I don't know,' said Lawrence. 'But knowing you, it would be perfect.'

Ronda surged with a sudden energy that felt impossible to contain. She sprang up and marched to Fergal's office and didn't even knock before barging right in.

'I'm in the middle of something right now, Ronda,' said Fergal, glancing up before returning to his computer. Ronda could see the reflection of the screen in the window behind him. He was playing his daily game of Wordle.

'You can't do this to Lawrence,' she said. 'Or to Fatima for that matter. She needs all the hours she can get. Even the pittance you pay us is better than nothing.'

'It's out of my hands, I'm afraid,' said Fergal, lifting both hands in the air to demonstrate. 'Besides, these people always find a way of landing on their feet, don't they?'

'You ignorant bigot.' She spat the words. Fergal was too shocked to react. Ronda walked with great purpose to his side of the desk.

'What are you doing?' Fergal shrieked. 'You're not supposed to be on this side of my desk.' She pulled his keyboard towards her and typed furiously. 'There,' she said, pointing at the screen. 'The word was PRICK. You of all people should have figured that one out.'

'Maybe you could talk to him, Ronda?' said Lawrence, looking at her with a flare of hope in his tired brown eyes.

'Me?' said Ronda.

Lawrence put his keyboard into a plastic bag. 'Sorry,' he said. 'I'm clutching at straws here.'

Then there was the price increase, sudden, and effective immediately. Ms Gallagher was fuming when Ronda called in to her room, on her rounds.

'Did you know about this?' she said, thrusting her tablet at Ronda. The email was from Healthcare Central Services Ltd, and was signed by someone called Chester Deavey. Green Gables was referenced in the subject line. 'If I don't cough up the extra, I'll be moved to a twin room and expected to share,' said Ms Gallagher, pointing to a line in the email that Ronda hadn't yet read. 'They'll have me in a top bunk at this rate.'

'That's terrible,' said Ronda. 'I'm sorry.'

'What good is your sorrow?' stormed Ms Gallagher. 'I need your anger. I need your fury. This is top-of-the-class capitalism. This is healthcare as commodity instead of basic human right. I need your rage, Ronda McCann, not your sympathy.'

'I'm s—' Ronda stopped herself just in time. 'I need this job,' she said instead. She hated the sound of her own voice. How small and defeated she sounded. But it was true. Truer than ever now, since she could be looking for a place to rent if she didn't start making a marked improvement behind the wheel of Margo's car.

Ms Gallagher thrust her hand out, patted Ronda's arm briefly. 'Don't mind me,' she said. 'I'm a curmudgeonly old witch.'

'You won't have to leave, will you?' asked Ronda.

'Why? Would you miss me?'

'I would,' said Ronda, risking Ms Gallagher's wrath. The woman was riled enough already without having to deal with sentimentality, which she despised.

However, no wrath was forthcoming from Ms Gallagher. Instead she said, in a quiet voice, 'I'd miss you too.'

It was like an incendiary device exploding. Ronda was shell-shocked. Before she could gather herself, Ms Gallagher opened her door wide and gestured Ronda out. 'Now go on with you,' she said, in her back-to-normal loud and gruff voice. 'I'm expecting a visitor.'

This too was shocking. Ronda kept walking.

The visitor was a college student who wanted to interview Ms Gallagher for her thesis. This was not the first such request Ms Gallagher had received, but it was the first one she had accepted. Ronda suspected it might have something to do with putting her affairs in order. A sudden yearning to have her presence felt in the world, perhaps. To leave her mark.

Or maybe she was just bored.

Either way, when Ronda passed by her bedroom later, Ms Gallagher was in full flow about the Women's Liberation Movement she had helped found in 1972, her flint-grey eyes full of light and a surge of colour stamped across her face.

The student cleared her throat before she asked her next question. 'So, I wonder if you would tell me about your relationship with Edel Scanlan?'

'What about it?' Ms Gallagher's voice lashed like a whip.

'Well, I just . . . I understand that you two worked closely together?'

As Ronda walked away, she heard Ms Gallagher emit a derisive snort. 'We worked together in the early 70s. We organised the contraceptive train to Derry. The setting up of the Women's Libreration Movement. And that was that. I haven't seen her in decades.'

When Ronda entered the kitchen, Fatima spun round, whipping her phone into her pocket.

'You okay?' asked Ronda.

'I thought you were Fergal or Tracey,' said Fatima. 'I've been trying to phone my solicitor all morning. I got the date for my Personal Interview,' she said. 'It's the fifth of March.'

'That's great news,' said Ronda. 'That's the last hurdle,

isn't it?' she asked. 'Before they make a decision on your asylum application?'

'Yes,' said Fatima, sounding more optimistic than of late.

'You'll ace the interview,' said Ronda. 'I know you will.'

Fatima took her phone back out and punched a number into the keypad. 'Hello, this is Fatima again, can you please call me back as soon as you can, thank you very very much, I hope you are having a wonderful day.' She hung up. 'Maybe he's on holidays?' she said.

'Maybe,' said Ronda.

'I better get back to work,' said Fatima. 'Lunch isn't going to reheat itself.' There was a tinge of resentment in her tone. Ronda didn't blame her. Even the residents with dementia were beginning to notice a change in the food at Green Gables.

Teresa put her hand over her mouth when Kim tried to entice her with what looked like a consommé but was, according to the label on the container it arrived in, farmhouse vegetable soup. 'It doesn't taste,' insisted Teresa, before clamping her hand across her mouth again. Ronda made her a cheese omelette, which was against rapidly increasing company regulations. Teresa wolfed it. She shifted Baby from one shoulder to the other and leaned forward so she could kiss Ronda's cheek. Ronda kissed her back, even though this was also against company policy now. Teresa's skin was delicate and soft, like the petals of Alice's climbing roses that were now at the bottom of one of the skips at the back of Green Gables.

'The house was beside the bakery,' Teresa said, reaching out as if she could see the house. As if she might open the front door. Ronda took her hand. It was cold. She pressed it against her face to warm it.

'You could smell the bread in the morning, couldn't you Teresa?' said Ronda, picking up Baby's blanket, which had slipped onto Teresa's lap, and carefully wrapping it around the doll. Teresa nodded as she closed her eyes and fell asleep.

'I hope you're still on duty when I'm in my dotage,' said a familiar voice. Ronda looked up. It was Donal, at the door of the dayroom, his battered satchel tucked under one arm.

'I'll have been put out to pasture by then,' said Ronda. The trolley rattled as she pushed it over the saddle board into the corridor.

'I'm not stalking you by the way,' said Donal, following her as she made her way to the dispensary.

'That's a relief,' said Ronda.

'Ernest asked me to give him a hand filling in some forms for a college grant,' went on Donal. 'He has his eye on a degree in Irish history and politics.'

'I'm delighted he asked you,' said Ronda. 'He's usually pretty shy.'

'He didn't ask, per se,' said Donal. 'We got chatting about a history podcast we both listen to and it sort of developed from there.'

'Ernest is a fast learner,' said Ronda. 'I'd say he'd do great in college.' She stopped at the dispensary and used her lanyard to unlock it. 'Well, this is me,' she said, suddenly awkward.

'You never called,' said Donal.

'Charlo never came back,' said Ronda.

'Oh, right,' said Donal, blowing his fringe out of his eyes. He could do with a haircut, Ronda noticed, as the fringe flopped back to its original position. He was wearing his usual jeans and T-shirt, but had donned a navy jacket that might once have belonged to a suit. It was a little roomy and in need of an iron. He glanced down at his jacket as if he could tell what she was thinking. 'I'm going to court with Carl this afternoon,' he explained, rolling the sleeves up so his hands could get a look in. 'I gave away all my suits after I stopped practising, so I bought this jacket in haste from the charity shop this morning. Is it awful?'

'It isn't too awful,' said Ronda, grinning. She pushed open the dispensary door. 'I'd better get going.'

'Oh, yeah, sure,' said Donal. 'Me too.'

'See you around,' said Ronda.

'I'd like that,' said Donal.

He was just that kind of person, Ronda thought, watching him lope up the corridor in that slightly falling apart way he had, all arms and legs. He said things like that. Things that made people feel . . . good about themselves. It didn't mean anything.

Still, Ronda couldn't help feeling good about herself.

CHAPTER 26

Shortly after Margo had given Ronda the driving hand-book – 'You owe me ten euros by the way, no hurry' – she applied for Ronda to sit the theory test.

Which cost forty-five euros.

'You don't have to give it to me right now,' Margo told her at their next driving lesson. 'You can give it to me when you do your theory test.'

Ronda presumed she would have a few weeks to prepare for the test. Instead, Margo informed her that it would take place in Santry the following Friday.

Which meant that Ronda had to study for the test and come up with forty-five euros in less than a week.

She didn't mind the studying bit. But there had been a lot of strain on her finances of late. Margo was correct when she said that thirty euros per lesson was a bargain, but it was still an extra thirty euros a week that Ronda had to find, on top of petrol, tax and insurance.

On Friday, Ronda cycled to the test centre, where she was given forty-five minutes to complete the test. She finished it in fifteen minutes, waited a further fifteen minutes, when she was told that she had passed.

In fact, she got forty out of forty.

'Typical,' said Margo, who was waiting in the corridor

when Ronda came out of the test centre. 'You don't even have to try,' she said.

'It's the only bit of the driving process I find doable,' said Ronda.

'You're getting the hang of the clutch control,' said Margo.

'You think so?'

'No,' said Margo, grinning.

'What are you doing here anyway?' asked Ronda. 'It's Friday night.'

'Malcolm's entertaining clients tonight,' said Margo. 'And the boys have gone to the cinema. One of those interminable Marvel films. Do you fancy going for dinner? I could talk you through the finer points of engine maintenance?'

'Thanks, but I've already eaten,' said Ronda, who was trying not to spend any more money until payday, which was still four days away.

'What did you have?' asked Margo, hurrying to keep up with Ronda's strides. She identified as 'vegetarian-curious'.

'Cheese on toast,' said Ronda. 'With anchovies,' she added, before Margo got started about scurvy or rickets or what-have-you.

'How did you get Mam to eat anchovies?' asked Margo. Annie McCann claimed to have a fish allergy, although quite how this occurred or manifested itself, nobody really knew.

'She was in bed when I got in,' said Ronda.

'Double pneumonia, I presume?' said Margo.

'Her note said palpitations,' said Ronda.

'It'd be gas if she actually keeled over of a heart attack, wouldn't it?' said Margo. When she grinned she looked like Ronda's little sister again, bouncing on the couch, begging Ronda for a piggyback to bed.

Ronda stopped at a lamppost in the car park where her bicycle was chained.

'We could go for a drink?' said Margo. 'Celebrate you passing your theory test.'

'I can't,' said Ronda. 'I'm meeting Fatima and Ada at the bowling alley.'

'Fine,' said Margo.

'You could come with me?' said Ronda, finding herself in the unusual position of feeling a little sorry for Margo, who seemed at a loose end.

'I don't think I'm a bowling alley type of person,' said Margo. 'Many reasons. But mostly the shoes. Why do they have to be so ugly? Not to mention unhygienic.'

Ronda's phone rang.

Margo waved as she headed off. 'Next lesson, Sunday morning at eleven,' she called back to Ronda. 'I'll pick you up.' She strode across the car park, ignoring an approaching car, which had to stop when it became obvious that Margo would not.

Ronda answered her phone. It was Fatima, cancelling. 'I have a cold,' she said.

'You don't get colds,' said Ronda. 'You're the healthiest person I've ever met.'

'That is true,' said Fatima.

'What is it then?' asked Ronda.

'I just don't feel up to it,' said Fatima.

'Why?' Ronda had never heard Fatima sound so flat. 'What happened?'

'My solicitor finally rang me back. He says he can't represent me any more, he has too many clients.' She sounded wrung out.

'Maybe it's for the best,' said Ronda. 'He's a terrible solicitor. All those delays with your application.'

'A terrible solicitor is better than none,' said Fatima.

Ronda didn't tell Fatima she was coming over. She knew
Fatima would try to dissuade her. Visitors were not encouraged at the direct provision centre. She jumped on her
bicycle and pedalled fast, noticing that her body was back to
its pre-accident condition. She sped along the roads, arriving outside the asylum accommodation in just under twenty
minutes. It had once been a budget hotel, a shabby building
on the main street with a featureless grey facade, studded
with numerous small windows, all closed with the curtains
tightly drawn. Ronda could see why. The pavement outside
the hotel was thronged with people. Some were carrying
placards, some held banners, some waved Irish flags. One
man had his whole face painted with the tricolour, while
others had daubed the green, white and orange in small
squares on their cheeks. All were chanting. Variations on the
same theme:

'Get them out!'

'Close the borders!'

'Ireland is full!'

Ronda got off her bike and pushed it through the crowd.
The protestors parted to let her through, perhaps assuming she was one of them. The main entrance into the centre
was a revolving door that had been locked. Inside the foyer,
Ronda could see two nervous security men on either side of
the reception desk. Neither of them acknowledged Ronda
when she knocked on the window.

'The citizens of this country aren't allowed in there,
love,' said a man, slamming his fist against the glass. He

roared through the window: 'Ireland for the Irish!' When he stopped shouting, he smiled at Ronda. 'I haven't seen you here before,' he said. 'You're welcome to join us.' He offered her a placard.

'I'm not protesting,' said Ronda. 'I'm visiting my friend.'

Confusion crossed the man's face like clouds rolling in.

'Your friend?' he said.

'She lives in there,' said Ronda. 'With her daughter. Ada. Ada's going to be thirteen soon. She wants to be a make-up artist when she grows up. She likes Irish dancing and Mario Kart and fizzy cola bottles and Tayto crisps. She speaks fluent English with a Dublin accent, and she knows all the words of "Amhrán na bhFiann".'

'What the fuck are you talking about?' said the man, moving closer to Ronda so that she could see stiff dark hairs sprouting out of his nostrils.

'"Amhrán na bhFiann",' Ronda repeated. 'It's our national anthem, I would have thought that even an ignorant racist such as yourself would know that much.'

The mob was chanting again.

'Ireland is full!'

'Close the borders!'

'Ireland for the Irish!'

The man smiled at Ronda. 'I haven't seen you here before,' he said. 'You're welcome to join us.' He offered her a placard.

'I took a wrong turn,' said Ronda.

'Speak up, I can't hear you,' said the man, stepping closer. Ronda turned and hurried away.

CHAPTER 27

Lawrence and the Machine had been replaced by a wide projector screen, set into the ceiling of the dayroom. During 'movie nights' – a new activity listed on the Green Gables schedule – the screen was lowered, the residents wheeled in front of it and a film projected onto it. Today it was Billy Wilder's *Some Like it Hot*, which initiated a heated debate on gender, kicked off by Sheila. 'They're only pretending to be ladies,' she declared.

There was outrage from Captain Grady during the scene where a mobster bursts out of a giant birthday cake and manages to gun several people down despite the thick rivers of icing cascading down his face and body. 'What kind of a soldier is he?' shouted Captain Grady, shaking his fist at the screen.

Ms Gallagher, who seemed distracted, stirred herself enough to throw in her tuppence worth. 'A clear case of gross female exploitation by entitled men,' she said, although without her usual blend of vitriol and fury.

'You okay?' asked Ronda, when she came around with her medication at two o'clock.

'You're not supposed to be doing that job,' said Ms Gallagher.

'Tracey is in a meeting,' explained Ronda. 'And Marie wasn't feeling well so she left, and Leona has to . . .'

'Fine,' said Ms Gallagher, putting up her hand to ward off

any further explanations. She seemed tired. Pale too. Her bouts of active MS had become more frequent in recent months, the episodes lasting longer.

'You sure you're okay?' Ronda asked.

'I said I was, didn't I?' said Ms Gallagher, watching as Ronda popped tablets out of various blister packs.

'Well, you didn't shout at Captain Grady when he made the universal man sign for large breasts,' said Ronda.

'Did I not?' said Ms Gallagher. 'Although – and I know I shouldn't objectify her – Marilyn's breasts were magnificent.' Ms Gallagher glared at Ronda then. 'Don't you go judging me, Ronda McCann. I'm only a human woman. We all have a weakness, and Marilyn is mine. Rest in power.' She held out her hand for her medication. 'They're not the usual brands,' she noted.

'No,' said Ronda, relieved to see her charge's observational skills were as sharp as usual. 'All the meds are coming from some company in the North now. Cheaper, apparently.'

'Hmmm,' said Ms Gallagher, unimpressed. Ronda felt the same way. Already, there had been delays, errors and confusion. Fergal referred to these as 'teething problems', which would be sorted ASAP. Since the Americans had arrived on the scene, he had begun using acronyms. ASAP was his favourite, with FYI a close second.

'Well,' said Ms Gallagher, 'if I seize up like the Tin Man, you'll know that they are ineffective as well as cheap.' She tossed the six pills Ronda handed her into her mouth and dry swallowed the lot. Her iPad binged and she glanced at the screen. 'It's another email from that upstart of a thesis student,' she said. 'She's been pestering me.'

'Why?' asked Ronda.

'Her mother is some class of a journalist. Patricia Glennon I think. She has a podcast and wants to interview me next week.' Ms Gallagher tried and failed to sound indifferent.

'She must have told her mother you were interesting,' said Ronda.

'I am interesting,' said Ms Gallagher.

'What's the name of the podcast?' asked Ronda.

'Whitewash, or some such nonsense,' said Ms Gallagher.

'Oh, I know that one,' said Ronda. 'It's good. A wide listenership.'

'Who the hell wants to hear the story of a bitter, cantankerous working-class, lesbian, communist, intersectional feminist like me, eh?'

'That's a lot of adjectives,' said Ronda.

'I'd say you could add a few more,' said Ms Gallagher.

'As I said before,' said Ronda, 'I need this job.'

As she was leaving Ms Gallagher's room, she saw Donal walking down the corridor. He waved when he saw her, smiling in that familiar way he had, as if she was just the person he was hoping to see.

'We're going to have to start charging you fees,' she said.

'I've got wind of a scholarship that Ernest can apply for,' said Donal, with his usual enthusiasm. 'I just need him to fill in a form. But I've time for a coffee afterwards, if you do?'

Ronda looked at her watch. 'I could take a quick break in about fifteen minutes,' she said.

'Perfect,' said Donal. 'I'll meet you in reception. Treat you to one of those instant coffees from the machine out there.'

'You shouldn't go to so much trouble,' said Ronda, smiling. She was pretty sure this might come under the heading of 'flirting'. It was unfamiliar terrain.

CHAPTER 28

'Today you're going to drive all the way to the industrial estate,' Margo informed Ronda when she arrived at eleven on Sunday morning.

Ronda's throat constricted. 'I'm not ready,' she said.

Margo ignored her and ran around the car to let herself in the passenger side. A car approached just as she pulled open the door. It kept coming, the driver clearly expecting Margo to close the door and flatten herself against it. Margo did neither of those things and, in the end, the car had to slow down before coming to a complete stop.

It was Joseph Murphy.

'Get in, Margo,' hissed Ronda. 'Quickly.'

Margo, noticing Joseph, did as she was bid. Joseph's car stayed where it was.

'How can you still give a damn what that 90s throwback C-lister thinks?' said Margo.

'I don't,' said Ronda, without much conviction.

'You do,' said Margo, with a great deal of conviction.

Margo was right. She did give a damn. But why? Ronda struggled to come up with an explanation.

'I feel like I'm this relic from his past,' she finally said. 'He must think I'm such a loser, still living at home. And now he's going to find out that I can't even drive. All the adults I know can drive. Even Mam.'

Margo looked at Ronda, and for a moment, she said

nothing. Then she rummaged in her bag and handed Ronda a lipstick. 'Put some on,' she said. 'And do something to your hair.'

'Like what?' said Ronda, looking in the mirror at the back of the sun visor. The lipstick wasn't her type of colour. Fire engine red. Glossy and conspicuous. Not a colour you could hide behind. She put some on.

Margo leaned over and mussed Ronda's thick fringe with her fingers, encouraged the sides behind her ears. 'There,' she said, sitting back and examining her work. 'That's a bit better.'

'Here's your lipstick back,' said Ronda.

Margo shook her head. 'I'm not having it back after you've been mauling it,' she said. 'Keep it.'

'Why is he not driving past?' whispered Ronda.

'He's texting,' said Margo, looking in the wing mirror. 'Oh, he's driving towards us now.'

'Don't look at him,' Ronda said, turning the key and checking her rear-view mirror. In her peripheral vision, she could see Joseph, peering into the car, waving at them as he drove past.

Margo looked resolutely ahead with her best imperious expression.

Ronda yanked the seat belt across her chest, clipped it in. She stepped on the clutch, put the car in first gear, revved the engine. Joseph's hand – the waving one – came to a stop and then lowered, disappearing below the window. A car behind him beeped. Joseph drove on. Ronda released the clutch until she could feel what Margo called 'the bite'.

'Steady,' said Margo, putting her hand on the wheel. 'He's eyeballing you in his rear view, try to look normal.'

'Do I not look normal?'

'You know what I mean,' said Margo. Ronda had no idea.

Joseph was a little ahead now, waiting for a delivery truck to execute a three-point turn before he could advance.

'Watch and learn,' said Margo, nodding approvingly. 'That truck driver knows his way around the classic three-point turn.'

The van drove up the road and Joseph followed it before seamlessly fitting his car in the tight space between Mr Freeman's Opel Corsa and Mrs Tiernan's Nissan Leaf.

'If you say that was a master class in parallel parking, I'm getting out of this car,' said Ronda.

'I was going to comment unfavourably on his post boy-band get-up.'

Ronda checked her blind spot. She released the handbrake and pulled out into the road just as Joseph's car door opened and one of his long, denim-clad legs made an appearance. Ronda kept her foot on the accelerator until they had passed him. The engine roared in frustration.

'Second gear,' barked Margo.

Ronda hauled the car into second gear, then third. She kept her foot on the accelerator until she had navigated the curve of the road and disappeared from Joseph's view. At the junction she stalled and could not persuade the car the start again. 'Will you please drive the rest of the way to the industrial estate from here?' asked Ronda. 'I have a headache.'

'A Mam-headache or an actual one?'

'An actual one.'

'You do look exhausted,' said Margo, peering into Ronda's face. 'Do you want a few painkillers?'

Ronda shook her head. 'I'll be fine once I'm not driving,' she said.

'You really do hate driving, don't you?' said Margo, as if she was realising this for the first time.

'I'm getting a bit more used to it,' said Ronda.

'You'd have the back of it broken by now, if you relaxed a bit. You're too careful of yourself.'

Margo opened the door and walked around to the driver's side. Ronda slid across the seat, hauled herself up and over the gear stick and belted herself into the passenger seat.

The nurse had said if she'd been wearing a seat belt she would have walked away from the crash with just a bit of bruising across her chest.

'I told her to put the belt on,' Gerry had said, glaring at the nurse. He did not like to be challenged and certainly not by a woman.

When she was being discharged, the nurse reached for Ronda's arm as she followed her father out the door. 'You be careful, Ronda McCann,' she'd said.

'I will,' Ronda replied. It was like an oath she was declaring.

A solemn vow.

One she had taken seriously.

CHAPTER 29

By the time the podcaster, Patricia Glennon, arrived at Green Gables the following week, Ms Gallagher had changed her mind about the interview and sent an email to that effect to Patricia the night before.

'I don't check my emails after five o'clock in the evening,' Patricia told Ronda when she arrived at Green Gables the next day. She was a big-boned woman in a long tweed coat, short skirt and knee-high boots. She didn't look like the type of person who took no for an answer. Ronda had been dispatched to reception by Ms Gallagher to get rid of her. She didn't fancy her chances.

Patricia took Ronda in with a glance. 'You could make her change her mind, couldn't you?' she said. 'You're one of those nurses, I can tell. Your patients adore you, don't they?'

Ronda shook her head. 'I'm a care assistant,' she said. 'And they're residents.'

Patricia nodded vigorously. 'Of course, of course,' she said. 'Residents. Yes. That was insensitive of me.' She peered at the name badge pinned to the front of Ronda's scrubs. 'Ronda,' she added, smiling. 'A Welsh name.'

'My maternal grandmother was from Cardiff,' said Ronda.

'You could put in a good word for me, couldn't you, Ronda?' Patricia asked, widening her dark brown eyes and pressing the palms of her hands together, prayer-like.

'Nobody can make Ms Gallagher do anything she

doesn't want to do, I'm afraid,' said Ronda, although she could feel her resolve crumbling beneath the woman's intimate gaze.

'Hmm,' said Patricia, stroking her chin. She took a different tack. 'What is she worried about do you think?' she asked Ronda, as if they were conspirators with a common goal.

'Well,' Ronda began. 'I think it's . . .'

'Go on, dear,' said Patricia.

'Off the record,' Ronda remembered to say.

'Of course,' said Patricia. 'That goes without saying.'

'She doesn't want to talk about Edel Scanlan,' said Ronda.

'Ah yes, the one that got away,' said Patricia. 'Nobody wants to talk about that one, do they?' Patricia looked at Ronda, straight at her eyeballs, like she could see right inside her. Like she knew everything about her.

From behind the reception desk, Monika coughed into her sleeve as if to distract Patricia from her probe. It worked, because Patricia pulled her gaze from Ronda's eyes and smiled at Monika, who nodded curtly, her hands wrapped around a mug of the liquorice tea she was convinced had age-defying properties.

'I'd better get back to work,' said Ronda, stepping out of Patricia's range and moving towards the double doors.

Patricia trailed after her. 'And yes, the whole Edel Scanlan storyline is interesting, I won't deny it. But Lyra Gallagher is a fascinating woman in her own right. There are lots of things we can talk about. Can you assure her that we'll only talk about Edel Scanlan if Ms Gallagher wants to, okay? She has my word.'

Ronda worried that even Ms Gallagher's guard could be

lowered by this woman. 'I'll tell her,' she said, pressing her lanyard against the security panel on the wall.

'Could I wait here?' said Patricia, pointing at a line of chairs along the wall. 'While you ask her? I don't mind waiting. I'm not in any hurry.'

The double doors opened and Ronda stepped through them. 'I can't promise anything,' she said.

'But you'll tell her what I said?' asked Patricia, as the doors began to close.

'I will,' said Ronda, heading down the corridor.

Patricia stuck her head through the doors and shouted, 'Thanks Ronda, you're a star.' She managed to extract her head just before the automatic doors sealed shut.

Kim waylaid Ronda on the way to Ms Gallagher's room. 'You will never believe who I had a date with yesterday,' she breathed at Ronda, grabbing her arms and forcing her to a halt.

'Who?' asked Ronda.

'You have to guess,' said Kim.

'I don't have time to guess,' said Ronda, although she couldn't help smiling. She sometimes found Kim's youthful high spirits infectious. Like now, with her high ponytail swinging about her head as she bounced on her toes.

'Just say a name,' she said.

'I have no idea,' said Ronda. 'And now I really have to . . .'

'Fergal's son,' blurted Kim. 'Ronan.'

'Oh,' said Ronda. The last time she had seen Ronan, he had been a scrawny, pimply, taciturn teenager. Although that had been a good few years ago.

'He's nothing like his dad,' Kim rushed on. 'He's super handsome for starters. And generous. He didn't scarper when the bill came.'

The bar was low, Ronda felt. 'Did you tell him you work for Fergal?' asked Ronda.

Kim shook her head. 'I only clocked it at the end of the date, and by then, I liked him and I didn't want to throw that into the mix.'

'So you're going to see him again?' asked Ronda.

Kim shrugged. 'If he doesn't ghost me in the meantime,' she said.

Ronda nodded as if she understood. Which of course she didn't. She had been on very few dates since the Joseph debacle, and only then when she felt under pressure. Like Monika setting her up with her cousin last year. 'I already told him you would,' she'd said, when Ronda's initial response had been a very robust, 'No.' 'He's okay looking. And he's quiet like you, so he doesn't go on many dates, but I showed him your picture. He said you had nice teeth.' Monika was ruthlessly frank, but she was also persuasive, not to mention mean when she didn't get her own way. You could suddenly find that your lanyard didn't work if you crossed her. In fairness, her cousin did turn out to be okay looking. But his quietness was not the reason he seldom dated, Ronda discovered. It was more likely to be his inappropriateness (he'd asked Ronda how much she earned), the strange smell he emitted (a curious mix of smoked trout and mothballs), his specialist subject (fly fishing) and his sly glances down the neck of Ronda's top when he thought he could get away with it. But she had to concede that he was polite and direct. He'd asked if he could sleep with her, and when she declined, he thanked her for her company and escorted her to her bicycle, parked outside the restaurant where they had gone

Dutch, at Ronda's insistence. She never liked them to feel she owed them anything.

The modern dating scene with all its apps and swiping here, there and everywhere filled her with a sinking sort of horror. It felt like putting your hand out to be slapped. Not just slapped but mangled.

'He paid for my coconut milk iced latte. And when I asked him to choose a bun for me, he picked a cinnamon bun, which happens to be my favourite, so that's definitely a sign,' went on Kim, checking her phone for messages. 'Oh, and he said my hair was beautiful.'

'Well, it is,' said Ronda.

'Yes, but he didn't have to say it, did he?' said Kim, pulling at the bobbin around her ponytail and releasing the long, silky sheet of her hair.

'Just be careful,' said Ronda.

'Where's the fun in that?' grinned Kim, slipping her phone back into her pocket.

'Is Ms Gallagher in her room?' asked Ronda.

Kim nodded. 'She's in foul form today,' she said. 'Fouler than usual, I mean.'

To get to Ms Gallagher's room, Ronda had to traverse the dayroom, where Sean and his son sat on either side of Captain Grady. The two men were watching an old Cliff Richard concert on the big screen while Eddie scrolled on his phone.

Sheila was singing along to 'The Young Ones'. 'Me and Noel saw him in Sound City in 1964,' she told Ronda with a rare gleam in her eye, as if she could still see it all clearly. As if it had happened yesterday. 'Do you want to see him?' she whispered to Ronda.

'Who?'

'Noel,' she said. She put her finger to her lips. 'Ssssh,' she said. She stood up and pulled up the cushion of her armchair. Underneath was a creased black and white photograph. A couple on their wedding day. The young woman could be Sheila, Ronda supposed. It was hard to tell.

'Eddie!' snapped Sean. Sheila stuffed the photograph back on the chair, covered it with the cushion and sat on it.

'Will you put that bloody phone down and say something to your grandad.'

'Why don't you say something,' said Eddie.

'You have to be at least eighteen before you can join the army,' said Captain Grady.

'I'm going to the loo,' said Eddie, standing up.

'Leave your phone here,' said Sean.

Eddie ignored him and left the dayroom, still scrolling.

Now, Cliff Richard was singing, 'We Don't Talk Anymore'.

'Are you a fan?' Ronda asked Sean. He shook his head. He looked tired, Ronda thought. And pale. Like he could do with a good night's sleep and some of Fatima's marrow soup. He glanced at his watch and Ronda knew he was calculating his exit time. 'Captain Grady,' said Ronda. 'Why don't you tell Sean about the choir that was here yesterday. Remember? They sang your favourite song, "Oliver's Army".'

Captain Grady registered no acknowledgement of Ronda's suggestion. She turned to Sean. 'Your dad sang along,' she told him. 'He knew all the words.'

'The army is all he remembers,' Sean said. 'He hasn't a clue who I am. And he never mentions my poor mother, God rest her.' Sean shrugged, his DPD branded T-shirt slipping down his narrow shoulder.

194

He looked at Captain Grady, who was reciting reams of army doctrine under his breath. 'Leadership is influencing people by providing purpose, direction and motivation while achieving the mission.'

'He likes it when you visit,' Ronda said.

'I've no idea why,' said Sean.

'His appetite is better on the days you visit,' said Ronda. 'And he sleeps through the night too. It really does make a difference.'

Ronda lifted a blanket off the arm of a chair and draped it across Captain Grady's knees. He got cold easily. 'Would you like some tea?' she asked them.

'I can't drink on duty,' said Captain Grady.

Sean shook his head. 'You've enough to be doing,' he said, trying to stifle a yawn.

'Were you working the night shift?' Ronda asked. For a moment, Ronda thought perhaps he hadn't heard her. Afterwards, she realised he was debating whether or not to tell her. She had no idea why he decided to in the end. Although in her experience, people often found it easier to talk to strangers.

'I haven't been sleeping,' he said. 'My wife and I separated recently. It's been a long time coming, I suppose.'

'Every person subject to military law who commits any act to the prejudice of good order is guilty of an offence against military law and shall be subject to dismissal from the defence forces,' declared Captain Grady, standing up so the blanket fell off his knees.

'That's hard on all of you,' said Ronda, picking the blanket off the floor.

Sean nodded. 'Especially Eddie. He hates when it's my

weekend with him,' he said. 'He always preferred Linda. That's his mother.'

'He probably just needs time to adjust,' said Ronda.

'I'm a chip off the old block, it seems,' said Sean, settling Captain Grady back into his chair. 'I was hoping I'd be a different kind of father, you know?'

Ronda could feel the potency of his sadness, and the clench of his body, trying to contain it. She tucked the blanket around Captain Grady's legs again.

'Sorry,' said Sean. 'You've enough to be doing without listening to me moaning.'

'There's a new Marvel film out,' said Ronda, straightening. 'My nephews saw it. They loved it, maybe Eddie and you could . . .'

'Is it time for a ration pack?' asked Captain Grady.

'I'll see if I can find some of Fatima's shortcake,' Ronda said.

Eddie returned, still on his phone.

As Ronda left the dayroom, she could hear Sean asking Eddie if he fancied going to the cinema later. 'There's a new Marvel movie out,' he said.

'Already seen it,' said Eddie. There was silence after that, apart from Cliff, who was still singing.

Kim was right. Ms Gallagher was indeed in foul form when Ronda eventually reached her room. 'Can I come in?' she asked, knocking gently.

'No,' snapped Ms Gallagher.

'I brought Fatima's shortcake,' said Ronda.

'How many pieces?'

'Two.'

'I suppose you'll be looking for one of them.'

'If you offer one to me, it would be rude to refuse,' said Ronda.

'Why are you still hovering around out there?' snapped Ms Gallagher. 'Come in if you're coming.'

Ronda didn't think she'd ever seen Ms Gallagher in bed before. Or in pyjamas. Although it wasn't pyjamas she wore, but a long, white flannel nightgown buttoned up to the neck. She was propped against pillows and had a shawl draped over her shoulders as if she were cold, which she never was.

'Are you sick?' asked Ronda, putting the plate of short-cake on the bedside table.

'My back's acting up a wee bit,' admitted Ms Gallagher.

'Do you need stronger painkillers?' asked Ronda. She lay her hand across Ms Gallagher's forehead, which felt a little hot to the touch.

'Is there tea to go with that shortcake?' said Ms Gallagher, waving Ronda away.

'Fatima will be here in a bit with the tea trolley,' said Ronda. 'In the meantime, you should know that Dr Patricia Glennon is in reception.'

'I told her I changed my mind,' said Ms Gallagher. 'I've said all I have to say, probably more than I should have, over the years.'

'Fine,' said Ronda, moving towards the door. 'I'll tell her to go.'

Ms Gallagher sat up a little straighter. 'What did she say to you?' she asked Ronda, idly pushing the cuticles back on her fingernails.

'She thinks you're fascinating,' Ronda said airily.

'I don't know if I'd go that far,' said Ms Gallagher. 'What else?'

Ronda paused and looked into the space above her head as if she were struggling to remember. 'She said there are lots of interesting things about you and there'd be no need to talk about . . . you know . . . anyone you didn't want to talk about.'

Ms Gallagher performed an impressive eyeroll. 'Edel's not bloody Lord Voldemort, Ronda, you can say her name.'

'So,' said Ronda, her hand on the door handle. 'Will I tell Patricia to leave?'

'I suppose I could spare her a few minutes of my time,' said Ms Gallagher, flinging the bed covers back and using the handle attached to the wall to pull herself into a sitting position. She pushed her legs over the edge of the bed, where they dangled, nearly a foot off the floor.

'Do you want a hand, getting dressed?' asked Ronda.

'Do I look like someone who wants a hand getting dressed?' demanded Ms Gallagher. 'No,' said Ronda, ignoring the wheelchair, the walking frame and the shelf crammed with bottles of medicine, boxes of tablets, creams and sprays.

'But if you want to make yourself useful, you could grab me a fresh pair of jeans from the wardrobe.'

Ronda did as she was bid and left to tell Patricia the good news.

Fatima was in the corridor, pushing the tea trolley towards the dayroom. Her step did not have its usual spring in it.

'Did you hear back from any of the solicitors you emailed?' asked Ronda.

Fatima shook her head. 'None of them can represent me,'

she said. 'But it will be okay, my case worker said it's not mandatory to have a solicitor at the Personal Interview.'

'Maybe we could ask Donal?' said Ronda.

'I don't want to take advantage of him,' said Fatima. 'He has a kind nature. He'll say yes, even if I can't pay him.'

Ronda nodded. She felt that was an accurate assessment.

CHAPTER 30

'Mam, I'm home,' said Ronda, struggling through the front door with two bags of shopping that evening.

'I didn't bother with dinner,' called Annie from the sitting room. 'My stomach ulcer's been acting up.'

'Are you hungry now?' asked Ronda, setting the bags on the floor and pulling off her helmet.

'What are you making?' asked Annie, turning the volume from raucous to merely loud.

'Bangers and mash,' said Ronda.

'Real sausages?' Anne asked.

'Pork ones, from Mr Hannigan's,' said Ronda, sticking her head around the sitting-room door.

'And the mash with the scallions and butter?' asked Annie, turning around as the credits rolled at the end of an episode of *Murder She Wrote*.

'Yes,' said Ronda. 'It'll be ready by seven, okay?'

The kitchen was cold. Annie was inclined to heat one room at a time, depending on which one she happened to be occupying. Ronda had the potatoes peeled and simmering and the sausages laid out on the grill pan before she took her coat off. Then she sat down and surveyed the chessboard. She was in a precarious position, which was proving difficult to manoeuvre her way out of. She was relieved when her phone beeped with a WhatsApp message, diverting her attention from the board. It was from Margo.

200

Lesson Thursday after work. I'll pick you up from No. 10 at 6 p.m. sharp.

Ronda felt the familiar resistance in her body and head. This would be the fifth lesson and the tension she felt inside the car had not abated. She wondered if it ever would. Before she could dissuade herself, she typed back, Yes, thanks, c u then.

What else could she do?

Margo sent a selection of emojis in response: the thumbs-up one, followed by a car, fingers crossed, gnashing teeth, eyeroll and a purple heart.

'Manifest,' Kim had advised her the other day when Ronda voiced her doubts about ever being able to drive like other people.

How could she know that Ronda was a dab hand at that bit? It was the rest of the process that she struggled with.

'Picture yourself behind the wheel, driving like a pro,' Kim had said. 'I'm in the passenger seat because you're giving me a lift to a shoot.'

'What shoot?' Ronda had asked, confused.

'In this manifestation, I'm a super model doing a photo shoot for *Vogue*,' said Kim. 'No, *Vanity Fair*.'

'And I'm driving with one hand on the wheel, like I'm not even nervous,' Ronda replied.

'That's the spirit,' Kim said, holding her hand out for a high five.

'Ronda? What's that smell? Ronda!' Annie's voice was shrill. Ronda jumped and dropped the queen that Berkley had relieved her of. Smoke poured out of the grill. Both the pork and vegetarian sausages were black and shrivelled

201

and no amount of paring and scraping would render any of them edible. The potatoes were pulpy and separating, but salvageable, once she drained them, lobbed a great pat of butter onto them, added a dash of cream and a sprinkling of nutmeg and mashed them.

'Jesus, Mary and holy Saint Joseph,' said Annie, coughing as she lumbered through the kitchen door. 'Are you trying to put the heart across me?'

'Sorry Mam,' said Ronda, opening the window in an effort to clear the smoke. 'Sit down and make a start.'

'Where're the sausages?' said Annie, examining her plate of mash and peas.

'They didn't make it,' said Ronda. 'Sorry.'

'Daydreaming I suppose,' said Annie, poking her fork through the mash. 'I don't see any scallions.'

'Oh, sorry, I forgot about them.'

Annie McCann shook her head and peered over the top of her glasses at her daughter. 'You'd want to get your house in order, Ronda McCann,' she said.

'I'm trying,' said Ronda, sitting at the table, opposite her mother.

'You're not trying very hard.' Annie shook her head as she speared a pea on the prong of her fork. 'Margo says you're still as anxious as a bag of cats in that car.'

The remark was a throwaway one, made casually and without much thought. Still, it felt like a slap across Ronda's face. 'I am doing my best, you know,' she said. 'I can't help feeling nervous.'

Annie took a drink of water. 'It was an accident, what happened,' she said. 'Your father felt terrible about it, sure didn't he join AA straight afterwards.'

It was true Gerry had apologised. Step nine. Make direct amends. 'Sorry,' he'd said, gesturing towards her face. He never really looked at her afterwards. Ronda presumed it was the scar, vivid in those days. Ronda hadn't known what to say, so she'd said nothing. He'd never mentioned it again.

'Did he really feel terrible?' asked Ronda. She was surprised at her mother's reference to the accident.

'Course he did,' said Annie. 'Now, would you get the bottle of brown sauce down from the press? My back is at me so I can't be stretching. Good girl.'

The doorbell rang. 'Are you expecting anyone?' asked Ronda.

'Who would I be expecting?' said Annie, matter-of-fact.

Ronda walked to the end of the hall and switched on the porch light, forgetting it didn't work any more. It probably just needed a new bulb, but the fitting required unscrewing and Ronda hadn't gotten around to it yet. She opened the door. There was no need for the porch light after all. Donal stood there beside his bicycle with a set of multicoloured flashing fairy lights strung around his jacket. She blinked in the glare.

'They are a bit garish,' said Donal, fishing a switch out of his pocket and turning them off.

'They're certainly . . . noticeable,' said Ronda.

He pulled a thick brown envelope out of one of the panniers. 'I did try and phone you earlier,' he said. 'I was going to just push this through the letter box, but it's too big. It's your mother's copy of the Enduring Power of Attorney.'

'Close the front door, Ronda,' called Annie from the kitchen. 'There's a terrible draught.'

'Thanks,' said Ronda, taking the envelope. It was freezing to the touch.

'Sorry for calling unannounced,' said Donal. 'Hope I'm not interrupting anything?'

'No,' said Ronda. 'I wasn't doing anything.' She wished she had said something else. Something a bit less dull.

'Who is it, Ronda?' called Annie.

'It's Donal Clarke.'

'The solicitor?' Ronda could hear the legs of her mother's chair scraping against the lino.

Annie opened the kitchen door 'Are you not going to ask the poor man in?' she said. 'He'll catch his death out there.'

'He was just leaving,' said Ronda. But Donal was already pulling the bicycle clips off the ends of his trousers and undoing the strap of his helmet. He lifted it off his head and patted his hair down. The thick thatch ignored his efforts.

'Temperature's going below zero tonight,' he said, wheeling his bike over to the fence to lock it.

The security light next door came on and Mrs Murphy appeared, pulling out the bin for the morning collection. She unlatched the garden gate, pausing when she noticed Donal and Ronda, her antennae twitching. Ronda grabbed a fistful of Donal's anorak, pulled him inside and shut the door. If Donal was surprised by the curtness of her actions, he did not say. He shucked off his jacket and tossed it across the bannisters. It slipped to the floor. As he bent to retrieve it, his helmet fell out of his arms and bounced down the hall. His jacket slid off his arm, back onto the floor. Ronda picked both items up and hung them on the coat stand at the door.

'Sorry,' said Donal. 'I'm usually way slicker than this.' He grinned. Ronda couldn't help grinning back.

She walked into the kitchen, acutely aware of him behind

her. The burnt sausage smell was not as strong as before, but the kitchen was cold again with an icy blast rushing through the open window. Ronda closed it. Annie was back in her chair, stroking Jessica Fletcher, who had jumped onto the table, hopeful of scraps.

'How are you, Mrs McCann?' said Donal. 'I hope that trapped nerve in your shoulder isn't still giving you grief?' He lifted Jessica Fletcher into his arms, petting her.

'Be careful,' said Ronda urgently. 'She scratches.' But she didn't scratch. In fact, Ronda could hear her purring, something she rarely indulged in.

'She's just as beautiful as you described, Mrs McCann,' said Donal, pulling softly at the cat's ears.

'She doesn't usually like anyone except me,' said Annie, her tone surprised and perhaps a little put out. Donal set her on Annie's lap. 'There're a few strays that come around my place. Maybe she can smell them off me.'

'She doesn't like cats either,' said Annie, stroking her. 'So, where is your place?'

The kettle whistled. 'Tea or coffee, Donal?' said Ronda.

'Tea, please,' said Donal, sitting beside Annie.

'I'd say you're a southside man,' said Annie. 'Would I be right?'

'I used to be all right,' said Donal. 'But I have a camper van now so I . . .'

'A camper van?' said Annie.

Ronda found a box of cherry bakewells. She tore it open, spilled them onto a plate and set it on the table between them. 'Do you take sugar in your tea?' she asked Donal.

'Is it like a trailer?' asked Annie. 'To pull your boat? Did you tell me you have a boat?'

205

'My sons do a bit of sailing all right,' said Donal reaching across the table and picking up a bun. 'But the camper van is my home.'

'What do you mean?' asked Annie.

'I live in it,' he said, then took an enormous bite out of the cherry bakewell.

Annie's mouth hung open as if her jaw had become unhinged. 'Why on earth would you do that?' said Annie.

'Will you have a cup of tea, Mam?' said Ronda, in a vain attempt to distract Annie. She needn't have bothered. Annie was like Jessica Fletcher stalking a bird through the branches of the laburnum tree.

'I like it,' said Donal, either not noticing or ignoring Annie's shock at his living arrangements. He picked up the pot. 'Tea for you Ronda?' he asked.

'Yes please,' she said as he poured.

'So you're living on the side of the road, like a . . .' Annie lowered her voice before she said, 'a Traveller.'

Donal nodded, blowing on the surface of his tea. 'I'm not as handy as they are when it comes to the open road,' he said. 'But I'm getting there.'

'Yes, but why?' asked Annie.

'Mam,' said Ronda, her tone pointed.

'I'm only asking,' said Annie, huffy.

'I don't mind,' said Donal. 'I'm always getting asked these kinds of questions.'

'See?' said Annie to Ronda. She looked at Donal again. 'You were saying?'

'Well,' began Donal, 'after me and Trish split . . .'

'Is Trish your wife?' asked Annie.

'My ex,' said Donal.

'Such a shame,' said Annie. 'When a marriage breaks down.'

'It was amicable,' said Donal. 'We just wanted different things, I suppose. We're still friends.'

'I see,' said Annie stiffly. Ronda wondered if she was thinking about her and Gerry. They'd never really been friends, as far as Ronda remembered.

'I didn't want us to have to sell the family home so I could afford a place,' Donal went on. 'So a pal of mine lent me his camper van. It was only supposed to be temporary while I came up with a plan. But I ended up buying if off him. I love it. I love not knowing where I might land up for the night. Waking up to a different view every morning.'

'What does your poor mother think about that?' asked Annie, shaking her head. She set Jessica Fletcher on the floor and used the table to haul herself up.

'She died when I was a boy,' said Donal. 'But, from what I can remember of her, I think she would have approved.' He stood up too and offered Annie his arm, which she leaned on.

'I'll take my tea in the sitting room, Ronda,' Annie said as Donal helped her through the kitchen door. 'And only one of those buns, I don't want to aggravate the ulcer.'

'Sorry about Annie,' said Ronda, when Donal returned to the kitchen. 'She doesn't have as many filters as I'd like.'

Donal picked up his teacup, took a slug. 'She has more than Ms Gallagher,' he said, smiling.

'That's true,' said Ronda, smiling back.

'I'm sorry about your mother,' said Ronda, pouring more tea for herself. 'And the smell in here.'

'What were you cooking?' asked Donal.

'Pork sausages,' said Ronda, nodding towards the blackened grill pan in the sink.

'I had you down as a vegetarian,' said Donal. Ronda couldn't help feeling pleased with the observation.

'I am,' she said.

Her phone beeped. It was a text from Fatima. She'd received another no from a solicitor.

'Everything okay?' said Donal.

Ronda knew Fatima was too proud to ask. But the Personal Interview was fast approaching.

'I have a favour to ask you,' she said. 'Please don't feel you have to say yes,' she added, pretty sure that he would say yes.

Donal did say yes.

'But I don't have much experience with asylum cases,' he added.

'You know the system,' said Ronda. 'That'll be a great help.'

'I'll ring Fatima tomorrow,' said Donal, draining his tea and standing up.

'She'll be resistant,' said Ronda. 'She'll want to pay you, but she doesn't have a lot of cash.'

'I don't accept payment, so that'll be fine,' said Donal.

'Why not?' Ronda couldn't help asking.

'I'm a recovering capitalist,' he said, matter-of-fact. 'Trying to bring back the barter system. We never should have tossed it.' He rinsed his cup and plate in the sink before putting them in the dishwasher. 'I have to go,' he said. 'There's a meteor shower tonight that I want to watch, it's going to be spectacular.'

'Most people watch Netflix,' said Ronda. She wasn't sure if she'd ever seen a meteor shower.

'You're a good chess player,' said Donal, examining the board on the small table near the door.

'I'm having a good game,' Ronda admitted. 'Which happens about as often as a meteor shower.'

'You have it set at advanced,' said Donal, impressed. 'My chess machine isn't speaking to me at the moment.' He looked at Ronda, grinning. 'I call her Cal. She can be a right imperious cow.'

'This is Berkley,' said Ronda. 'He's firm but fair.'

'An excellent combination,' said Donal, heading into the hall. 'Goodnight Mrs McCann,' he called through the sitting-room door. Annie couldn't hear him over the blare of the television. He opened the hall door and waved goodbye at Ronda. Then he unlocked his bike, walked it out through the gate, turned on the fairy lights and cycled away.

There was a crunch of feet against the gravel in Mrs Murphy's driveway. It was Joseph, taking his car off the charger and inspecting Donal's retreating form with the same curiosity Jessica Fletcher displayed when she poked and prodded at a mouse she had lured from its bolthole. Ronda backed towards the front door but Joseph turned his head her way.

'Ah, there you are, Ronda,' he said, as if he'd been looking all over for her. He walked up to the fence dividing their gardens, his hand tucked inside his suit pocket and a navy wool coat draped over his arm. His winter tan had faded; they had been in the Maldives in November, Ronda had seen the photographs on Instagram. 'How are you?' he asked.

'Fine,' said Ronda.

'That your boyfriend?' he asked. 'Stephen Roche up there?' When Ronda didn't respond right away, he sighed and shook his head. 'Sorry, I've no right to be so nosy,' he said. 'I'm turning into my mother.' He smiled at her. 'I don't suppose you fancy a drink? We could catch up? I'm going out of my mind in there.' He nodded dismissively towards his parents' house. Many possible responses flashed through Ronda's mind, some less polite than others. In the end, Ronda didn't use any of them. Instead she looked up. Joseph followed her gaze, his eyes raking across the sky, obscured with cloud and light pollution. 'What are you looking at?' he asked.

'There's a meteor shower tonight,' Ronda told him, as she walked back inside her house. 'It's going to be spectacular.'

CHAPTER 31

The following few days were busy ones. All the usual jobs at work, plus another of the meetings Fergal was so fond of since the takeover, called at short notice. These meetings nearly always ran over, leaking into Ronda's lunch break. Leaving her less time to quiz Fatima on the questions Donal had sent her in preparation for the Personal Interview. Fatima had written sample answers on flash cards and memorised them.

'What do you think?' asked Fatima when she got through all of the answers without the slightest hesitation.

'Do you not think you should sound a bit more . . .?' began Ronda.

'A bit more what?' snapped Fatima, whose usual bright and positive constitution was showing signs of wear and tear in the lead-up to the interview with the International Protection Office.

'I just wondered if your answers should sound a little less rehearsed, you know?'

'But I have to rehearse them,' said Fatima. 'Otherwise, the English words will desert me and I will forget everything.'

'You could do the interview in your own language, couldn't you?' said Ronda. 'Get an interpreter to translate?'

'No,' said Fatima. 'I want to sound as Irish as possible. Do you think I do?' She looked anxiously at Ronda.

'You sound great,' Ronda assured her.

Kim arrived into the kitchen in her usual exuberant manner, twirling and leaping. 'I have news,' she declared. 'Starting with the super duper first date I had last night.' She stretched out her arms and took a deep bow so the ends of her hair trailed against the floor.

'What happened to Ronan?' asked Fatima.

'He ghosted me after I told him I worked here,' Kim said.

'That's shabby behaviour,' said Fatima.

Kim shrugged. 'Better to find out people are not your one true love sooner rather than later,' she said. She fished in the pocket of her scrubs for her phone and stabbed at the screen. 'Allow me to introduce you to my date.'

Fatima and Ronda peered into the screen. This one was skinny with long red hair in a ponytail. He wore a maroon velvet suit and looked at the camera with enormous, liquid eyes, his long, slender hand placed delicately across his chest, as if he were feeling for a heartbeat.

'His name is Scott,' Kim told them. 'We went to The Flagstones. It's a karaoke bar. His idea, which was the first sign. There we are singing "Islands in the Stream",' said Kim, scrolling to another photo. 'Another sign.'

'A sign of what?' Fatima wanted to know.

'Of true love, of course,' said Kim with gravitas. 'Isn't he the most gorgeous thing you've ever seen?'

'He looks . . . very sincere,' said Ronda.

Kim scrolled through more photographs. 'Now for the next piece of news. Look, here we are ordering drinks, and guess who I see?' She zooms in on the photograph and points at a man on a stool, propping up the bar. 'Look,' she said. 'It's Charlo. He nodded at me and then scurried into a snug at the back with his pint.'

Ronda wondered how this was news, but Kim had only paused to take a drink of water. 'Next,' she went on, 'a couple of Travellers arrived and the bar woman ordered them out. My Scott was the only one who stood up for them. He told the woman that she was being racist and that hate speech was a crime now. He was ah-mazing. Look.' Kim scrolled through several more pictures. 'There she is,' she said, pointing at a photograph of a middle-aged woman with long blond hair, tight black leather trousers and a bright red T-shirt with a headshot of Johnny Depp over the words, 'I'm Team Johnny'. A name tag declared her to be Flossie, the manager. She looked directly at the camera, her finger pointing towards the door.

'That was just before she threw us out,' Kim explained.

'Did Scott call the police?' Fatima wanted to know.

Kim nodded. 'We waited outside for ages, but they never came. Which leads me to my next revelation.' She scrolled through more photographs on her phone.

'Go on,' said Fatima.

'While we were waiting for the police, Charlo came out. And guess who he was wrapped around?' Kim found the photograph she was looking for and showed it to Ronda and Fatima. It was Charlo with his arm around Flossie. Her hand was over her face as if she was about flick her hair.

'Hang on,' said Ronda, taking Kim's phone and zooming in on Flossie's hand.

'What?' said Kim, peering over Ronda's shoulder.

Ronda pointed to the ring around Flossie's finger. 'That looks exactly like Sheila's engagement ring,' she said. 'The one she inherited from her mother.' She showed the photo to Fatima, who nodded. 'It's even got those tiny little

213

emeralds,' she said, pointing at the diamonds, which were indeed topped with bright green stones.

'OMG!' shrieked Kim.

'Maybe that's why Sheila insists she's a widow,' said Fatima. 'Charlo is dead to her.'

'And he's a thief,' said Kim.

'We don't know that for sure,' said Ronda, who was pretty sure he was.

'Are you saying we do nothing?' said Kim, her eyes flashing at Ronda.

'For the moment, yes,' said Ronda.

Kim sighed and flounced towards the door. When she got there, she turned back. 'I nearly forgot to tell you,' she said. 'There's something going on with Ms Gallagher.'

'What do you mean?' asked Ronda.

'It's her mood,' said Kim. 'It's . . .' Here, she paused to consider her next words. Then she said, 'Not as foul as usual.'

As soon as Ronda had unwrapped an almond Magnum for Sheila, brought Captain Grady for his daily manoeuvres – a lap of the building – changed Baby into dry clothes after Teresa baptised her by pouring a glass of water over her head, and got the TV working again after Captain Grady reefed wires out of the back – the enemy is spying on us – Ronda knocked on the door to Ms Gallagher's room.

'What?' came the sharp voice from inside.

'It's me,' said Ronda.

'What do you want?'

'I was just passing.'

'So?'

'Kim said you were in good form,' said Ronda.

'No she didn't.'

'She said you weren't in foul form,' said Ronda.

'That sounds more likely,' said Ms Gallagher. 'Come in if you're coming.'

Ronda opened the door. Ms Gallagher was in her wheelchair by the window, reading. The sun had made a last minute appearance in the day, casting a soft light across her face, robbing it of its usual harshness. Ronda did not tell Ms Gallagher this. She would not take it well.

'So?' said Ronda, perching on the edge of the bed. 'To what do we owe this sunny disposition of yours?'

'Maybe I've resigned myself to my fate,' she said.

'You're not one for resignation,' said Ronda. 'When is the podcast coming out?' This elicited a smile from Ms Gallagher, which she tried to cover by pretending to yawn.

'It went well I take it?' said Ronda.

'It went better than expected,' said Ms Gallagher. 'But as you know, my expectations are low.'

Ronda, who also operated a low expectation philosophy, nodded. 'Do you need anything?' she asked as she stood up. She thought Ms Gallagher was holding her body more rigidly than usual.

'A wee reefer would be most acceptable right about now,' said Ms Gallagher, shifting carefully in her wheelchair.

'Are you in pain?' asked Ronda.

'Nothing a toke wouldn't cure,' said Ms Gallagher.

'I could ask the doctor to come and take a look at you?' said Ronda.

'Did I ever tell you about the day I knew I was a good,

old-fashioned, through and through, card-carrying lesbian?' said Ms Gallagher.

Ronda sat back down.

'It was in the accident and emergency room,' said Ms Gallagher, looking out of the window as the ghost of a smile crossed her face. 'I was thirteen years old, getting stitches on my forehead, just there.' She pointed to the skin just above her eyebrow. 'You can't make them out now. I got a dig from the butt of a soldier's rifle so I did. He took exception to me telling him to fuck off back to where he came from. Although I mightn't have put it that politely.' Ms Gallagher's grin broadened, as she remembered. 'The nurse who tended to me, she put thirteen stitches in my head. One for every year, she said. Bernadette. That was her name. She was only young. Not even twenty, I'd say. She kept asking if she was hurting me. "You can tell me to stop," she said. She was so careful with me. Tender. That was the first time I ever had cause to use such a word. I remember thinking things about her skin. And her smell. Things I'd never thought about before. I never told her to stop. And when she did I nearly howled with the pain of it. I tried to kiss her. She slapped me in the face and told me I was a filthy article. And lo, another lesbian was born.' Ms Gallagher finished with a flourish of her arms that Ronda could see was a struggle for her.

'I don't think there's any weed in the medical stores,' said Ronda, opening the door. 'But I'll see if I can find anything good.'

'Fine,' sighed Ms Gallagher, picking up her book. 'And if you dare tell anyone my cute little coming-of-age lesbian story, I'll have you kneecapped. I still know people.'

Over the next few days, whenever Ronda thought about Charlo and his treachery, she indulged in a fantasy of telling Ms Gallagher, who would immediately arrange to have Charlo dealt with. Instead, Ronda brought Sheila some of her favourite things: coconut snowballs and packets of candy popcorn and cans of Club Rock Shandy and Catch bars and liquorice pipes and a box of After Eights. Sheila never asked what she had done to deserve the sugar-soaked windfall. She methodically ate her way through the stash.

In the meantime, Charlo had not returned to Green Gables with his documents for Sheila to sign. But Ronda knew that it was only a matter of time.

CHAPTER 32

On Thursday, Ronda got delayed at work. Fergal had called an impromptu meeting at a quarter to five to explain the workings of the new clock-in-clock-out system that had recently been installed. He said it would only take five minutes. Now it was a quarter past five and Ronda was cutting it fine for her lesson. Margo had said she'd pick her up at No. 10 Casino Place at six p.m. sharp. Ronda sped out the back door and ran towards the bicycle shed, along the muddy track at the back of the building that skirted the hoarding around the construction works.

It was only when she started cycling she noticed the back tyre was flat. As she pumped it up, she could hear the air hissing out.

'Puncture?' Donal, walking through the car park, noticed her. Ronda nodded.

'I'll throw it on the van and give you a lift,' he said, rummaging in his pocket for his keys.

'Are you going my way?' asked Ronda.

'I am now,' said Donal, securing her bike beside his on the rack at the back of the van. Through the window, Ronda caught a glimpse of the inside, then looked away, not wanting to seem nosy.

'Would you like the grand tour?' asked Donal.

'I should get going,' Ronda said. 'I'm meeting Margo for a driving lesson.'

'The tour takes forty-two seconds,' said Donal. 'Come on.' He pulled at a handle and most of the side of the van slid open, revealing the interior.

'My mother told me never to get into a strange man's van,' said Ronda. It sounded like something Margo might say. Still, it landed okay because Donal laughed.

'And your mother definitely thinks I'm strange,' he said.

Ronda stepped inside. It was brighter than she'd imagined. Pale grey laminate on the floor, white panelling on the walls, windows along one side, each with their own roller blind and curtains, reminding Ronda of the dolls' house Margo got for Christmas one year. A bite-sized two hob induction oven. Overhead bins, miniature versions of the ones you get on planes. A wet room with a shower and built-in toilet, low to the ground and just wide enough to accommodate a modest posterior. There was a white table with yellow cushioned benches on either side. Ronda assumed it must turn into a bed. She noticed the chess set on the table. Cal, she presumed. A stack of books. Legal reference books, mostly. A Maeve Binchy paperback. A book of short stories by Kevin Barry. A well-thumbed DIY manual with the front cover hanging on by a few threads. A recipe book: *The Camper Van Cookbook*.

'It's compact,' said Donal. 'But I can always find my car keys now.'

Ronda's phone rang. It was Margo. 'I better take this,' she said.

'Sure,' said Donal. It had started raining, so he closed the door of the van, turned on the lamp, slotted himself in at the table and studied the chessboard.

'Hi Margo,' said Ronda. 'I should be there in twenty minutes, okay?'

'I'm really sorry, Ronda, I can't make the lesson today,' said Margo.

'What happened?' said Ronda. 'Are you okay?'

'I'm fine, but there's a Covid outbreak at the hospice. Two of our nurses are down with it, and three of the residents. I have to stay.'

'Of course,' said Ronda. 'I understand.' She did. The Covid chapter of Green Gables still felt raw. It had been a long and painful period, even though they'd had fewer deaths than most of their counterparts. But fewer wasn't none, and Ronda did her best not to think about that time.

'We can do the driving lesson another time,' said Ronda.

'Try not to sound too euphoric,' said Margo, a touch of her old self bubbling up. 'And will you let Mam know I won't make it around tonight. I said I might, earlier in the week.'

'Sure,' said Ronda.

'How is she?' asked Margo.

'Her plantar fasciitis is at her today.'

'How?' said Margo, exasperated. 'She literally walks nowhere.'

'Maybe that's how?' offered Ronda, although she was as much in the dark as her sister when it came to her mother's assortment of ailments.

'If only Dad hadn't died,' said Margo then. 'He'd have been great company for her, taken her out of herself.'

'Oh, my pager's going off, I better go,' said Ronda.

Talking about Gerry McCann to Margo was something that Ronda indulged in as seldom as she could get away with. It was like they'd had two different fathers. Which, Ronda supposed, they had. Margo had little memory of Gerry before he stopped drinking, the day after the accident.

He had been evangelical when it came to AA. His new religion. One day at a time until the lung cancer got him. He'd managed to kick the booze, but cigarettes had proved more difficult. If there had been an AA for smokers, perhaps he might have stopped. Ronda remembered his fingers, stained orange with nicotine. And the way he tapped each cigarette on the face of his watch before he struck the match, cupping his hand around the flame. The ceremony of it. And the pleasure. The way the first drag would ease him against the back of the armchair in the kitchen, the smoke settling over his head in layers.

Donal lifted his knight to capture a pawn. 'Sounds like you're off the hook,' he said.

'Are you sure you should do that?' asked Ronda, examining the board.

'No,' said Donal. 'But if I don't, Cal will take the knight. She's like that.'

'You could castle,' suggested Ronda. 'Then your rook can defend your knight.'

'Oh,' said Donal, studying the board. 'Yes. That's a better plan.' He picked up his rook and king, made the switch. 'Who taught you?' he asked.

'I taught myself,' said Ronda, putting her phone back in her pocket.

'Aren't you going to check your pager?' He smirked at her. Ronda flushed.

Donal stood up. 'I'll drop you home,' he said.

Ronda was surprised to find that she was not her usual sack of nerves in Donal's van. She supposed this could be down to a few things. For starters, she was a passenger, not a learner driver. So while she continued to scan the road for potential danger, and kept an eye on oncoming cars in case they veered into their lane, and hovered her foot over an imaginary brake, ready to screech to an imaginary halt should the need arise, she felt a lot more relaxed than she did in Margo's car.

Maybe not a lot more.

That was probably overstating it.

But a bit more, all the same.

Also, the camper van had wide, squashy, airplane-style seats, with armrests and cup holders. The seat belts were padded with memory foam to cushion passengers from any jerks or bumps. But there were no jerks or bumps, because that was another thing. Donal's driving. He drove as if he had no place to be and no particular time to be there. His hands were in the requisite ten to two position on the wheel, but they were not clenched. Nor were his knuckles white. His fingers tapped the beat to the song on the radio. Which happened to be 'Islands in the Stream'. Ronda smiled, remembering Kim's prediction about the song. It was a banger, as Sebastian would say. It took her mind off all the gruesome scenarios it usually produced when she was in a moving vehicle. She found herself leaning back against the seat and releasing the breath she had been prepared to hold for the length of the trip in one long, gentle sigh.

'You okay over there?' asked Donal. He asked the question without taking his eyes off the road, which further increased Ronda's feeling of calm. Not quite calm, but nearby. The suburbs of calm.

'You seem to enjoy driving,' said Ronda.

'I find it relaxing,' he said.

Ronda laughed.

'What's so funny?' Donal asked.

'Nothing,' she said. 'I just . . . I don't think that'll ever happen to me.'

'It might,' said Donal.

'Who taught you?' she asked.

'Tricia,' he said. 'My ex.'

There was a cyclist up ahead and Ronda's nerves woke up and stretched. Then clenched.

The cyclist was dressed in black, with no helmet. There were no lights on the bike. If the van hit a pothole, or the cyclist swerved out to avoid some impediment on the road, like a discarded can of Coke, or a . . .

Donal indicated, checked his mirrors and pulled out, giving the cyclist a wide berth so that they passed without incident.

'Tricia couldn't believe I couldn't drive when she met me,' Donal said. 'I had no interest in learning to be honest. I like bicycles and public transport.'

'Me too,' said Ronda.

'But it was handy,' said Donal, 'being able to drive, when the kids came along.'

He pulled in, put the handbrake on. Ronda was surprised to see they had arrived outside No. 10 Casino Place.

'Thanks for the lift,' she said, unclipping her seat belt. She put her hand on the door handle. Then she hesitated.

'Donal,' she said, turning back towards him.

'Yes Ronda?'

'Are you hungry?' she said.

'I'm starving.'

'Do you like risotto?'

'What kind?'

'Mushroom?'

'That's my favourite dinner.'

'And do you like vanilla ice cream with butterscotch sauce?'

'That's my favourite dessert.'

'Are you just saying that?

'No.'

'Do you want to come inside?'

'I thought you'd never ask.'

'Great,' said Ronda. Her smile reached across her face and up and down her body and soaked through her skin and filled up her insides with a warmth that felt like summer blooming. That hadn't been so difficult, had it? Maybe this could be the beginning of something. Maybe she could be someone who . . .

'Yes Ronda?' Donal was looking at her expectantly, waiting for her to say the thing that she had turned around to say.

'Oh,' she said. 'I just . . . There's no need for you to get out.' She put her hand back on the door handle. 'I'll get the bike off the rack.'

'It's no problem,' said Donal, unclipping his belt.

'No, no, it's fine,' said Ronda, opening the door. 'I've delayed you long enough. I'm sure you have plans.'

Donal looked at his watch. 'I'm meeting Tricia in a bit,' he said. 'We try to have dinner together once a week. Talk about the lads, you know. Check in.'

'That sounds cordial,' said Ronda, climbing out of the cab, stepping onto the road.

'Ah yeah,' said Donal. 'If it hadn't been for my courtroom

meltdown, the loss of my corporate ambition, and my spectacular about-face in terms of ideology and general hopes
and dreams, I'd say we'd still be arguing about whose turn it
is to take out the bins or unload the dishwasher.' He glanced
over Ronda's shoulder. 'Watch your back,' he said. Ronda
pasted herself against the side of the van as a car passed, so
close the back draught lifted her fringe.

It was Joseph.

'That guy wasn't taking any prisoners,' said Donal. 'You
okay?'

'I'm fine.'

'Well, enjoy your unexpected evening off,' said Donal,
turning over the engine.

'Thanks again.' Ronda lifted her bicycle off the rack at the
back of the van. Donal waved as he drove away.

Annie must have been watching out for her because she
opened the front door before Ronda had even locked her
bicycle to the fence.

'Did you hear about the outbreak at the hospice?' she
said. 'I'm worried now that I might have Covid too. Margo
was here the other day, she could have given it to me then,
couldn't she? She could be a carrier.'

'You had your booster shot recently,' said Ronda. 'You
should be fine.'

'I've got a scratchy throat,' said Annie, her voice heavy
with worry. 'And feel me, I'm hot, amn't I? I think I should
do a test.'

'I don't think we have any left,' said Ronda. Annie was a
keen Covid tester.

'You wouldn't go and pick some up, would you?' Annie
asked.

*

Ronda walked to the pharmacy. Night had fallen without her noticing. It started to drizzle. She pulled up her hood and pushed her hands into her pockets to warm them. She thought about Donal, having dinner with Tricia. She was sure it would be a companionable event, with wine maybe. The two of them laughing over something the twins had done. An achievement they'd managed. Or some obstacle they had overcome. She tried to imagine her and Joseph like that. Talking across a table about the children they hadn't stayed together long enough to have. What would that have been like? She was unable to conjure up the image in her head. She sped up. She didn't know why she was having these thoughts. She supposed it was because Joseph was around. She kept seeing him. He was like a ghost, haunting her.

Haunting the life they'd never had together.

Annie tested negative and celebrated with an early night.

Alone downstairs, Ronda tried to concentrate on her chess game, but thought about Donal instead. She wondered if he would mention her at dinner? Maybe she would feature as an amusing anecdote. A grown woman. Middle-aged. Learning how to drive. With a banjaxed bicycle and no plans for the evening.

No, she didn't think he would do that. It was more likely that he wouldn't mention her at all. Why would he?

CHAPTER 33

By Saturday, the worst of the Covid outbreak at the hospice had been contained. Margo's slavish attitude to rules and regulations combined with her keen work ethic and attention to detail made her exceptional at her job, especially in stressful conditions. While Ronda was delighted with this outcome, the speed with which Margo resumed the frantic pace of her life and attended to her many responsibilities was breakneck. One of those responsibilities was Ronda's driving lessons. 'We need to get you back in the saddle straight away,' Margo told her when she rang the doorbell – two short blasts, followed by a long, impatient one – at nine o'clock on Sunday morning.

'Come in,' said Ronda. 'Have you had breakfast?'

'When I say straight away, I mean right now,' said Margo, stepping into the hall, yanking Ronda's jacket off the newel post and ushering her out. 'I've literally got thirty minutes.'

Margo had parked in front of the Murphys' house, the L plate lit up by the unexpected warmth of the March sun. Through the sheer net curtains of the front bedroom, Ronda could see a silhouette. Tall enough to be Joseph. Ronda darted to the passenger door of Margo's car.

'Can you please drive to the business park?' begged Ronda. She couldn't bear Joseph to be a witness to her stammering, stuttering efforts to pull out onto the road.

Margo didn't put up much of a fight. Ronda suspected she

too had seen Joseph. 'But the stabilisers are coming off after this one,' said Margo, arranging herself behind the wheel. 'I've enough people to be mammying.'

Ronda admired how Margo pulled out and drove up the road without any of the angst that plagued Ronda's efforts.

'Could you reach into my bag and hand me my water bottle?' asked Margo, flying through a junction.

'Sure,' said Ronda, obliging.

Margo took an enormous swig out of the bottle. 'I've a bit of a head on me. It was the AGM of the Tidy Towns last night. They may be a lacklustre bunch, but they can put away an unmerciful amount of wine, I'll say that for them.'

'Was it a late night?' asked Ronda, trying to sound unconcerned.

'Got in some time after one, far as I remember,' said Margo, yawning.

Ronda closed her eyes and tried to do the breathing Fatima recommended and not worry about the slant of the sun making it difficult to see or the alcohol content that may or may not still be coursing through her sister's veins.

'Are you listening to me at all?' said Margo, jerking to a stop at a red light.

'Yes,' said Ronda. 'You were talking about booking yourself in for a facial peel and wondering if you could get some work done on your right eyelid that seems to be drooping of late. You got up early to have breakfast with Malcolm – you'd made breakfast bowls with toasted quinoa, almond, blueberries and coconut milk, but he didn't have time to eat because he was rushing to a golf tournament. Oh, and you've lost a kilo since last week although you were disappointed it wasn't two, but you're going to cut down on wine and replace it with vodka and slimline tonic.'

'Jesus,' said Margo, yanking on the handbrake. 'You make me sound so bloody boring and self-absorbed.'

'I was just letting you know that I am listening to you,' said Ronda.

'Do you see what I mean about my eyelid?' asked Margo, turning her face towards Ronda and closing her eyes.

'No,' said Ronda.

'Malcolm says it's only a minor procedure, I'd be in and out.'

'You're beautiful,' said Ronda. 'You don't need to change anything.'

'Do you really think so, Ronda?' It was strange to hear the uncertainty in Margo's voice.

'I do,' said Ronda.

If it hadn't been for the sudden appearance of a squirrel on the main road in the industrial estate park, the lesson would have gone without a hitch. Ronda only noticed the small grey squirrel as it was streaking across the road. She jammed on the brake. In her panic, she forgot to clutch in. The car cut out. The driver of the car behind them narrowly missed colliding into the back of them, and he leaned on his horn to demonstrate his displeasure. Margo pulled down her window and waved him past. 'You can't just stop like that in the middle of the road,' she told Ronda.

'Would you prefer me to kill a squirrel?' asked Ronda, gripping the wheel to hide the shake in her hands.

'As a driver, you have to be prepared to kill squirrels,' said Margo.

'That guy behind was driving much too close,' said Ronda.

'I agree,' said Margo, 'but other drivers' stupidity and aggressiveness is just something you have to factor in.'

'I suppose you think I'm not trying hard enough,' said Ronda.

'What?' said Margo.

'Mam told me.'

Margo sighed. 'Prove me wrong then,' she said.

Ronda watched the squirrel jump onto the lid of a bin. It crouched there, watchful, as if waiting for the next disaster to present itself.

'I can't kill a squirrel,' Ronda said.

'You mightn't ever have to,' said Margo brightly. 'Now drive on.'

Ronda would have admired Margo's tenacity were she not directly in its sights.

She drove on.

She still found it nerve-racking, how responsive the car was. Every action she made produced an immediate reaction, no matter how ill-advised that action may or may not be.

She got up into third gear, which was the highest one she'd managed so far. The idea of fifth terrified her. How would you get down from there?

'You're overthinking,' said Margo. 'Just go up one gear at a time and don't worry about how to get back down.' The engine was straining and there was nothing on the road ahead. No other cars. Or pedestrians. Or squirrels. Ronda pushed the clutch down and gripped the gear stick.

'Go on,' said Margo. 'You can do it.'

Ronda pulled the gear stick straight down as Margo had

demonstrated and eased up on the clutch. Slowly, slowly, until she felt the bite, then she lifted her foot all the way up. The car kept going. There was no protest from the engine, no juddering motion in the chassis.

'I'm in fourth gear,' she shouted.

Even Margo was impressed. 'I didn't think you'd actually do it,' she said. She held up her hand, palm outstretched.

'I can't high five you,' said Ronda.

'Take one hand off the wheel and high five me,' ordered Margo.

'I'm supposed to keep both hands on the wheel,' said Ronda.

'Just do it,' said Margo. 'My arm is getting tired.'

'Can I do it when we stop?'

'No.'

'Why not?' said Ronda.

'Because I said so and I'm in charge,' said Margo.

Ronda prised her left hand off the wheel and held it up. The minute Margo's palm made contact with her own, Ronda's hand flew back to the wheel, gripping it even tighter than before. Then, without allowing the thought to gain traction in her brain, she pushed the clutch in, grabbed the gear stick and guided it into fifth gear. She couldn't shout about it this time because her throat had constricted and her mouth was dry and she didn't think she'd be heard over the thudding of her heart in her chest. Instead, it was Margo who shouted, 'You're in fifth!' Which made Ronda jump and bite her tongue, although, with the adrenalin rampaging through her body, she wouldn't feel the pain of it until later.

'I don't know how to get back down,' she shouted.

'You do,' said Margo calmly, as they approached a junction near the entrance of the industrial estate.

It wasn't the smoothest manoeuvre. There was a bit of clanking and revving, and the stop itself was jerky and sudden. But Ronda managed to climb down through the gears without anyone beeping or cursing or swerving or screeching.

'Keep going,' shouted Margo.

'But we're at the entrance of the business park,' shouted Ronda.

'Keep. Going,' shouted Margo.

And Ronda did. The lights were green and she drove through them and then kept on driving.

'You're doing it,' shouted Margo.

'I'm not high fiving you again,' shouted Ronda.

'Fine,' shouted Margo.

Ronda drove through two junctions, three sets of lights, one yellow box and a chicane. It was true that she earned the ire of the drivers behind her given her sluggish speed, but she didn't care about that. She was driving.

She might be a late learner but she was driving. On a real road.

In real life.

CHAPTER 34

And suddenly, it felt like spring. Ronda noticed it around the grounds of Green Gables despite the noise and din of the construction work behind the hoarding. It was there in the nodding heads of daffodils, crowds of them lining the avenue up to the nursing home, like Ronda's very own welcoming committee.

And in the weather, still unpredictable but with hints of warmer, brighter days to come.

Fatima was putting the finishing touches on preparation for her Personal Interview. Ada had decided it would come down to Fatima's make-up. And her eyebrows. 'You can't underestimate the importance of a well-manicured brow,' Ada proclaimed in the dayroom. She was there most days after school. Fatima didn't like her being at the direct provision centre on her own. Once she had finished her homework, Ada practised make-up on the residents. All of them loved it, even Captain Grady, whose eyelashes – the longest in the dayroom – Ada raved about.

Ronda thought it was the attention they loved. The gentle stroke of a make-up brush against worn out skin. The closeness of another human being. Being the sole focus of somebody's attention.

These things were invaluable. Perhaps because they were rare.

Today it was Teresa's turn. She sat obediently in her

armchair, one hand resting on Baby, fast asleep in the crib beside her.

'Close your eyes for me,' Ada said, her fingers holding Teresa's narrow chin as she studied Teresa's face.

Teresa closed her eyes. Like everyone else, Teresa did everything Ada told her to. Ada picked up a wand and dipped it in powder, brushing a shimmering bronze eye-shadow across Teresa's eyelids.

'Ta-daaaa,' Ada sang when she was finished. Everybody clapped. Teresa peered at herself in the mirror Fatima gave her, cupped her hand over her mouth and giggled like a schoolgirl. For a moment, Teresa – the real Teresa, the before version – was right there, in the room. Ronda could only describe it as a power surge. A spike in the grid. Ronda could see Teresa. Everybody could. The vibrancy of her, all her bright colours coming into sharp focus.

Just for a moment.

And then she was gone.

'I'm not wearing that much stuff on my face at the inter-view,' laughed Fatima, backing away as Ada came at her with her make-up bag.

Ronda knew that Fatima would wear whatever make-up Ada deemed fit. Ada had already dissuaded her mother from wearing a green, white and orange head wrap.

'I want them to know how much I wish to stay in Ireland,' argued Fatima.

'Yes, but you don't want them to know you're mad,' said Ada. 'Which is what they will think if you arrive at the inter-view with your head wrapped in an Irish flag.'

'You like the wrap, don't you?' said Fatima, looking at Ronda, who kept a straight face as long as she could before she and Ada started laughing and couldn't stop. After a while, Fatima joined in.

'What's all the noise?' said Tracey, marching into the dayroom.

'It's laughter,' Ms Gallagher told her. 'You should try it some time, it might soften those frozen facial features of yours.'

Tracey's face flooded with blood. Ronda almost felt sorry for her. She grabbed at the handles of Ms Gallagher's wheelchair. 'You look like you could do with a nice cup of tea,' she said, pushing her out of the dayroom.

'If I drink another cup of tea, I swear I'll lose whatever's left of my mind,' groaned Ms Gallagher.

'I thought you might like a cup while you're listening to the podcast,' said Ronda.

Ms Gallagher whipped her head around, glared at Ronda. 'The podcast is out?' she said.

Ronda nodded.

'Well, why didn't you say so?'

'I presumed you knew,' said Ronda. 'Patricia emailed me with a link to the interview. She emailed you too.'

'Who has time to check emails with my busy schedule?' said Ms Gallagher but there was a trace of a smile on her face.

Ronda settled her by the window in her room, with a pot of tea and a toasted ham, cheese and tomato sandwich, her favourite lunch. Ms Gallagher turned on her tablet and found the link to the podcast in her Gmail. The clipped voice of Patrica Glennon poured through the Bose speaker on the windowsill. 'Hello and welcome to another episode of Whitewash. Today I've got an absolute treat for you.

It is my pleasure and privilege to introduce the legend that is Lyra Gallagher, one of the founders of the Irish Women's Liberation Organisation, set up in 1970. Gallagher is also chiefly responsible for organising the contraceptive train from Dublin to Belfast on an early summer's day back in 1971, returning to Connolly station with her pockets full of condoms and spermicides and pills and all sorts of other prophylactic treats. Lyra Gallagher, you are very welcome to Whitewash.'

There was silence for a bit after that. Ronda imagined that Ms Gallagher had done one of her stiff nods after the exuberance of the introduction. Then Patricia Glennon asked a question: 'So, Lyra . . . Is it okay if I call you Lyra?'

'You just did,' came the familiar, disgruntled voice.

One of those nervous laughs followed, then Patricia cleared her throat and got into gear. 'You grew up the daughter of a single mother in Belfast back in the forties and fifties, can you tell us what that was like?'

'My mother said I was born shouting and roaring and that I never let up,' Ms Gallagher began, as Ronda tiptoed to the door. There was an amused expression across Ms Gallagher's face, as if she was catching up with someone she knew long ago.

Someone she liked.

CHAPTER 35

After the high-five day, the next couple of lessons were uneventful. Which is to say that Ronda had given Margo no reason to raise her voice, roll her eyes or grip the handbrake in a pre-emptive strike. After the latest lesson, instead of shovelling Ronda out of the car and scorching off to complete the next item on her interminable 'To-do' list, Margo remained in the passenger seat and studied Ronda's face as if she was committing it to memory.

'What?' said Ronda, uncomfortable with the scrutiny. She wiped her fingers across her mouth. 'Do I have something caught in my teeth?'

'I never thought I'd say this, but you're actually starting to drive like a normal person,' said Margo.

'Go easy on the positive feedback,' said Ronda.

Margo picked up her handbag. 'There's a slim chance that you could – maybe – pass the test,' she went on.

The moisture inside Ronda's mouth evaporated. 'No,' she said. 'It's much too soon. There's no way I'm ready.'

'I'm going to book you in,' went on Margo as if Ronda had said nothing.

'You can't,' said Ronda. 'I've only had ten lessons. Amn't I supposed to have done twelve before I can apply?'

Margo waved away Ronda's concerns, like she was swatting at a fly. 'There's a backlog,' she said, whipping her mobile out of her bag. 'It'll take months for a test to come up, and by then, you'll have done your twelve and more besides.' Margo's certainty was catching, and Ronda found herself bewitched by it. Nearly believing it. By the time she snapped out of it, it was too late. Margo had already booked her in for the test.

'You owe me eighty euros,' she told Ronda. 'You can—'

'Revolut you, I know,' said Ronda.

Now that the driving test was booked, Margo insisted on doubling down on the lessons. 'Two a week,' she said in a tone that was not to be argued with. Oddly, Ronda did not feel like arguing, even if she had been the argumentative type. For starters, what would have been the point? She'd never won an argument with Margo. Also, wasn't this the point of the enterprise? To undergo a driving test? Get her licence, stay at No. 10 Casino Place? There was a certain fatalism about the whole thing now. No going back. All Ronda could do was hope for the best.

'It's about time you applied for that test,' said Ms Gallagher in the dayroom the following afternoon. She'd lost a bit of weight, Ronda thought. The chest infection she'd had recently had taken a bite out of her.

'It feels much too soon,' said Ronda, pouring popcorn into a bowl and handing it to Sheila, whose eyes were glued to the big screen where Gene Kelly was singing and dancing in the rain.

'When you get to my age, you'll realise there's no such thing as too soon,' said Ms Gallagher. 'Time is of the essence, Ronda.'

'Wouldn't you think he'd put the brolly over his head?'

said Sheila, shaking her head. 'He's soaked to the skin, so he is.'

'It's a film,' snapped Ms Gallagher. 'Nobody was struck down with pleurisy in the making of it.'

'My poor husband died of pleurisy, I'll have you know,' sniffed Sheila.

'Your husband is alive and kicking, more's the pity,' said Ms Gallagher.

'You got post today,' said Ronda, wheeling Ms Gallagher out of Sheila's earshot.

'Post?' Ms Gallagher looked confused. She rarely got post.

'There's a pile of it,' said Ronda. 'I think it might be fan mail. People who heard you on the podcast.'

Ms Gallagher snorted.

'I'll leave you in your room and I'll go collect it from reception, okay?'

'I suppose so,' said Ms Gallagher, doing her damnedest to sound nonchalant.

On the corridor, Ronda met Fergal. He looked and smelled like he was going somewhere nice for lunch.

'We have a leak,' Ronda told him. 'One of the sinks in the toilets.'

'The visitor toilets?' asked Fergal, slowing from a stride to a trot.

'No, it's the staff one beside the storage cupboard. I think we need a plumber.'

'Don't worry,' said Fergal airily. 'Ernest will fix it.'

'Ernest tried. He says we need a plumber,' said Ronda.

'Isn't Ernest a plumber?'

'He's a handyman.'

'Exactly,' said Fergal, looking at his watch. 'I'm popping out for an hour or so. Tracey is out too, so I'm leaving you in charge of the unit, Ronda. I'm sure you'll be glad of an opportunity to flex your managerial muscle, show us what you're made of.'

'Yes, of course,' said Ronda. 'And perhaps we could talk about that supervisory role when you get back?' she added, trying to inject a bit of Margo into her voice.

Fergal patted her arm. 'Let's not run before we can walk,' he said, quickening his pace as he set off up the corridor again. 'I'll be gone about two hours, three, tops.' He darted through the double doors before Ronda had a chance to tell him that her shift ended in two hours. Now she would have to stay late, and, under the new regime, there was no paid overtime any more. There was nothing to be done but get through it as best she could. Show Fergal how she could handle the responsibility without any problems.

The strategy worked very well until visiting time.

CHAPTER 36

The day began to disimprove around four o'clock, as the closing credits of *Singing in the Rain* scrolled up the big screen. Ronda, who had thrown windows open earlier in a flurry of spring, now ran around closing them against the chill wind that had picked up. The sky darkened and a light drizzle fell. By the time the visitors started to arrive, rain lashed in sheets against the windows, making it difficult to see through the glass. Ronda helped Fatima with the afternoon tea round. According to the newly edited policy booklet, they were no longer supposed to offer visitors a cup of tea or coffee or one of the muffins that now came wrapped in plastic with condensation forming along the inside of the packaging. But it was not in Ronda's gift to pass people over when it came to tea and buns, no matter how unappetising the buns happened to be. In Ronda's experience, the visitors were grateful for any warm drink or sweet treat they might receive at Green Gables. A bit of comfort. Something to do with their hands as they wracked their brains, trying to come up with something new to say. Or resigning themselves to a repeat of the conversation they'd just had, the threads of it already lifting away, like kite tails, impossible to catch. The visitors always thanked Ronda for the warm drinks, wrapping their hands around the cups, as if it were cold, which of course, at Green Gables, it never was.

A woman arrived. She stepped inside the dayroom and

looked around. Ronda was pouring tea for Captain Grady and Sean when she noticed her. The woman was younger than Ronda, perhaps in her late thirties. She was a bit thrown together, as if she'd left home in a hurry. She wore loose-fitting clothes, grey track pants and a hoodie tied around her waist, her fair hair falling down the length of her back in a long ponytail. Her T-shirt was black, and Ronda spotted a pale circular stain on the shoulder, the unmistakeable call-ing card of a newborn baby. She remembered Margo's boys throwing up on her shoulder, the handful of times Margo let her wind them. She recalled the warm, sweet smell of it, marvelling at how even a baby's sick was somehow adorable and brand new.

The woman glanced around the room and made her way towards Ronda. 'Excuse me?' she said. Her accent was English. Perhaps northern.

'Hello,' said Ronda. She made sure to smile warmly at the woman, who had a look of flight-risk about her, as if she might bolt out the door at any minute.

The woman took a breath, pushing at a strand of hair that had escaped the ponytail. 'I'm looking for Teresa Keogh.'

'Room Number 23,' Teresa called from the corner of the room where Fatima was helping her change Baby's nappy. 'The house was beside the bakery. We could smell the bread in the mornings.'

'She's over there,' said Ronda, gesturing towards Teresa. The woman seemed to study Teresa, who appeared oblivi-ous to the scrutiny.

'Are you a relative?' Ronda asked.

The woman looked at Ronda again. 'I'm a . . . family friend,' she said.

'I'm sure Teresa will be happy to see you,' said Ronda. 'She doesn't get many visitors, apart from her sister of course.'

The woman looked again at Teresa, who was rocking Baby to sleep in her arms, singing 'Rock-a-bye Baby'.

'Is she . . . okay?' the woman asked.

'She has dementia,' said Ronda. 'But she's physically healthy. I'll bring you over.'

The woman seemed disinclined to move. Teresa looked up, perhaps feeling the weight of the woman's stare after all.

Captain Grady began an argument with Sheila, who refused to stand to attention and salute him.

'You're not the boss of me,' said Sheila, pointing her finger at him.

'This is insubordination,' said Captain Grady, struggling to get himself out of his chair. Sean pulled him back down. 'Stop shouting,' he hissed at his father. 'You're not scaring anyone any more.'

'If my husband was alive, he'd put manners on you,' said Sheila.

Fatima slotted herself between Captain Grady and Sheila. 'How about a game of musical statues?' she said.

'Bagsy doing the music,' said Kim, making a beeline for the stereo.

'R and R,' said Captain Grady, smiling as he rubbed his hands together.

Sean looked at his watch and stood up, 'I'd better go,' he said. 'I'm on a double shift today.'

'Are you not staying for the rest and recreation?' Captain Grady asked, his smile slipping.

'I mightn't be here next week,' said Sean.

'You're not going AWOL are you?' said Captain Grady.

'It's mid term,' said Sean. 'Linda's going away with her . . . with a friend of hers. I thought I'd take Eddie to my cousin's mobile in Brittas for a few days. Not that he wants to go.'

'Are you coming back?' asked Captain Grady, looking worried.

Sean nodded. 'Yeah,' he said. 'I'll come back.'

Ronda crouched beside Teresa's armchair. 'Teresa,' she said. 'You have a visitor. It's . . .' Ronda looked at the woman, who had come to a stop, about two metres from Teresa's chair.

'Kate,' the woman said. The name tugged at some strand of memory in Ronda's head although, at that moment, she couldn't remember where she'd heard it. Teresa seemed to stare through and past the woman, as if she wasn't there at all.

'Hello Teresa,' said Kate, taking a step closer.

'Sssh,' said Teresa. 'Baby's asleep.'

'Oh,' said Kate, whispering now. 'I'm sorry.'

'Kate's come to visit you,' said Ronda, dragging an armchair beside Teresa's. 'Sit down there,' she said to Kate. 'I'll bring you a cup of tea.' There was something a bit spent about the woman. She was pale and thin, the outline of her clavicle visible beneath the thin cotton of her T-shirt. She looked like she could do with some food. Ronda thought there might be a fruit scone left over from earlier. And Fergal and Tracey weren't around to object. Ronda was in charge.

When Kate smiled, she looked younger. 'That's so kind,' she said to Ronda, lowering herself into the armchair. 'Thank you.'

*

In the kitchen, Ronda cut the last scone in half and slathered butter and cherry jam on both sides. She was pouring tea into a cup when she heard something. A raised voice? Perhaps just a dispute over one of Fatima's musical statue judgements, which happened not infrequently. Ronda arranged the tea and scone onto a tray and opened the kitchen door. The noise was immediately amplified. Someone shouting. And music, blaring. Freddie Mercury asking, 'Is this a kind of magic?'

Ronda ran down the corridor, into the dayroom, the cup and plate rattling around the tray.

Kim was no longer standing by the stereo, her finger hovering over the Pause button. Instead, she and Fatima were doing their best to calm Teresa down.

It was Teresa who was shouting, louder than Ronda would have thought. She leaped to her feet, like a much younger, agile version of herself. It was Kate she was shouting at. 'Liar, liar, liar,' she shouted, stabbing her finger towards Kate. She kept saying it, over and over. Even Baby was forgotten in the scorch of her fury. The doll lay on the floor beside Teresa's slippered feet.

Kate stood in front of Teresa, rigid, her hands clamped across her mouth. She was even paler than before.

Fatima and Kim tried to persuade Teresa back into her chair, but she pulled herself free of their hands and took to her heels. Ronda watched as Teresa stopped momentarily in front of a table where newspapers and magazines were displayed. She swiped at them, until they were all in a heap on the floor. Kim, following her, slipped on the face of Sharon Horgan, who was on the cover of that month's *VIP* magazine. 'I'm fine,' she said, as Ronda rushed over to her.

Freddy Mercury got to the end of the song. Some of the dancers froze in place. Some, upset by the bedlam, put their hands over their ears. Some kept on dancing. All of them watched Teresa as she rampaged around the room. Any cups and saucers Teresa encountered on footstools and occasional tables, she picked up and flung. They made a tremendous crash as they shattered on the floor, spilling their dregs in puddles. Following in her wake was Fatima, impeded by a terrified Sheila, who had her two arms clamped around Fatima's waist as she cowered behind her back.

Teresa pushed her way into the throng of dancers. For a moment, it seemed as if Captain Grady might be the one to call a halt to the bedlam. He was one of the dancers who had remained still as a statue once the music dribbled away, being keen on rules and regulations. However, as Teresa came his way, he released himself from his stance and stepped in front of her.

'This calls for a court martial,' he declared with great authority.

Teresa stopped running and stood in front of him, no longer shouting. Then she reached up and grabbed the peaked military hat Captain Grady wore indoors and out, pitched it on the floor, stamping on it until it was as flat as one of the silver medals on his lapel. With each stamp of her foot, Teresa shouted her one-word mantra, 'Liar. Liar. Liar.' Now the rest of the dancers took up the mantra too, as if it was the chorus of a song they all remembered from their dance hall days.

Ronda reached Teresa and put her arms around her, half hug, half restraint. Teresa howled as Ronda pulled her back so her foot could no longer reach the flattened hat. Captain

Grady was roaring at her, something about disobeying a direct order, and Ronda in the middle, trying to talk them all down.

'What on earth is going on here?' Ronda looked up to see Fergal standing in the doorway. The noise of the room dribbled away, like water down a drain. The dancers stopped dancing, Teresa stopped shouting, Kim picked herself off the floor, brushing dust off her skirt.

Fatima recovered first. 'Come on everybody,' she said, clapping her hands. 'Take a seat and I'll put a Daniel O'Donnell DVD on.'

Teresa was the only one who didn't move. She stood rigid, like a musical statue, her body heaving with her breath. It was only then that Ronda realised that Kate was gone.

'I think this little one needs her bottle,' Ronda said, picking Baby off the floor and handing the doll to Teresa. Teresa nodded and allowed herself to be led back to her chair.

'The house was beside the bakery,' Teresa whispered against the hard plastic of the doll's head. 'We could smell the bread in the mornings.' Her voice was hoarse after the shouting. Her pale, milky eyes shimmered with tears, and when she blinked they rolled down her face, hung from the thin line of her jaw before dropping onto the doll's face, so that it looked like Baby was crying too. Ronda reached for a box of tissues.

'My office,' Fergal hissed at Ronda. 'Now.' He swept away before Ronda could respond. She pulled a tissue out of the box, wiped Baby's cheeks, then held it against the delicacy of Teresa's face, blotting her tears.

'You go on,' said Fatima, taking the box from Ronda's hands. 'I'll look after these two.' She handed Teresa Baby's bottle. Teresa shook it on her wrist, licked the transparent skin there, checking that the milk was not too warm and not too cold. It must have been just right because Teresa slipped the teat carefully into Baby's mouth.

Ronda hurried up the corridor after Fergal. Ms Gallagher sat in her wheelchair at her bedroom door as Ronda walked past. 'Don't let the bastards grind you down, Ronda,' she called after her.

At the door to his office, Fergal paused and told Ronda, in a clipped tone, to give him five minutes, he had an important phone call to make first. He never said he had a bog-standard phone call to make. They were always important ones. Ronda was right about him being out for lunch. There was a piece of gristle caught between his front teeth.

'Sure,' said Ronda, hoping he would use at least some of the five minutes to brush his teeth. She continued up the corridor, through the doors and into the reception area. Monika caught her eye and pointed towards the ladies' toilets, then at a name, printed in the visitors' book. Kate Deering. Under the address section, Kate had written, 'Manchester, UK.'

'Thanks Monika,' said Ronda, as she walked towards the ladies.

Kate was at the washbasin, collecting cold water in her hands and sluicing her face. When she was finished, she groped her hand towards the paper towel dispenser. Ronda handed her one. Kate wiped her face and looked at Ronda's reflection in the mirror. Her eyes were puffy and red.

'I'm sorry,' she said. 'I shouldn't have come here.'

'Why don't you sit down for a minute,' said Ronda, gesturing towards a small leather couch along the wall.

'I should go,' said Kate.

'How do you know Teresa?' asked Ronda gently.

'I don't,' said Kate. 'I was born in a mother and baby home. I'm pretty sure Teresa is my birth mother.'

Ronda nodded. That made sense.

'Teresa wasn't delighted to hear the news, as you just witnessed,' said Kate.

'Teresa has dementia,' said Ronda. 'She's not herself.'

'I know,' said Kate. 'I just thought, maybe . . . She might see me and then . . . I don't know what I was thinking really, it was such a long time ago. I was only in the home for four months before I was adopted.' She looked down at her chest. Two damp patches spread across the front of her T-shirt. 'I have to go,' she said. 'My daughter needs feeding.' She threw the paper towel into the bin and walked to the door.

'Will you come back?' Ronda called after her. 'Teresa might be in better form another day.'

Kate shook her head. 'Thank you for being so kind,' she said, opening the door. She crossed the reception area towards the exit, stabbing at the door release like she couldn't wait to get out. Ronda didn't blame her. Outside, Kate sprinted towards an old Vauxhall estate, its engine idling. A man sat behind the wheel, anxiously tracking Kate's progress across the car park. Ronda could see a car seat in the back. Kate opened the back door, tucked herself in beside it, leaned down. A tiny hand reached up to pull at a strand of Kate's hair. The engine revved and the car disappeared down the avenue.

Ronda jumped as Monika's voice boomed through the tannoy. 'Ronda to Fergal's office. Ronda McCann to Fergal Hutch's office immediately.'

'I'm right here,' said Ronda, walking towards the reception desk.

'Fergal asked me to make the announcement over the PA system,' said Monika.

Ronda sighed.

'He is not in a good mood,' said Monika.

Ronda smoothed her hair with her hands and rubbed at a tea stain on the front of her scrubs. She straightened and pulled her face into a smile.

'How do I look?' she asked.

Monika shrugged. 'Same as always,' she said.

Fergal was behind the desk in his office, his arms folded tightly across his chest. He had not brushed his teeth.

'What the hell was all that?' he asked.

'I'm sorry,' said Ronda.

'Sorry?' Fergal repeated, like the word was a mouldy grape he had unwittingly bitten into. 'You were supposed to be in charge. I trusted you. You said you could handle it. And I come back to this . . . this . . . this circus.' The tip of Fergal's nose became paler and paler until it was a bloodless circle of pure white. Ronda tried not to look at it.

'Well?' said Fergal, his voice gaining volume now. 'What have you got to say about any of this?' He waved his arms over his head, like a soldier, shot but not yet fallen.

Ronda felt anger surge through her veins. She went to stand up, then realised she was already standing. Fergal hadn't even offered her the courtesy of a seat before lambasting her. Nor had he offered her the benefit of the doubt by asking for an explanation. The anger surged again. Ronda thought she might burst with it.

'What do you expect?' she said, and her voice was low and deliberate, shocking in its intensity. It also seemed to shock Fergal, shutting him up and pasting him back against his chair like a centrifugal force. 'There aren't enough staff to take care of the increased number of residents you've admitted since the sale,' she went on. 'The staff we have are completely overworked, underpaid, unappreciated, unsupported, disrespected.' Ronda counted the adjectives on her fingers, only stopping when she had used up all the digits on her left hand. 'And still, they do their best,' she raged on. 'Because they care about the residents. You are taking advantage of their beautiful, generous natures. They show up here every day and do their best to do their jobs. In spite of your death by a thousand cuts policies that have been introduced since the takeover. Those cuts are as painful as the toilet paper in the staff loos. You could cut your arse with it.'

Ronda stopped to draw breath. She didn't think she'd ever said 'arse' before. And she'd really spat the word, so it sounded even more coarse. It felt good. Ronda could feel a smile splitting her face in two. She tried to rein it in, but it was too strong. Her blood surged down her vessels like a stampede of buffalo. She could barely contain it.

'Ronda.' Fergal's voice was a sliver. Ronda looked at him. The arms that had been over his head were lowering now, the soldier registering the shot, falling in slow motion. He clutched at his chest, grabbing handfuls of his shirt. A button flew off.

'Ronda,' he said again, his voice rasping now, as if Ronda had taken all the oxygen in the room and there was none left for him. The white spot at the tip of his nose had spread to the rest of his face and his lips were tinged with blue.

251

Ronda rushed to him, pulled him off the chair and dragged him out from behind his desk. She laid him across the floor, grabbed the tight collar of his shirt in two hands and yanked it open, revealing a white vest. His neck was long and sinewy and there was a birthmark in the shape of a canoe at the top of his skinny, white chest. Ronda knew that, whatever happened, Fergal would always hate the fact that Ronda had seen his vest. She put one hand on top of the other, interlocked her fingers and placed them on Fergal's chest, pressing down fast and hard.

'Fergal,' she shouted at him. 'Can you hear me?' His eyes were open and staring. Ronda kept pressing, calling for help through the door of Fergal's office. 'Can anybody hear me?' she roared, as she pushed her hands into Fergal's chest. 'Help me,' she shouted over and over again, to the rhythm of her hands, pressing into the soft cotton of his vest.

The door flew open and there was Fatima, looking down at them, taking in the situation. Relief flooded through Ronda. Fatima hurried to the phone on Fergal's desk, picked up the receiver and dialled.

'I need an ambulance,' she said, giving the Green Gables Eircode and address. 'Yes,' she said, her eyes travelling across Fergal's blue-white face and limp body.

'It is an emergency.'

CHAPTER 37

Fergal was kept in hospital for three days. During his absence from Green Gables, Tracey stepped into his shoes as though they were slippers that he had warmed by the fire for her. Fergal was sent home with a stent in his coronary artery and strict orders not to smoke, drink, eat any of the food he liked, have sex with his wife or return to work for at least a month.

He didn't mind not having sex with his wife.

Kate did not return to Green Gables. Teresa never mentioned her.

'You seem a bit distracted,' said Margo a few days later, as Ronda drove towards No. 10 Casino Place at the end of a driving lesson.

'I'm fine,' said Ronda, indicating to pull in.

'Something's up,' said Margo. 'You didn't have a conniption when the guy on the motorbike undertook you at the junction.'

'I thought I wasn't supposed to be having conniptions when I'm behind the wheel?' said Ronda, turning off the engine.

'Yes, but that never stopped you before,' said Margo. 'Something's eating away at your foundations.'

Ronda sighed. 'Fatima's Personal Interview is next week.'

'That's good isn't it?' said Margo.

'Not if her application is rejected,' said Ronda. 'Then there's Fergal.'

'I thought he died,' said Margo.

'He's coming back to work this week,' said Ronda.

'Didn't he have a cardiac arrest?' said Margo.

Ronda shook her head. 'Angina,' she said. 'He was supposed to be off for a month.' She opened the car door.

'Wait,' said Margo. 'I have news.'

'Is it good or bad?' asked Ronda.

'It depends on your disposition I suppose,' said Margo.

'Bad then,' said Ronda, closing the door.

'I got a date for your driving test,' said Margo, her eyes gleaming.

'What?'

'I know,' said Margo. 'I was surprised too.'

'When?' asked Ronda, her fingers tightening around the wheel.

'Don't worry,' said Margo. 'It's not for another three weeks.'

'Three weeks!' Ronda shouted.

'It'll be fine,' said Margo. 'You just need to calm down and—'

'You said it would take ages to get an appointment,' said Ronda. 'Months, you said.'

'Well, they've obviously improved the system,' said Margo. 'More good news, right?'

Ronda slumped against her seat. Before now, the driving test – the actual doing of it – had seemed like some vague, theoretical, distant aim. Like meditation. Something you talk about but never actually get around to doing.

'Well?' said Margo, picking lip balm out of her handbag and smearing it across her lips. 'How do you feel?

Ronda's mouth was so dry, she didn't think she could peel her tongue off the roof of it.

'You're not going to hyperventilate, are you?' Margo peered into Ronda's face. 'I didn't think you could get much paler, but there isn't a drop of blood in your face.'

Ronda reached for her water bottle and took an enormous slug.

'I won't pass the test,' she finally managed to say.

'That's the spirit,' said Margo, grinning.

'Do you think I'll pass it?'

'It doesn't matter what I think,' said Margo.

'It matters to me,' said Ronda.

There was silence after that declaration. Margo looked surprised before she collected herself.

'I don't fail,' she told Ronda. 'Which means, neither will you.'

CHAPTER 38

'How do I look?' It was the day of Fatima's interview at the International Protection Office. She stood in front of Ronda, ramrod straight with her arms held stiffly at her sides. She was wearing a black suit she had borrowed from one of the refugees at the centre. The jacket was a little tight and the colour a little faded. This suit was no stranger to the interview rooms at the IPO.

'You look perfect,' said Ronda.

'What about my hair?' asked Fatima. She had straightened it and pulled it into a bun at the back of her head.

'No Irish flag head wrap?' asked Ronda, trying to make Fatima smile. It didn't work. 'How are you feeling?' asked Ronda.

'I'll feel better once it's over,' said Fatima.

'Don't forget to breathe,' Ronda said.

The interview would be difficult, Donal had warned. Long too. An hour. Maybe even longer than that. Her reasons for seeking asylum were personal rather than political. That meant the questions would be personal. But Fatima would have to answer them. She would have to tell her story, tell them about the coercive control and the domestic abuse, the stalking and the spying, the cold, clammy fear in the pit of her stomach when she woke up every morning, and the suffocating helplessness that smothered her when Noah started looking at Ada, not like a father but a predator, in the months before they made their escape. She couldn't leave anything out, she had to be consistent, recall exactly what she had written in the reams and reams of forms she had filled in when they had arrived. She had to stay in control, be authentic, make them believe her.

She looked at her watch. 'I'd better go,' she said. 'Donal's picking me up outside.'

Ronda reached for Fatima's hands and they stood like that for a moment, holding hands, not speaking.

Then Fatima turned and left.

Ronda got back to work. She was already behind on her rounds. Eight more residents to see before lunch. With the new timetable in place, there was very little wriggle room for things that were not planned activities. Things that just happened. Like conversations with Ms Gallagher. Or watching the finches with Sheila, after she'd scattered nuts and seeds along the windowsill outside her bedroom window.

Every time the door to the dayroom opened, Ronda looked up to see if it was Fatima, back from her interview. Or maybe Kate Deering. Ronda held out a sliver of hope that Kate might return to see Teresa. To the casual observer, it looked like Teresa was her usual self, feeding Baby, winding her, changing her nappy. But there was something lacklustre about her, Ronda felt. It was perhaps in the way she held the doll. Loosely by the hand, instead of tucked tight into the crook of her elbow. And Ronda hadn't heard her sing 'Rock-a-bye Baby' since Kate had left.

Ronda hurried towards the dispensary to get Captain Grady's medication. He should have had it an hour ago, but

Tracey had been delayed at a meeting. Halfway down the corridor, a familiar voice behind her.

'There you are, Ronda.' It was Fergal.

Ronda had not seen him since the cotton vest day. Today was his first day back. Tracey had issued strict instructions that he was not to be besieged with enquiries about his health or his speedy return to work. 'He's fine,' she'd assured them.

'Hello,' said Ronda, smiling like nothing out of the ordinary had taken place between them. Like she had not seen his soft little cotton vest that covered a chest so skinny it was almost concave.

'I just wanted to say . . .' began Fergal, straightening his already straight tie. 'You know, thanks and all that,'

'You're welcome,' said Ronda. Fergal nodded and moved back towards his office, then stopped abruptly and turned. 'I had the weirdest dream,' he said. 'When I was, you know, having that little turn.'

'A dream?' said Ronda, confused.

'Yes,' said Fergal. 'You were shouting at me, can you imagine?' He chuckled as he recalled the exchange. 'Something about toilet paper,' he said, mostly to himself, shaking his head at the absurdity of the dream.

Ronda was rigid, as if she was frozen to the spot. She had assumed that her diatribe had been all in her head. Fergal didn't appear to notice her discomfiture.

'Crazy, eh?' he said, smiling.

'Eh yes,' Ronda managed, with a weak smile.

'I'm afraid I do have to write up a report on what happened in the dayroom when you were in charge,' went on Fergal. 'It's standard procedure. I'm sure you understand.'

'Of course,' said Ronda.

'Where is Fatima?' asked Fergal then. 'She wasn't in the kitchen when I passed it.'

'She's on a half day,' said Ronda, not mentioning the interview at the IPO. She didn't want to give him an opportunity to express his concern about Ireland's 'open door' policy as he called it, conveniently forgetting that the majority of his staff were immigrants.

Fergal sighed as if it were he who was going to have to do the scrubbing and sweeping and reheating in the kitchen.

'I should get back to the dayroom,' said Ronda.

'Of course, of course,' said Fergal. 'The wheels of industry aren't going to turn by themselves, are they?'

Captain Grady had removed the medals from his jacket to polish them, but was unable to put them back exactly as they had been before, and he was becoming agitated. 'I need to get them back on before the colonel carries out the inspection,' he said, looking at the door as if the colonel might appear at any moment. There was a framed photograph of Captain Grady outside an army barracks on his bedside table. Ronda picked it up and studied the positioning of the medals.

'At ease, soldier,' he told her, as she pushed one of the pins through the thick material of the lapel of his uniform.

'I am at ease,' she said, reaching for the next medal.

Captain Grady shook his head. 'No,' he said. 'You are not at ease.' This surprised Ronda. Not because it wasn't true. It was true. She had shouted at Fergal. Actually shouted at him. In real life. She hadn't just imagined it. She'd gone ahead and done it. There seemed to be a glitch in her filter. Some kind of malfunction. Was it a one-off? There was no way to know.

'You're right, Captain Grady,' she said. 'I'm not at ease.'

He patted her arm. 'It's only to be expected,' he said. 'When you're in no-man's land.'

'Am I in no-man's land?' Ronda couldn't help asking the question.

'Yes,' said Captain Grady, standing up and running his fingers across his newly polished medals. 'All we can do at this point is soldier on.'

Fatima soldiered on when she returned to Green Gables after the interview. She kept a low profile in the kitchen, having been warned of Fergal's premature return to work by Monika. So Ronda didn't have a chance to ask about the interview until later in the afternoon. Fatima said it had gone really well. But it was difficult to know if this conclusion was reached because of Fatima's optimistic disposition. Or if it was an accurate assessment of the interview itself.

They would know soon enough.

CHAPTER 39

While Patricia Glennon was true to her word, carefully editing out any mention of Edel Scanlan on the podcast, she had made no promises regarding the column she wrote for a glossy magazine that came with one of the weekend newspapers. The following Sunday, Patricia's column was headed, 'Love in the Time of Contraceptive Trains'. It was, for the most part, a plug for the podcast, shot through with voluptuous details of the explosive love story of one Lyra Gallagher and Edel Scanlan, as a way of baiting the readers and leading them by the hand to the interview.

Ms Gallagher, being old school, had several newspapers delivered to her room every morning. And even though she called the Sunday paper in question, 'a rag', she nonetheless went through it each week, just in case.

'In case of what?' Ronda had asked. But Ms Gallagher had withered her with one of her looks and returned to an article about washed-up reality TV stars under a 'Where are they now?' headline.

It was Margo who alerted Ronda to Patricia's column, ringing her at eight o'clock on Sunday morning. Ronda, who was not on duty until lunchtime, was in bed, not quite asleep, but not fully awake either, an enjoyable halfway house where the drudge of the day ahead was only a vague possibility.

She could hear purring and wondered, in her dreamy, heavy-limbed state, if it was her.

It was Jessica Fletcher, who had shouldered her way into Ronda's bedroom, taking advantage of the loose latch on the door some time during the night. Ronda turned in her narrow single bed and Jessica Fletcher, dislodged from her position behind Ronda's knees, stopped purring and was now sitting on Ronda's hip, kneading her body with both paws.

When the phone rang, Ronda sat up, forcing Jessica Fletcher to seek attention elsewhere.

'Have you seen the article?' It was Margo.

'What article?' asked Ronda, rubbing sleep out of her eyes as Jessica Fletcher hissed at her from the floor, her back arched, high as a viaduct.

'That woman, from Whitewash,' Margo went on. 'Patricia Glennon. She's written all about your Ms Gallagher and her lady love, Edel Scanlan.'

Ronda flung back the duvet, fully awake now.

'I don't know where she got the photograph, it's stunning,' Margo went on. 'All moody in black and white, and the pair of them draped across a sofa smoking their heads off.'

'I have to go.' Ronda hung up and swung her legs out of bed, narrowly missing Jessica Fletcher, who continued to hiss and spit, albeit to an empty room now as Ronda flew into the bathroom. It was early enough. There was a chance she could get to Green Gables before the newspapers arrived. Ms Gallagher had been almost happy recently. Yes, she was still doing her damnedest to be her cantankerous self, but she was finding it more difficult than usual. Ronda put this down to Patricia's interview. And the student working on her thesis. Donal's visits too, putting the finishing touches to her affairs. A bit of affirmative attention. Such a small thing. But it was like tending to a neglected flowerbed, choked with weeds. It didn't take much for a shoot to unfurl.

'Why are you here?' asked Monika in her deadpan, disinterested voice as Ronda charged through the front door. 'Your shift does not begin for three hours and one half.'

'Have the newspapers been delivered?' panted Ronda, who had cycled to Green Gables in ten minutes less than it usually took her.

'Yes,' said Monika.

Ronda grabbed her lanyard and made a lunge at the double doors. There was still a chance that Ms Gallagher hadn't read the column yet.

'You have not clocked in, Ronda,' Monika pointed out, reasonably.

'I'll do it later,' said Ronda, scanning the lanyard. The doors remained stubbornly shut, despite Ronda's repeated scanning of the lanyard against the panel on the wall.

'It will not admit you until you clock in,' said Monika, not looking up from her nails, which she was filing. Ronda raced to the other side of the reception area where the new clocking-in machine was affixed to the wall. She rummaged in her pockets for her staff card, punched it into the machine. This time, there was a click when she held her lanyard against the panel. The double doors began to inch open.

'You will not be paid for overtime even though you have clocked in early,' Monika said, blowing dust shavings off her nails and reaching for a bottle of electric blue nail polish.

'I know,' said Ronda, resisting the urge to yank the handle as she waited for the doors to open wide enough for her to slip through. She shot down the corridor, flew past the day-room, where Fatima was clearing up after elevenses, sprinted by Fergal's office, turned right at the end, third door on the left. The door was closed. Not a good sign. Nor was the silence that seemed to emanate from the room like a thick fog. Ronda knocked on the door.

There was no answer.

'Ms Gallagher?' she called. 'It's me. Ronda.'

Nothing.

Tracey rounded the corner. 'You're not due in until lunch-time,' she called out.

Ronda knocked on the door again. 'Ms Gallagher?' she said, louder this time.

Tracey hurried towards Ronda, carrying a large cardboard box of nappies. 'Now that you're here, you might as well make yourself useful,' she said, holding the box out. 'Can you unpack these? And give the storeroom a bit of a tidy up while you're at it.'

'I'm not on duty,' Ronda said.

'What are you doing here then?' said Tracey.

The door opened and Ms Gallagher appeared. 'Didn't the girl just say she wasn't on duty?' she snapped at Tracey before pulling Ronda by the arm inside the room and slamming the door shut.

'Thank you,' said Ronda.

'It should be you, defending yourself from the likes of that one,' said Ms Gallagher. She sat upright in her wheel-chair, wearing a long nightdress with an Aran cardigan over it and a pair of slipper socks on her feet. Her hair was wilder than usual, as if she'd been reefing at it with her fists.

'I suppose you've heard?' she said.

Ronda looked around the room. Strewn across the bed, newspapers. 'Yes,' said Ronda, quietly.

'That sly old witch,' spat Ms Gallagher. 'She gets the job done, Patricia Glennon, I'll give her that.'

'Maybe Edel won't see it?' ventured Ronda.

Ms Gallagher shot a scathing look her way. Ronda couldn't blame her. The only way that Edel wouldn't hear about the article was if she lived in a cave in the Arctic Circle.

CHAPTER 40

Hope is the last thing to die. Ronda had worked in enough nursing homes for enough years to know how true that was. The hope in this instance emanated from Ms Gallagher, sitting by the window every day, keeping an eye on the comings and goings up and down the avenue. She had been on tenterhooks since Sunday, fully expecting – hoping, Ronda felt – Edel Scanlan to barge her way into Green Gables and let her have it, both barrels. Any time Ronda knocked on her bedroom door now, Ms Gallagher's habitual, 'Who is it?' contained a modicum of nervous hope that Ronda found difficult to hear.

With each passing, uneventful day, Ms Gallagher grew more and more agitated.

'Why isn't she coming to lambast me?' she wailed. Ronda wondered if perhaps this might be Edel Scanlan's revenge. Indifference.

Hope wormed its way into Ronda's thinking about the driving test. She was convinced she would fail. But, in spite of her conviction in this matter, she found herself hoping that she wouldn't.

Hoping that she might pass.

Then there was Charlo. Ronda had hoped he would not return with his forms and his treachery. But of course, it was only a matter of time before he did.

He arrived at Green Gables, oozing out of a three-piece wool suit with a black attaché case swinging from his hand and a brisk smile nailed to his face. Monika asked him to sign into the visitors' book. While he was thus occupied, she rang Ronda's mobile. 'That package you were waiting for has arrived,' she hissed into the mouthpiece, then hung up. It took Ronda a moment to understand Monika's cryptic message. She rang Donal. The call went straight to his voicemail.

I can't take your call. Leave a message and I'll call you back. Unless you're a telemarketer in which case I won't. This is in no way reflective of your worth as a human being. I just happen to have everything I need, thank you.

Ronda didn't leave a message. She rarely did. She wasn't very good at it, inclined to wander around the reason for the phone call and often getting cut off in the middle of a sentence because she had failed to articulate the point she was striving for in time. Or at all.

She rushed into reception, where Monika was doing her best to keep Charlo at bay by flattering him. 'This bag makes you look like important business person,' she said stiffly, pointing at his attaché case.

'Oh, yes, well, you ladies have your handbags, us men have our briefcases,' said Charlo, patting his toupée gently. 'Oh, hello Ronda.'

'Hi Charlo, let me bring you a cappuccino, Sheila's just—'

'I'm afraid I don't have time for niceties today,' he said briskly. 'I need to see Sheila straight away.'

'Of course,' said Ronda. 'It's just . . . it's a bit busy here at the moment, and—'

'Ordinarily, I could watch you work all day,' said Charlo, allowing his gaze to travel down Ronda's body. 'But today,

Sheila and I have important matters to discuss, so if you don't mind . . .' He moved towards the double doors.

'I do mind,' said Ronda, not moving.

'Sorry?' Charlo turned back towards her, certain that he had misheard.

'Elder financial abuse is a crime that's taken very seriously by the court system in this country,' said Ronda.

'Elder abuse?' said Charlo, his jovial tone gone. 'What exactly are you suggesting?' He glared at Ronda, but there was an edge of worry around his words.

Ronda took out her phone, found the photograph of Flossie.

'She's wearing Sheila's engagement ring,' said Ronda, zooming in.

'Have you been spying on me?' Charlo's face pinked, then reddened. Soon, he was the colour of the pickled beetroot Annie liked to put in her salad.

'One of our staff saw you in the bar,' said Ronda.

'What I do in my private life is none of your concern,' he spat.

'I'm afraid it is when it concerns one of my residents,' said Ronda.

'Sheila is my wife,' said Charlo, puffing his chest up.

'Maybe you should let your fiancée know?' said Ronda.

'I'll report you,' said Charlo. 'I'm going straight to Fergal's office and I'm going to tell him everything.'

Ronda hesitated. She wasn't sure how Fergal would react to this. Even though Ronda was certain that Charlo was up to no good, her evidence was circumstantial.

Charlo smirked, sensing her reluctance. He marched to the double doors. 'Open these immediately,' he barked at Monika.

Monika looked at Ronda for a signal. Ronda nodded at her.

As the doors opened, Charlo glared at Ronda before sweeping through them and down the corridor. He stopped outside Fergal's office and knocked on the door, two furious raps of the knuckles, then opened the door and let himself in. He slammed the door shut.

The corridor was empty now, the double doors shut. There were no voices shouting, no doors slamming, no sound at all really. Even Ronda's breathing was calm. Measured. It would be easy to conclude that the interaction hadn't taken place.

After all, Ronda had form in such matters.

It would be easy to decide that Charlo had never been here.

Apart from one thing.

The lingering cloud of Charlo's sickly sweet cologne.

Even Ronda couldn't imagine that stench.

CHAPTER 41

Ronda had fully expected to be hauled into Fergal's office as soon as Charlo told all his tales, but Monika said that Fergal had left Green Gables shortly after his conversation with Charlo. He'd been holed up in his office since his return, with his new 'Do not disturb' sign hanging crooked from a hook he'd asked Ernest to nail to the door. Still, Ronda knew it was just a matter of time.

'That's it,' said Ms Gallagher, when Ronda called into her room with fresh towels. 'If Edel won't come and lambast me, I'll go and see her.'

'Do you think that's wise?' asked Ronda.

'Of course not,' roared Ms Gallagher. 'You'll have to take me.'

'Me?' said Ronda.

'Who else?' snapped Ms Gallagher. 'You've seen the visitors' book, it's not like people are lining up outside my door seeking an audience.'

Ronda had wondered about this, but had never asked.

'Aren't you going to ask me why I never have visitors?' said Ms Gallagher, eyeballing Ronda so hard, she thought her retina might combust.

'I burnt bridges, that's why,' she went on. Her hands were balled into fists on the arms of the wheelchair.

Ronda reached for the keffiyeh, strewn across the bed, handed it to Ms Gallagher. She sometimes plaited the tassels when she was agitated. Ms Gallagher took the scarf and exhaled. 'Will you take me?' she asked in a smaller voice than before.

'I don't think now is a good time for me to be asking for time off,' said Ronda.

'Why not?'

Ronda told her about Charlo and what she might have said to him.

'What do you mean, might have said?' asked Ms Gallagher.

'Well, it's not exactly my usual patter,' said Ronda.

'And all the better for that,' said Ms Gallagher.

'I don't think Fergal will agree,' said Ronda.

'What's the worst Fergal can do?' asked Ms Gallagher.

He could fire her. Ronda could feel her insides clench. She'd never been fired before. This seemed like a particularly bad time to start.

'Where does Edel live?' she asked, anxious to change the subject.

Ms Gallagher took a battered, worn-out address book from the top drawer of her bedside locker. It fell open on the S page, and she pointed at Edel's name at the top, in Ms Gallagher's tangled cursive.

'Oh,' said Ronda. 'She lives in Howth.'

'You sound surprised,' said Ms Gallagher.

'Well,' said Ronda, wondering how to put it. 'You don't seem like the type of person who has friends in the leafy 'burbs.'

'Thank you,' said Ms Gallagher, pleased. 'Edel did a complete 360 when I outed her, as she called it. She married a barrister for starters. A wee fella with a few bob in the bank. They had a wain, moved to Howth and lived happily ever after, just like in all the best stories.' If Ms Gallagher believed that to be true, she had neglected to tell her face, which retained an expression of deep scepticism.

'So Edel wasn't "out" when you "outed" her, was that the problem?' asked Ronda, perching on the edge of the bed.

Ms Gallagher nodded, leaning her head against the back of the wheelchair. 'It happened on the first of May, 1973,' she said, like she was reciting a poem buried in the rich soil of her memory bank. 'International Workers' Day. I was being interviewed on the radio. All I did was answer the question he asked me at the end. I didn't want to make a big deal about it, refuse to answer, any of that. So I just said yes, me and Edel were together and we were happy. Simple as that. I thought she'd be relieved. She was gone by the time I got home. All her stuff was gone too. Like she'd never been there. Like I'd dreamed her.' Ms Gallagher said the last sentence in such a soft voice, Ronda wondered if she'd misheard, the words being so different in tone from Ms Gallagher's usual battering ram sensibilities.

'So,' said Ms Gallagher, clearing her throat and straightening herself in the chair. 'Will you drive me to Howth?'

'I can't,' said Ronda. 'I don't have my licence yet.' The word 'yet' at the end of the sentence gave Ronda a jolt. As if it was just a matter of time before she got a licence.

'Donal might drive me,' said Ms Gallagher. 'I'd say his van is wheelchair friendly, he's the type.'

Ronda thought this was likely.

'Will you ask him?' said Ms Gallagher. 'He'll say yes to you.'

'You should ask him,' said Ronda. 'He wouldn't dare say no to you.'

Ms Gallagher allowed a hint of a grin to glance against her face.

Monika's monotone came over the intercom. 'Ronda to Fergal's office please, Ronda McCann to Fergal Hutch's office immediately.'

'I'll go with you,' said Ms Gallagher. 'Put that little pip-squeak in his place.'

'No,' said Ronda, even though the idea of Ms Gallagher's protection was tempting.

'Come in,' said Fergal, when Ronda knocked on the door of his office. She walked in. 'I'm very busy Ronda, what is it?' he said, peering at her over the top of his computer screen.

'You sent for me,' said Ronda.

'Oh yes, sorry, so I did,' said Fergal, massaging his temples. 'I might make it look easy, but senior management in a global organisation can sometimes be taxing Ronda, let me tell you that for free.'

He clicked his mouse around his screen. 'It's Charlo I want to talk to you about. He came to see me earlier.'

'Yes,' said Ronda, her mouth parched with nerves.

'He wants to move Sheila,' went on Fergal.

'Oh,' said Ronda. She hadn't been expecting that. 'Did he say why?'

'He's moving house,' said Fergal. 'He wants to move Sheila closer to his new place.'

Relief rushed through Ronda. Charlo hadn't reported her.

But the relief was tempered with unease. The reason he hadn't reported her was because everything she had accused him of was correct. He was abusing Sheila. Manip-ulating her financially. And now he wanted to move her so he could continue doing it without any interference from Ronda.

'Paperwork has to be filled in for Sunset Boulevard,' went on Fergal. 'That's where Sheila is moving to.'

Sunset Boulevard did not have a good reputation, but it was popular, being the cheapest nursing home in Dublin. 'I don't have time at the moment, so I'm emailing it to you. That okay?' This was above Ronda's pay grade. But Fergal wasn't asking. He pecked at the keyboard with his two index fingers, then pressed Return. 'No hurry,' he said, leaning back in his chair. 'If you can get it done by the end of the week, that would be great.'

CHAPTER 42

On her break, Ronda went outside. She needed to think. She couldn't let Charlo take Sheila away. But she couldn't stop him either. Neither could she think of a solution in the hot-house conditions inside Green Gables. She needed some air.

The back of the building was still a building site, with signs of the new build emerging through the freshly laid foundations. Instead, Ronda walked out the front door, down the avenue and through the gates. Today, spring was struggling to make an impression, the sky low and grey, the delicate heads of the tulips at the base of the cherry blossom trees that Ernest had planted some years back, bowed under the weight of raindrops from a recent downpour. Still, the air was fresh after the soupy heat of Green Gables. Ronda pulled her phone out of her pocket. Donal hadn't rang back.

She reached the bottom of the avenue and cast about for somewhere dry to sit and eat the egg and tomato sand-wich she had made that morning. Best to eat it in the open air, given the robust odour of the hard-boiled eggs. The bus stop across the road was empty. It had a long, narrow steel bench, sheltered by heavy sheets of plastic on three sides and a curved Perspex awning overhead. It looked dry and pro-tected from the sharp edge of that easterly blowing up the road into her face. She walked past it. She usually avoided this bus stop, which was easy enough, since she cycled to and from work. But now she found herself wondering

275

why. Just because it happened to be not dissimilar to the bus stop Gerry had careered into all those years ago? So what? Ronda wondered. The bus stop where the accident had happened wasn't a bus stop any more. Gerry was dead, the car long gone to the scrapyard, crushed and shredded, making up numbers in a landfill somewhere. And look at Ronda herself, doing a passable imitation of someone who knows what she's doing behind the wheel of a car. Ronda stopped walking so suddenly that, had there been anyone behind her, they would have smacked straight into her. She crossed the road, sat inside the bus stop and rummaged in her backpack for her lunchbox. It was an uneventful meal, the sandwich soggy and the bread stained pink from the juice of the tomato. The cheeks of Ronda's bum got cold, then uncomfortable, then numb. No would-be passengers arrived. No buses passed. Even though she wasn't actually waiting for a bus, Ronda found herself lamenting the decline in public transport services and, while this made her both sad and angry, she was happy too. That she was able to think of such things, sitting at a bus stop that was not dissimilar to the one Gerry McCann had careered into all those years ago.

Ronda felt she had passed some kind of test.

Made some progress.

On the way back to work, her phone rang. It was Donal. 'Sorry, I was in court, I'm only seeing your missed calls now.'

'Thanks for ringing back,' said Ronda.

'You didn't leave a message,' he said.

'No,' said Ronda.

'What would you have said? If you had left a message?'

'I would have said, Hi Donal, it's Ronda here. Ronda McCann. From Green Gables. Margo's sister. You're doing the Enduring Power of Attorney for Margo. Margo McCann-Waters. Remember?' Ronda stopped. 'See?' she said. 'This is why I don't leave messages.'

'Ah yeah, that makes sense now,' said Donal. 'How about just talking on the phone? Is that any better?'

'Not much,' admitted Ronda.

'You nearly finished your sandwich?'

'How did you know I . . .?'

'I passed you,' said Donal. 'I'm parked outside Green Gables, I have a meeting with Fatima.'

'Did she hear back?' asked Ronda, tightening her grip on the phone.

'No, don't worry,' said Donal. 'The IPO want a few more documents, so we're going through them today.'

'I can't believe I didn't hear the camper van,' said Ronda.

'You were deep in thought all right,' said Donal. 'Come on up and you can talk to me in person, you're good at that.'

'I think that's overstating it,' said Ronda. She hung up and kept walking. She couldn't help noticing her gait, quicker now. She tried to slow it down but found it difficult. She had to admit what she had suspected for quite some time. About Donal Clarke. He was someone who had aroused her interest. She felt herself drawn to him. She thought it might be something to do with his humanity. The way he wore it, light and loose. Not like a cape. There was nothing super-hero-ish about it. More like a comfortable pair of jeans that sit on your hips without any necessity for a belt. Old ones, the denim worn but not worn out. Soft against skin. The analogy embarrassed her. She could feel her face flush a bright red even though there was nobody there to bear witness to her discomfiture. She hadn't said anything out loud. She was only thinking these nonsensical thoughts in the comfort of her own head. This made her flush harder, as if her insides were scorched by her own foolishness. Not just because she felt herself drawn to Donal Clarke and admired his loosely-worn humanity, but also because she found him handsome.

The sun had broken through the cloud and Ronda was warm by the time she walked up the avenue to Green Gables. The camper van was in the car park, and Donal was in the driver's seat with his bare feet up on the dashboard, listening to Dolly Parton on the stereo.

'There you are,' he said, leaning his head out of the window when he saw her. She tried not to feel singled out by the warmth of his greeting. This was how he greeted people. She knew that.

'Hello,' she said.

'Ronda, isn't it?' he said, grinning. 'Ronda McCann. From Green Gables. You're Margo's sister, aren't you? I'm doing the Enduring Power of Attorney for Margo. Margo McCann-Waters. Remember?'

Ronda smiled. 'You're making fun of me,' she said.

'Just a little bit,' said Donal.

The front door of Green Gables opened and Fatima appeared, waving at them. 'I'll be there in two minutes, Donal,' she called across the car park. 'I'm just waiting for Fergal to sign a form for me, okay?'

'Sure,' Donal called back, opening the door of the van and stepping out. He slid the side of the van open and pulled out two fold-up camping chairs. 'Step into my office,' he said, gesturing Ronda into one of the chairs. He sat on the other one. 'Now,' he said. 'You were looking for me?'

Ronda told him about Charlo.

'You must have really unsettled him,' said Donal.

'Maybe,' said Ronda.

'But you're right,' went on Donal. 'You only have circumstantial evidence, so you can't prevent him from moving Sheila.'

Ronda nodded.

'You need direct evidence,' said Donal. 'A signed document, a transcript, a recording, something along those lines.'

'Or I need Charlo to think I have direct evidence,' said Ronda slowly.

'As a reformed corporate solicitor, I couldn't possibly encourage that kind of thing,' said Donal formally, winking at Ronda.

'There's one other thing,' said Ronda, wriggling her arms out of her backpack.

'Go ahead,' said Donal.

'I feel bad asking,' said Ronda, setting her bag on the ground by her feet. 'We're like your full-time job now.'

'Believe me, this is way better than my old full-time job,' said Donal.

'How come you gave up?' asked Ronda. Donal didn't reply immediately. 'Sorry,' said Ronda. 'It's none of my business.'

'It's common knowledge,' said Donal. 'At least in legal circles. Believe it or not, I was really good at my job. I got a banking mobster off on an impressive litany of charges. Fraud, tax evasion, bribery, corruption, insider trading, I could go on. Anyway, when the not guilty verdict was handed down, I had a bit of a turn in the High Court. My therapist said the correct terminology is a mental breakdown. Although it didn't feel like a breakdown, to be honest. It was more like a throwing down of arms. Not giving up, but just . . . getting out, you know?'

Ronda nodded, although she didn't know. She had no idea what that might feel like.

'I probably shouldn't have said all that,' said Donal, glancing anxiously at Ronda.

'Why not?' she asked.

'Some people think I was a fool, throwing it all away,' he said. 'Tricia couldn't understand it. She's a real workhorse. And my father of course. Although in fairness he probably always thought I was a fool.'

'You seem pretty workhorsey to me,' said Ronda.

'Thank you,' he said, smiling his disarming smile at her. She knew it was a disarming smile because she felt disarmed.

Donal rooted through a pile of paperwork on the table. 'Tell me all,' he said.

Ronda gave him a brief outline of the Ms Gallagher / Edel Scanlan story.

'That's a bit . . . heartbreaking,' said Donal.

Ronda nodded. 'It is,' she said.

'So,' said Donal. 'What can I do?'

'Could you drive us to Howth?' Ronda asked. 'Ms Gallagher will pay you, of course.'

Donal shook his head. 'I'm afraid I don't accept cash or any major or minor credit or Visa cards.'

'She'll insist,' said Ronda. 'Otherwise, she'll feel like she's taking advantage of your kind nature. We all feel like that, to be honest.'

'That's just capitalism messing with you,' said Donal. 'It makes us believe that if we're not paying through the nose for something, it's worthless.'

'Yes, but how are you actually paying for anything? Like food?' Ronda asked, a reasonable question she felt.

Donal shrugged. 'I don't have many overheads,' he said. 'Plus I don't eat all that much.'

'What are you talking about?' said Fatima, arriving out of breath. 'I've seen the way you charge through a plate of my gingerbread.'

'That's different,' said Donal, his voice grave. 'Nobody could resist that.'

Fatima smiled. 'I brought all the paperwork,' she said, pulling a file out of her handbag.

Ronda jumped up. 'You can have my seat, Fatima,' she said.

'What day were you thinking?' Donal asked Ronda. 'For Ms Gallagher?'

'Would Friday suit?' asked Ronda.

'Sure,' said Donal. 'I'll pick you both up at around four, when your shift ends, okay?'

'That's perfect,' said Ronda. 'I owe you.'

'No you don't,' said Donal. 'But Ms Gallagher can chip in for petrol, if that makes her feel better, okay?' He did his wide smile then, the one that seemed to slide off the edges of his face, make all his freckles converge. Ronda could see herself reflected in the bright green of his cats' eyes. Her smile was wide too. With the sunlight on her face, she couldn't make out her scar.

Fatima coughed discreetly. 'Ahem.' An amused expression on her face.

Ronda grabbed her backpack off the ground. 'I'll let Ms Gallagher know,' she said. 'Thanks so much.'

'You're welcome,' Donal called after her, and Ronda could feel his eyes on her as she walked away.

The feeling was not unpleasant.

CHAPTER 43

The not unpleasant feeling continued into Ronda's next driving lesson.

'What are you looking so happy about?' Margo asked when she picked her up.

'Do I?' asked Ronda.

'Well, you certainly don't look like you're about to get behind the wheel of a car,' said Margo. She climbed across to the passenger seat and Ronda arranged herself in the driver's seat, She pulled the chair closer to the wheel, put on her belt, adjusted the mirrors and positioned her hands in a strict ten-to-two arrangement. She turned the key in the ignition, got the car into first gear and trundled down the avenue towards the gates.

'Can we hurry it along?' said Margo. 'Malcolm and I are going out to dinner this evening.'

'I'm going as fast as I can,' said Ronda.

'I could stilt-walk faster than this,' said Margo, although Ronda was pretty sure she was joking.

The lesson went well. Or rather, nothing happened that elicited a shout, curse, groan or shriek. In fact, Margo was moved to say, 'Nicely done,' when Ronda's attempt at a hill-start was successful. Although it was more of a gentle incline than a hill. Margo kept up a steady hum of conversation throughout the lesson. Things she had to do in the main.

Spring was always a busy time for the Tidy Towns, and there was a new treasurer on the committee whose grip on the purse strings was airtight. Sebastian was going skiing with his class and his passport needed renewing. A new drop-off area in the school car park was wreaking havoc, resulting in yet another emergency meeting of the PA. An outbreak of a vomiting bug at the hospice was restricting visiting times, causing upset for patients and relatives. Then there was Malcolm and his hectic work schedule. She worried about burnout and, of course, he invariably forgot to take any of the minerals or vitamins she bought for him in the health shop. Margo did not seem to expect any response to her many and varied observations, and even if she did, Ronda could not supply any, since she had not mastered the skill of doing anything else other than drive while driving, and was pretty sure she never would. Still, Margo's monologue formed a type of white noise that Ronda found curiously comforting as she concentrated on the myriad tasks she had to perform to keep her and Margo – and all the road users they encountered – alive and unhurt.

Now, Margo was talking about their mother. It seemed she was regretting her rash offer of driving Annie to and from her appointments with Dr Anderson. There was another appointment scheduled for this Friday, Ronda learned as she indicated – too early, according to Margo – to pull out – too far out, according to Margo – to pass a cyclist.

'Blood tests this time,' said Margo. Ronda couldn't see her sister's face, but felt sure she was doing one of her impressive eyerolls.

Ronda didn't blame her. Their mother insisted on having her blood extracted and tested so regularly, Ronda worried that she might one day run out of the stuff. Margo laughed when Ronda voiced this observation – they were stopped at a traffic light – and the sound it made was a pleasant one, giving the atmosphere in the car a bit of a Sunday-drive vibe. Like they weren't stuck in thick traffic on a damp Thursday afternoon. 'You're getting better at traffic,' remarked Margo.

'Let's face it, I couldn't have gotten any worse,' said Ronda.

'That's true,' said Margo, with a wry smile.

Ronda's phone rang from the well between the two front seats.

'That's supposed to be on silent,' said Margo.

'Sorry,' said Ronda. 'I forgot.' She stopped at a T-junction, pulled up the handbrake. Margo snatched up the phone. 'It's the Solicitor-at-Large.' She punched the green button. 'Hello, this is Margo McCann-Waters speaking, Ronda is driving so I'm afraid she can't come to the phone, can I take a message?' A pause, then Donal, talking. Ronda could hear the low murmur of his voice. She concentrated on the road. She was approaching a crossroads, which was one of her least favourite driving events. Margo lifted her hand, indicating that Ronda should turn right, which was Ronda's least favourite turn at a crossroads, especially when there was no filter light. The light was green, but there was a long line of oncoming traffic through the junction. Ronda indicated right and waited. Margo nodded approvingly at her as she talked into the phone.

'I'm sorry to hear that,' she said.

'Yes, of course, she'll understand.

'When?

'Yes, that's only to be expected.

'Okay then.

'Thank you, I will.

'Yes, you too. Goodbye.'

She hung up, put the phone back in the well. 'You've got a gap there,' she said.

'I won't make it,' said Ronda.

'You will, you've loads of time.'

Ronda stepped on the clutch, manoeuvred the gear stick into first and began easing her foot up, listening for the sound of the bite. By the time she heard it, the light was red. 'Sorry,' she said.

'Don't be,' said Margo. 'That was a test, and you passed.'

'The guy in the car behind me doesn't look thrilled about it,' said Ronda, looking in her rear-view mirror.

'Don't mind him,' said Margo, adjusting the mirror so Ronda could no longer see the man. 'Never do anything in the car that you're not comfortable with, no matter what anyone tells you. Even me.' Her phone beeped and she fished it out of her handbag. 'Malcolm's meeting is running over, he won't make dinner,' she said, flinging her phone back into her bag.

'Sorry to hear that,' said Ronda.

Margo shrugged. 'We'll go out another night.'

'Course you will,' said Ronda.

'Oh, and Donal's wife's brother died.'

'Was that why he rang?' said Ronda.

'He can't give you and Ms Gallagher a lift to Howth tomorrow,' Margo said. 'He's going to Clare for the funeral. He'll be there for a few days, he said.'

The light went green, and this time Ronda scorched across the junction before the oncoming traffic could get a move on.

'Nicely done,' said Margo, surprised and perhaps a little taken aback by the speed of the manoeuvre. Ronda was surprised too. She usually waited until the coast was so clear, you could drive a couple of articulated trucks though the gap.

'Is that what he called her?' said Ronda.

'What?' Margo looked confused.

'His wife?'

'Oh, yeah, I think so. Why?'

'No reason,' said Ronda quickly. 'I just . . . she's his ex-wife, as far as I know. That's what he usually calls her.'

Margo shrugged. 'Maybe he did,' she said. 'He sounded a bit shook. I got the feeling it was unexpected. You should call him.'

'Did he ask me to?' asked Ronda.

'I think so,' said Margo.

'He either did or he didn't,' said Ronda.

'Fine,' said Margo. 'He did.'

'You sure?'

'What difference does it make?'

'I don't want to call him if he didn't ask me to.'

'He did, okay?' said Margo.

'Fine.'

'I'm pretty sure.'

Ronda sighed.

'Don't slow down,' said Margo. 'The lights are about to turn green.'

'It's a junction, I should slow down.' Ronda lifted one of her hands off the wheel and quickly wiped the sweat against the leg of her scrubs. She had no idea how people drove with only one hand on the wheel, the other holding one of those travel mugs maybe. Or a cigarette. Or just draped oh-so-casually over the gear stick. She would never be one of those people.

'Here,' said Margo, when Ronda stopped at the lights. 'Hold out your hands.' Ronda did as she was bid and Margo sprinkled talcum powder over her palms. 'That'll help with the sweat,' said Margo, rubbing the sweet-smelling powder into Ronda's hot, damp hands.

When Ronda pulled in outside No. 10 Casino Place, she put the car in neutral, pulled up the handbrake and turned the engine off.

'Done like a pro,' said Margo. 'You're totally going to pass the test.'

'Don't say that,' said Ronda, who was not a fan of expectations.

'You can ask me, you know,' said Margo, checking her phone again.

'Ask you what?'

'To give you and Ms Havisham a lift to Howth. Since I'm bringing Mam to the clinic tomorrow.'

'You've got a lot on,' said Ronda. 'I don't like to overstep.'

'You should ask for what you want, Ronda,' said Margo emphatically. 'Actually you should demand it.'

'Eh, okay then, I demand that you take Ms Gallagher and me to Howth tomorrow,' said Ronda. 'How's that?'

'Bit presumptuous, but fine,' said Margo, hauling her diary out of her handbag and leafing through it. 'I was going to grab Mam around half three, after my meeting with HIQA. Their meetings never run over on a Friday, so I should get to Green Gables just before four, okay?'

'That'd be great, Margo, thanks,' said Ronda.

Margo snapped her diary shut. 'From what you've told me about Ms Havisham, I don't think she'll like me,' she said.

'She definitely won't if you refer to her as Ms Havisham,' said Ronda.

'She'll have me pegged as a yummy mummy,' said Margo.

'She'll admire your industry,' said Ronda.

'She might be good for Mam though,' said Margo.

'What do you mean?' asked Ronda.

'Make her see what an actual sick person looks like.' It took Ronda a moment to realise whom Margo was referring to. She had never thought of Ms Gallagher as a sick person.

CHAPTER 44

Ronda did call Donal back, but not until the following afternoon, since she was not at all sure if he wanted her to or not.

'Hello?' Donal answered on the first ring.

'Hello,' said Ronda.

'Oh,' said Donal. 'Hi.' His 'Oh' was sufficient evidence. He had not requested a call back. She could hear voices in the background. The clank of china and cutlery. A kettle whistling.

'Margo said you wanted me to ring you back,' said Ronda, 'but it doesn't sound like a good time.'

'Hang on,' said Donal. Ronda heard a door close and the babble of voices faded away. Now she could hear the clip-clip sounds of Donal's shoes against gravel.

'They're waking him in the house,' said Donal, stifling a yawn.

'I'm sorry for your loss,' said Ronda.

'Thanks,' said Donal. 'Pat was a lovely person, Trish is in bits here, he only found out he had cancer six weeks ago. We thought he had more time.'

Silence down the line. Ronda struggled to come up with something to say to staunch it, but could think of nothing that didn't sound trite. She could hear Donal breathing. A steady sound. Like a clock. He didn't seem to mind the silence.

'Donal?' A woman's voice, low and melodic, cut through

the silence on the line. 'Auntie May is leaving. She wants to say goodbye to you.'

'I'll let you go,' said Ronda then. 'I'll see you when you get back to Dublin.'

'Thanks for calling,' said Donal.

'Take care.' Ronda hung up and shoved the phone into the pocket of her scrubs. She went to collect Ms Gallagher, who was waiting at the door of her room looking pointedly at her watch even though it was precisely four o'clock.

'What ails you?' she said as Ronda reached her. 'You look like someone spat in your porter.'

'No one spat in my porter,' said Ronda. 'You look nice.'

Ms Gallagher was dressed in her usual black with the keffiyeh tied around her neck. And while her hair remained thick and bushy, there was a distinct possibility that she had dragged her fingers through it. It was tamer than usual. Also – and this was unheard of – she had applied lipstick. Some of it was on her front teeth, but the overall effect was one of effort.

They made their way to the front of the building where Margo had parked. Annie waved from the back seat. Ronda knew better than to offer Ms Gallagher help in front of other people. She wheeled the chair as close to Margo's car door as she could get. Ms Gallagher used the armrests to pull herself up and out of the wheelchair, then stood for a moment without moving, looking around as if she were admiring the few hardy crocuses that had not been flattened by the construction site traffic driving up and down the avenue. She used the roof of the car, the top of the door, the back of the passenger seat, and Ronda's discreetly offered arm, to support, manoeuvre and negotiate herself into a seated position in the front of the car. 'Well,' she said, breaking the uneasy silence that had prevailed during her protracted entry. 'What about ye?' She grinned at Margo, then at Annie, both of whom smiled back with their mouths tightly closed, as if they were worried they might say the wrong thing. Perhaps Ronda had given too much detail, in the anecdotes she had told them over the years.

'This is my mother, Annie,' said Ronda. Annie held out her small, bony hand and Ms Gallagher took it in both of hers and subjected it to her usual vigorous pump action. Annie took it well, and only winced when Ms Gallagher released her hand and turned her attention to Margo.

'So,' she said, 'you're the multitasker?' Margo smiled her dangerous smile.

'I am,' said Margo. 'And you're the caustic contrarian.' Ms Gallagher looked at Ronda, her eyebrows raised.

'I never said that,' said Ronda, flushing.

'Nobody would blame you if you did,' said Ms Gallagher, grinning. She looked back at Annie again. 'You've raised two fine girls, Mrs McCann,' she said. 'You should be proud.'

Annie smiled. Ronda, climbing into the back beside her, thought her mother seemed more vivid outside of the confines of No. 10 Casino Place. She had applied two lines of blush, accentuating her high cheekbones and the delicacy of her skin, which was clear and not particularly lined, a testament to a sedentary life, rarely subjected to the elements. A dash of her usual frosty pink lipstick and a silk scarf tied jauntily around her neck in pastel shades of green. A gift from Gerry in the summer of 1972, when his horse came third in a complicated accumulator bet.

Annie wore her 'going out' outfit, which, these days,

meant 'going to Dr Anderson's outfit'. A skirt-and-cardigan-combination in mauve. Over that, her 'good' coat, a woollen one in pale grey, bought in the sales in Switzers in the eighties, still as good as new.

'So, Mrs McCann?' said Ms Gallagher, twisting around in her seat and grinning at Annie. 'Ronda tells me you're a hypochondriac.'

'I beg your pardon, Mrs Gallagher?' said Annie, her bright pink cheeks growing pinker.

'It's Ms actually,' said Ms Gallagher. 'The reason I mention it is because my auntie Belinda was one too. She could actually manifest a rash down her left leg at will, could you credit that?'

Annie glared at Ronda. 'I never said you were a hypochondriac,' Ronda told her.

'It's nothing to be scundered about,' said Ms Gallagher. 'It's a medical condition. A real one, I mean.'

'Dr Anderson takes all my medical problems very seriously,' said Annie, her voice high and shaky.

'Och, you know these quacks,' said Ms Gallagher. 'They'll say anything for their twopenny bits.'

'How about some music?' said Margo, turning on the radio.

Ms Gallagher cracked the window. 'It's good to get out of that place, all the same,' she said.

'A change is as good as a rest, they say,' Annie piped up from the back seat. And even though her hair blew across her face, she did not mention the draught and how it might give her Bell's palsy or a crick in her neck or just a common-or-garden cold.

*

Edel Scanlan lived in an estate of well-maintained houses with speed bumps, neat, well-stocked gardens, and garages with corrugated doors at the side.

'It's this one,' said Margo, pulling up outside the last house on the block. 'Number thirty-six, isn't that what you said?'

'Aye,' said Ms Gallagher, her sharp eyes fixed on the house, taking everything in. There was a car in the driveway. A Fiat Punto.

'Who lives here?' asked Annie, peering out the window.

'A friend of Ms Gallagher's,' said Ronda, unclipping her seat belt.

'We were lovers,' said Ms Gallagher. 'Long time ago.'

'Oh,' said Annie. 'It'll be . . . nice, I'm sure . . . to see him again.'

'He's a she,' said Ms Gallagher.

'Oh,' said Annie again.

'And I'm not a bit sure she'll be pleased to see me,' went on Ms Gallagher, opening the door. 'There's a wee touch of Marmite about me, people either hate my guts or else they learn to tolerate me, like Ronda here. Isn't that right, Ronda?'

'Marmite gets bad press,' said Margo. Ms Gallagher grinned at her.

'We'll be about forty-five minutes at the clinic,' Margo said, examining her watch. 'I'll come back for you then, okay?'

'I suppose I should thank you for the lift,' said Ms Gallagher, swinging her legs out of the footwell, planting them firmly on the tarmac of the road.

Ronda jumped out of the car, opened the boot and lifted

the wheelchair out. Ms Gallagher lowered into the chair and pushed herself onto the footpath. Ronda followed her.

'I do not need a chaperone,' snapped Ms Gallagher.

'I know you don't,' said Ronda. 'I'll wait until Edel answers the door and then I'll head off, okay? There's a coffee shop up the road, I'll wait for you there.'

'Good luck,' Annie called from the back seat.

'Hands on the wheel at ten-to-two,' said Ronda. Margo grinned and pulled up the window. The car scorched up the road.

'Well?' said Ms Gallagher, glaring at Ronda. 'How do I look?'

'Formidable,' said Ronda.

Ms. Gallagher nodded briskly. 'That's the vibe I was going for,' she said.

Ronda did not make it to the coffee shop. Before Ms Gallagher got halfway down the garden path, the front door opened and a woman appeared. Not particularly tall, but with a regal bearing. Perhaps it was her long-sleeved, round-necked navy dress that ended just past her knees and matched her navy court shoes. Or maybe it was her rigid posture. Or the silver hair pulled into a neat bun at the back of her neck. Her eyes were narrowed and fixed upon Ms Gallagher, her face set and without expression. She had been expecting them, Ronda felt.

'Edel,' said Ms Gallagher. Her voice held none of its usual ferocious certainty.

'What are you doing here?' said Edel, in a clear, neutral voice, all traces of her Belfast accent long gone.

'I came to say I'm sorry,' said Ms Gallagher.

'For which particular transgression?' snapped Edel, her composure slipping for a moment.

'Everything,' said Ms Gallagher. 'All of it. I'm so sorry, Ed.'

Ronda's palms were sweaty. It was awful, standing there, bearing witness.

'I'll go,' she said.

'Make sure you take her with you,' said Edel, glaring at Ms Gallagher.

'Ed, listen to me,' said Ms Gallagher. 'Patricia Glennon did not have my permission to print any of that stuff about you, you have to believe me. It was off the record. I was very clear about that.'

'My name is Edel. And what I'm not clear about is why you were talking about me in the first place?' said Edel. 'Or why you're here now?'

'Because I . . .' Ms Gallagher's voice faltered, then came to a full stop. Ronda had never known her to be at a loss for something to say. Even Edel looked surprised.

'Look,' said Ronda, reaching for a bright, breezy tone. 'There's a coffee shop down the road, why don't we go there? You two could talk, and . . .?'

'No,' said Edel. 'I don't think there's anything further to say, do you, Lyra?' Ronda didn't think she'd ever heard anyone call Ms Gallagher, Lyra. The word, coming from Edel Scanlan's pursed mouth, had the finality of a full stop about it.

Ms Gallagher did not respond. It was, after all, a rhetorical question. Edel's nod was a curt one as she stepped back inside the house and closed the door.

*

Usually, Ms Gallagher insisted on wheeling herself, since she didn't tolerate people pushing her around, either meta-phorically or physically. But she did not object when Ronda turned the wheelchair and pushed it out of the driveway. When they reached the pavement, Ronda continued walking. Anything she came up with to say seemed trite and ineffec-tual. She said nothing and kept walking. In this way, she did a loop of the housing estate. That didn't take long enough, so she pushed the chair into the park across the road, stopping briefly to text Margo and let her know where they were. Ms Gallagher sat very still and did not speak. In the park, Ronda noticed how bright and mild the afternoon was. She didn't share this observance with Ms Gallagher. She kept walking. Eventually, at a bench, she stopped and perched on the edge of it. After a while, Ms Gallagher looked at Ronda.

'Is this the bit where you tell me there's plenty more fish in the sea and then we hug?' she said, with a touch of her old gruff self.

'I wasn't going to say the bit about the fish,' said Ronda.

'My mother grilled mackerel every Friday,' said Ms Galla-gher. 'Wile bony creatures.'

'And I'm not much of a hugger,' Ronda added.

'Me neither,' said Ms Gallagher. This struck them both as funny for some reason and their laughter rang out on the still air. It was such a bright, light sound that, for a moment, Ronda thought she saw Edel Scanlan, running towards them along the path, her arms flailing, shouting at Ms Gallagher to wait, she was sorry, she didn't mean it, she was glad to see her.

She was so glad.

*

Margo didn't ask any questions when she picked them up. Instead, she hauled the wheelchair into the boot as Ms Gallagher struggled into the passenger seat. It took longer this time, as if Ms Gallagher, like the parades of daffodils in the park, was wilting on the stem.

'You tired?' Ronda asked and, instead of snapping at her and telling her to mind her own business, Ms Gallagher nodded and let Ronda pull the seat belt around her and clip it in. The drive back to Green Gables was a quiet affair. Even Annie, usually invigorated after some attention from Dr Anderson, didn't regale them as she otherwise would with a step-by-step account of the medical procedures she had undergone or the ones she believed she should have been offered. At Green Gables, Annie leaned forward and tapped Ms Gallagher's shoulder. 'It was lovely meeting you,' she said.

'Really?' Ms Gallagher sounded surprised. Annie grinned, which is something she did very rarely. It lifted the air of malady off her, made her seem healthier.

'Very . . . refreshing,' said Annie, after giving some consideration to the adjective.

'Pity Edel Scanlan doesn't agree with you,' Ms Gallagher said.

'Don't you worry,' Annie said, her hand still on Ms Gallagher's shoulder, patting it now. 'There's plenty more fish in the sea.'

CHAPTER 45

Ronda still hadn't done the paperwork for Sheila's transfer to Sunset Boulevard.

And Fergal hadn't asked her about it because he assumed that she would do as she was bid, as she always did. Of Charlo, there was no sign. Sheila, oblivious, ate her way through a fruit cake that Fatima had made and smuggled in to her. Ronda knew she couldn't put it off for ever, but, for the moment, that's what she did.

What she had been doing, systematically, was marking off the days on the wall calendar Annie received from the local pharmacy every Christmas. Now, there was less than a fortnight to go before the test, and she still hadn't mastered the act of reversing around corners.

'Why on earth would anybody reverse around a corner?' she raged on Monday evening after she'd attempted the manoeuvre a dozen times in a row, ending up a metre from the kerb every time.

'Let's take a break,' suggested Margo. 'I could do with a drink.'

'No,' said Ronda. 'I have to learn this. Besides, you can't, you're driving home.'

'Jesus Ronda, I just meant one lousy glass of wine.'

'Even one will impair your driving,' said Ronda.

'It won't,' said Margo.

'I just don't want you to have an accident,' said Ronda.

Margo sighed.

'Can I try it a couple more times?' asked Ronda.

'I should go,' said Margo. 'Malcolm is out at a work thing tonight. If I don't make an appearance, the boys will end up ordering those filthy spice bags from the takeaway. They stink up the entire house.'

'Just one more time then?' said Ronda. 'Please?'

'Look at you,' said Margo, suddenly grinning. 'Who would have thought there'd ever come a day you'd be begging to drive a car backwards around a corner?' Ronda agreed that it did sound a little preposterous.

She reversed around the corner again. This time she ended up half a metre from the kerb.

'It's an improvement,' said Margo, opening her door to inspect the gap.

'Is there any chance I won't be asked to do that in the test?' asked Ronda.

'No,' said Margo.

'But I can't do it,' said Ronda.

'Yet,' said Margo. 'You keep forgetting to add that word to the end of your sentences.' She walked around to Ronda's side, opened the door.

'I can give you another lesson at the same time tomorrow?' she said.

'Really?' said Ronda, getting out of the car.

Margo tossed her hair as she settled herself behind the wheel. She turned the key in the ignition, used the rear-view mirror to reapply her lipstick, and put the car into gear.

'Thank you,' said Ronda, admiring the fluidity of her sister's movements. 'That would be . . .'

Margo waved as she roared up the road.

'. . . great,' finished Ronda.

'What's great?' Joseph stepped onto the path, closing the garden gate behind him.

'Oh, hello,' said Ronda, using the grass verge to sidle past him. But Joseph stepped onto the grass, stood right in front of her.

'Are you learning how to drive?' asked Joseph.

Ronda nodded.

'Good for you, Ronda,' said Joseph, in his soupy TV voice.

'I have to go,' said Ronda, trying to negotiate a way past him.

'Do you think we could ever be friends again?' he asked. He was so close, Ronda could feel his breath against her face. But if she stepped backwards, she would be on the road.

Suddenly, anger flared like a firework inside her.

'We were never friends, Joseph,' she said. 'Now, can you move? You're in my way.'

Joseph's mouth fell open, but he stepped back so that Ronda could get past without so much as glancing against him. She walked away. She didn't rush. She strolled, as if she had a surplus of time and self-assurance.

'Do you?'

Ronda blinked and there was Joseph, still in front of her, but now with a puzzled expression across his face.

'Sorry?' she said.

'Think we could be friends?' Joseph repeated. It started to drizzle. Ronda could feel her boots sink into the cold grass. 'We were just kids back then,' said Joseph. 'Isn't it time we let bygones be bygones?'

It did sound reasonable, Ronda supposed. 'Okay,' she said.

Joseph laughed. 'Try not to sound too enthusiastic, won't you?'

'Sorry,' said Ronda. She wished she could stop saying sorry.

'I'm glad we got that out of the way,' said Joseph, stepping back so Ronda could get past him. 'See you around, Ronda.'

'Bye,' she said, making a beeline for the garden gate at No. 10 Casino Place. It creaked and resisted and Ronda had to pull at it so it would widen sufficiently to admit her. Ordinarily, she oiled it once a week, but she had let things slip of late. She could feel Joseph's eyes on her as she rummaged for the door key, finally finding it in the zip pocket inside the main section of her backpack. Then came the careful manipulation of the key into the lock, twisting it first this way, then that, pulling it out ever so slightly and turning it again, then the shoulder heave and, when the door finally opened, it was sudden so that Ronda stumbled into the darkness of the hallway.

'I could take a look at that lock for you, if you like?' There was an amused edge to Joseph's voice from across the fence.

'It's fine,' said Ronda, switching on the hall light, blinking in the sudden glare. 'Goodnight.' She pushed the door closed and leaned against it.

'Hi Ronda,' called Annie from the kitchen. 'You're just in time, I've made stew. With lentils.' There was a pause after this statement, as if they both needed time to process it.

'I didn't think you liked lentils?' Ronda finally managed.

'I thought I'd give them another chance,' said Annie. 'Margo says they're a superfood. Wash your hands and come in, I'm dishing up.'

The lentils were a bit on the mushy side, but the carrots,

turnip and tomatoes were tasty with the mash Annie had made with her secret ingredient that everybody knew was a sprinkling of nutmeg.

'What's all this in aid of?' asked Ronda, when Annie produced a tub of vanilla ice cream and a tin of fruit cocktail afterwards and scooped some of each into two bowls.

'It's only dinner and dessert,' said Annie, taking off the housecoat she wore to protect her clothes from the smell of cooking. It had been a long time since she'd worn it. 'Even hypochondriacs have to eat, right?'

Ronda put her spoon on the table. 'I didn't tell Ms Gallagher that,' she said.

Annie leaned across the table and placed her hand on Ronda's shoulder. 'I know you didn't, love.'

Ronda couldn't remember the last time they had touched, even brushed against each other by accident.

'How is she, by the way?' asked Annie. 'It must be hard for her, with the MS.'

Ronda was surprised. Annie didn't usually have time to enquire about anybody else's health, being too preoccupied with her own.

'She's doing well,' said Ronda.

'She seems like someone who's made of stern stuff,' said Annie. 'I hope she's not too down about her . . . friend?'

Ronda hadn't commented on Ms Gallagher's swollen, red eyes when she called into her room with a cup of tea after they got back from Howth. 'I think I'm coming down with a cold,' Ms Gallagher had said. She agreed to Ronda's suggestion of rest, and allowed Ronda to help her to bed.

'She's okay,' Ronda said to Annie.

Annie jumped. 'What was that?'

'What?' said Ronda.

'Did you not hear something outside?' said Annie.

'Like what?'

'Maybe a knock on the door,' said Annie.

'I didn't hear anything,' said Ronda.

'Maybe it's your friend with the camper van,' said Annie. 'He's the only one who calls unannounced.'

Ronda shook her head. 'He's in Clare,' she said. 'His wife's brother died so they've—'

'I thought he was divorced?' said Annie.

'He is. Or maybe just separated. I'm not sure.'

'He's a bit of a fly-by-night, isn't he?' said Annie, shaking her head grimly.

Ronda didn't think so, but then, what did she know?

'I'll go see if there's anyone at the door,' she said, anxious to get away from the conversation.

Through the mottled glass of the hall door, she could see the branches of the laburnum tree, flailing around in the strengthening wind.

Ronda glanced up and down the road. It was empty.

It started to rain.

She wrapped her cardigan tighter around her body and closed the door.

CHAPTER 46

The next day, the manager of Sunset Boulevard rang Green Gables, wondering where Sheila's paperwork was. Luckily for Ronda, Fergal was out. His calendar said, 'Meeting with MD of Sanitation Services'. This meeting was taking place on the championship links course at The Island Golf Club in Donabate. The club served 12oz fillet steaks and boasted a well-stocked wine cellar. Fergal had his company credit card. He would not be back any time soon.

Monika took a message, then paged Ronda.

'Ronda to reception please,' Monika called through the intercom. 'Ronda McCann to reception immediately.'

'You have to give them the paperwork,' Monika told Ronda when she arrived at reception.

'I know,' said Ronda.

'Today,' said Monika.

'I will,' said Ronda.

Back in the dayroom, Ronda brought Sheila over to a chair by the window so she could watch the antics of the local birds in the bath that Ernest had made on the patio. Every time one of the birds dive-bombed into the bath, Sheila laughed. She had a hearty laugh. 'What kind of birds are they?' asked Ronda.

'Starlings,' Sheila said. 'Me and Noel saw a murmuration of starlings once. At Lough Ennell. It was like a mythical creature, rising up out of the lake.'

It sometimes still astonished Ronda, the clarity of some of her charges' memories. The articulation of them.

What made these ones unforgettable while so many others fell away, as if they'd never happened?

'Do you like it here, Sheila?' asked Ronda.

Sheila smiled. 'I like the birds,' she said.

Sunset Boulevard was in the middle of an industrial estate near the airport. There were no trees to hang a bird table from.

Margo texted to ask if she could pick Ronda up for her lesson at lunchtime instead. She had thought Malcolm would be able to attend Tiernan's parent–teacher meeting this evening, but HQ had called an impromptu Town Hall meeting that he couldn't get out of. Margo would give Ronda a quick lesson at one, chair a work Zoom meeting on her way to Tiernan's school, and then do a lap of his teachers.

'I don't mind going to the parent–teacher meeting, to be honest,' said Margo when she picked Ronda. 'I could sit there all day and listen to his teachers heap praise on him. It's like the best performance review ever.'

'You were going to miss his parent–teacher meeting?' said Ronda. 'To give me a driving lesson?'

'You need all the help you can get,' said Margo.

'That's . . . really kind of you,' said Ronda.

'Yeah well, I'll make it to the meeting after all,' said Margo, 'so it's no biggie.'

'Thank you,' said Ronda quietly.

'You won't be thanking me when we're done,' said Margo grimly. 'Today it's all about reversing around corners.'

'The whole lesson?'

Margo nodded. 'It's the only bit you really need to work on,' she said.

'What about the parallel parking?' said Ronda. 'I'm awful at that too.'

'You are,' said Margo, 'but it's not on the test curriculum.'

'But shouldn't I know how to do it?' said Ronda, who would rather do anything other than reversing around corners.

'Nah,' said Margo. 'You can just park perpendicularly.'

By the end of the lesson, Ronda had reversed around thirteen corners. The closest she had got to the kerb was seventy-four centimetres.

'Twenty-four centimetres to go,' said Margo, measuring the gap with her pocket tape.

'I'm never going to get it,' said Ronda.

'You will,' said Margo.

'I won't.'

'You will.'

'I won't.'

'I have to go,' said Margo. 'Can you walk back to work from here?'

Ronda couldn't get out of the car fast enough.

Traffic was heavy. Ronda reckoned she'd be quicker walking back to Green Gables. But instead of walking towards the nursing home, she found herself turning the other way, heading in the opposite direction, as if her mind and body had disconnected.

In fifteen minutes, she was outside The Flagstones. She hadn't given much thought to what she would do once she got there. She stood outside. She didn't go in to see if Flossie was behind the bar.

She rang Charlo. It rang twice before he cut her off.

She didn't know what she had been thinking. And now she would be late for work. Ronda hurried back up the road. At the top, she stopped. She returned to the pub, took a photograph of the sign over the door.

The Flagstones.

Then she sent it to Charlo.

She had twenty minutes to make it back to Green Gables. If she ran, she might make it.

She was stopped at a pedestrian crossing, waiting for the green light, when a man in the window of a French patisserie caught her attention. At first she couldn't be certain it was Malcolm. The light went green and pedestrians crossed the road, so Ronda could only catch glimpses of the café through gaps in the throng. She saw Lazy Susans laden with colourful macaroons. The sign over the door. Chez Antoinette. The side profile of the man in the window. He picked up an espresso cup, tossed it back like it was a shot, the same way Malcolm did. He wore a three-piece pinstripe suit, similar to the ones Malcolm favoured, and had the same gym-keen build. As Ronda crossed the road, she saw that there was someone else at the table. A woman. Young. Late twenties maybe. Petite and pretty, with long, brown hair, which appeared to be a recent recipient of a curly blow-dry. The man laughed, then leaned towards the woman, wiping froth from her top lip with his finger, licked it clean. He looked at the woman with performative intensity. Ronda moved out of the flow of pedestrians, stood beside a postbox. She must be mistaken. Malcolm had a Town Hall meeting at his office in the city. Isn't that what Margo had said? The man pointed at something out of the window. Ronda ducked behind the postbox. She waited a moment, then straightened and peeked over the top. Now the man was talking. In the same fluent, authoritative way that Malcolm did. The woman hung on his every word. It couldn't be him, Ronda concluded. Malcolm wasn't that interesting. She looked at her watch. She had to get a move on or she would be late for work. With the new clocking-in system, it would be noted on her file, which Fergal would bring up if she ever got to talk to him about that supervisor role. Before she slipped away, she took one more furtive glance over the top of the postbox. At the table, the man rummaged in the inside pocket of his suit jacket.

'Do you mind?'

Ronda spun around.

'I'm trying to post a letter,' said a woman, peevish in a pink tracksuit, with a rolled-up yoga mat under her arm.

'Sorry,' said Ronda, stepping back.

Now she was in plain sight. But the man wasn't looking in her direction. From the inside pocket of his jacket, he pulled out a phone. A bright blue phone.

Cornflower blue.

He flipped the phone open with his thumb. One slick flick.

There could be no doubt.

It was Malcolm.

CHAPTER 47

Ronda didn't remember getting to Green Gables. Fergal, lounging by Monika's desk in reception, informed her that she was seven minutes late. Monika, relieved to have been divested of his attention, returned to eBay where she was bidding for a stair gate for her preternaturally active nine-month-old.

'It's not that I mind,' said Fergal, as Ronda trudged through reception. 'As you know, I pride myself on flexibility in my management style. But the Americans are a different animal altogether Ronda. You'd do well not to make a habit of this.'

Ronda walked past him towards the double doors behind the reception desk. She rummaged in her pocket for her lanyard.

'Ronda?' said Fergal, following her. 'Did you hear what I said?'

She nodded as the doors opened.

'Did you get that paperwork over to Sunset Boulevard?' Fergal called after her.

Her phone rang as she stepped through the doors, into the corridor. She pulled it out of her pocket. It was Charlo. 'I have to take this,' she called to Fergal, as the doors closed.

'Hello?' Ronda's voice was calm and even. She was unable to muster any anxiety about Charlo. He was just another man, being unfaithful to a woman.

'Are you trying to blackmail me?' Charlo was already shouting.

'I think Flossie has a right to know what kind of man you are,' said Ronda.

'She knows about Sheila,' said Charlo.

'Well then, she won't be surprised when I bring Sheila in to see her,' said Ronda.

'You wouldn't dare,' said Charlo.

'I saw they have steak and kidney pie on the menu,' said Ronda. 'That's Sheila's favourite dinner.'

'I'm phoning my solicitor,' said Charlo. 'This has gone far enough.'

'Speaking of solicitors,' Ronda went on, 'Sheila is being represented by Donal Clarke. Make sure you let your solicitor know.'

Down the line, Ronda could almost hear the sound of Charlo's eyes bulging, his wet, fleshy lips flapping.

'What is it you want?' he said eventually, his voice lower now.

'Let Sheila stay at Green Gables,' said Ronda.

'Is that it?'

'Yes,' said Ronda.

'And you won't say anything? To Flossie?'

'No,' said Ronda.

'What are you getting out of this?' asked Charlo, baffled.

'My job is to look after Sheila,' said Ronda. 'That's what I'm doing.'

She hung up.

It was a win. A small one perhaps. One that Sheila would never know about. But a win nonetheless.

Ronda should have felt good.

All she could think about was Margo.
She'd have to tell her.
She couldn't tell her.
She knew she should.
She had no idea how.

The good thing about working at Green Gables when you were in need of distraction was the heavy workload. Ronda went from task to task, stopping only to see if Fatima had heard anything. The IPO's decision was due any day now.

'No news is good news,' said Fatima who was also rushing from task to task, trying to get all her jobs done within the reduced hours she was now working.

Once Ronda's charges were warm, clean, fed, hydrated and distracted, they were unlikely to notice any signs that Ronda's mind was elsewhere.

This was not the case with Ms Gallagher, however, whose powers of observation had not been diminished by recent events.

'What's eating you?' she asked, as Ronda helped her into her wheelchair.

'Nothing,' said Ronda, crouching to place each of Ms Gallagher's feet onto the rests.

'You've a face like a smacked arse, so you do.'

'I'm fine,' said Ronda. 'Do you want a blanket to tuck around you?'

'It's hotter than hell in this place,' said Ms Gallagher. 'If I put another layer on, I'll burst into flames.'

'Can I do anything else for you?' asked Ronda, standing up.

'You can tell me what ails you,' said Ms Gallagher. 'I could do with some distraction.'

'Ronda?' Tracey paused outside Ms Gallagher's door, peered in. 'If you're at a loose end, you can get a urine sample from Captain Grady. He's in terrible form today.'

'Sean hasn't been around lately,' said Ronda.

'Why?' asked Tracey.

'He's away with his son,' said Ronda. 'That's probably why Captain Grady is a bit out of sorts,' she added.

'Well, whatever it is, he won't let me near him,' said Tracey. 'So you'll have to do it.'

'She can't,' said Ms Gallagher. 'She's wheeling me around what's left of the garden. My arms aren't up to wheeling this contraption today.'

'What's wrong with them?' asked Tracey.

'None of your business,' said Ms Gallagher. 'Let's go, Ronda.'

Ronda pushed the chair out the door, stopping at the cloakroom to put on her coat and hat. Ms Gallagher refused to put hers on. 'I like the cold,' she said. 'Reminds me that I'm still alive, albeit barely.' A sharp easterly wind whipped Ms Gallagher's words away, and already Ronda could see goosebumps, rising along her arms, where she'd pulled the sleeves of her jacket up to her elbows. Still, there was no point in arguing with her. Ronda had never managed to change Ms Gallagher's mind about anything.

The hoarding was still in place but the roof of the new build could now be seen over the top of it. Men in hard hats crouched on it, their mouths full of nails as they hammered tiles in place. A generator emitted smoke as well as a choked rumbling sound. Ms Gallagher wheeled herself away from the noise and Ronda had to stride to keep up with her.

'Your arms are all better then?' she said.

Ms Gallagher allowed a small smile to dart across her face as the wind whipped her hair into a tangle of tumbleweed. She stopped at the sturdy wooden bench Ernest had made at the bottom of the garden.

Ronda sat down.

'Well?' said Ms Gallagher, locking the brake and folding her arms expectantly. Ronda knew there was no point in dodging Ms Gallagher's questions. Captain Grady would call them heat-seeking missiles.

'It's private,' said Ronda. This admission did nothing to deter Ms Gallagher.

'Who am I going to tell?' she asked. 'Everyone I know is either dead or not speaking to me.'

That could be true. Ms Gallagher was disinclined towards exaggeration.

'It's Margo's husband,' Ronda began.

Ms Gallagher shook her head. 'He's playing away,' she said.

'I can't be one hundred per cent certain,' said Ronda. 'I saw him in a café with a woman. He's supposed to be in a meeting.'

'Younger?' asked Ms Gallagher. Ronda nodded.

'A stunner no doubt?'

Ronda nodded again.

'He's playing away,' said Ms Gallagher, grimly.

'Maybe she's a work colleague?' said Ronda, blowing into her hands to warm them. Ms Gallagher withered Ronda with a cynical expression.

'When are you going to tell Margo?'

Ronda felt every muscle in her body clench. Ms Gallagher's question was like a finger poking at an open wound.

'I could be mistaken,' said Ronda.

'You have to tell her,' said Ms Gallagher.

'She's mad about him,' said Ronda.

'She probably already knows,' said Ms Gallagher. 'Women usually do, we're cursed with insight.'

'But what if she doesn't?' said Ronda. 'She seems . . .' Ronda stopped. She had been about to say, 'happy'. 'She never says anything negative about Malcolm,' she said instead.

'Keeping up appearances,' said Ms Gallagher, sighing. 'Another thing women are gifted at.'

'What if you're wrong?' asked Ronda.

Ms Gallagher grinned, so wide that Ronda could see the fillings in her molars. 'Well then, I suppose there's a first time for everything.' She lifted a hand and patted Ronda's arm awkwardly, proving that there was indeed a first time for everything. 'You're frozen to the bone, girl,' she said. 'If we were going to my house, I'd make you a bowl of my carrot soup with turmeric and ginger. Edel loved that one, when she was poorly. It would warm the cockles of any heart, so it would.' Ms Gallagher kept her voice gruff. But behind the words, Ronda could hear a yearning for home. She made a point of not asking the residents about their old lives; she found they told her what they wanted her to know. Or what they could remember. And maybe it was a way to protect herself too. Because now she was imagining Ms Gallagher's kitchen. An empty room. Bare and cold, with a thick layer of dust covering the surfaces, a sweeping brush leaning useless against a wall, and pots and pans hanging by handles over a range, swaying in a chilly draught, waiting for her to come back. To come home and make soup that could warm the cockles of any heart.

Ronda stood up and turned away from Ms Gallagher's scrutiny. She made a great show of brushing off the back of her coat, as if some splinters of wood might have attached themselves to the fabric.

'You'll tell Margo?' said Ms Gallagher when Ronda turned around.

'I will,' she said in a small voice.

Ms Gallagher leaned against the back of the wheelchair as if she were suddenly exhausted. When Ronda put her hands on the handles and pushed her back towards the building, Ms Gallagher did not object.

CHAPTER 48

Ronda would have loved to ask Donal for his advice. There was a touch of the agony aunt about him she sometimes thought. He had an ability to listen without prejudice, a rare skill. She wondered what was keeping him in Clare. He was helping out, no doubt. That was the problem when you were a helpful person. People asked for your help.

Ronda also knew that there was no need to ask Donal – or anyone else – for advice. Ms Gallagher was right. She had to tell Margo.

She didn't want to tell her in the confined space of the car, so she waited until the end of the next driving lesson, a mere six days away from the test.

The decision to wait until the end of the lesson was a mis-step. The lesson finished at the hospice, since Margo had a lunch meeting with one of her most valued fundraisers. 'You don't mind making your own way back to work again, do you?' asked Margo, directing Ronda into the car park at the hospice, where Ronda managed to park – perpendicularly – between two white lines.

Ronda turned off the engine. 'Margo, there's something I need to tell you. It's about—'

'Can we walk and talk?' said Margo, checking her watch. 'The woman I'm meeting is a volunteer and doesn't have a lot of time.' She got out of the car and strode towards the

317

main entrance, leaving Ronda with no choice but to hurry after her.

A young man wearing a turban smiled when Margo pushed through the front doors. 'I have a few messages for you, Margo,' he said, holding out a couple of yellow stickies. 'And your lunchtime appointment has been pushed back to one fifteen p.m. if that's okay with you?'

'Thanks Ashneer,' said Margo, not stopping but slowing sufficiently to take the messages.

'Let me know when you want the sandwiches sent up, okay?' He called after her as the phone rang.

'Will do,' said Margo.

'Good afternoon, St. Bridget's Hospice, how can I help?' said Ashneer, smiling a greeting at Ronda.

She hurried after Margo, wondering what the hell she was doing here. What was she thinking? She couldn't tell Margo here. At her place of work. Before a meeting. It was out of the question. But if not now, then when? She should have told her by now. Margo would want details. She would want to know when Ronda had seen what she had seen. Then she would demand to know why. Why Ronda hadn't told her before now. Margo stopped at the lift and Ronda bumped into the back of her.

'Sorry,' she said.

'You okay?' said Margo, stabbing the call button. 'You seem distracted.' The lift pinged and the doors slid open, revealing an elderly man in an immaculate suit.

'Ah Margo,' he said, tipping his felt hat at her as he made his slow way out of the lift. Margo held the door for him.

'How's Rose doing?' she asked.

'I read Keats to her this morning,' he said.

'"Heard melodies are sweet, but those unheard are sweeter",' quoted Margo. 'That's the line I remember from school.'

'*Ode on a Grecian Urn*,' said the man, smiling. 'One of Rose's favourites.'

Margo stepped into the lift. Ronda followed her. 'See you later, John,' Margo said as the doors slid shut. 'So,' Margo turned to Ronda, pressing the button for the top floor, 'what did you want to talk to me about?'

'Well,' said Ronda, shifting her backpack from one shoulder to the other. 'The thing is—' She was interrupted by the lift, jerking to a stop at the next floor. A woman in a bright orange jumpsuit and a blue buzz cut got in, carrying a bundle of files.

'I'm just waiting on one more donor to get back to me and that report will be good to go, Margo,' the woman said. 'I'll email it to you later this afternoon.'

'That's great, thanks Caroline,' said Margo. 'This is my sister, by the way. Ronda.'

'You're nothing alike,' said Caroline, glancing from one to the other.

'We get that a lot,' said Margo.

Caroline got out at the next floor. Ronda could see comfortable couches, bookshelves, a small, tidy kitchenette where someone was making a pot of coffee. Music drifted down the hall. Massenet's 'Méditation'.

There was no time to say anything between that floor and the next one, which is where they got out. Margo walked briskly down a brightly lit corridor, greeting various staff members as she went. 'Welcome to my lair,' she said, opening her office door. 'I can't believe this is your first time here.' She glanced at the clock on the wall. 'You have exactly thirteen minutes,' she said.

Ronda wasn't superstitious, but that seemed like another reason why here was not a good place to tell Margo. Why now was not a good time.

'I saw Malcolm with a woman,' she blurted out. Margo said nothing. Ronda kept it as short as possible, the details scarce. The café. The day and time. The young woman. Malcolm. She didn't mention how the young woman had never dropped her eyes from Malcolm's face. How Malcolm had touched her hair, twirled the fine strands around his fingers. How he had made her laugh. And when she laughed, how she had tipped her head so that her hair cascaded down her back in magnificent, undulating waves as Malcolm admired the pale delicacy of her neck.

'Are you for real?' Margo's voice was dangerously low.

'I'm sorry,' Ronda whispered.

'You wait until you get your pound of flesh out of me before you drop your bombshell.'

'That wasn't why I—' began Ronda.

'I don't know why I'm surprised,' Margo said. 'You've always been jealous of me.'

'That's not true,' said Ronda.

'You feel that I got everything and you got nothing and now you're trying to take me down a peg or two.'

'No,' said Ronda. 'It's not like that at all.'

'And you've never liked Malcolm,' Margo said. 'You think he's pretentious, I know you do.'

'Malcolm's a good father to the boys,' Ronda said in response, which, she realised, was the same as saying that Malcolm was pretentious. That she'd never liked him.

That he had never been good enough for Margo.

'The young woman's name is Madeleine Halpin,' said Margo. 'She is Malcolm's protégé. She shadows him. To meetings and whatnot. That's what you saw. That's what was going on there.' Margo sounded out of breath, her chest rising and falling with the force of her breathing.

'I'm sorry,' said Ronda. 'I really am. I thought, since you'd mentioned Malcolm being in the Town Hall meeting and that being the reason he couldn't go to Tiernan's school that afternoon, I —'

'Just stop,' said Margo. 'Stop talking. I've heard enough. I want you to go.'

She held the door open as Ronda let herself out.

CHAPTER 49

'Fatima to reception, please,' came Monika's flat drawl through the tannoy at Green Gables at lunchtime the following day. 'Fatima Nwodo to reception immediately please.'

Fatima was on the floor in the dayroom, groping under Teresa's chair for Baby, who had slipped down the side. She picked up the doll and offered it to Teresa, who shook her head and turned her face away.

'Maybe it's your case worker,' said Ronda, taking Baby from Fatima. 'You'd better go.'

'I'll be as quick as I can,' said Fatima, setting off at a trot.

'Take your time,' said Ronda. 'It's quiet in here today.'

It was true that a low mood seemed to have pervaded the dayroom. Ms Gallagher sat in the corner, turning the pages of a newspaper. The movement was a listless one, and she no longer peered out of the window whenever she heard a car coming up the driveway. Hope, it seemed, had finally died.

Captain Grady was slumped in his chair with one of the buttons of his jacket in the wrong hole and a ketchup stain on the trousers of his uniform. Ronda stood in front of him, clicked her heels together and saluted. This roused Captain Grady enough to perform a small salute back at her.

'Sean will be back soon,' she told him, leaning down to fix his button.

'He's a good boy,' said Captain Grady.

Ronda straightened Captain Grady's hat. 'You can tell him that when he comes back.'

'Tell him what?' said Captain Grady, looking blankly at Ronda.

Only Sheila seemed her usual self, glued to an episode of *Columbo* on the telly, and making fast work of the sharing bag of jellies Kim had given her. Charlo hadn't made an appearance since Ronda's phone conversation with him. Sunset Boulevard had cancelled their transfer request, and the paperwork that Fergal had asked Ronda to prepare had been shredded in the new machine at reception that Monika had ordered on eBay.

Ronda's phone beeped and she wrestled it out of the pocket of her scrubs, stabbing at the screen to see if it was Margo, returning her calls. And texts. And WhatsApps. But it wasn't. It was a telemarketer. Which reminded her of Donal. No word from him either. Ronda told the telemarketer she had everything she needed, thanked him and hung up.

Fatima didn't come back. When Ronda went to look for her, Fergal told her she had gone home.

'Why?' asked Ronda, her heart thudding inside her chest.

Fergal expelled a dismissive breath. 'She claimed to have a headache,' he said. 'I told her to man up and take paracetamol like the rest of us do, but no, she turned on the water works and that was that.'

'When did she go?' asked Ronda.

'A few minutes ago,' said Fergal.

Ronda ran up the corridor.

'Where are you going?' Fergal shouted after her. 'You can't go, you have to cover for Fatima.'

'I'll be back in a minute,' Ronda called over her shoulder.

She flew through reception, out into the car park and down the avenue. Fatima was sitting at the bus stop. Ronda skidded to a halt in front of her. 'Fatima?'

Fatima rubbed furiously at her eyes. Ronda found a clean tissue in her pocket, handed it to her.

'I'm so sorry, Fatima,' Ronda said.

Fatima nodded. 'So am I,' she said. Her tone was flat. Resigned.

'What happens now?' asked Ronda.

'They will send out a deportation date,' said Fatima.

'When?'

Fatima shrugged. 'My case worker wasn't certain, but she thought it would happen sooner rather than later. A matter of weeks, she said.'

'Does Donal know?' asked Ronda. 'Maybe he can—'

Fatima stood up, putting out her hand as a bus approached.

'What can I do?' asked Ronda.

The bus pulled up, the doors opening. Fatima shook her head.

'Nothing,' she said.

At No. 10 Casino Place, Annie was packing an overnight bag. She was spending the night with Margo, since she had an early appointment with Dr Anderson the next morning.

'Good for me to get used to staying there,' said Annie, packing her bag with enough stuff for a week. 'Since I could end up living there soon.'

'I haven't failed the test yet,' said Ronda, feeling that Margo would be pleased with her use of the word, 'yet'.

'Best to be prepared,' said Annie, grimly.

Margo didn't come inside the house when she arrived to

pick Annie up. Nor did she get out of her car. She looked straight ahead when Ronda opened the passenger door and helped Annie in.

'Bye,' said Ronda.

Margo drove away before Annie had finished putting her seatbelt on.

Later, Ronda rang Fatima, but it went straight to voicemail. She thought about ringing Donal to tell him. But she didn't. It wasn't her news to tell.

She played a game of chess, but neglected to develop her knight and bishop early enough. Berkley, not one to make allowances in any circumstances, had her on the ropes and kept her there while he crept to victory in his fastidious way.

She crossed another day off the calendar. Five days to the test and her driving instructor wasn't speaking to her and she still couldn't reverse around a corner properly.

The phone rang at half ten. Ronda hurried to her backpack to get the phone out. Half ten was never a good time for a phone call.

It was Fergal.

'I'm afraid I have some bad news,' he said.

CHAPTER 50

'Which one of them is it?' said Ronda. Her mind raced through the possibilities. Captain Grady? Sheila? Teresa? It could be any of them.

'Fergal?' she said. 'Which one?'

'It's Ms Gallagher,' he said.

'Ms Gallagher?' Ronda repeated.

'In her sleep,' said Fergal. 'Sudden. She wouldn't have felt any pain, the doctor said.'

Ronda couldn't think of anything more ludicrous. Someone as vibrant and loud and colourful and relentless as Ms Gallagher just . . . coming to a stop like that. Without a roar. Without even a murmur.

'An hour ago,' said Fergal. 'I rang you as soon as the coroner came and confirmed everything.'

Ronda pressed the phone against her ear so she could feel the hard heat of it.

'Ronda?'

'I'm here,' she said.

'Do you want to . . . see her?' said Fergal. 'I mean, before she's removed to the morgue.'

'Yes,' said Ronda.

'I'm sorry, Ronda,' Fergal said. 'I know you two were close.'

*

326

Ronda cycled to Green Gables. The roads were quiet and the night was dark and cold but dry. A clear night with a dusting of starlight across the sky and a delicate curve of moon. Ronda concentrated on the push of her feet against the pedals. The way her breath erupted from her mouth in a foggy cloud every time she exhaled. She didn't rush because there was nothing to rush for. Ms Gallagher was gone and she hadn't said goodbye to her. She tried to remember the last time they'd spoken. Ms Gallagher in her chair, leafing through the newspaper, not reading it. Not looking out of the window any time a car drove up the avenue. Ronda had said something, hadn't she? Some meaningless observation about the weather. 'It's to rain later.' A person says something stupid like that, and it ends up being the last thing.

Ms Gallagher was in her room. In bed, as if she were asleep. Ronda touched her face, her hands. There was still a trace of warmth there. A tear fell onto Ms Gallagher's cheek, like she was the one who was crying. Ronda kissed it away, then rubbed furiously at her eyes, blew her nose, straightened herself up. Ms Gallagher would not care for Ronda's sympathy. Nor would she want a prayer or a hymn or a moment's silence. She would want Ronda to be practical and professional, so that's what Ronda did.

Ms Gallagher had died in her nightdress, which she would have disapproved of. Ronda carefully removed the nightdress. She filled a basin with warm, soapy water, dipped a sponge into it.

She took her time. She started with Ms. Gallagher's arms, lifting each in turn, running the sponge gently from the shoulder to the wrist, along her hands, in between her fingers.

Her legs were heavy. Ronda lifted first one, then the other. She washed her feet, in between Ms Gallagher's toes, no longer ticklish. There wasn't a sound in the room, save the occasional splash of water when Ronda rinsed the sponge. Ronda did not feel alone. She had a sense of Ms Gallagher. She wasn't long gone.

Ronda left her face until last. Ms Gallagher was wrong. Ronda could make out a faint line where Bernadette had sown the stitches.

Thirteen stitches.

Ronda moved her fingers gently over the ancient scar, determined to be as tender as Bernadette had been all those years ago.

Afterwards, she rubbed lavender-scented lotion into Ms Gallagher's skin, then dressed her. A fresh pair of jeans, a T-shirt, her leather jacket and, of course, the black and white keffiyeh, which Ronda tied loosely around her neck. The white in the scarf matched the white of Ms Gallagher's hair, which was its usual thicket. Ronda ran her fingers gently through it, trying to make it look like it did that day.

The Edel Scanlan day.

Ronda heard footsteps in the corridor. She knew she didn't have much time left. She stood by the bed and picked up Ms Gallagher's hand.

Then she began to sing.

Ronda did not have a great singing voice. She was much too self-conscious for one of those. Still, she sang the song as best she could.

'Come Out, Ye Black and Tans'.

It had been Ms Gallagher's party piece from her life before Green Gables, when parties were a possibility.

When everything was a possibility.

Against the window, Ronda could hear the rain, starting up. She had been right after all. It did rain later. Except Ms Gallagher was no longer around to hear it fall.

CHAPTER 51

Ms Gallagher's funeral was crowded with politicians, journalists, trade unionists, academics and activists. The crematorium wasn't big enough to accommodate them all.

Ronda couldn't tell if Ms Gallagher would have been annoyed or amused by the turnout. Probably annoyed, since that was her default reaction. But also amused, since she was a committed contrarian.

As far as Ronda could tell, no family came. She was relieved. She felt it would have fallen to her to tell them to go fuck themselves since Ms Gallagher wasn't there to do it herself. They had been loud in their opinions of her sexuality and their opinions had not been positive ones. Ms Gallagher had been well able for bigots. Edel Scanlan had not. Ronda had hoped that Edel might come to the funeral. Instead, she had written a letter.

Dear Ronda,

Thank you for letting me know about Lyra's death. I cannot come to the funeral. I feel it would be a great disservice to Lyra, whose love and companionship I spurned for the greater part of our lives. She was the bravest person I ever met. I found it incomprehensible that she loved me. But she did. This much I know. Regret is a useless, monstrous thing, especially now, when there is nothing to be done about it. I regret that Lyra never knew just how much she

meant to me. If only I could have been the person she saw
when she looked at me. I regret what I said that day, when
you brought her to see me. I regret not telling her what I
should have told her a long time ago.
That she was the love of my life.
Yours sincerely,
Edel Scanlan

Ronda made sure she didn't cry at the funeral. Ms Galla-gher would be unimpressed with such a crude display of emotion. Instead, Ronda sang along to 'Mandinka', one of Ms Gallagher's favourite Sinéad O'Connor songs, when the coffin moved inside the chamber and the curtains closed. She belted it out. Everybody did. She saw Patricia Glennon near the front, her eyes closed as she sang along.

Afterwards, Ronda tapped her on the shoulder. 'Excuse me,' she said. She wished she didn't sound so timid and polite.

Patricia looked at her. 'Yes?' she said, struggling to place Ronda. 'Oh, you're one of the staff at Green Gables, aren't you?' said Patricia. 'A Welsh name, isn't that right?'

'You upset Ms Gallagher. She told you those things off the record,' said Ronda.

'Correct,' said Patricia. 'That's why I didn't put it on the podcast.'

'But you wrote it instead, in your column. You—'

'Oh, would you excuse me?' Patricia said, waving at somebody over Ronda's shoulder. And then she was gone. Ronda stood in the room as the crowd moved past her and around her.

She'd never felt more alone.

She looked at her watch. She should go, her shift was starting in thirty minutes. Fergal had said only one person could go to the funeral, since they were so short-staffed. Nobody pointed out that the staff shortages fell under the auspices of the 'Productive Rationalisation' policies brought in by the Americans.

Ronda glanced around. There was no sign of Donal. She had rung to let him know about Ms Gallagher. It didn't seem like the kind of news that should be texted. He hadn't picked up and she hadn't left a message. He'd rung back when she was showering Sheila, and she'd missed the call. Then, on RIP.ie, she saw a message of condolence from him, which meant he knew, which meant there was no need for her to phone him again.

'Ronda!' The crowd seemed to part like water and suddenly there was Margo and Annie, both elegant in black suits and white blouses. Ronda had to struggle not to cry then.

'What are you two doing here?' she managed to say.

'Mam told me about Ms Gallagher,' said Margo. 'I'm sorry, I know how much you loved her.' She slipped her hand into Ronda's and squeezed gently.

'I can't believe she's gone before me,' said Annie, shaking her head. 'She was so full of life.'

'Anyway,' said Margo. 'We wanted to pay our respects.'

'Ms Gallagher would have appreciated that,' said Ronda.

'She would have reprimanded me for not having anything better to do,' said Margo, matter-of-fact.

'And she'd tell me to catch myself on and stop bellyaching,' said Annie. She looked around. 'I'm going to go and light a candle for the repose of Ms Gallagher's soul.' She

332

disappeared into the crowd before Ronda could tell her that Ms Gallagher had not believed in souls and, even if she had, there were no candles in the crematorium to light for their repose.

Now it was just Ronda and Margo. Ronda studied her feet and Margo examined her nails. The silence between them stretched. They both spoke at the same time.

'I'm really sorry about—' said Ronda, while Margo said, 'The test is—'

They smiled.

'You go,' said Ronda.

'I was just going to say we should probably have one last lesson before the test,' said Margo. 'It's the day after tomorrow in case it's slipped your mind.'

Ronda's throat constricted. She had neglected to mark off the last couple of days in her calendar. 'That would be great,' she said. 'And I'm really sorry about—'

'It's forgotten,' said Margo.

'So, everything's okay then?' said Ronda.

'Of course,' said Margo. 'I already told you and I don't want to get into it again. And I certainly don't want to bother Malcolm with conspiracy theories, he's got enough on his plate with the AGM coming up.' She whipped a diary out of her bag. 'Let's see, how about a quick lesson tomorrow? After your shift?'

'That would be good.'

'Great,' said Margo, tossing her diary back into her bag. 'Now, I have to dash, there's a golf club dinner dance tonight, and I have to be there since they're making the announcement about my captaincy.'

Ronda was about to say something. Congratulations.

Something like that. But Margo was gone so suddenly it was possible to suspect that maybe she hadn't been there at all.

With the absence of Ms Gallagher's family, Ronda felt obliged to stay until the end. She hated the way the curtains closed after the coffin passed through them, everything so silent and still, as if that might make the burning of a body a little more decorous.

Outside, Ronda consulted her watch and hurried through the car park. If she was quick, she might make the next bus. In the distance, a clanking sound, like tin cans rattling along the ground. The noise got louder as Ronda reached the exit. It was coming from a seen-better-days camper van.

'Ronda!' Donal shouted, leaning through the window. 'I'm so sorry I'm late.'

Ronda felt her spirits lift, as if the wind had got hold of them.

Donal stopped the van and jumped out in a crumpled dark blue suit that looked as if it had been expensive once.

'Ms Gallagher will haunt me,' he said.

'She wouldn't waste her time haunting someone with such poor timekeeping skills,' said Ronda. Donal grinned, which Ronda had been hoping for. It was cheering.

'There was a herd of goats on the M50,' explained Donal. 'I didn't realise their horns could do quite so much damage. Probably the stress, poor things. Anyway, it took an age for the guards to round them up, and then there were tailbacks for miles.'

A horn blared. 'Get that contraption out of my way,'

shouted a man, leaning out of his car window and shaking a fist. Donal smiled and waved at the man, as if he had said something else. Something complimentary.

'I need to talk to you,' Donal said, turning back to Ronda. 'Do you have a minute?'

'I'm due back at work,' said Ronda.

'I'll give you a lift,' said Donal. 'I need to speak to Fatima too.'

The man was leaning on his horn now, producing a continuous and raucous blast. Donal opened the passenger door of the camper van and Ronda bolted inside. Donal blew a kiss at the man by way of apology, although Ronda did not think the apology had been accepted, judging by the man's blood red face. Donal got in, turned over the engine and pulled away.

'I'm so sorry for your loss,' he said. 'I can't believe she's gone. So suddenly. Are you okay?'

Ronda nodded. She was well acquainted with death. In her business, it was often a release when it came. She didn't feel relief now. She felt loss. It was heavy, the feeling. But also potent. You must have loved to have lost, Fatima always said.

'I loved her,' said Ronda suddenly, surprising herself.

Donal covered Ronda's hand with his own, held it for a moment. His hand was warm, the weight of it a comfort.

'She left something for you,' he said, pointing at the glove compartment. 'Take a look.' Inside was a manila envelope. Ronda lifted it out. Her name was written on the front in Ms Gallagher's familiar hand.

'What's this?' she asked.

'It's a copy of Ms Gallagher's last will and testament.

That's what I was helping her with. I didn't think I'd be executing it quite so soon.'

Donal stopped at traffic lights and pulled up the handbrake.

'She said she was giving everything she had to People Before Profit,' said Ronda.

'They're beneficiaries all right,' said Donal. 'But so are you.'

'Why?' asked Ronda.

'She said you never patronised her,' said Donal.

'I wouldn't dare,' said Ronda.

The lights went green and he drove through the junction.

'What did she leave me?' asked Ronda.

'A fund,' said Donal.

'I presume there are conditions?' asked Ronda.

Donal nodded.

'What does she want me to do?' asked Ronda.

'You sound worried,' said Donal.

'I won't want to do it,' said Ronda.

'How can you be so sure?' asked Donal.

Ronda shrugged. 'That's just who I am,' she said.

'You don't seem like that to me,' said Donal, looking at her with something like respect. Or admiration. Or a heady mix of both. Ronda wanted to tell him to stop looking at her. To keep his eyes on the road. But, for a moment, she felt herself elevated. As if she could be that person. The person Donal saw when he looked at her like that.

'It's an education fund,' Donal went on, his eyes on the road again. 'To pay for you to finish your degree in nursing.'

'Oh,' said Ronda.

'She said you'd be surprised,' said Donal.

'I did want to be a nurse,' said Ronda. 'But that was a long time ago.'

'You must have mentioned it to Ms Gallagher,' said Donal.

Ronda nodded slowly. 'I must have,' she said.

'So that means you still want that,' said Donal.

Nurse McCann.

For an instant, Ronda allowed the idea to gain a foothold in her head. Maybe she could specialise in geriatrics. Look at all the experience she had with the residents at Green Gables. People said she was good with them. Ms Gallagher had thought so too. 'You've the patience of Saint Brigid,' she'd said when she came upon Ronda doing something she considered arduous. Like talking Captain Grady down when he went on manoeuvres around the corridors. Persuading him to take his medication. Holding his hand when he had to have an injection. He hated needles.

Donal pulled his window down and the wind blew inside the cab, tossing Ronda's fringe into her eyes. She shook it out of her way and doused herself in the cold waters of reality.

'I can't afford to be a student,' said Ronda. 'Especially at the moment. I could be looking at a serious rent hike soon.'

'Not if you pass your driving test,' said Donal, reasonably.

'I'm too old to go to college,' Ronda went on.

'Ms Gallagher said you'd say that,' said Donal.

'What else did she say?' Ronda asked, curious.

'That you'll be a great nurse.' Donal indicated and drove up the avenue towards Green Gables. He pulled up at the front door.

'I should really have done this in a much more formal way,' said Donal. 'A meeting in my office sort of thing.'

'Unorthodox,' said Ronda, remembering.

'What?' asked Donal, confused.

'That's how I described you to Ms Gallagher. She said it was a good characteristic in a solicitor,' said Ronda.

'I've been called a lot worse,' said Donal.

'Thanks for the lift,' said Ronda, opening the door and getting out of the van.

'Ronda?'

His face looked paler when he was being serious. His hair had been treated to a recent trim and that, coupled with the uncharacteristic formality of the suit, gave him the earnest look of a schoolboy on the first day of term.

'Ms Gallagher wanted you to have this money,' he said. 'She said you deserved it.'

'I was just doing my job,' said Ronda. She couldn't help feeling warmed by his words.

'I'd better go park this yoke.' Donal smiled, attracting her attention to his mouth. It was a wide mouth, his lips full and stained the deep pink of oxygenated blood. She found herself wondering what he would taste like.

'What?' asked Donal. 'Do I have something stuck in my teeth?'

Ronda shook her head. 'I was just wondering . . . Would you mind if I . . .' She paused there, unsure quite how to phrase it.

'Would I mind if you what?' Ronda could tell she had aroused his curiosity.

'If I kiss you?' asked Ronda.

'Not at all,' said Donal in his cheerful, amenable way. 'Are you coming in here or should I get out?'

'I'll come in.'

Ronda stepped up into the van, sat on the passenger seat

and reached over the handbrake until she was close enough to feel his breath on her face. He pushed her fringe to the side. He was looking right at her. Not impatient or anything. Just . . . waiting.

'I feel a bit . . . awkward,' Ronda said then.

'No need,' said Donal. 'Unless . . . you don't want to now?'

'I do.'

'Okay then.'

'Okay.'

'Whenever you're ready.'

'I'm ready now.'

Ronda breached the space between them. His mouth was firm against hers. It tasted like . . . she wasn't sure. Something fruity maybe. Sweet. She put her hands on his face, raspy with stubble. The kiss deepened. It was delicious.

Like biting into a peach.

The sound of the engine starting up startled her.

'Would I mind if you what?' asked Donal, looking at her standing there on the drive, clutching the Manila envelope with Ms Gallagher's will inside.

'If I think about it,' she said, nodding at the envelope.

'Sure,' said Donal. 'Take your time.'

'Do I only get the money if I go back to college?' asked Ronda.

Donal nodded. 'But Ms Gallagher seemed pretty convinced you would go back,' he said.

'Even death can't stop her from being a bossy cow,' said Ronda.

They grinned at each other.

'It's nice to have you back,' Ronda said before she could stop herself.

'It's a brief visit,' said Donal. 'I'm heading back to Clare later this afternoon.'

Disappointment felt like a lift going down inside Ronda's body.

'Things are a bit complicated,' said Donal, his face furrowing. 'There's a family business that Trish's brother Pat ran. A café. So that needs to be wound up and sold. Or, I don't know, find someone to run it maybe. And then there's the family home. Pat lived there, so now it has to be cleared out and packed up. Trish isn't doing well. She asked me to stay and help.'

The front door of Green Gables opened and Fatima shot out.

'Why did you want to see me?' she said, running over to Donal's van.

'Hang on,' said Donal. 'I'll park and come in.'

'I don't have time,' said Fatima. 'My break is fifteen minutes, and I've already used four of them.'

'I'll leave you two to it,' said Ronda.

'Stay,' said Fatima, holding out her hand to Ronda. 'Hold my hand, in case it's bad news.'

'I wrote to the International Protection Appeals Tribunal about your case,' Donal said.

'And?' said Fatima, squeezing Ronda's hand, her trademark optimism creeping into her voice.

'We got leave to appeal,' said Donal.

'I can appeal?' said Fatima, her voice catching on the words.

Donal nodded. 'I brought the forms with me,' he said. 'If you sign them now, I can get them over to the Appeals

Tribunal office before I head back to Clare.' He opened his satchel and pulled a sheaf of papers out and handed them to Fatima.

'I can appeal,' she said again, in a louder voice.

'The chances are slim,' said Donal, trying to rein in Fatima's expectations. 'You have to do another interview.'

Fatima laughed, the breadth of her optimism too wide to be compromised. 'Did you hear that?' she said, turning to Ronda. 'Maybe Ada and I can stay.' Her smile was dazzling. Ronda looked away. She could hardly bear to watch Fatima's hope bloom once more, like a delicate rose reaching up through a rocky crevice.

'Let me sign them now,' said Fatima, pulling a pen out of her pocket. She put the form on the passenger seat and signed the back page. 'Thank you,' she said to Donal.

'Can I have a quick word with you before you go back to work, Fatima?' Donal said. Fatima looked at her watch. 'I have seven minutes,' she said.

'I'd better get back to work,' said Ronda.

'Good luck with the driving test,' Donal called as she walked towards the building. 'I'll see you soon I'm sure.'

Ronda wanted to know how soon and how sure. She knew these were not the type of questions people asked. And even if they were, she wasn't the type of person who asked them. Instead, she waved and smiled like people did.

Donal caught her eye and for a moment they did nothing but look at each other. Then he nodded and it felt like an assurance. That he would see her soon. That he wanted to.

CHAPTER 52

At Green Gables, life went on as it always did. It was as if Ms Gallagher had never lived there. In the dayroom, Tracey was stomping about looking for the TV remote. Ronda could see it poking out of the sleeve of Captain Grady's military jacket. Kim sat on a stool beside Baby's crib, gently brushing Teresa's hair. 'Room number 23,' Teresa said.

'The house was beside the bakery, wasn't it?' said Kim.

Teresa nodded. 'We could smell the bread in the mornings,' she said.

Sheila sat at the window watching the finches argue over the seeds she had scattered in the birdhouse earlier. Ernest had made it from the same material as the birdbath.

'You haven't seen Charlo in a while,' said Tracey, looking under Sheila's chair.

'Who?' said Sheila.

Somebody else who hadn't been seen in a while was Sean. Captain Grady noticed him first, walking down the corridor and in through the doors of the dayroom. 'Private Grady,' he shouted, whisking his hat off his head and lifting it into the air like some sort of victory salute. His excitement was infectious.

Even Sean smiled. 'At ease, soldier,' he said to his father.

'How was Brittas?' Ronda asked.

'It wasn't terrible,' said Sean.

'That sounds better than you were expecting,' said Ronda, smiling.

'There was no Wi-Fi.'

'How did Eddie cope?'

'There was a chess board in the caravan,' said Sean.

'A great game of military strategy,' Captain Grady piped up.

'Do you play?' Ronda asked him.

Captain Grady shook his head, worry darkening his face. 'The colonel said games were for girls,' he said.

Sean sat down beside him, took his hand. 'The colonel isn't here any more,' he said. Captain Grady looked around the dayroom. 'Are you sure?' he asked.

'Yes,' said Sean. 'I'm sure.' He pulled the TV remote out of Captain Grady's sleeve.

'Where did you find the remote?' asked Tracey, taking it out of Sean's hand. Captain Grady looked alarmed.

'On the floor,' said Sean, innocently.

Tracey tutted as she pointed the remote at the TV and jabbed at buttons until a film came on.

It was *My Fair Lady*. Nobody seemed to think it was strange when Ms Gallagher didn't charge into the dayroom in her wheelchair, rail about the vile sexism and classism in the film not to mention Henry Higgins' rampaging misogyny, then demand to have it turned off, but not before Eliza Doolittle sang 'Just You Wait'.

She had a sweet spot for Audrey Hepburn too.

'I'm only a human woman.' Ronda could nearly hear her say it, in her loud, indignant voice.

Now, everybody sang along to, 'Why Can't a Woman Be More Like a Man,' as if they had never heard Ms Gallagher heckling and booing Henry Higgins from the dayroom sidelines.

It wasn't personal, this forgetting. It was just dementia, being good at its job. Ronda distracted herself by being good at hers. In this way, she managed to clear out Ms Gallagher's room to make way for a new resident, who was moving in on Friday.

'Need a hand?' Fatima popped her head around the door as Ronda was putting clean sheets on the bed.

'I'm fine, thanks,' said Ronda.

Fatima came in anyway. She picked up a pillow, fed it into a case. 'Donal told me that Ms Gallagher left me money,' she said.

'I'm glad,' said Ronda. She didn't tell Fatima about the fund. Fatima wouldn't let up until Ronda was in the front row of a lecture theatre in DCU.

'It is a lot,' said Fatima. 'Maybe enough for a nice place to rent. If I win my appeal, I could . . .'

'Don't,' said Ronda.

'Don't what?' asked Fatima.

'Make plans,' said Ronda. 'At least, not until you know what's going to happen. For sure.'

Fatima shook her head. 'What's the point of that?' she asked.

'To avoid disappointment,' said Ronda.

Fatima thought about it, then shook her head. 'You're forgetting one little thing,' she said.

'What?'

'Hope,' said Fatima, winking at Ronda.

It was as if Donal had never said anything about slim chances.

It was true.

About hope.

Being the last thing to die.

Margo picked Ronda up after work the next day for the last driving lesson before the test. Even Ronda couldn't help feeling a brief flutter of optimism afterwards.

The lesson went well.

In fact, it was flawless.

Margo said as much.

Hope flared like a match and, for a moment, Ronda allowed herself to indulge it.

What if she passed?

Doubt arrived almost immediately, pitching the match on the ground and stamping on it. 'What's wrong?' asked Margo, watching as doubt stole across Ronda's face like fog.

'I'm just not sure I can pull it off again tomorrow,' Ronda said. 'The dress rehearsal is supposed to be bad, isn't it?'

'This isn't a Broadway musical, Ronda,' said Margo. 'Now get out, I've to pick Tiernan up from his flute lesson in fifteen minutes.'

Ronda got out.

Margo stuck her head out of the window and did her best *Annie* impression, belting out 'Tomorrow' like she was in the comfort of her own shower and no-one was listening.

CHAPTER 53

If it hadn't been for the squirrel, things might have been different.

The test centre was in an industrial estate.

Margo did not hang around. 'I've a Teams meeting to chair in ten minutes,' she told Ronda, jumping out of the car. 'There's a café up the road, I'll work from there, I'll see you in forty minutes, good luck.' She strode away, then stopped and ran back. 'Two things,' she said. 'Don't forget to breathe, and the talcum powder is in the glove compartment. Okay?'

Ronda nodded, and Margo left for good this time, her high heels making a satisfying *clip-clip* sound against the concrete path. She didn't look back. Ronda knew she was doing what she had done to the boys when they were little and didn't want to stay at a summer camp or attend one of their many and varied extracurricular activities. Keep it brief. Don't linger. Smile. Stay positive.

Ronda cast a critical eye around the interior of the car. It was immaculate as usual. The smell of lavender was intense, coming from a small cut-out cardboard tree hanging from the rear-view mirror. It swayed whenever Ronda sighed. She removed it, put it in the glove compartment, took out the tin of talcum powder and sprinkled some on her hands, rubbing them together. The smell of the talc was sickly sweet.

Her mouth was bone dry. Her eyeballs felt gritty. She examined her watch.

Two minutes to go.

The passenger door opened and the inspector got in. A man. Somewhere north of thirty. A rattle of keys in his pocket. A button missing on his shirt. A milky stain in the middle of his tie that ended in an upward curve along the swell of his belly. When he opened his mouth to speak, Ronda got the sharp tang of kipper. He said his name was Ray, which Ronda felt was informal for a driving test examiner. She felt he should elongate it to Raymond.

After a series of questions – tyre pressure, emergency stops, hand signals – all of which Ronda answered verbatim, as if she were reading them straight from the manual – they got out of the car and she showed him how she would go about changing the oil and where the water tank was and how to tell if the tyre tread was low.

Ray had a clipboard and a pen. After each task, he scribbled something.

They got back inside the car and put on their seat belts.

After a while, Ray looked at Ronda. 'Are you going to go?' he asked.

'I was waiting for you to tell me to go,' said Ronda.

'I'm telling you now,' said Ray, with a bit of a Margo eyeroll in his tone.

Ronda drove away from the test centre, careful to check her rear-view mirror, her wing mirrors, back to her rear-view mirror, then out through the windscreen, eyes on the road, hands at ten-to-two on the wheel, straight-backed, alert. She was already exhausted, and she hadn't reached the entrance of the industrial estate. Her hands were hot and damp. She should have used more talc. Even so, she could smell it, the dense sweetness of the powder aggravating her gag reflex. She gripped the wheel so it couldn't slip through her hands, indicated and turned right out of the industrial estate.

Traffic was heavy, which was just as well because Ronda couldn't remember what the speed limit was on any of the roads. Her mind was like interference on a TV screen, all jumbled lines and white noise. She crawled along. She could feel sweat bloom under her arms, between her thighs, the soles of her feet.

'Turn left,' Ray said, as they approached a junction.

His voice was low, the tone flat.

The lights turned red.

Ronda stopped, indicated left. Then she remembered what Margo had said, and took a breath, exhaling it so long and so hard that the pages on Ray's clipboard fluttered in the draught.

'Are you all right?' he asked.

'Yes,' said Ronda. Her voice sounded unfamiliar, like the voice of somebody else, someone from another land, distant and strange. She cleared her throat. 'Thank you for asking,' she managed to add, because Margo also told her to act normal and be polite to the inspector.

The lights turned green and Ronda turned left and the manoeuvre felt smooth and calm and normal.

She drove on.

She surprised herself by performing a passable hill start and managing a tight-fitting and monotonous seven-point turn. The reversing around a corner piece proved just as pointless and problematic as it had ever been, but nonetheless, Ronda completed the manoeuvre. The inspector opened his door and studied the distance between the car and the kerb. Ronda wasn't sure if it was within the requisite fifty centimetres, but it was true to say that it was closer than Ronda had ever managed before. Ray made another notation on his page.

The incident involving the squirrel happened on the way back to the centre. By then, Ronda couldn't help noticing what she thought might be relief, trickling through her body.

She was almost finished. She'd nearly got through it. The questions, the queries, the manoeuvres, the directions, the constant vigilance. She had done it.

But of course she hadn't done it.

She had nearly done it, and that was a different thing altogether.

The squirrel was red this time. Perhaps that had something to do with it. Ronda was used to grey ones. They were the only kind she saw when she cycled through the Botanic Gardens or St Anne's Park. She had understood the red ones to be in decline. Perhaps even extinct. That was not the case. It was a shame that she had to discover this fact during her driving test.

The road to the industrial estate was narrow. It twisted and turned like a branch in a storm. Ronda navigated these inconveniences with not quite ease, but a degree of quiet competence that surprised her. Sometimes she had to pull out onto the other side of the road when she came across a parked car. She indicated and checked her mirrors before executing each manoeuvre, thus earning herself further ticks on the clipboard. Ronda became convinced that these ticks had a lighter touch, and this perhaps encouraged an ever so slight lowering of her guard.

The red squirrel was perched on the branch of a horse chestnut tree on the right-hand side of the road. The tree was thinking about blooming, swollen buds dotted along the boughs, about to burst. The squirrel squatted on its hind legs, taking occasional nibbles from a walnut, clamped between its front paws. Ronda did not see the red squirrel. Or the walnut. She was busy manoeuvring the car past a delivery van, parked a little haphazardly at the side of the road. Once past the van, Ronda accelerated.

She was nearly there.

The red squirrel jumped along the branch of the tree, its bushy tail like an upside down question mark bouncing behind it. It settled halfway down the branch, where it narrowed.

Then, a cat.

Stockier than Jessica Fletcher. A big tom. He crept, stealthy, through the tree, and suddenly there he was, stepping carefully towards the squirrel. The squirrel dropped the walnut and fled, a streak of russet red. There was nothing to do at the end of the branch but jump, which is what the squirrel did. A great leap of faith. That it was doing the right thing. That everything would work out fine in the end.

This was the moment when the red squirrel caught Ronda's attention. The small mammal executed a near perfect landing in terms of technique, if not direction, ending up in the middle of the road. This was the moment Ronda observed that the squirrel was red. She even managed to register surprise at the colour. Then, in direct contravention of Margo's instructions in relation to squirrels or any other animals that might cause an impediment, Ronda jammed on the brakes and swerved to avoid hitting the small creature.

What she did not manage to avoid was the kerb, which she mounted with a violent jolt. Nor did she manage to avoid the lamppost, which she crashed into. The screech of the bumper against the aluminium was guttural. It drowned out all other sound. Apart from the shriek of the inspector, which was high-pitched and sustained. Ronda's eardrums rang with the reverberations.

There followed the briefest moment of silence. It was the purest silence Ronda had ever experienced. Like being under water. Deep down. Dense. Then the sound of Ray's voice, faraway and distorted at first, getting closer and clearer until the noise of the world burst like a bubble on the surface of Ronda's consciousness, flooding it. A volley of barks from a German Shepherd, straining on his lead. A horn, blaring. A pedestrian, shouting and pointing at Ronda. The sharp screech of a siren, in front or behind, Ronda couldn't be sure.

'Ronda?'

She looked at Ray. 'Did I hurt anyone?' she asked. Her voice shook, it was difficult to get the words out.

'No,' said Ray. 'Are you okay?'

Ronda opened the door and leaned out. She threw up. Bile mostly. Behind her, she could hear Ray on the phone, asking one of his colleagues to come and pick them up. Ronda's mouth felt dry and coarse, like sandpaper. 'I'm sorry,' she managed.

Ray shrugged. 'You'll have better luck next time,' he said.

'There won't be a next time,' said Ronda. She rose on unsteady legs, got herself out of the car.

'Wait,' shouted Ray. 'Where are you going?'

Ronda walked away. It took less than five minutes to reach the test centre. She'd been so close. Margo was pacing outside the building, stopping after every couple of steps to pull up the sleeve of her jacket and check her watch. She froze when she saw Ronda.

'Ronda?' Margo took a step towards her. 'What are you . . .? What's going on? Where's my car? Is that vomit on your jacket? What the hell happened?'

It was difficult to know how to begin. Margo crossed her arms and pursed her lips. Ronda knew she would wait as long as it took for Ronda to begin. In the end, Ronda mumbled something about the squirrel.

'I distinctly said you have to be willing to kill squirrels,' said Margo, her confusion clearing, the floodgates of her anger swinging wide open. 'Remember? Remember me saying that?'

'I'm just . . . I'm not a driver,' said Ronda, when Margo stopped to take a breath.

'Of course you're a driver,' said Margo. 'You just have to try harder.'

'I did try.'

'You can try again,' said Margo.

Ronda shook her head. 'I can't do it,' she said. 'It was a mistake to think I could.'

Margo planted herself in front of Ronda, glared at her. 'So, what? That's it? You're just going to let Mam move into the Kube and you pay an extortionate amount of your hard-earned cash to rent some hovel of a room in a house full of strangers? Is that what you want?'

'It's the way it is,' said Ronda.

'It's not,' said Margo. 'Why do you have to give up so easily?'

'That's not fair,' said Ronda, stung. 'I did my best. I nearly killed a squirrel.'

'But you didn't kill a squirrel,' said Margo. 'That's the important thing. Isn't it? Nothing terrible happened.'

'Something terrible could have happened,' said Ronda.

Margo put her hands on Ronda's arms, eyeballed her. 'Loads of people fail their test the first time round. They just do it again. So can you.'

'No,' said Ronda. She didn't mean to shout, but that's the way it came out.

Margo lifted her hands away, stepped back.

'No,' Ronda said again, softer this time, but no less resolute.

CHAPTER 54

Annie surprised Ronda by being surprised she had failed the test.

More than surprised in fact.

Disappointed.

'I actually thought you might pass it,' she said.

'You never mentioned it,' said Ronda.

'I even told Mrs Murphy I might give the choir a go,' Annie went on. 'Since there was a chance I could be staying at No. 10.' She laughed now at such a ridiculous notion.

'I thought she'd stop asking you,' said Ronda. Mrs Murphy was the founding member of the church choir and its chief recruiter.

'It was actually me who approached her this time,' said Annie, and there was an element of amazement in her voice, as if she couldn't quite believe it. Neither could Ronda.

'I think it's something to do with Ms Gallagher,' said Annie then, as if she realised an explanation was necessary. 'Dying so suddenly. It just . . . it makes you think, doesn't it?'

'About what?' said Ronda.

'About . . . life, I suppose,' said Annie.

Margo left Ronda to calm down for a few days. She didn't even send her the invoice for the car repairs with her usual accompanying text about Revoluting. When she did ring, she presumed she would be able to persuade Ronda to re-sit the test. But Ronda was adamant.

It was true that she had not hurt anybody. But she might have.

'But you didn't,' railed Margo.

Ronda refused to move from this position and in the end, Margo did something she had never done before.

She gave up.

Shortly thereafter, Margo assumed her usual role of Juggernaut, picking the earth off its axis with her bare hands and readjusting it so they were immediately set on a different course.

Now, there was a For Sale sign in the front garden of No. 10 Casino Place. The estate agent – the same pimply youth who had put up the sign – told them that houses in the area were selling 'like hot cakes'.

Donal rang the day after the test. Ronda didn't answer. She knew he was ringing to congratulate her. Or tell her it was a simple matter of sitting the test again. He and Fatima and Margo were cut from the same cloth. They thought anything was possible.

At night, Ronda dreamed about Fatima's hot cross buns. Sitting on a tray, in the window of the estate agent's office while hoards of people formed an untidy queue out the door and up the road and around the corner and over the hill and down the lane and . . .

Ronda walked and walked but could never reach the end of the queue.

It just kept going.

The For Sale sign meant that, in the butchers and the newsagents and the supermarket, there were questions. The questions made Ronda want to clamp her hands against her ears, shut her eyes and maybe even shout a bit. Or a lot. She didn't do that, of course she didn't. She nodded and smiled and gave vague, brief answers to the questions she could answer and an apologetic shoulder shrug to the questions she couldn't. Like where Ronda was moving to.

Annie said that she could stay in the house until the sale went through, but who knew how long that might be? Not long, if the estate agent's comment about hot cakes was in any way accurate.

Now, the house at No. 10 Casino Place was cluttered with big brown cardboard boxes that Annie kept filling, emptying, then filling again as she dithered over what she should take with her to Howth and what she should discard. The outhouse in Margo's back garden had been razed and the Kube was rising from the detritus, exactly as per the blueprints that Margo's architect had drawn up.

As for Margo herself, Ronda hadn't seen her in a while. There was every chance that Margo had taken Ronda's test fail as a slight on her teaching capabilities. Also, that business with Malcolm in the café with the young woman. That hadn't gone away, Ronda was sure. No matter what Margo said. Mostly, Ronda wished she hadn't said anything. They'd been . . . nearly friends, her and Margo.

And now look at them.

At work, Fatima gave Ronda a 'Congratulations on passing your driving test' card. She'd bought it before Ronda's disastrous test. 'It will do for the next time,' she said, as if she knew something about Ronda that Ronda herself did not. Inside the card, Fatima had put a scratch card.

Ronda did not win anything.

'I will come with you to view the rooms,' said Fatima, texting Ronda a list of places to rent on the north side of the city. There weren't many in Ronda's price range. In the time it had taken her to learn how to drive and fail her test, rents had increased by more than ten per cent. Now, there was nothing she could rent for €500. The cheapest room was €575 a month. It did not come with a bed, and was two bus rides away from Green Gables. The photograph was grainy, but not grainy enough to hide the mould spores gathered like little black clouds in the corners of the ceiling.

'Shall we make an appointment to see it?' asked Fatima, looking at the room on her phone. Her finger hovered over the 'Enquiry' field.

Fatima's resilience was always a source of wonder to Ronda. There she was, raising a child, living in direct provision, her application for asylum refused, her appeal pending, her future dependent on a committee of bureaucrats that could send her back to Nigeria, where she and Ada would be easy targets for Noah and his influential family.

And yet, here she was, working all the shifts she could get her hands on, wheeling the tea trolley down the corridors, finding Teresa's slipper, saluting Captain Grady, and bringing Sheila to the prayer room to light another candle for the repose of her poor husband's soul.

'I got the date for my appeal,' said Fatima, smiling as if she'd won the lottery. 'It's the fourth of April. A Saturday. Ada was born on a Saturday. It's my lucky day.'

'That's great,' said Ronda, doing her best to sound as

enthusiastic as her friend. Fatima was not fooled. 'What is it?' she asked. Ronda shook her head. 'Nothing,' she said.

'Tell me,' said Fatima.

'I was just thinking about how much I'd miss you,' said Ronda. 'You and Ada. If you . . . go.'

'We are not gone yet,' declared Fatima.

Yet.

It sounded so positive, the way she said it. A declaration. As if she could change the world with the courage of her conviction.

Fatima's finger wavered over the 'Enquiry' button. 'Well?' she said.

'Go ahead,' said Ronda.

Fatima lowered her finger and pressed.

CHAPTER 55

It was the first Friday of April. When Ronda arrived at Green Gables that morning, she was shocked to find two goats, an alpaca, three lambs, a basket of kittens, a hutch of rabbits and a coop of chicks, positioned variously about the dayroom.

'This will cheer everybody up, won't it Ronda?' said Fergal. 'And the petting zoo aren't charging us,' he added. 'So it fits nicely into our cost-cutting strategy. Everyone's a winner here.'

Ronda had a vague memory of Fergal mentioning something about a zoo at one of his interminable meetings. With everything going on, she had completely forgotten it was happening today.

While Ronda was a believer in the comfort-giving qualities of animals, especially cute, fluffy ones, she and the rest of the staff were all too familiar with the extra work involved in the endeavour.

'Do we have extra staff on duty?' asked Ronda, but Fergal had already swept away, mumbling something about an important phone call.

The goats had already left two neat piles of droppings on the floor on either side of Captain Grady's armchair. Fatima was on her way, armed with floor wipes and anti-bacterial spray. If you didn't know, you couldn't tell that she was due to appear before the Appeals Tribunal tomorrow. Saturday.

Her lucky day.

Just as Fatima reached him, Captain Grady stood up and stepped on one of the mounds with his ferociously polished brogue. He walked the squashed droppings across the floor before Ronda managed to waylay him. She tucked her hand around his arm.

'Unhand me,' he demanded as he turned around. His face relaxed into a smile. 'Ah Ronda, it's you,' he said. 'I thought you'd gone AWOL.'

'I have some intelligence,' said Ronda, leading him to a chair and easing him into it. 'I need to de-brief you.'

'Well, why didn't you say so?' asked Captain Grady as she crouched to untie his shoe lace. 'But if it's of a sensitive nature, perhaps we should repair to my quarters?'

'No, no, here is fine,' said Ronda, as Fatima handed her the wipes and spray. She set to work, wiping the sole of Captain Grady's shoe clean.

Captain Grady, who had forgotten about the intelligence Ronda had promised him, looked around the room. 'Have the barracks been secured?' he asked her, anxiety raising his voice. He was fixated on something over her shoulder. Ronda followed his line of vision. He was looking at one of the petting farm employees, a tall, bulky man, with dark hair and big hands. In one of his hands hung a black lead, which he was attempting to attach to the collar of one of the lambs. The lamb had broken rank and was kicking and jumping its way across the dayroom.

'Come back here, Larry,' said the man. His voice was big too.

Beside her, Ronda could feel Captain Grady tense, pressing

himself tightly against the back of the chair as if he was trying to disappear into the fabric. 'It's okay,' Ronda told him, reaching up to rub his arm.

The lamb clattered by in a frenzy of hooves and the man followed, the lead dangling from his hand. Now he was beside them, his shadow falling across Captain Grady who stood up, holding his arms in front of his face.

'I'm sorry Colonel,' he shouted. He kept shouting it, over and over again. It was the voice of a boy, coming from the body of an old man.

The man with the lead stopped and stared at Captain Grady, unsure of what he should do.

'Put that bloody lead down.'

Ronda looked up. It was Sean. He had arrived with Eddie, who was peering over the screen of his phone at his distressed grandfather.

Sean took the lead from the man's hand and tossed it onto a chair. 'Can't you see he's upset?' he said, waving the man out of the way. He took Captain Grady's hand and led him back to his armchair. 'You okay Dad?' he asked, stroking his arm.

Eddie picked up a box of tissues from the windowsill and pulled one out, handed it to Sean who wiped tears from his father's face.

'You okay Grandad?' asked Eddie.

A chick ran by and Ronda bent and scooped it up. She showed it to Captain Grady. He opened his palms so Ronda could place the chick in the cradle of his hands. The little thing settled there, its head burrowed under a wing as if to shield itself from the worst of the world.

On the other side of the room, Fatima managed to catch the lamb. Ronda ran to her, held the lamb's wriggling body firmly in her arms while Fatima secured the lead to its collar.

'Thanks for catching him,' said the man.

'You need to be careful with people in here,' said Ronda, setting the lamb on all fours on the floor.

'I know,' said the man. 'I'm really sorry.'

Ronda looked over at Captain Grady, who was still holding the chick in careful hands while Sean and Eddie crouched on either side of him. Eddie was stroking the chick's head with the soft pad of his thumb. All three men smiled at the chick. There was nothing else to be done with such a bright, fluffy creature.

Ronda picked a kitten out of the basket and perched on the arm of Teresa's chair. Teresa was staring out of the window, Baby lying face down in the cradle beside her. Ronda held the kitten out. 'Want to hold her?' she asked.

Teresa looked at Ronda. 'I can't remember the number,' she said.

'Twenty-three,' said Ronda. 'Room number twenty-three.'

'That's it,' said Teresa, sitting a little straighter. 'Beside the bakery.' She looked at the kitten and smiled. 'Where's your mammy?' she said. The kitten mewed. Its eyes were a startling blue. 'There, there,' said Teresa, as Ronda placed the furry bundle in Teresa's arms. 'Rock-a-bye baby,' Teresa whispered.

'I'll be back in a bit, Teresa, okay?' said Ronda, scanning the dayroom to see where she was most needed. That's when she saw Donal. He was with Sheila, helping her feed a lamb with a bottle of milk. Ronda noticed a sensation inside her, like hummingbirds, colourful and airborne.

'Hello,' she said, walking towards him.

'Oh, hi Ronda,' he said.

'I wasn't expecting to see you here,' she said.

'Well, you won't answer my calls, so you left me no choice but to drive up from Clare to see how you got on.'

'Sorry,' said Ronda.

'Did I tell you that I failed three times before I got my licence?' said Donal.

'How do you know I failed?'

'You would have called me back if you'd passed,' said Donal.

'Can we not talk about it?' said Ronda.

'You do know that not talking about things isn't considered best practice by the medical profession?'

Ronda smiled. 'It's nice to see you,' she said. It really was.

'You too,' said Donal. 'I'm up for Fatima's appeal tomorrow. Is she around? There're a few things I need to go through with her.'

'She's in the kitchen,' said Ronda.

'Look at this,' said Sheila, tugging at the end of Donal's jacket and laughing at the vigorous way the lamb sucked on the teat. There was a youthfulness in her laugh. She looked happy.

'I thought Charlo might come in today,' Tracey had said to Sheila earlier.

'I don't know anybody of that name,' Sheila had replied. Now she examined Donal's face. 'You'd be a fine looking fellow,' she told him, 'if you tidied yourself up a bit.' She looked at Ronda. 'Wouldn't he, Ronda?' The lamb took a break from the bottle to sniff at a narrow rip across the knee of Donal's jeans. Ronda bent to tie the lace of Sheila's

363

runners. 'You could do a lot worse,' Sheila said, handing the bottle to Donal.

'She could do a lot better,' he said, guiding the teat into the lamb's mouth, turning the bottle as the lamb suckled, the way you would with a baby.

'My husband died,' Sheila told him in a conspiratorial whisper.

'I'm very sorry to hear that,' said Donal. His phone beeped and he glanced at the screen. 'I need to ring Carl,' he said. 'I'll make the call from the van and then I'll come back and talk to Fatima.'

Sheila reached for one of Donal's hands, turned it over. 'My Noel had good, strong hands too,' she said. 'They arranged them across his chest in the coffin. A beautiful corpse, he made.'

Donal handed the bottle to Ronda, pulled gently on the lamb's ears by way of goodbye.

'Noel loved animals too,' piped up Sheila, beaming at Donal, as Ronda ran after an alpaca, which had escaped from its pen and was making a beeline for the kitchen.

'I'll come back and see you before I go, Sheila,' said Donal, waving as he ran to the pen, opening the gate wide as Ronda herded the alpaca back inside.

'I think you're in with a chance with Sheila,' Ronda told Donal.

'Still got it,' said Donal, pretending to straighten an imaginary tie, before ducking out of the room and up the corridor.

Sean and Eddie were leaving too. Captain Grady struggled out of his chair and put the chick – asleep now – into Eddie's hands and Eddie walked carefully to the coop to place the chick inside.

Captain Grady swivelled towards Sean and saluted. 'Private Sean Grady,' he said with gravitas. 'It has been an honour and a privilege to serve with you on this mission.'

Sean performed an awkward return salute. If he didn't, Captain Grady would keep on saluting until he did. Sean knew that now. In a place where progress was difficult to measure, Ronda felt that this counted.

The tannoy crackled with static. 'Ronda to reception please,' Monika's monotone cut through the cacophony of animal noises. 'Ronda McCann to reception immediately.'

CHAPTER 56

When Ronda arrived in reception, Monika looked at her pointedly and, with the help of her vivid eyebrows, directed her towards the couch near the door.

Kate Deering sat there with a baby held in the crook of her elbow. The baby was asleep, a tiny fist curled around one of Kate's fingers.

'You came back,' said Ronda, smiling as she walked towards them.

'I wasn't sure if I should,' said Kate. She had a look of night feeds about her, pale skin pulled tight across her features, darker in the hollows beneath her eyes. 'But I want Alanna to meet her grandmother.' She drew her finger down the baby's cheek. 'And then I lost my nerve,' she said, looking at Ronda. 'So I asked for you instead.' The baby's eyes opened all of a sudden, intensely blue, shaped like almonds, framed by long, fine eyelashes. They were Teresa's eyes.

Ronda picked up one of Alanna's feet, jiggled it a little, which made the baby smile, revealing two rows of soft pink gum.

'I think Teresa would love to meet her granddaughter,' said Ronda. 'But maybe . . .'

'I know,' said Kate. 'I won't say anything this time.'

'I know it's hard,' said Ronda.

'I've been doing more research on the mother and baby home,' said Kate.

'Where is it?' asked Ronda.

'London,' said Kate. 'Near Putney. It's an office block now.'

'I think Teresa was in Room 23,' Ronda said.

The baby's arms and legs were moving now, jerky and uncoordinated.

'What makes you say that?' she asked.

'Was there a bakery next door?' asked Ronda.

Kate nodded. 'Yes,' she said. 'Burtons Bakery.'

'Teresa remembers that,' said Ronda. 'And she remembers you. When you were a baby. I'm sure of it.'

There was a ring on the doorbell. Ronda glanced through the glass at the front of the building. It was Donal. Monika pressed the door release button and he bounded in. 'Carl didn't keep me long,' he said.

'I told Fatima you were here,' said Ronda. 'Her shift ends in half an hour, she was wondering if you could wait?'

'Sure,' said Donal. 'I'll treat myself to one of those terrible coffees from the machine.' He pulled a fistful of coins out of his pocket. 'I don't suppose you're due a break, Ronda?' he asked. 'I have enough change for two terrible coffees. It'd be lovely to catch up with you, I promise I won't mention the you-know-what.'

Ronda noticed Kate smiling at him. People didn't seem to be able to help themselves.

'Can you give me two minutes?' Ronda said.

'Of course,' said Donal.

Ronda turned to Kate. 'Will you and Alanna follow me?' she said.

Teresa was in the same place Ronda had left her, the kitten gone and Baby lying across her knees.

'You've got visitors, Teresa,' Ronda told her, pulling an armchair beside Teresa's chair and settling Kate and Alanna into it.

Teresa did not acknowledge the new arrivals. She continued staring out of the window. Alanna started crying. Teresa turned her head. Her eyes fastened first on Alanna, then on Kate. She picked up Baby, draped her over her shoulder, then pointed to Alanna. Kate followed suit and settled Alanna in the same position, over her shoulder.

'Rock-a-bye baby, on the tree top,' Teresa began.

'Will you be okay?' Ronda asked Kate.

'When the wind blows, the cradle will rock,' sang Teresa, poking Kate's arm with her finger.

Kate nodded. 'We'll be fine,' she said. Then she turned to Teresa and sang, 'When the bough breaks, the cradle will fall.'

Teresa smiled.

'Down will come baby, cradle and all,' they sang in unison. Alanna had stopped crying.

'Room Number 23,' Teresa said. She placed her hand on Alanna's back, rubbed her gently. 'The house was beside the bakery,' she told Kate. 'We could smell the bread in the mornings.'

Kate nodded, putting her hand on Teresa's. 'I know,' she whispered.

Ronda darted into the staff toilet on the way up the corridor, examined herself in the mirror. She splashed water on her face and, in the absence of a brush, pushed her fingers through her hair. She reached into her pocket for a chewing gum and found the lipstick Margo had given her. It seemed like such a long time ago now. She ran it carefully along her lips. Fire engine red. Margo was right, it did brighten up her face. She hunted for one of Fatima's perfumes in the cupboard behind the mirror. She found one that claimed to smell like wild roses, and she dabbed some behind both ears. She looked at herself in the mirror. 'What do you think you're doing, Ronda McCann?' she said. There were so many things she should be doing. Or worrying about because she wasn't doing. And yet here she was, mooning over some man. It was most unusual. Ronda smiled at her reflection to make sure she had nothing on her teeth. She didn't.

She kept smiling, all the way up the corridor.

CHAPTER 57

Donal was sitting where she had left him, scribbling in a notebook, paperwork spread across his lap and his satchel on the floor between his feet.

A courier handed Monika a package. She pressed the door release button to let him out. As the courier left, a man appeared and managed to slot himself through the front door before it closed. He was tall, powerfully built and strangely formal in a black suit and an immaculate white shirt. Something about the way he held himself, coiled tight, as if he was struggling to restrain himself, set off a warning flare inside Ronda's head.

The phone rang. 'Good afternoon, Green Gables, Monika speaking, how may I be of assistance?' said Monika, all the while watching the man walking towards her. He stopped at the reception desk, drumming his fingers against the counter as he waited for Monika to get off the phone. She hung up. 'Can I help you?' she asked.

'I want to speak to Fatima Nwodo,' the man said. His voice was loud, the accent a louder, more pronounced version of Fatima's.

'What is your name?' Monika asked, picking up the phone.

'Monika, wait,' said Ronda, walking towards the reception desk. She looked at the man. 'Are you Noah?' she said. She recognised him from a photograph Fatima had shown her. The man stepped towards her. There was barely a foot between them now. Ronda could feel heat coming off him in waves. He bent down. His face was inches from hers. She could see a sheen of sweat glistening on his forehead. His breath was hot and sour.

'I do not wish to speak to anyone but Fatima,' the man said. His voice was low and deliberate.

'Fatima's not here today,' said Ronda.

'That is not true,' he said, his voice gaining volume.

'She's on a day off,' said Ronda. 'You can leave a message if you—'

The man banged the flat of his hand on the reception desk. The harsh sound reverberated around the room, and Ronda couldn't help flinching.

'Do not lie to me,' he said.

Donal jumped to his feet. 'Hey, take it easy,' he said, putting his hand on the man's arm.

Noah flung it off. 'How dare you touch me,' he said.

Donal put his hands up in a conciliatory gesture. 'I meant no offence,' he said. 'Why don't we sit over here.' Donal pointed towards the couch he had just vacated. 'Come on,' he said, taking a step back from the reception desk. 'I can contact Fatima. Let her know you're—'

'It's you, isn't it?' shouted Noah, making a lunge for Donal. 'You're the one.'

'What do you mean?' asked Donal, still in his usual, low-key voice, as if they were having a perfectly normal back and forth and there weren't flecks of angry spittle around the edges of Noah's mouth.

'You have been sleeping with my wife,' said Noah, pushing his finger against Donal's chest.

'Hey,' said Donal. 'Let's calm down, okay?'

371

'Don't tell me what to do.'

Noah, easily half a head taller, bore down on Donal. He raised his fist. Ronda made a grab for his arm. He pushed her away and she staggered backwards, nearly falling.

'Stop,' shouted Donal, putting his hands on Noah's shoulders.

Noah flung them off, curled his fist and drove it into Donal's face. Donal staggered backwards, landing on the tiled floor with a sickening thud.

Monika screamed.

Blood spurted from Donal's nose.

Noah advanced on him.

Behind reception, Monika leaped to her feet, her chair flying back, hitting the wall. Her face was frozen in a scream.

Without planning to, Ronda planted herself squarely in front of Noah. 'Fatima was right about you,' she said.

For a moment, she thought he was going to bulldoze his way past her. Instead, he stopped.

'What did you say to me?' he said.

'She said you were a bully,' said Ronda. Her breath was harsh in her throat, her heart hammering against her chest. She steeled herself and managed to stand her ground. Noah was taller than Ian Paisley. And just as broad. She lifted one of her thick-soled trainers, holding Noah's contemptuous glare as she drove the heel of the shoe down onto his foot with all the force she could gather. He let out a roar and bent forward, which is when Ronda jerked her knee – her hard, bony knee – up, keeping it rigid, pulling it up, up, up, fast as she could, until it connected with Noah's nose. Ms Gallagher had been right. She heard the crack of the bone breaking and it was a most satisfying sound.

Noah reared up, screeching in pain, his hands covering his bloody nose. The sound cleared the red mist from Ronda's mind. She realised she had no idea what to do next. Ms Gallagher hadn't counselled her on that bit. Noah was coming at her again, angrier than before. Behind him, Donal, still laid out on the floor, wasn't moving. Noah lunged at Ronda, grabbing her by the collar of her scrubs.

'Press the panic button,' Ronda shouted at Monika, who remained standing, rigid as a statue.

Noah said something as he shook Ronda, but she couldn't hear him over the sound of the alarm ringing through the building, loud and piercing.

Noah shoved Ronda out of his way as he cast about the room.

'The police are on their way,' Ronda shouted over the noise.

Noah spat at her before making a lunge for the door. It wouldn't open.

'Open it,' he roared.

Monika looked at Ronda. Ronda nodded. Monika pressed a button and there was a click.

Noah yanked at the handle and hurled himself though the doors, racing down the driveway.

'Lock the doors, Monika,' Ronda shouted as she crouched on the floor beside Donal. His eye socket was already swelling and his hair was matted with the blood from his nose.

'Donal?' She put her hands gently on his head, palpating his skull with her fingers. There was a sizeable bump on the back.

'Donal,' she said again, louder this time. She tapped his cheek with her fingers, softly at first, then more insistently.

'Donal?' she said again. 'Donal! Come on, it's time to wake up.'

'Ring an ambulance,' she said to Monika. When she turned back to Donal, his eyes were opening.

'Are you okay?' Ronda asked.

Donal blinked a couple of times, did his best to focus on her. 'I'm clearly not much use in an emergency,' he said, sitting up. He grinned, then winced. 'Hurts to smile.'

Ronda helped him up, got him onto a chair. He was pale, his freckles a bright orange against the white of his skin. Blood from the gash on the back of his head dripped onto the collar of his T-shirt. Monika ran over with tissues, which Donal held against his nose. She handed Ronda a tea towel, which she folded and pressed gently against the back of Donal's head.

'Does that hurt?' Ronda asked.

Donal nodded.

The double doors opened and Fatima rushed through them. 'What's going on?' she asked, looking at the blood on the floor and Ronda administering first aid to a blood-spattered Donal. 'What happened?'

In the distance, the sound of sirens, getting louder.

'Was it Noah?' Fatima said then, her voice nearly a whisper. 'Was Noah here?'

'He's gone now,' said Donal. 'Ronda saw to it.'

Fatima's eyes scanned Ronda's face. 'Did he hurt you?' she asked.

'I'm pretty sure Ronda broke his nose,' said Donal, grabbing another fistful of tissues.

Fatima cupped Ronda's face with her hands. 'You are brave, Ronda McCann,' she said.

'You're the one who's brave,' Ronda said. 'Escaping from that man.'

'It is true Ronda,' said Monika, coming out from behind the reception desk on shaky legs. 'You are brave.' There was a tremor in her usual detached monotone. Ronda led her to an armchair, sat her down.

Fatima shook her head and wrapped her arms tightly about herself. 'I am sorry,' she said, her eyes filling with tears. 'I have brought trouble to your door.'

'You have nothing to be sorry about,' said Ronda, reaching her hand out. Fatima clasped it.

'This isn't all bad, you know,' Donal said, as narrow trails of blood ran down his face.

Fatima handed him a clean tissue. 'Even I can't think of anything good about this situation,' she said.

'It'll help with your appeal,' said Donal.

'How?' asked Fatima.

'We have proof now,' he said. 'About Noah. How abusive he is. We'll get a Garda report and . . .'

There was a sharp rap on the front door. Everybody jumped. Two uniformed police officers peered through the glass.

Monika let them in and Ronda gave them an account of what had happened. Fatima took her phone out of her pocket and showed them a photograph of Noah.

'Do you have family here?' one of the officers wanted to know.

Fatima nodded. 'Ada,' she said. 'My daughter.'

'Is she at school?' the Garda asked.

'Yes,' said Fatima. 'Why?'

'We'll go over to the school now,' the Garda said.

'You think Noah will go there?' said Fatima.

'It's just a precaution.'

Fatima got her coat out of the cloakroom.

'I will go too,' she said, her voice brooking no argument.

The phone rang. 'Good afternoon, Green Gables, Monika speaking, how may I be of assistance?' said Monika, who had assumed her composure and her position behind the reception desk.

Ronda looked at Donal, still bleeding from the back of his head. 'You need an ice pack,' she told him.

'Well, I'm hardly going to argue with you, am I?' said Donal, standing up. He swayed a little. Ronda offered her arm, which he held onto as they made their way to the kitchen. 'Sit on the couch,' she instructed, rummaging in the freezer and pulling out two ice packs. He did his best not to grimace as he pressed one against the back of his head and the other at the side of his face.

Ronda opened the first aid box and found some arnica. 'You probably already know this,' she said, handing him the cream. 'But arnica is a great all-rounder for cuts and bruises.'

'That was the first time we met, wasn't it?' he said. 'In my office.'

'Yes,' said Ronda, pushing two ibuprofen tablets out of a blister pack. She handed them to him with a glass of water.

'Three months ago,' said Ronda.

'It feels way longer than that,' he said.

Ronda nodded. It did.

'Thanks by the way,' said Donal.

'For what?'

'Saving my life.'

'I don't think it was quite that dramatic,' said Ronda.

'It looked pretty dramatic from where I was standing,' said Donal.

'You were lying down as far as I remember,' said Ronda.

'Funny,' said Donal. 'But seriously, thank you. I don't know how you managed to take that guy down, he was pretty enormous.'

'You should thank Ms Gallagher,' said Ronda. 'She taught me everything I know.' She could feel Donal's eyes on her as she made her way to the sink to wash her hands.

'Fatima and Monika are right about you,' he said. 'You are brave.'

Ronda concentrated on her hands, scrubbing the blood off them. 'I'm not usually,' she said.

'Well, you definitely were today,' said Donal, squeezing arnica out of the tube. He stood up, put the ice packs on the draining board. 'I should let you get back to work,' he said. Beside him, she felt like a taller version of herself. Stronger. Invigorated and full of possibility. Perhaps it was the aftermath, adrenalin still pouring through her body. Whatever it was, it was a glorious feeling, heady and hot and fizzy. She could see her face reflected in the brightness of his eyes, and she felt that it might be true. She might be brave. She felt light and free, like she had slipped her moorings and was floating away. The feeling was like dancing, but easy. Effortless. Ronda wasn't sure if she was the one turning around and around or if she was standing still, and it was the world, spinning on its axis around her.

Donal was looking at her with curiosity. 'You okay, Ronda?' he asked.

She took a breath. 'I like you,' she said. 'The things I like about you are as follows, in no particular order.' She took a moment to notice that this was not how she expressed herself ordinarily. Not just what she said, but the way she said it, her voice light and free and unburdened by her awkward self-consciousness.

'For starters, you're smart and handsome and interesting and funny. You're thoughtful and kind. You're exactly yourself, and that's so refreshing. Also, you have integrity, which is not all that easy to come across. I think that's my favourite bit.'

There was a sudden draught as the door opened. 'Fergal heard what happened, Ronda,' said Kim, sticking her head around the door, one of the rabbits in her arms, its ears up like antennae, twitching.

It took Ronda a moment to remember the petting zoo. It felt as though days had passed since the animals had arrived.

'He wants to see you in his office,' Kim went on.

Ronda put her hand on the counter to steady herself, although there was no need. The world was not turning and neither was she. Donal picked up his satchel, getting ready to leave. Everything was fine. Nothing had been said that shouldn't have been said.

Oddly, the first feeling she felt was disappointment.

Then relief.

'You should let the paramedics examine you when the ambulance arrives,' she told Donal. 'And if you get drowsy later, go straight to A&E, okay?' There was her voice, sounding as it always did. Quiet with a touch of worry about the edges. Everything was fine.

Kim left, Ronda picked up the ice packs.

Donal's face was flushed. Probably a bit of shock settling

in. When he got to the door, he stayed there, his hand on the handle. 'The thing is, Ronda,' he began. 'Tricia wants to give it another go.'

'Oh,' said Ronda. Now it was her turn to flush.

'She wants us to try again, in Clare,' Donal went on, not quite meeting Ronda's eye. 'She thinks maybe we could run the café together. Or she could work remotely from there, she's not sure. Everything's a bit, up in the air, I suppose.'

'That's . . .' began Ronda.

'It's not what I was expecting either,' said Donal. 'It's Pat, dying so suddenly. It gave Trish an awful shock. Then, down in Clare, there was a bit of space to think, I suppose. She says she's reconfiguring things.'

'Reconfiguring?' said Ronda. Her voice sounding nonsensical in her ears.

'Something like that,' said Donal. 'We've spent a bit of time together, and the thing is . . .'

Donal said other things. Ronda wasn't sure what. It didn't matter really. It was just different versions of the same thing. Ronda wanted him to stop. She wanted to tell him that she got it, there was no need for him to go on and on. She became aware of the bones in her body, heavy, like weights. She was tired. She wanted to sit on a chair. Lie on a couch. Donal put the strap of his satchel over his head. He looked at her. 'And I also just want to say,' he struck up again, 'it was lovely, all those things you said.' Ronda's insides caved in. Blood flooded her face. 'Nobody's ever said anything like that to me before,' Donal went on. 'It was so, well, I just wanted to say, thank you.'

Ronda opened the door. It seemed to take Donal forever to reach it. Ronda willed him not to pause, to keep going, to walk straight through the doorway and up the corridor and be gone.

He didn't pause. He kept on going and didn't say anything else, other than a brief, 'Bye,' when he cleared the door.

Ronda didn't respond. She couldn't trust herself to speak. Who knows what she might end up saying next?

CHAPTER 58

Ronda cycled home. It rained all the way. It wasn't until she reached No. 10 Casino Place that she realised she'd left her backpack in her locker at work, with her house keys inside. She rang the doorbell. After a while, she rang it again. The third time she kept her finger pressed against it. There was no movement inside the house. She peered through the window of the good room. There was nobody there. She rapped her knuckles against the glass. The pads of her fingers were pulpy and water-logged with rain. She sat on the step. There was no point seeking shelter. She couldn't get any wetter.

The For Sale sign was in her sights. Whatever way she turned her head, she could see it. Ronda pulled her phone out of her pocket. Fatima had texted. She and Ada were at the centre and a garda was parked outside, keeping an eye on them.

'Is that you Ronda? What are you doing sitting out here in this weather, you'll catch your death.' Mrs Murphy stood on the other side of the garden fence, practically dressed in a long, belted raincoat holding a golf umbrella over her head. 'Did you forget your keys?'

Ronda nodded.

Mrs Murphy looked at her watch. 'You'd better come inside,' she said. 'Your mother won't be back from choir practice for at least another hour.'

'Choir practice?' Ronda said. She was pretty sure this

conversation was taking place in real life. It felt as real as the cold rivers of rain running down the strands of her hair, dropping inside the collar of her jacket and dripping down her back.

'I know,' said Mrs Murphy. 'I'm delighted too, I've been at her to join for ages. I hope she didn't get drenched. She wouldn't take a lift, said she fancied a bit of fresh air.' As she prattled away, Mrs Murphy was on the move. Down her garden path, onto the pavement and then through the gate at No. 10. She stopped when she reached Ronda, surveyed her for a moment, like a map she was holding upside down.

'Are you all right, Ronda?' she asked.

Ronda was unsure how to answer. She knew people didn't say, 'No,' when asked that question in polite company, but had no idea what else to say.

Mrs Murphy held out her hand. 'Let's get you inside, shall we?'

Ronda remembered the last time she had been inside the Murphys' house. Three days after the itching had started. One day after Ronda had made the appointment to see Dr Anderson and get a prescription for what she had assumed was a UTI.

The house had changed quite a bit since then. It was what Annie's house might have looked like if Gerry had been a good provider like Mr Murphy. And if Ronda or Margo had been architects with contacts in the business like Joseph. There was a great impression of space and light inside the house, any bit of brightness left in the fading evening falling through the skylights slotted variously about the ceiling. The walls were freshly painted. Ronda fancied she could smell the paint, vibrant white with a delicate hint of peppermint.

There was an extension at the back so that the kitchen – fitted with soft-close doors and drawers in a glossy teal finish – spanned the width of the house, the back of which was made entirely of triple-glazed glass, looking out at the yard that had the same dimensions and aspect as that of the McCanns'. Otherwise the yards had nothing in common, the Murphys' being covered with great slabs of sandstone and filled with an assortment of vividly flourishing potted plants and rigorous climbing vines and burgeoning window boxes, the splendour of which even the dank evening could not diminish.

The only artefact that had survived the waves of modernisation that had crested and crashed through this house was the holy water font by the light switch. A ceramic one, with a statue of Jesus on a plinth, dressed in a red robe with a matching exposed red heart in the middle of his chest, disproportionately huge. Ronda remembered Mrs Murphy pushing her fingers into the font as far as they'd go, blessing herself with a guttural Jesus, Mary and Joseph when Ronda told her the wedding was off.

Now, here she was, back in the kitchen, dripping onto the terracotta tiles. Mrs Murphy handed Ronda a towel – a big, soft, fluffy one, like the ones you might see in an ad for a fancy hotel – and some clothes. 'Mary left a few bits behind,' she said. 'I don't know if they'll fit, but they'll be warm.' She pointed to a door that opened into a wet room that was thankfully dry.

Ronda undressed. Even her knickers were wet. She shouldn't have sat on the step. Annie would tell her she'd get a cold in her kidneys. Or double pneumonia. When she was wrapped in Mrs Murphy's beautiful bath towel that felt like it had never endured a hot wash, she glimpsed herself in the massive mirror over the sink, surrounded by glaring Hollywood style bulbs. Ronda's hair looked blacker when it was wet, her face paler. Her reflection seemed far away, as if Ronda was smaller than usual. Everything about her was diminished, she felt. As though she was barely there at all.

'You okay in there, Ronda dear?' Mrs Murphy knocked on the door. 'I've to go to choir now.' When Ronda didn't answer immediately, Mrs Murphy went on, 'I promised your mother a lift home. Mr Murphy is at the bridge club, but Joseph is here. Is that okay? I told him to make you some tea. All right dear?'

'Yes,' said Ronda, injecting as much gratitude and volume into her voice as her diminished reflection would allow. 'Thank you.'

She heard the front door open, then close, then silence. Ronda put on Mary's clothes. Joseph's older sister had been broader and taller than Ronda when she emigrated to Australia years ago. Ronda rolled the bottoms of the jeans up and secured them around her waist with the belt from a dressing gown hanging from a hook on the back of the door. The T-shirt was fine, plain white and baggy. Mrs Murphy had also provided an Aran cardigan, which made Ronda's arms itch. Still, the weight of it around her shoulders was a comfort. She listened at the door for a bit. She could hear nothing. After a while, she opened the door and stepped into the kitchen.

'There you are,' said Joseph, smiling. He was in his bare feet and wore the dregs of that day's suit; a pair of trousers, a tie, loosened and the top buttons of his white shirt undone. His hair was carefully tousled, the ends brushing against his collar. A shadow of stubble darkened his face, intensified the blue of his eyes. He was at the island in the middle of the kitchen, expertly opening a bottle of Barolo with a complicated looking corkscrew. It made a loud, celebratory pop. He poured the wine into two large glasses, handed one to Ronda. 'Have a seat,' he said, hopping up on one of the bar stools at the island. 'Mum said I should give you tea, but I thought wine would be better,' he said.

Ronda sat down. The stool was uncomfortable, more style than substance.

'What'll we drink to?

Nothing occurred to Ronda.

'How about your driving lessons?' said Joseph. 'How are they going?'

'I failed my test,' said Ronda.

'Well, we can't drink to that,' said Joseph. 'How about me, finally persuading you to have a drink with me?' Joseph looked pleased with himself as if he had personally arranged for Annie to join the choir, Ronda to leave her backpack in her locker with the door keys inside, not to mention the rain, which he had drawn down with the merest click of his fingers.

'Well?' said Joseph, his arm outstretched. 'Don't leave me hanging here.'

Ronda set the glass down on the island's granite surface. She looked at Joseph.

'Why did you do it?' she asked.

'Do what?' asked Joseph, not quite looking at her. Ronda made no move to reply. She had nothing to lose. She could wait. Eventually, Joseph lowered his arm. 'It was a horrible thing to do,' he said. 'I shouldn't have done it.'

'I know that,' said Ronda. 'But what I don't know is why?'

Joseph opened his mouth, then closed it again, as if he couldn't remember his lines.

'Is it me?' Ronda asked. 'Is it because I'm unlovable?'

Joseph put his glass on the island and picked up both of her hands. 'No,' he said, and his voice was urgent. 'Of course not, how could you say that?'

Ronda shrugged and pulled her hands out of his grasp. 'Why then?' she asked. 'I really want to know.'

Joseph ran his hands through his thick, luxurious hair. 'There wasn't any reason,' he said. 'It just . . . happened.'

'Nothing just happens,' said Ronda. 'People do things and make things happen.'

'Okay,' said Joseph, shifting uncomfortably on the bar stool. 'You were . . . somewhere, I can't remember, and . . .'

'I brought my mother to Wales on the ferry. We were visiting my aunt Tess in Cardiff,' said Ronda. 'She was recovering from jaundice.'

'Really?' said Joseph. 'I don't remember that.'

'Go on,' said Ronda.

'Let me think,' said Joseph. 'Em, I was in the pub, Eileen was there, she was celebrating something, I can't rem—'

'She'd gotten a promotion at work,' said Ronda. 'Claims handler at Axa.'

'Oh, yes,' said Joseph. 'Anyway, it was kicking out time and Eileen suggested we go back to hers and have a few more drinks, her parents were . . . I don't know, somewhere in Wicklow . . .'

'Courtown,' said Ronda. 'It's in Wexford.'

'Right,' said Joseph. 'The thing is, I thought everyone was going back to Eileen's, but it ended up just me and her. And, you know, one thing led to another and then . . .'

'And then you slept with her.'

Joseph looked at Ronda. 'I was very drunk,' he said. 'We both were. That's the reason.'

'That's not a great reason,' said Ronda.

Joseph nodded. 'I know,' he said. 'I'm sorry.' He picked up Ronda's glass and handed it to her. 'Let's have a proper toast,' he said, bending towards her so she could feel the warmth radiating from his body. 'To the very loveable Ronda McCann.' He clinked his glass against hers and drank from it until it was empty, then set it on the counter and took Ronda's hands in his. 'Your fingers are cold,' he said, rubbing them between his warm, soft ones.

Ronda tried to pull her hands away, but he persisted, and she relented since her fingers were actually warming up in the rub of his hands.

After a while, he put his hands on either side of her face, leaned towards her and kissed her, his tongue pushing through her lips, into her mouth and around. It was so familiar, the manoeuvre. Even now, all this time later. As if she and Joseph had never broken up, had never stopped kissing each other. At the same time, she felt like a bystander. An observer on the sidelines. Looking at herself being kissed by Joseph. She remembered his tongue. The insistence of it, probing and searching, like a SWAT team, ransacking a place for drugs. She noticed how her arms hung loosely down her sides, her hands dangling at the end as if they weren't sure what to do with themselves. Joseph's hands were much more decisive, disappearing inside Mary's T-shirt, up and up until they came upon her breasts, then setting to work on them, kneading thoroughly. She heard the sounds he made, deep in his throat. Little grunts. This carried on for a bit.

After a while, she put her hands against his chest and pushed gently. His mouth came away from hers with a loud, sucking sound. He was breathing hard.

'You okay?' he asked.

Ronda nodded.

He looked at her then. Right at her. Ronda remembered this. The intensity he could bring to a look.

'You broke my heart, you know,' he said. 'When you called the wedding off.'

'You started going out with Danielle pretty soon afterwards,' Ronda reminded him.

'Rebound,' he said, smiling a sad sort of a smile into the middle distance. Ronda had the distinct impression that it had been practised, that smile. In front of a mirror.

'Oh Ronda,' he said in a ragged, hoarse sort of voice, leaning his forehead against hers. 'You're driving me crazy.'

Ronda couldn't help giggling. This surprised her. She was not exactly the giggling type.

'What's so funny?' asked Joseph.

'Nothing really,' said Ronda. 'It's been a strange day.'

'Must be stressful,' said Joseph. 'Being a nurse.'

'I'm not a nurse.'

'I thought you were doing a nursing course?'

'I dropped out.'

'How come?' said Joseph. 'You were really into it, as far as I remember. Weren't you?'

Ronda nodded. 'And I was good at it too,' she said. 'I was top of my class.'

It seemed so long ago. She had left that girl behind, abandoned her, just when she was getting going.

'I wouldn't blame you,' said Joseph, picking up the wine

and refilling his glass. 'All those sick people, moaning all the time. But you'd look super sexy in a nurse's outfit.' He swallowed a mouthful of wine, then another. 'I'm slammed at work at the moment,' he said. 'Shooting the new season and doing all the promo work for it, and then Danielle rocks up today, barges into the studio, and just like that, dumps the kids on me because she has a meeting with her solicitor. Her divorce solicitor, she was keen to tell me.' Joseph shook his head and looked at Ronda. She recognised the look. A pouting, plaintive one. It had made a smoother landing on his face when he was younger.

Ronda set her glass on the island and looked back at him. It wasn't a glare. Not even a sneer. It was just a look. Casual. Objective with perhaps a touch of pity to it.

'I'm glad you gave me syphilis,' she said.

'What do you mean?' said Joseph, his face flushing. 'It was Eileen who . . .'

'You were a fantasy in my head for so long,' said Ronda. 'You were the popular boy, handsome and cool. The boy next door. When you came back from London, I couldn't believe that you'd be interested in someone like me. And you weren't. I should have trusted myself. I was a stopgap back then. And you want me to be a stopgap again, but I'm not going to be. I deserve better than you.'

Ronda got off the stool and hoisted Mary's jeans up on her waist.

'Don't say that,' said Joseph, the plaintive pout on show again.

Ronda looked at him. 'Say what?' she asked.

Joseph looked confused now. 'What you just said, you're not just a stopgap.'

'Good,' said Ronda, nodding. 'I was just checking.'

'Checking what?' said Joseph.

'That I said what I meant to say.'

'And did you?' asked Joseph, with a touch of hope.

'I did,' said Ronda.

And then she left.

CHAPTER 59

Ronda slept late the next day and was awakened by the morning sun easing its way through the window and spreading across her duvet. She allowed herself to lie there for a while, marinating in the unexpected warmth of the spring sunshine. She stretched like Jessica Fletcher after one of her lengthy naps along the branches of the laburnum tree.

The events of the previous day arrived in the inbox of her mind in a single drop. She sat up, threw off the duvet and swung her legs out of bed. She had a quick shower and brushed her teeth. It was her day off, so she dressed in her usual off-duty uniform of jeans and a T-shirt. She spied Margo's lipstick on the windowsill. Fire engine red. She put it on in the bathroom, using the age-spotted mirror over the sink. She looked as if she'd slept well. She wet her fingers and encouraged her fringe to lie down against her forehead, which it did eventually. She grinned at herself in the mirror and her reflection grinned back. She bounded down the stairs, two at a time. 'I'll be back later,' she called out as she opened the front door and stepped outside. She breathed in. The air was warm and rich with the possibility of summer all of a sudden. Ronda clamped her helmet on her head and unlocked her bicycle. She cycled up the road, not bothering to check if Joseph's car was there or if his blinds were open or closed.

*

Monika looked surprised to see her when she strode through the front door of Green Gables. 'You look different,' she said suspiciously. 'It is improvement.'

'Thank you,' said Ronda. Her smile was different too. Wider. There was a good bit of teeth on show.

'You should not be here,' said Monika. 'You need rest after yesterday.'

'I need to see Fergal,' said Ronda.

'You have appointment?' said Monika.

'No,' said Ronda, standing at the double doors. 'But don't worry, I won't keep him long.'

'Tell him I tried to stop you to no avail,' said Monika, pressing the button on her desk that opened the doors.

'Thanks Monika,' said Ronda. She walked down the corridor and stopped at Fergal's office. She rapped on the door.

'Who is it?' he called, his tone unenthusiastic. Ronda opened the door and stepped inside. Fergal glanced over the top of his computer screen.

'Ah Ronda, our local hero, how are you?'

'Fine,' said Ronda. 'Any feedback from the police?'

Fergal shook his head. 'I rang them this morning,' he said. 'Noah is still at large.' He picked up the mouse, moved it around the pad. 'Was there anything specific, Ronda?' he said. 'I'm quite busy here.'

He was playing Wordle again. She could see the reflection of the screen in the window behind him.

Ronda sat down without being invited, pulled an envelope out of the inside pocket of her jacket and placed it on his desk.

'What's this?' he asked, peering at the envelope as if it might be a letter bomb.

'I'm handing in my notice,' said Ronda.

'You're resigning?' said Fergal, his mouth hanging open.

'Yes,' said Ronda.

'No!' said Fergal.

'I've got leave, so I'd like to use that in lieu of notice,' said Ronda.

'You're leaving right away?' said Fergal.

'Yes,' said Ronda.

'No,' said Fergal again. He buried his face in his hands, shook his head.

After a bit, Ronda cleared her throat. 'Fergal?'

'This is not what I need right now,' he said, his voice muffled.

'I'll ring the agency if you like,' said Ronda. 'They'll send a replacement by this afternoon, it'll be fine.'

'Wait,' said Fergal suddenly, his eyes widening. 'I don't have to accept your resignation, do I?' He stood up. 'I don't accept it,' he said. 'I don't accept it at all. Not one little bit.'

Ronda did not interrupt. She knew him. He had to run out of steam by himself. It didn't take long. He paced from one side of the office to the other before sighing and collapsing back into his chair. When he spoke again, his voice was quiet. 'I did not see this coming,' he said, shaking his head. 'There have been so many changes around here, but I never thought you'd be one of them.'

'You'll have another carer here by the end of the week,' said Ronda brightly.

'But they won't be like you,' said Fergal. 'They'll be . . . You know what I mean.'

'No I don't,' said Ronda, who knew exactly what he meant.

'Why are you leaving?' Fergal asked then. It was more of a plea than a question.

'I'm going to complete my nursing degree at DCU,' said Ronda. Her smile felt wide across her face.

It was the first time she had said it out loud. It sounded great.

'Hang on,' said Fergal, straightening. 'You'll need a part-time job surely?'

'Yes,' said Ronda.

'That's perfect,' said Fergal, smiling now. 'You can work here. Part-time.'

Ronda shook her head. 'I need a fresh start,' she said.

'We'll fit your shifts around your course,' said Fergal.

'I don't think I—'

'I'll pay more,' said Fergal.

Ronda looked at him. 'How much more?' she asked.

'Name your price,' said Fergal grandly. 'Within reason,' he added.

Ronda studied his face. 'You really want me to stay, don't you?'

Fergal nodded slowly. 'You're . . . good at your job,' he said.

'I know I am,' said Ronda, standing up. 'But it's nice to hear all the same.'

'Besides, if you leave, the rest of them might follow suit,' said Fergal grimly.

'You could pay them more too?' suggested Ronda.

Fergal glared at her.

Ronda felt it was a good time to leave, so she did.

*

She ducked into the kitchen. Fatima was where she always was, at the sink, stacking crockery into the dishwasher.

'I just wanted to wish you luck,' she said. 'At the appeal this afternoon.'

'Thank you,' said Fatima, smiling. 'But I won't need it. You heard what Donal said yesterday.'

Ronda felt a glimmer of hope ripple through her, as if Fatima's positivity was contagious and she had caught a dose of it.

'Any developments on Noah?' asked Ronda. Fatima shook her head.

The back door opened and Kim and Ernest walked into the kitchen. There was lipstick around Ernest's mouth. It was the same colour as the trace that remained on Kim's lips.

'You two look cute together,' said Fatima.

Ernest smiled. Ronda was pretty sure this was the first time she'd seen him do this. He excused himself before Fatima could make any further comment.

'I presume it's off with Scott then?' said Fatima, flicking Kim with the edge of her tea towel.

'Scott turned out to be gay,' said Kim, picking a mandarin out of the fruit bowl. 'He's going out with a tattoo artist now. We're still pals.'

Ronda marvelled at her ability to adapt and move on. 'I want to be just like you when I grow up,' she told her.

Kim beamed. 'And I want to be a badass like you,' Kim said, doing a series of high kicks and karate chops across the kitchen floor.

'Flick her with that tea towel for me, Fatima,' said Ronda as she left the kitchen.

Halfway down the corridor, she stopped. Doubt crept into her head. The meeting with Fergal had gone much too well. Surely it was too good to be true.

She turned back and rapped on the door of Fergal's office once again.

'Who is it?' he called, his tone unenthusiastic. Ronda opened the door and stepped inside. Fergal glanced over the top of his computer screen. He was still struggling with Wordle.

'I suppose you came back for this,' he said, picking up her letter of resignation and handing it to her.

Ronda darted forward and took it out of his hand. Fergal studied her face. 'Did you resign just so I'd give you a pay rise and a part time job?'

'No,' said Ronda, trying not to look too delighted. She'd done it. She'd really done it.

'Go on,' said Fergal, his face disappearing behind his screen again. 'Before I change my mind.'

'It's arise by the way,' she said.

'A rise?'

'The Wordle word,' said Ronda. 'It's arise.'

CHAPTER 60

On her return to No. 10 Casino Place, Ronda could hear the sounds of industry. She hung her helmet and jacket on the coat stand and walked down the hallway. Annie was in the kitchen, standing on a chair washing the tops of the presses, humming a song from West Side Story.

'You're full of beans,' said Ronda.

'That choir practice is after giving me a boost of energy,' said Annie, plunging her cloth into a bucket of warm, sudsy water.

'I can't believe you went,' said Ronda, putting on the kettle.

'Sure, aren't you and Margo always on at me to do this, go there, join that,' said Annie, her tone a little defensive.

'I'm glad you went,' said Ronda. 'That's all I meant.'

'Your father would have loved it,' said Annie. 'We sang "Crazy". Gerry loved Patsy Cline, so he did.'

'I can't see him in a choir,' said Ronda, reaching into the press for the teabags.

'You never have a good word to say about him,' said Annie, shaking her head.

'You say enough good things about him for the both of us,' said Ronda.

'I suppose that's a dig?' said Annie.

'No,' said Ronda. And it was true. She did not feel any animosity towards her mother. People imagined all sorts of things. Ronda could attest to that.

Annie paused in her cleaning and looked at Ronda. 'You look better,' she said.

'Better than what?' Ronda said.

'Than usual,' said Annie, getting down off the chair. She didn't exactly leap down, but neither did she sigh or wince.

'So do you,' said Ronda.

The doorbell went. Two short blasts, followed by a long, impatient one.

'Margo,' they both said at the same time.

'You were right,' Margo said as soon as Ronda opened the door. 'Malcolm was having an affair.'

'You spoke to him?' Ronda pulled her inside and closed the door. Margo nodded as she took off her coat and draped it carefully across the bannister. She took a lipstick out of her bag and examined her face in the mirror over the hall table.

'I look awful,' she said.

'You don't,' said Ronda. Margo might have been paler than usual, but this only served to accentuate the high, delicate line of her cheekbones and soften the arctic blue of her wide eyes. 'You look beautiful.'

'Grief becomes me,' said Margo, sighing.

'I wish I hadn't been right,' said Ronda.

Margo ran the oxblood lipstick across her mouth, smacked her lips together. 'Me too,' she said.

'What did he say?' asked Ronda.

'What men always say,' said Margo briskly. 'He didn't plan for it to happen, it meant nothing, it was a one-off, he was stressed in work, it'll never happen again, blah-blah-blah.' She put the lid on the lipstick and tossed the tube back into her bag.

'And what did you say?'

'I told him to leave,' said Margo, folding her arms tight across her chest.

'Where is he now?' asked Ronda.

'He's in the Kube.'

There was silence for a bit after that short statement. And then the pair of them collapsed laughing, staggering around the narrow hallway, clutching each other, their bellies aching, the muscles contracting hard. Each time it looked as if they might be able to stop, one of them would say, 'The Kube', or, 'The fucking Kube', and they'd be off again, howling.

Eventually, they did manage to stop.

Ronda leaned down with her hands on her knees, winded, as if she'd run a marathon. Margo put her back against the wall and slid down until she was sitting on the floor. 'I suspected,' she said, when she got her breath back. 'I just . . . I didn't want to know.'

Ronda sat down beside Margo, curled her hand around her sister's arm. Margo didn't shift it.

'I thought if I just keep busy, keep everything going, keep everything perfect, then it would turn out okay. You know what I mean?'

'I do,' said Ronda.

'But nothing was perfect,' said Margo. 'I did all the running, all the stuff with the boys, the house. I did it all. Even sex. If it happened, it was because I initiated it. It was exhausting. I'm exhausted.'

Ronda rummaged in her pocket for a tissue. She handed it to Margo, who blew her nose and wiped the tears off her face. 'Look at the state of me,' Margo said, shaking her head.

'Crying over a poxy man.' She balled the sodden tissue in her hand.

'Don't be so hard on yourself,' said Ronda. 'You're allowed to be sad.' She handed Margo a fresh tissue. 'Just don't be like me and forget to stop.'

'You've had things to be sad about,' said Margo. She mopped up the last of her tears, blew her nose again and hauled herself up off the floor.

'I've stopped now,' said Ronda. 'Being sad.'

'Are you sure?' said Margo with mock sincerity. 'These things shouldn't be rushed.' And they were off again, leaning against each other and heaving with the laughing, whacking the other's back like they were trying to find an off switch.

'What in the name of all that's holy is going on out here?' The kitchen door opened and Annie appeared in the hall. She had to raise her voice to be heard over the din. Margo got her breath back first, which Ronda was glad about because she didn't want to be the one to break the news.

Annie had always considered Malcolm a great catch.

Margo sat at the kitchen table and broke the news to Annie.

Ronda made tea.

'Well, I must say you're taking it very well,' said Annie, shaking her head. 'If my Gerry had done anything like that, I would have—'

'You would have done nothing,' said Margo. There was no anger or malice in her tone, it was merely matter-of-fact. Annie stiffened. 'I don't know why you'd say that,' she said.

'Well, you did nothing when he was drunk and crashed the car and injured Ronda,' said Margo.

'It doesn't matter now,' said Ronda, setting the teapot on the table. 'Who wants toast?'

'What was I supposed to do?' said Annie, glaring at Margo. 'Gerry was my husband.'

'Ronda was your child,' said Margo.

'Would you have liked me to leave? Where would I have gone? With two children? On my own?'

'It's ancient history,' said Ronda. 'It's not a big deal, I—'

'It is a big deal,' said Margo. 'You didn't see Ronda in the car when she started learning. She was terrified, it was awful, I felt dreadful because I never realised just how big a deal it was until then.'

'Well,' Annie began in her injured tone, 'I must say—'

But whatever it was that Annie McCann must say went unsaid as Ronda banged her fist against the table and shouted, 'Stop', drawing the word out until she ran out of breath.

Afterwards, the kitchen was quiet, the *tick-tock* of the clock loud as hobnail boots on a concrete floor.

Ronda picked up the teapot. 'I'm just glad we're all here,' she said, eyeballing the two of them in a way that was not dissimilar to Margo.

Annie sighed, but not in an aches-and-pains way. More like the release of a breath she'd been holding for a long time. 'So am I,' she said, in a voice as quiet as the kitchen.

'Me too,' said Margo.

Ronda nodded. 'Now,' she said, 'who's for tea?'

'Thank you, Ronda,' said Annie, holding out her teacup. 'I'd be lost without you.'

The toaster popped and Margo got plates out. The kitchen filled with the smell of warm buttered toast and the sound of crunching as the three of them sat around the table,

Jessica Fletcher moving stealthy under their chairs, waiting for handouts.

'I can't believe that Malcolm,' Annie said after a while. 'In my Kube.'

Margo and Ronda didn't look at each other for fear they'd set each other off again.

Margo collected herself first. 'His mother won't let him stay because she's redecorating. And also, let's face it, she's a cow. And at least if he's on the grounds, the boys can see him. They're really upset, especially Tiernan.'

'How long is he going to be in the Kube?' asked Annie.

Margo shrugged. 'I'm sorry Mam, but I don't know.'

'Don't you worry, love,' said Annie, patting Margo's hand. 'I've been toying with the idea of staying at No. 10.'

'What?' asked Margo. 'Why?'

Annie looked around the kitchen. 'It's my home,' she said. 'I know my neighbours, and Mr Hannigan always throws a little something extra in the bag whenever I call in.'

'You're making this life decision based on a bit of black pudding?' said Margo.

'He sometimes gives me kidneys,' said Annie. 'Lambs' ones. Or a few rashers. But it's not just that. I've been thinking a lot recently. Since your friend died, Ronda. Mrs Gallagher.'

'Ms,' said Ronda.

'That's it,' said Annie. 'Anyway, I want to do a bit more with what few days are left to me.'

Ronda and Margo caught each other's eye and grinned.

'I think I'd like to join that choir,' Annie went on. 'They were very welcoming to me yesterday.'

'But what about Dr Anderson?' asked Margo. 'Ronda

can't drive you over to him, and I'm a single mother now, I won't have time to do it.' Margo stopped talking. 'Oh Jesus,' she said. 'I'm a single mother.'

'I'll help you,' said Ronda.

'So will I,' said Annie.

'There's never been a single mother lady captain at the golf club before,' said Margo.

'You'll be a great single mother lady captain,' said Annie, reaching across the table to pat Margo's hand. 'And I'm done with Dr Anderson,' she added, doing a great Margo eyeroll. 'I rang for an appointment with his lordship the other day and was told the next available slot for me was May. Sure I could be dead by then. And did I tell you he has a timer now? Fifteen minutes is all we're allowed.' She shook her head. 'I'm better off taking my chances with the Indian girl in the local clinic.'

'She's from Pakistan,' said Ronda.

'Exactly,' said Annie. She smiled at Ronda. 'So you don't have to move out after all,' she said.

'I have also made decisions,' said Ronda. Annie and Margo stared at her with a degree of confusion. Ronda supposed she couldn't blame them. She didn't normally make such declarations.

'Well?' said Margo, recovering first. 'Are you running away with the circus or something?'

'I've resigned from Green Gables, I'm going to complete my nursing degree and I'm moving out.' Ronda used a solemn voice to deliver her news. It felt like an oath she was taking. A vow. She couldn't go back now. 'I'm going to rent a room in a house with strangers like other people do. In the real world.'

'Wow,' said Margo, impressed. 'That's a lot of decisions.'

'But how are you going to afford rent?' said Annie. 'If you're in college?'

'I'll get a few shifts at Green Gables,' said Ronda. 'And I have savings.' €8,339 now, after the driving related expenses.

'That money is supposed to be for a rainy day,' said Annie.

'A rainy day is for an emergency,' said Ronda. 'This is an emergency. My life has been passing me by, and I've just . . . I've let it. But I'm not going to let it any more.'

Margo whooped. 'Go Ronda,' she shouted.

'And I'm going to re-sit my test,' Ronda added.

Margo's jaw dropped. 'Really?' she said.

Ronda nodded. 'Someone told me that loads of people fail their test the first time round,' she said. 'Apparently, they just do it again.'

Margo looked at her sister with a mix of admiration and surprise. 'You're not hanging around, are you?'

'No,' said Ronda. 'There's been quite enough of that.'

CHAPTER 61

In the dayroom, Captain Grady wanted to know what was different about Ronda.

'Nothing,' said Ronda although the correct answer was, 'Everything.'

He pointed at her head. 'Your hair is not regulation length,' he said. It was true that her hair had grown over the summer. It was down to her shoulders now, with curtain bangs. She found the style easier to maintain than the blunt fringe and since she'd started her nursing course, time was scarce.

'It's . . . nice,' said Captain Grady, begrudgingly.

Sean and Eddie arrived, saluted Ronda, then saluted Captain Grady, who clipped his heels smartly together and saluted them, turning to salute Ronda, who saluted all of them. It was a ritual between them now.

'You need anything, Sheila?' asked Ronda, perching on the arm of Sheila's chair. Sheila shook her head. She was glued to a documentary about puffins, and eating her way through a sharing bag of Maltesers that she refused to share with anyone. In her other hand was the photograph of her and Noel on their wedding day. Since Ronda had put it in a silver frame, Sheila no longer hid it under the cushion of her chair. She told Ronda about Noel. How handsome he had been. How clever and witty and charming. And she blushed when she talked about the way he had looked at her in the ballroom when she told him yes, and they danced together all night.

Sheila never mentioned Charlo and neither did Ronda.

Teresa was asleep in her chair, emitting gentle snores. Baby's blanket had slipped onto the floor. Ronda picked it up and tucked it around the doll. Teresa opened her eyes. 'The house was beside the bakery,' she whispered.

'Kate and Alanna are coming to visit you this weekend,' Ronda said. Teresa smiled. It was impossible to know if she understood. Kate, Robbie and Alanna got the keys of their first home in Manchester two weeks ago. 'The number of the house is 23,' wrote Kate in her last email to Ronda. 'I know it's just a coincidence but isn't it something, all the same?'

Teresa put her hand on Ronda's face, traced her fingers along the scar. 'Does it hurt?' she asked.

Ronda shook her head. 'No,' she said. 'Not any more.'

Monika's detached voice crackled across the intercom. 'Ronda to reception please,' she said. 'Ronda McCann to reception immediately.'

Ronda picked up Teresa's cup and plate from the table beside her armchair. 'All finished?' she asked. Teresa nodded as she bent to kiss Baby's head.

Ronda popped her head around the kitchen door. Fatima was there, cleaning out the fridge. 'Any news?' she asked. There had been long delays at the Appeals Tribunal over the summer but Donal had said Fatima should hear from them any day now.

Fatima shook her head. 'No news is good news, right?' she said, smiling.

She was even optimistic about Noah, even though he

hadn't been seen or apprehended by the police since the petting zoo day. Fatima was convinced he'd managed to slip through the ferry port, maybe with a fake passport, and returned to Nigeria. 'No way he would stay here after getting beaten up by a scrawny Irish woman,' she'd told Ronda.

'Bowling on Friday?' asked Ronda.

'Of course,' said Fatima. 'Ada wants to talk to you about your course, she's decided she wants to be a nurse too.'

'See you then,' said Ronda, waving as she left.

As she passed Fergal's office, he poked his head around the door. 'How's the course going, Ronda?' he called after her.

'Good,' said Ronda, turning around. She didn't have time to tell him that she was top of her class in all subjects except pharmacology. But only because they hadn't been assessed in pharmacology yet.

'Great,' said Fergal. 'Oh, and good luck this afternoon. Let me know how it goes, my door's always open as you know.' He nodded towards his office door, ajar. Since Ronda had – unsuccessfully – tendered her resignation, Fergal had been at pains to make sure nobody else followed suit. Staff shortages were chronic across the industry, Fergal had told the Americans. Better terms and conditions were needed to maintain their team. 'Green Gables is only as good as the talented people who work here.' This was his new mantra. The toilet paper in the staff toilets had been replaced with a softer product. There was talk of a Christmas bonus. 'Sorry, I mean end-of-year bonus,' Fergal corrected himself, remembering that some staff were not Christians. The bonus would not come close to paying for all the textbooks Ronda would need next term. Still, it was a start.

In reception, Monika pointed towards the couch at the front window. 'Your sister is here,' she said in her grave voice.

Margo looked her usual impatient, impeccable self. 'Do you mind if I rain check the charity shop shopping on Saturday?' she said, texting furiously into her phone.

'You can just call it shopping,' said Ronda. Margo pitched her mobile into her handbag. 'You know the way Malcolm is always trying to get me to like him again?' she said. Ronda nodded. Malcolm was still in the Kube and, even though Margo told him he could only stay there temporarily and then he would have to find his own place, Ronda knew he viewed this stay of execution as an opportunity. This was what made him good at persuading people to invest vast tracts of money in munitions companies in the American Midwest.

'Well,' went on Margo. 'He's managed to get reservations for Charcuterie on Sunday. That French place in Portobello. Impossible to get a table unless you book a year in advance. Or you happen to be the owner's financial consultant.'

'We can go shopping another time,' said Ronda.

'Thanks,' said Margo, hugging Ronda. 'Now, let me have a look at you.' She took a step back and looked Ronda up and down. She fished a tissue out of her pocket and wiped her lipstick off Ronda's cheek. 'You're ready,' she said.

'I don't know,' said Ronda, suddenly flooded with nerves.

'It wasn't a question,' said Margo in her authoritative voice.

'What if I fail again?' said Ronda.

'Chances are, if you do fail, you'll fail better this time. Which means you'll probably pass the next time.' Margo's certainty was like a high, brick wall that Ronda could not scale.

'Don't look so worried,' said Margo. 'What's the worst that can happen?'

'I'll let you down,' said Ronda, her stomach churning.

'You've never let me down,' said Margo. 'I don't see why you should start now.'

CHAPTER 62

'Missed me, did you?' The passenger door of the car opened and the inspector got in. It was the same one as before, with the same kipper breath and the same milky stain in the middle of the tie that still ended in an upward curve on the swell of his belly.

'Hello Ray,' said Ronda.

'I'm going to take us on a different route this time,' he said. 'Where the chances of encountering squirrels are lower.'

'So there's still a chance we could encounter squirrels?' said Ronda.

'There's always a chance of encountering squirrels,' said Ray. 'That's a metaphor, by the way, I'm reading English at the Open University.' He smiled, displaying a mossy green piece of semi-masticated spinach on a front molar.

Ronda's stomach roiled.

She checked her mirrors, put the car in first gear, took off the handbrake and drove away.

Margo was wrong. The second time was just as nerve-racking as the first. Perhaps more so, because she knew what was coming. Like the possibility of Ray belching, which he did as they approached a busy junction. Even though he cupped his hand over his mouth, the stench of kipper filled every inch of Margo's small car and made Ronda want to throw up even more than she already did.

'Did you say turn left?' asked Ronda.

'No, I said, "pardon me",' he said. 'Because I belched.'

'So I'm going straight through the junction then?'

'Let's go right, shall we?' Mercifully, he jacked his window.

As the smell of kipper abated, Ronda was surprised to realise that she had completed the hill start, the turnabout and the hand signals. She had even reversed around a corner, although she had no idea how far she'd ended up from the kerb this time. Now, she was on her way back to the test centre. It had gone by in a blur.

Was this a good or bad sign?

Ronda had no idea.

As she drove down the road, her phone rang. She jerked, banging her knee off the base of the steering wheel.

'Your phone is supposed to be on silent,' said Ray, clicking his pen and making a great show of writing on his clipboard.

'Sorry,' said Ronda. The phone kept ringing. It was Fatima's ringtone. Ronda hadn't told any of them she was re-sitting her driving test. She couldn't bear to have to tell them she'd failed again.

The phone fell silent for a moment, then started up again. Ronda's fingers tightened around the wheel. Fatima never rang. She always texted. It must be important. Ronda tried not to think about it, willed the phone to stop ringing, which it eventually did. Ronda drove on for as long as she could before indicating, checking her mirrors and pulling in.

'Sorry,' she said, putting the car in neutral and pulling up the handbrake. 'I have to return that call.' Ray was too shocked to reply. Ronda grabbed her phone out of her bag, punched in the number. Fatima answered on the first ring, but it took Ronda a moment to make out what she was

411

saying. It was a jumble of words and tears and laughing. But Ronda got the gist. She'd heard back from the International Protection Appeals Tribunal.

It was good news.

'You can stay,' said Ronda, shutting her eyes tightly in an effort not to cry.

'And I've been thinking about you,' said Fatima. 'Looking at all those grotty rooms to rent. Why don't we look together, you, me and Ada?'

'Really?' said Ronda.

'I saw a little house in Artane we could rent,' said Fatima. 'It's more money, but I have my inheritance from Ms Gallagher.'

'And I have eight thousand three hundred and thirty-nine euros,' said Ronda.

Fatima whooped and Ronda pictured her in the kitchen at Green Gables, punching the air. Ronda whooped back.

From the corner of her eye, she could make out Ray's shell-shocked face.

'I have to go now Fatima,' said Ronda. 'I'm in the middle of my driving test, I'll ring you back later, okay?'

Ronda hung up. Silence hung like a thick mist in the space between her and Ray.

'That was most unorthodox,' Ray said eventually. He scanned the page on his clipboard, perhaps wondering what box he could tick for this particular misdemeanour.

'Unorthodox?' said Ronda.

'Yes,' said Ray. 'It means . . .'

'I know what it means,' said Ronda. 'I just . . . it's a good word.'

'I'm glad it meets your approval,' said Ray, impatient now. 'Do you need to make any other calls or can we continue?'

Ronda drove on, trying to concentrate, torn between exultation for Fatima and disappointment for her and Margo.

Still, Margo had been right. She had failed better this time.

At the test centre, Ray slid his pen behind his ear. The mashed spinach was still stuck to his tooth.

'Reverse into that parking space,' he said, pointing to a narrow space between a 4x4 and a truck. Ronda did as she was bid, then put the car into neutral, lifted the handbrake and turned the engine off.

'Well,' said Ray, with a deep sigh that rustled the pages on his clipboard.

'At least no squirrels were injured,' said Ronda.

'That's true,' said Ray. He scribbled something at the bottom of his page and released it from the clipboard. He handed it to Ronda. 'You need to hand this in to the office there. At the hatch. Okay?'

Ronda took the paperwork and reached for the door handle.

'Most people can't wait,' said Ray. 'They beg me to tell them.'

'I don't think there's any need for that here,' said Ronda, opening the door.

'You might be surprised,' said Ray. Ronda stared at him. He was grinning. 'Your behaviour during a test may have been unorthodox, but it wasn't unsafe,' said Ray. 'Congratulations Ronda.'

Ronda got out of the car. She walked towards the test centre, but it was like the walking you do in a dream where your legs are moving but you're going nowhere. She stopped and ran back to the car where Ray was still sitting in the

413

passenger seat, putting his clipboard into his briefcase. She opened the passenger door.

'Sometimes I imagine things,' she said.

Ray got out of the car and grabbed at the edge of the L plate, ripped it off the window. 'That real enough for you?' he asked, handing it to Ronda. The red of the L had faded over the last few months.

A lot had happened over that time.

Terrible things.

Wonderful things.

Surprising things.

That was life, Ronda supposed.

That was real life.

CHAPTER 63

Margo said Ronda could have the job at the hospice now that she had her driving licence. She could use Margo's car. Catherine, who had been persuaded to stay for a while, had once again tendered her resignation, the draw of Julia Roberts' rude good health and effortless beauty in *Eat, Pray, Love* outgunning any further perks Margo could offer at the hospice.

'I'm going to be a nurse,' Ronda said. It still made her smile, every time she remembered.

'I know, but you could do the job part-time while you're studying,' said Margo.

'I have a part-time job.'

'Minimum wage,' said Margo dismissively.

'Actually no,' said Ronda. 'I got a raise.'

'Really?' Margo looked at Ronda with something like admiration. 'Good for you,' she said. 'But I still want you to have the car,' she said. 'Consider it a gift for passing your test.'

'No,' said Ronda. 'But thank you.'

'Why not?' said Margo.

'I can drive,' said Ronda. 'But I'm more of a bike and bus kind of person. You know that.'

Margo nodded. 'I suppose I do,' she said. She dropped Ronda at Green Gables where she collected her bicycle and cycled to No. 10 Casino Place.

It was one of those autumn days, when summer reaches back for a moment, her swan song full with promise, even as the leaves – shades of shining golds and glossy browns and russet reds – hung on by their fingertips.

Ronda felt as if she was marinating in sunshine as she cycled along, warmth flowing through her body like a sugar rush. Anytime she stopped at a junction or a traffic light, she wanted to knock on a car window and tell the driver that she had passed her test.

That she had never thought she would but then she did.

She didn't knock on anybody's window. She smiled at everybody instead and she even waved once, at a window cleaner at the top of a ladder outside a dry-cleaners. The window cleaner waved back, like she knew something pretty wonderful had happened.

As Ronda cycled past Hannigan's, she remembered the helmet she had left there.

It felt like a lifetime ago.

She stopped outside the butcher's and leaned her bike against the shop window.

'Ah Ronda, is it yourself?' said Mr Hannigan, wiping bloodied fingers down the bib of his apron.

'Hello, Mr Hannigan,' said Ronda.

'You're looking well, have you been away?'

'No,' said Ronda. 'I've been busy, doing different things.'

'A change is as good as a rest, they say,' said Mr Hannigan. 'What can I get you?'

'I was wondering if my bicycle helmet was here?' Ronda asked.

'I think I saw one ages ago,' said Mr Hannigan. 'I'll go check in the back.'

'Thanks,' said Ronda.

The bell jangled as the door of the shop opened and an

elderly lady walked inside, pulling a shopping bag on wheels behind her.

'Is himself gone on strike?' she asked Ronda, pointing behind the counter.

'He'll be back in a minute,' said Ronda.

The woman leaned towards Ronda, peering at her face.

'What happened, love?' she asked, her voice low and fearful.

'Car accident,' said Ronda.

The woman took a sharp intake of breath and shook her head. 'Must have been a bad one,' she said.

'It was a long time ago,' said Ronda.

'Here it is,' said Mr Hannigan, holding her helmet aloft like a trophy.

'Thanks,' said Ronda, taking it and heading towards the door.

'You mind yourself love,' said the woman as Ronda opened the door.

'You too,' said Ronda.

'And tell poor Annie we were asking for her,' said Mr Hannigan. 'How is she?'

'She's well,' said Ronda.

Mr Hannigan was too surprised to respond. Ronda waved as she stepped outside, back into the sunshine.

Annie was at the kitchen table, elbow deep in paint colour cards. 'I can't decide,' she wailed when Ronda arrived. 'There're too many colours to choose from.'

'It'll look lovely when it's all done,' said Ronda.

'So long as I'm still alive to enjoy it,' said Annie, sorrowfully.

'I took my test again,' said Ronda.

'You never mentioned it,' said Annie, holding one of the cards up to the light.

'I passed,' said Ronda.

'Didn't I say you would?' said Annie, smiling. 'Your father would be very . . .' She stopped then, stood up and put her hands on Ronda's shoulders. 'I'm very proud of you,' she said.

'Thanks Mam,' said Ronda. 'And Fatima wants us to look for a house together.'

'A house?' said Annie. 'Can you afford that?'

'Maybe,' said Ronda. 'Fatima said she can cover me if I can't. I can pay her back when I've finished my course and I'm working full-time as a nurse.'

'I wish I had a friend like that,' said Annie.

'You have Mrs Murphy,' said Ronda. It was true that, since Mr Murphy's stroke and Joseph moving out shortly thereafter, the relationship between Annie and Mrs Murphy had improved.

'That reminds me,' said Annie, standing up and stretching. 'I need to practise my songs for the concert in Liberty Hall on Saturday.'

'I can see you're going to miss me terribly,' said Ronda, grinning.

It was true that Annie McCann had been dreading the day Ronda left home for the second time. She would finally be alone, and a woman on her own is a pitiable thing, she felt. But then Jessica Fletcher pressed herself against Annie's legs. Annie bent and picked her up. As she stroked the cat, it dawned on her that she would never again have to endure one of Ronda's vegetarian stews, the tofu bobbing along the surface like the bodies of bloated snails.

'Of course I'll miss you,' said Annie, setting Jessica Fletcher back down on the floor. 'But you know me, I don't like to complain.'

The doorbell rang. 'I'm not expecting anyone,' said Annie, glancing at the kitchen clock.

'It's probably a salesperson,' said Ronda. 'I'll answer it.'

When she opened the door, there was nobody there. She stepped outside, momentarily blinded by the sun pouring through the branches of the laburnum tree.

There was a van parked on the road.

A camper van.

The back of it was open and she could see a man, rummaging for something inside. A long, narrow man with sandy hair that could do with a trim. There were freckles everywhere. He wore shorts, a T-shirt and flip-flops and seemed to have gone out of his way to get the colours to clash. He had done a good job.

'Ah Ronda,' he said, straightening as her shadow fell across him. 'I brought chocolates for Annie but I can't find them now.' He looked at her with his usual blend of interest and curiosity.

'Shouldn't you be in Clare?' said Ronda, flushing, remembering in vivid detail the litany of accolades she had poured over him. What had she been thinking? Who said stuff like that? Her inner critic was roused now, in full swing.

'I've moved back to Dublin,' said Donal.

'Oh,' said Ronda. She hadn't expected that.

'The reconfiguring didn't turn out to be such a great idea after all,' said Donal.

When Ronda didn't respond – she could think of nothing appropriate to say – Donal went on. 'I think death just did a bit of a number on us,' he said. 'It was so sudden and Tricia sort of freaked out and then I freaked out and bad decisions were made. You probably don't understand that, Ronda, you're good at death.'

Ronda nodded. That was true.

'Plus,' Donal went on, 'it turns out I make really bad coffee. The customers were up in arms.'

'What about Tricia?' said Ronda.

'She thinks that I make really bad coffee too,' he said. 'We've agreed that we're better off as friends.'

'I see,' said Ronda.

'Ah, there they are,' said Donal, pulling an enormous box of Black Magic out of the van.

'Why did you bring chocolates for my mother?' asked Ronda.

'I want her to like me,' said Donal.

'Why?'

'Because then she won't mind that I like you.'

'Black Magic are her favourites actually,' said Ronda.

'I have more things I want to say,' said Donal.

'Okay,' said Ronda.

Donal took a breath. 'Ronda McCann,' he began solemnly, 'I want you to know that I find you smart and attractive and interesting and funny. You're thoughtful and kind. You're exactly yourself, and that's so refreshing. Also, you have integrity, which is not all that easy to come across. I think that's my favourite bit.'

'Anything else?' Ronda asked him with a smile that let them both know she was *flirting* with him.

'Well, if it's okay with you, I propose we get to know each other a bit better,' said Donal.

'I agree,' said Ronda. 'When should we start?'

'I was thinking right away?' said Donal.

Ronda smiled.

'I think that would be best,' she said.

Loved *Late Leaner*? Don't miss out on *Queen Bee*.

'Bridget Jones meets menopause . . . sharp, funny and real' Cecelia Ahern

When fifty-year-old Agatha Doyle starts keeping a diary, it records only the ways she doesn't know who she is any more. Her glorious empty nest is full of people. And her head is full of brain fog. All it takes to tip her over the edge is a pair of red velvet heels and a man who won't stop talking.

Standing up for herself, Agatha unwittingly becomes a heroine for midlife women everywhere.

But with a distant husband, and an even more distant sex life, can she also become the heroine of her own life?

Read on for an extract!

22 May, 4 a.m.

Symptoms: Insomnia, rage, resentment, night sweats, resentment

How's that for starters?

What else?

Oh yes, resentment. Did I mention that?

23 May, 4 a.m.

Symptoms: Insomnia, boiling (heat and rage)

Brain fog: Does my phone number start with 086 or 087?
Also: Resentment

Everyone else in this house is fast asleep. My sons (like, hadn't you two moved out?). My father, ensconced in the spare room, in the throes of his a-bit-late-in-the-fucking-day midlife crisis. And beside me in the bed, Luke has the gall to smile in his sleep. Like he's dreaming about the hairy bacon and cabbage he's cooking in the café tomorrow.

He's also snoring.

He has no idea how close he is to being smothered with a memory-foam pillow.

24 May, 4 a.m.

Symptoms: Insomnia, rage, resentment, hot flush, resentment
Also: Repetitive. Like, I'm supposed to be a writer and I can't
even come up with new words for my symptoms
Also: Frustration. How is this supposed to help? This stupid
symptoms diary? Riddle me that, Dr bloody Lennon

And no, I will NOT call you Susie. You're my GP, not my friend.

Besides, I already find it difficult to take you seriously with your child hands and persistent air of hope.

Fuck you 'Susie'.

25 May, 4 a.m.

Symptoms: Weary, sweaty
Also: Resentful. This is a complete waste of time, I could be
watching *First Dates*. Or *Gogglebox*. Or *Queer Eye*

I could even be writing. Proper writing, I mean. After all, I am contractually obliged to deliver the first draft of my sixteenth novel to my editor in ten weeks' time. Which of course I assured her was no problem during our last conversation:

ANNA: How's the book coming along, Agatha?
ME: So, so, so good, it's literally pouring out of me . . . like
     . . . I don't know . . . lava! Out of a volcano!
ANNA: Wow! I'd really like to rea . . .
ME: NO! I mean . . . no. Not yet. It's . . . not quite . . . you
     know . . .

ANNA: Is the deadline still working for you?
ME: YES! Definitely. I love the deadline. It's so . . . do-able
   . . . you know?
ANNA: I wish all my writers were as disciplined as you.
ME: Hahahahahahahaha . . .

Pause.

ME: Yeah. That would be . . . nice.
MAM: See? Wasn't I right, Agatha? Oh, what a tangled web
   we weave when first we practise to deceive . . .'

Technically, it's Sir Walter Scott who was right on that score.
   Anyway, Anna's been an editor for decades, surely she
should be less gullible when it comes to writers and the
stories (read: blatant lies) they tell?

26 May, 9.05 a.m.

Symptoms: Impatience

All anyone really needs to know about the new GP –
Dr-Lennon-call-me-Susie – is, when I ring the clinic, she
answers the phone. And, like, she has people for that.
Receptionists and whatnot. She has probably given everyone
the day off and a pay rise.
   That place has gone to the dogs since Dr Hardiman retired.
   Although he didn't retire so much as die of old (read:
ancient) age.
   I miss Dr Hardiman. He was taciturn. Such an underrated
characteristic. Consultations would take five minutes after

which he'd shove a prescription for antibiotics across the desk, no matter what ailed you.

Until I caught a dose of menopause. Then he snapped his prescription pad shut with a snap.

DR HARDIMAN: You're just menopausal. It's part of the ageing process. You'll be fine.
ME: When?
DR HARDIMAN (shrugging): Hard to say.
ME: I've heard HRT might help?
DR HARDIMAN: With your family history, you'll most probably get breast cancer and die if you take HRT.

Thanks a bunch, Mam.

'Susie', on the other hand, thinks it's good to talk.

'Good morning, Hearty Healthcare, Susie speaking, how may I help you?'

That's another thing about 'Susie'. She sounds like she really, really wants to help.

ME: The writing down of menopausal symptoms isn't helping.
'SUSIE': Think of it more like a diary.
ME: Do I seem like the kind of woman who keeps a diary?